Ostrich

∎ ∎ ∎

D1516820

Western Literature Series

Ostrich

■ ■ ■

MICHAEL A. THOMAS

▲▲
University of Nevada Press
Reno & Las Vegas

Western Literature Series

University of Nevada Press, Reno, Nevada 89557 USA
Manufactured in the United States of America

Library of Congress Cataloging-in-Publication Data
Thomas, Michael A.
Ostrich / Michael A. Thomas.
p. cm.—(Western literature series)
ISBN 0-87417-351-5 (alk. paper)
1. Basque Americans—Fiction.   2. Ostrich farming—Fiction.   3. Sheep ranchers—
Fiction.   4. Ranch life—Fiction.   5. Nevada—Fiction.   I. Title.   II. Series.
PS3570.H5739O88 2000
813'.54—dc21
00-008599
The paper used in this book meets the requirements of American National Standard
for Information Sciences—Permanence of Paper for Printed Library Materials, ANSI
z39.48-1984. Binding materials were selected for strength and durability.

09 08 07 06 05 04 03 02 01 00
5 4 3 2

*To my parents, Ed and Azalia, who showed
me the funny edge of the world and the
importance of family*

Acknowledgments

Many thanks to:

Enrique Lamadrid, Becky Noland, Laura Fashing, and Sharret Rose: they read the book and told me how to make it better.

Minda Stillings, my wife: she read every word, every draft. She offered generous and unfailingly accurate advice, often in the face of stiff resistance.

Margaret Dalrymple, Editor in Chief at the University of Nevada Press: Margaret helped me develop patience with processes beyond my control.

Two anonymous readers for the University of Nevada Press: their advice helped.

Jennifer Hengen, my agent, who coincidentally sustained a monkey bite around the time she'd taken on this book. Jen is the greatest.

My sisters, Terry, Kathy, and Molly: we laugh together, always have.

The many animals who graciously provided demonstrations of the behaviors I document in these pages: Fidel, Rayos, Cruz, Cancion, Ginny Mae, Nicky, Chauncy, Fancy, Daisy, Looie, nameless legions of sheep, anonymous coyotes, etc.

CHAPTER ONE

■ ■ ■

A staccato "Pop! Pop! Pop-pop! Pop!" cut short Everett Crume's consideration of the eviction notice. He lunged into the forty-watt gloom of VJ's cramped apartment. Blinking and off balance, he then stumbled over a metal folding chair and nearly fell. Ev's two hundred and thirty-five pounds were crammed into cut-rate jeans that restricted movement and added an element of danger to the business of walking. Bringing all his strength to bear, he was able to keep his feet if not his composure.

Upright but shaken, Ev lacked the confidence to proceed. For several moments he stood just inside the door panting and cursing. He made a point to specifically mention the manufacturers of the metal chair and the man who'd placed it so carelessly in his path. Staring into the murky half-light, sunlight streaming around him, he smelled an odor, fish and Pinesol, an astringent, bracing stink. Now he understood. VJ's swamp cooler was on the blink and five-ounce Jojobalueca Liniment bottles were exploding in the undiluted fervor of the midday heat.

Hot, short of breath, and still shaky on his feet, young Crume endured the stink and thought of his great-uncle. "You can't count on a guy who's scrawny," the old gentleman had said. The remembered words impressed Everett as profound, prophetic. Ev had been a chunky, responsible child and had developed into a portly, reliable young man. Scrawniness and irresponsibility were attributes the Crumes managed to avoid.

This was not the case for Virgil Jose ("VJ" or "Virg") Eckleberry. Ev regarded his friend with a deflating sigh of resignation. Likable as he was, VJ Eckleberry was one of the thinnest and most unreliable human beings ever to have cared for sheep on the ranchlands of Nevada or peddled Jojobalueca products on the sun-roasted streets of Albuquerque. Now, according to the notice VJ's landlord had evidently nailed to the door, Ev's friend had just under thirty days to "vacate the premises." Ev was far from surprised. The timing, in fact, was perfect. They were leaving that very day for a visit to the Eckleberry family ranch in Nevada. Maybe VJ would make peace with his father and stay.

VJ, the subject of these ruminations, sat at the foot of an unmade sofa bed. Gaunt arms angled out of a purple-flowered cowboy shirt. Pink longjohn bottoms betrayed the easy lifestyle of a man who washes clothes democratically, in a single load. His face was unshaven. His long black hair was going in all directions in an apparent attempt to escape from his head. He began twirling an unruly handful into a rough bun on the right side. He showed no signs of having noticed his friend, the liniment explosions, or the brash, exuberant stink that pervaded the apartment. In Ev's experience, the absentminded hair twirling was a sure sign of trouble. Instantly wary, he noted with horror that VJ was reading. This was going to be bad. Ev's head began to ache.

It was twelve noon. Outside, the high sun tracked the endless pavement and sent heat shimmers into the air, distorting vision and causing headaches. VJ had avoided headaches and the many other risks of venturing outside his apartment. His attention was fixed on a dog-eared copy of *Stockman's Universe,* with feature stories titled "Spotscald in Feedlots" and "The Environmentalist Threat to Our Traditions."

Anyone familiar with Virg Eckleberry would expect him to show right-thinking, if passing, concern for the ravages of spotscald in feedlots. Still, Ev did not imagine that his friend would give much attention to the topic. VJ simply would not find articles on spotscald particularly gripping. Similarly, as far as Ev knew, VJ Eckleberry had not reflected deeply on environmentalists or "our traditions." He hadn't, in fact, reflected deeply on much of anything. His metabolic level seldom allowed it. In a Wyoming bar someone *had* called VJ an environmentalist and there *had* been trouble. Still, Ev did not think that VJ was likely to be reading up on the subject. In Ev's experience VJ had confined his reading to concrete, practical documents such as the daily racing form and inspirational pieces on Jojobalueca marketing. Ev was puzzled. What about this particular issue of *Stockman's Universe* could exert such force on the ever-wandering mind of VJ Eckleberry?

Several minutes passed and VJ didn't move. He didn't so much as nod to acknowledge Ev's presence. Ev's eyes adjusted, and he again noted the undiminished virulence of the smell. He could understand why VJ's landlord and former business associate, the slight and indomitable Chingleput Gupta, had decided to evict his erstwhile supplier of Jojobalueca products. Even in a depressed market for apartment rentals, there is a point when a landlord must act to guard his investment.

VJ had conceived of his Albuquerque apartment as the "Southwest Regional Headquarters" for Jojobalueca Products. One such product was "Jojobalueca Miracle Performance Liniment for Horses and Show Bovines." This liniment was one of the less prominent products, but every one of the thirty "Opportunity Kits" that VJ kept in his closet had a five-ounce bottle. The bottles, Ev supposed, could not contain the miracle. Happily, the explosions that had ushered Ev into the apartment were benign except for the powerful stink they loosed into the world.

That smell! Neighbors, reporting the odor to both landlord and police, had characterized the smell as something like a limit of trout rotting in a bucket of Pinesol. Mr. Gupta had apparently lost his enthusiasm for both the product line and VJ Eckleberry. Ev empathized.

Smelling the fresh evidence of the liniment (VJ had made earnest, if not sustained, efforts to clean up the mess every few days), Ev nevertheless felt brave enough to continue into the depths of the apartment. He shut the door behind him and crossed the front room into the fetid "kitchenette" where VJ had stored some of the Opportunity Kits. He made himself a cup of instant coffee and stood in the kitchen doorway. Every few minutes, VJ would idly stroke the sensitive area behind the only ear of a large, grimy, and battle-scarred tomcat. Foreman regarded Ev with a purity of disdain that Ev found both amusing and incomprehensible. Thus meeting the minimal needs of the purring, snot-colored cat, VJ continued to stare with rapt, complete attention at the soiled magazine. Ev watched and sipped coffee. They were to be in Nevada by noon the next day. There was a birthday party for VJ's old man. Ev had hoped to drive in the cool of the day. Since the cool of the day was gone, he was content to pass the hot hours enveloped in a cloud of smelly liniment. He would sip coffee, bear up under the withering gaze of Foreman, and watch VJ read. It was a novel experience, if a bit slow.

At length, the time for reading evidently passed. The magazine fell from Virgil's hands. He lifted his gaze to the fly specks and cobwebs on the wall or a vision of paradise beyond.

"Ev," he said, correctly surmising that his friend had joined him, "your parents can get rid of that tacky trailer. You can sell that ratty pickup. You can get some comfy, decent Five-oh-one Levis instead of those K-mart seconds that never fit. You can quit pinching every penny and buy a beer or two for someone else. I'll see you in a beaver hat, a silver quadruple-X with a hatband and everything. I swear that wool felt thing looks like a cat sleeping on your head. Go ahead and shit-can it before Foreman gets romantic. You can also get old four-eyes Susie some contact lenses, or better yet, get a new girlfriend. That Susie may not be good-looking," he shot a sideways glance at Ev, "but she sure can be a bitch. Now that you're going to have a pot to piss in, you can get a woman with manners."

"Whoa," Ev finally said, cutting his friend short. He was used to VJ's insults, but usually his slim friend managed to spread them out a bit, throwing one here, then one there, over the course of the day. VJ smiled a big face-busting grin and lifted his shoulders sheepishly.

Ev liked VJ. His energies and enthusiasms were infectious, and he'd always been the perfect antidote to Ev's unhappy bias toward pessimism. Still, he could be exasperating at times, and this was one of those times. Experience told Ev that he should not squander his powers by challenging any of Eckleberry's outrageous statements. He ought to keep his mouth shut.

The room was close and uncomfortably warm. Young Crume had narrowly missed a ruinous fall. His stamina was compromised.

"VJ," he raised his voice, "I've told you a dozen times. Susan is *not* my girlfriend. Get it through your head. She's got a boyfriend, some guy with earrings in his eyebrows." Ev closed his eyes and rubbed his head.

VJ was not slowed, just deflected, by the interruption. He leapt to his feet and began to pace. The cat followed suit, trotting in and out between VJ's legs and purring.

"I guess you saw the paperwork on the door," he said. "Old Chingleput's evicting me. I have thirty days. It's a shame. He had potential. He was already my best salesman." The limited dimensions of the room did not leave young Eckleberry much latitude. Three steps turn, three steps turn: that's all there was, and he made the best of it. Twisting at his hair, he began whistling "Volare" with as much volume as he could muster.

Ev stood in the kitchen door, sipped coffee, and watched. Things had picked up. He smiled. Mr. Gupta had been the *only* person VJ had convinced to sell Jojobalueca products. Recalling VJ and Chingleput as partners and their plans to "change the rules" in the South Asian household product market, Ev's smile broadened.

VJ continued to pace and whistle. It was entertaining for a couple of minutes but soon began to get on Ev's nerves. He was surprised that he was not genuinely angry about the insults.

While Virg paced up and down, he gazed at his old friend through brown eyes that glowed with warmth and fellow feeling. Ev shook his head. The last volley of insults had a rare and unexpected purity about them. Certainly, the outburst was appalling. Ev hoped his pal would henceforth find the forbearance to keep them to himself, but they were not malicious. Virg was simply excited, overexcited, and Ev still didn't know why.

"Virg!" Ev broke the silence sharply, hoping to end the ridiculous pacing. "What's put you into this state? Stop the damned workout and settle down. We ought to be to Monticello by now. What the *hell's* going on?"

The lanky man stopped the march. He lifted his eyes as though to heaven and took a deep breath. He continued to whisper the words of "Volare" under his voice.

Let's fly 'way up to the clouds
Away from maddening crowds.

Finally, VJ met Ev's gaze. Why! he thought, old Ev hasn't heard the plan! No wonder he looks so crabby.

VJ was a man of compassion. He decided at once to end this disturbing ignorance. Fixing his friend with eyes that simply radiated brotherly love, he smiled in a fond way and said, "Ostriches."

Ev had to admit that his friend had found the word for the occasion. Ostriches have a reputation for avian single-mindedness of the type VJ had shown in his attention to *Stockman's Universe*; they bury their heads. Likewise, following their own inscrutable impulses, they will suddenly run to the far horizons, an embodiment of speed without reflection. VJ had taken a similar approach to his own twenty-two-year span on the planet. Beyond that, Ev noted that his friend's eyes were glazed in that look of vacant absorption one so often finds in poultry. "Ostriches," indeed. No word could better characterize the appearance and behavior Ev had witnessed. Impressed, but far from satisfied, Ev urged his friend to flesh out his description.

"What do you mean, 'ostriches'?"

"We're going to be rich," VJ explained. "But let's get the flock out of here." He stepped to the door. "Go on, Foreman, there's a good kitty." The cat had apparently lived in the midst of Central Avenue traffic since the days of the Old Testament. Young Eckleberry, as everyone knew, was a marvel with animals. According to landlord Gupta, VJ was the only human being ever to have touched the cat without sustaining injury. VJ had both fondness and admiration for the cat he'd christened "George Foreman." The cat stalked out, not failing to bare his teeth and hiss as he walked past Ev.

VJ shut the door and fixed Ev with a knowing gaze. "Chop-chop, Ev. We'll have to scrape the sisters off the ceiling if we miss the old man's party. You know who they'll blame. I'll tell you about it while we drive."

Ev agreed, Rosa and the others would blame him. He got a sick, hopeless feeling in the pit of his stomach. He'd been sweet on Rosa Eckleberry as long as he could remember. It was his secret and it was hopeless. She was inaccessible, older by two years, a seeming chasm of time. Besides, all the guys were sweet on Rosa. She was beautiful, smart, and confident, and she was an Eckleberry. In addition to having the finest ranch in Basque County, Nevada, the Eckleberry family had something else. Call it confidence, charisma, or just a glow, it was a family trait. VJ had it, in spite of himself, and Rosa had it in spades. Ev admired her with fervent resignation. He didn't have a chance. Still, he did not want her mad at him, and that was a distinct possibility.

"Yeah," sighed Ev, fatigued and forlorn, "let's go, shake a leg. If we don't hurry, we'll miss driving in the heat of the day. I figure we've now got six full hours to spare. No need to waste it resting in cool comfort here."

VJ ignored the bitter tone of irony that Ev attempted to convey. Old Ev was often and inexplicably moody. VJ had to get ready to go! Chop-chop! He started packing: sniffing shirts, searching for mates to any of the socks strewn about, putting everything into a paper bag that held a new pair of jeans. VJ avoided doing laundry. He'd found he could put it off a while by buying new clothes.

"Don't worry." He stuck his head into the kitchen to see that the stove was off. "I want to stop and see Mama on the way."

"What!?!"

"I want to stop and see Mama on the way."

"In Phoenix!?!"

"That's right, that's where she lives, Evertly Ev."

VJ was out the door. Ev followed, his large frame bent with trouble.

VJ stood for a moment and admired his pickup before getting in. It was a brand-new, metallic-blue Ford one-ton, with dual rear tires.

"Hell of a truck," he said, "no damned king cab, either." VJ took great pride in the fact that the pickup did not have a king cab to spoil the lines.

"Hell is right," Ev replied bitterly, getting into the blisteringly hot, nonking cab. "It looks to me like a guy paying twenty-eight thousand dollars for a truck could get one with an air conditioner."

"A man might," VJ shot back, "if he wanted to junk up a nice truck with unnecessary trash and waste his daddy's good money."

It must have been a hundred and fifty degrees inside.

They took off into the Friday swell of traffic. A thousand or so dollars worth of stereo equipment blared "I Got Friends in Low Places" into their skulls. Ev snapped it off. "Yeah," he said, "it'd be a shame to junk up your nice pickup with unnecessary trash." It was so hot the knob burned poor Everett's sausagelike fingers. "And now you can explain to me how Phoenix is 'on the way' to Basque County, Nevada. The town's evidently shifted a bit north."

"It only adds a couple of hundred miles," VJ answered, swerving in and out of traffic to sail cheerfully south, away from their destination. "I want to see that Mama knows about this from the get-go. We can triangulate to Nevada and get there just in time for the old man's party. If we hit the ranch too early, Rosa will have us cutting hay in the morning dews. Sudan hay, if I hear right."

CHAPTER TWO

■ ■ ■

Once on the freeway, VJ cranked up the speed to his customary eighty-five and pointed the pickup south. They headed to Socorro and hung a big right for Arizona. VJ used the time to apprise his friend of the new possibilities.

"The West's going to hell," he said, deciding to ease gradually into the subject of ostriches. Ev would need some preparation for the topic.

Ev had long noted that people with plenty of money and endless acres of land always seem to yap about how bad things are going. Now Ev would have to listen to this crap from VJ. It figured. As rich as the Eckleberrys were, the topic was bound to come up. "Uh," he said. He hoped that the minimal response would encourage VJ to hurry the "West going to hell" topic and get to the "ostrich" business he'd mentioned at the apartment.

"No water," VJ went on, determined to make his point. "I

mean, think of it. My old man has to have better than thirty sections just for a few mangy sheep."

"A rural tragedy," Ev replied, "a terrible plight. Here you are, heir to a thirty-thousand-acre ranch, and you can't afford an air conditioner in your pickup."

VJ ignored the tone of irony.

"It's the sheep! We shouldn't have sheep on that land. Hell, in Spain, they'd only need five hundred acres for the few sheep we're able to run. No, really, the smart people in the western U.S. are getting away from sheep and cattle. They're starting to raise animals suited to dry country. They're getting rich at it, too, and that's what I plan to do."

"VJ, you're already rich."

"Correction. Daddy's rich, not me. And what about you? A fellow gets sick of having their friends' whole families in such a sorry state."

"Virg! My family is not poor, and they damned sure are not sorry. My folks rented their house out and bought that RV because they wanted to travel. I am going to UNM. That means I have to pay to work rather than the other way around. That does not mean I am in want."

"And poor Mom, think of her over there in Phoenix clipping those damned poodles day and night. The Mexicans think that Basques are all misers and tightwads. Now, that may be prejudice, but I'm starting to think that the Mexicans are right. My old man is one tight Basque when it comes to Mommy's alimony."

"Your mom is just fine!" Ev interrupted. "She loves her poodle business, and it's less work than she did at the ranch. And it isn't alimony! They're separated. God knows they love each other."

"I'm starting from scratch," VJ continued. "I damned sure ain't rich. You will recall that Daddy ran me off the ranch with a salad fork. I have to get rich on my own, just like my daddy did. But I'm damned if I'm going to do it with idiot, smelly, panicky, god-damned sheep. The old man never made a dime out of sheep ranching anyway. He had more imaginative ways of getting rich, and I reckon I will too."

"Listen, Virg, however angry old Sabine gets, he is not going to disinherit the son he's brought up to take over the family ranch, and you know it. Even if he wanted to, do you think your sisters would allow it?"

The truck hurtled up the little two-lane. Ev and VJ took a silent moment to consider VJ's sisters. No man alive could stand up long to the sustained pressure of those women. If it served their purposes, they would make mincemeat out of their poor father. The thought of it made VJ smile and Ev shudder. He fixed VJ with a stare, as though that would make Young Eckleberry listen.

"You know that no Basque in history ever disinherited his only son. Your grandpa changed his name to Eckleberry, but that didn't get the sheep out of your blood. Anyway, your family's done well with sheep, especially since Rosa's been involved. Sabine may not have started with sheep, but you can't say he's gone broke with them."

VJ frowned. Ev had ventured into a touchy area. VJ did bear a prejudice against sheep. He'd picked it up hanging around rodeos and country music bars. Being a sheep shagger was about as bad as being a goat roper. Virg was down on sheep, even though he was a superb shepherd with a sixth sense about the well-being of his animals. That made him a little testy.

"Ev," he snapped, "with the Euzkadi, it's not the *sheep,* it's the freedom. The sheep are the excuse, the pathway to a life under the skies and stars, without bosses or responsibilities."

Ev was annoyed that they were talking about sheep rather than ostriches. He was aware, of course, that VJ was restless, on the prod, needing a new project. Virg had lived three months in Albuquerque. During that time he had lost interest in the Jojobalueca venture without regaining any enthusiasm for his daddy's sheep ranch. He worked on a casual basis as a groom for the state fair and Albuquerque Downs. He made enough money (barely) to rent the little apartment, cover his tab at the Wonder Bar, keep his truck gassed, and buy the clothes he needed. He got by, but with the collapse of the Jojobalueca bubble, he was feeling the lack of challenge, drama. Now, of course, he was faced with the eviction. This would provide some drama, but not enough. VJ aspired to visionary goals. He felt the tugs of destiny. Ever since his hasty departure from the Nevada ranch, VJ's three sisters had been pressuring him to come home to team up with Rosa and relieve old Sabine of the day-to-day worries of running the place. This, VJ proclaimed, was a cowardly and unimaginative choice. Even if old Sabine apologized about the fork incident, which he wouldn't, VJ wouldn't have been interested. The article on ostriches had popped up at just the right time. Virgil grasped the revolutionary possibilities of ostriches on western range. He'd long since accepted his fate as a "breakthrough person," the kind of man who (the motivational tapes claimed) would implement the great ideas of the age.

He continued. "What I want is freedom from the damned woolies. To hell with the ranch. To hell with my bossy sisters. To hell with my tightwad daddy. To hell with the brainless sheep. To hell with shepherd chores. Especially to hell with the endless damned fencing the sheep require. There's no animal alive with less respect for a damned fence."

He looked over at Everett and smiled. In VJ's view, Ev wore his fat well, like a five-hundred-dollar overcoat. He had a big old head (hat size 7⅝), soft honest eyes, and full lips that were presently all twisted down. That twist showed how leery Ev was of his pal's big ideas. VJ did love that expression; it was so familiar. Ev was not the kind to warm instantly to new ideas, however brilliant. It was Ev's way. He was not a fickle guy, and VJ liked that. It made him a hell of a friend, though exasperating.

"I also figure I can do some other people some good. People who have it coming. That suit you?" VJ said. "So maybe your parents are set for life. Maybe you're not hurting either, and I have to admit that clipping poodles is easier than shearing sheep. But that's not the point! I have higher goals than getting greedy rich. I figure I'll do my bud and my family some good. My family needs a shot of money to balance things up. Old Sabine *is* tight. Anyway, it's the future of the West I started in on. This is arid land, compañero, arid land."

Ev found this line of reasoning difficult to refute. They were crossing the plains of San Agustín in central New Mexico. Grassland, but dry, dry.

"I was wondering when you'd get back to the West going to hell. You know, this land's been arid for about eight thousand years. So I guess it's been going to hell all that time and you just heard about it. You might as well quit beating around the bush and tell me about this ostrich scheme you're cooking up. You can spare me the part about the water problem, unless raising ostriches is going to somehow increase rainfall."

"That's what I like, College Boy. You're a deep one. That article said the same damned thing, the West's been arid for eight thousand years. But you have to love this country. Beat to shit, overgrazed, underwatered, eroded, and still it raps you right in the noggin it's so damned pretty. But you know, Ev, eventually I am going to need you for just that kind of thing, knowing about the eight thousand years. You just keep going to school. If that Anderson School of Business is as good as people say, it'll prepare you to manage all the money I'm going to make. I've got the vision, Ev, and you've got the brains."

Ev rolled his eyes, but he did agree with this assessment. "VJ," he urged, "will you get to the point? You don't need to butter me up."

"Well, I know you won't like it, not at first. The point I was getting at, when I started in on the West going to hell, is that ostriches are the solution to the problem. They're arid-climate animals. They're real easy keepers. The plumes bring a good price. The skin, well, just *price* ostrich-skin boots. The eggs are huge and low in cholesterol, and you can sell the empty eggshells for novelties. They're poised to be the next big thing in meat. Turkeys took over their market share in the twenties. It'll be ostriches for the millennium. The meat is low cholesterol and better than beef. And they've got a nice disposition, they're docile, and they love people. Well, maybe 'love' is not the right word, but they are really sweet until they are a year or two old, and they are curious, intelligent birds. They can live seventy years. Just imagine the money in eggs over sixty-five, seventy years. You don't need much space for them, either. Just a few hundred acres is enough to make a man rich beyond reason."

Ev Crume looked at his friend and was annoyed to feel affection crowding at his reasoned resistance. Virgil Jose's face was always relaxed, even when he was off on one of his wild notions. It was a face that Ev always found fascinating. As he drove, VJ's dark eyes were bright, dancing. He had his usual wide, winning, ear-to-ear smile, and the energy just crackled off him. When VJ got fired up, full of spunk and completely sure of himself, he took a lot of resisting. He sat erect, his shirt open to catch the cool air of the mountains along the Arizona border. What a pistol! If people like VJ could direct their energy toward fruitful ends, they'd probably be able to bring about world peace, end hunger, and cure cancer and AIDS in a few days, max. Instead, people like VJ attract vicious tomcats, buy ostriches, go on macrobiotic diets, take up with loud drunken women, fix up cars to run a quarter mile in 5.9 seconds, pester their friends about Jojobalueca soap franchises, and end up with multiple listings in the *Guinness Book of World Records*.

Ev had the questions, and he just couldn't bring himself to ask them. Questions like, "So, VJ, how many pounds of ostrich meat were sold in the U.S. last year?" And "Is there really any product or are the present ostrich farmers raising ostriches to sell to people like you, VJ?" And a whole litany of other tiresome, dismal inquiries into practical concerns. If the birds were "sweet" until they were "one or two years old," then what were they like for the sixty-eight years after the sweetness wore off?

Rather than squabble all the way to Phoenix, Ev let VJ run with it.

"Well," he said, "it sure *sounds* great."

"Damn straight," VJ replied. He knew Ev didn't like the idea and was thankful his buddy didn't come up with an endless laundry list of doubts and objections. Things like that bring a person down and can keep a guy from thinking in color. It was nice of old Ev to cut him some slack. He went on, determined to address some of Everett's unspoken objections. It was the least he could do.

"You know, Ev, this time I'm going to take care. I know I'm not a detail man, so I have to be extra careful. With the Jojo-balueca, I wasn't careful, I just didn't have the zeal for the product. I also learned from that problem I got into with the FFA. Hiring that rainmaker, I wasn't careful there either. I didn't check his background and didn't ask before I spent the FFA money. It was too bad they kicked both of us out; hell, it wasn't your fault. This is going to be different. I'm going to start small, way small. The price of ostriches right now is through the roof. Folks are getting twenty to sixty thousand dollars for a proven pair of breeders, so I want to get into the deal pretty cautious. I figure I should start with chicks, unsexed juveniles, and eggs. That'll keep my costs reasonable. I plan to get started pretty soon now. I want to see how I do with them, what they're like."

Ev was amused. VJ was attempting to show that he was reasonable. He was talking at a measured clip, emphasizing his cautious deliberation. He made his points with slow, open-handed gestures that conveyed a sense of earnestness.

"I'm low on start-up money anyway. I damned sure won't ask my old man for a loan. But you know, Ev, I can't wait too long. The way you make money is raising ostrich-emu breed stock for folks getting into the business. The meat-eggs-hide business is still down the road."

VJ warmed considerably. Gradually giving up the pretense of reasonableness, he chattered and flailed, emphasizing his points with an assortment of winks, snorts, and hoots. As entertaining as VJ's enthusiasm was, Ev missed the caution. He felt uneasy and tried to remember what emus were.

"The price," VJ went on, "is going nowhere but down as folks breed more and more of them. I need to act. There's a concern up near Stansville that raises ostriches. So either before or just after the birthday party, I figure we can just drift over to Stansville and look at an ostrich or two."

Everett Crume's face had gradually darkened. He was not much enjoying the hectic pace of the trip. Animated and happy to be on the road, VJ had pushed the speed to just above ninety miles an hour. The frantic pace annoyed Ev, but even worse was VJ's habit of suggesting frequent, pointless stops that Ev invariably opposed. Ev liked to travel at a leisurely but consistent sixty. If VJ had his way, he'd drive better than ninety and average well under fifty. This was, for Ev, an annoying way to cover ground, and he hated having to argue VJ out of stopping every five or ten minutes. Resignedly, he adapted to circumstances and accepted his role as the voice of reason. He even felt a little smug as they blew across the Arizona border. It was 11:00 P.M., cool and dark, with no moon and no traffic.

Sure enough, this ostrich business was pyramids with feathers, about as sound an investment as a chain letter. It was a relief to know that VJ probably wasn't going to lose more than a few thousand dollars and some months of futile labor. He'd end up, of course, back at the family ranch, mending fences and arguing with Sabine and Rosa. Ultimately, he'd run the ranch. Sabine had raised him to run the ranch. He had the brains. He had the knowledge and the inclination. He knew how to care for land and animals. All he lacked was maturity and patience. The advantage of the ostrich business, so far as Ev could see, was that VJ would fail fast, clean, and cheap. The experience would demonstrate the merits of thoroughness and practicality. VJ did not learn those lessons very readily, but the cumulative effects of fiascoes like Jojobalueca, the degradation of *Jeopardy,* and this benighted ostrich scheme were bound to bring the point across. Valuable educational experiences, Ev ruefully recalled, are inevitably expensive. Ev had to pay a hefty out-of-state tuition at UNM; VJ would pay "tuition" for his lessons as well. It was only just, and this notion cheered young Everett. Feeling peaceful at last, he went to sleep in the cool mountains at Show Low, Arizona, just as VJ gunned the truck over the summit for the long, breakneck descent into the Salt River Canyon.

There are places hotter than Albuquerque in early July. One of them is Phoenix. The young men arrived around 3:00 A.M. Ev Crume awoke with a start from that terrible, hot, neck-rolling sleep one gets in a pickup truck (excepting, of course, trucks with king cabs, layback passenger seats, and climate control). Banishing a feverish dream, Ev took stock.

Camelback Road, he remembered the name. Yes, they were in or around Phoenix. Approaching metropolitan Phoenix, the Salt River Valley is an irrigated hothouse. The desert blooms. Transpired water soaks the air and holds the heat. Often a week or more will pass with the temperature never dipping as low as one hundred degrees. It stays hot all night. Americans cannot live in such places without refrigerated air. Phoenix sucks a billion years of stored energy to lower summer temperatures fifty or so degrees. Ev was sinking to a subhuman level of anguished, brute existence. A bright bank sign emerged from the black night to warn that it was one hundred two degrees. They'd soon get to Mrs. Eckleberry's Scottsdale digs, thank God. It'd be air-conditioned.

VJ suddenly swerved into a gas station, stopped, jumped into his jeans, and hopped out. They'd both shed their clothes a couple of hours back, and it took a moment for Ev to retrieve his pants. Getting them on was no cinch either. Bargain-basement jeans do not slide easily over large, sweaty thighs, and neither do they button readily. Ev jumped out of the cab barefoot, holding his pants up. Visions of Diet Coke consumed his attention. VJ looked like a ghost pumping gas in the neon glare.

Ev shuffled toward the office of the all-night minimart intending to pay for the gas and the Diet Cokes that so occupied his mind. One, two, three hesitant steps and then, rodeo time! The 3:00 A.M. pavement would have fried eggs. Ev danced some steps never seen on the dance floor at the Wonder Bar. He swore oaths, called on saints (despite the fact that he was not Catholic), and colored the air with imprecations. Tiptoeing his way, he pranced back to the truck. VJ watched. The dance of the hippopotami from *Fantasia* came unbidden to mind. Ev launched himself through the truck's open door and fell onto the seat. VJ finished pumping, paid for the gas, and bought a cold six-pack of Diet Cokes. He'd had the foresight to put on his boots. He'd not done a perfect job—the boots were on the wrong feet—but they did put a crucial barrier between foot and pavement.

Ev had things to say about the mothers of the men who'd established Phoenix. He rubbed and fanned his blistered feet. VJ drove in silence, listening sympathetically.

"Mesa," VJ finally said.

"What?" An application of Diet Coke, both internal and external, had slowed Ev's invective. He sipped his second can and soothed his feet by resting them on the others.

"Mesa," said VJ. "That station is in Mesa, not Phoenix. Hell, we're not really going into Phoenix."

"Well, I don't give a jolly god-damn if it's Tempe, Mesa, Phoenix, or Christly Scottsdale," said Ev with withering sarcasm. "You figure that the pavement is cool in Phoenix, I guess? It's all Phoenix to me, and it, by Jesus, shouldn't be here. People who put a city in a place like this, Jesus! So don't tell me 'Mesa,' because I don't give a rat's ass about Mesa. We might as well go to Morocco, Algeria, Libya, let me blister my feet on a bloody Sahara sand dune while you hunt your idiot ostriches. It's you, your fault. We ought to be in Nevada by now."

VJ listened without comment, impressed that his friend found a way to blame him for the balmy climate Arizonans so enjoy.

CHAPTER THREE

■ ■ ■

While her baby, Virgil Jose, quietly accepted responsibility for the climate of central Arizona, Magda Zumwalt-Eckleberry applied an ice pack to the Baron de Saint-Germain d'Alsace's injured leg. When the ice was properly placed, she turned on a timer. Twenty minutes, that's what the vet said, twenty minutes of ice every six hours. The little dog could even make the trip to Nevada as long as Magda could keep the icing schedule.

Magda supposed that she would go to Nevada. It was Sabine's birthday, after all, and she did miss him, stubborn as he was. Besides, she was worried about Rosa. How could she ever learn to nurture and manage intractable animals if she didn't have a husband to practice on? She wanted to run the ranch, which was fine, but she needed to get married. Anyway, Magda's girls—Rosa, Felice, and Celia—were clamoring for Magda to come to the party. It made the girls nervous to have one parent in Arizona and the other in Nevada. And that was just fine. Magda could count on their help in the ongoing project to get Sabine to winter with her in Scottsdale.

She repositioned the ice pack and reset the timer. She was happy to care for her "Sassy-Wassy." Getting up at three in the morning was a small enough sacrifice. Her poodles certainly deserved it. Anyway, Magda still had the habits and expectations of a ranch wife. It'd been decades since she'd expected an uninterrupted night's sleep. Sheep, children, dogs, birds, horses, husbands, and other livestock all tended to feel their deepest and most desperate needs during the hours between midnight and 6:00 A.M. Magda prided herself on always being there to relieve sufferings, soothe nerves, and provide needed comforts. The dog boutique and clipping service she ran in downtown Scottsdale was merely the commercial aspect of a capacity that Magda had refined through her entire life.

The current object of Magda's maternal concern was a competitor, a winner. The Baron de Saint-Germain d'Alsace was a white toy poodle who thrived in the glare of the show ring. At present he was a dog at risk. His career and perhaps even his life were on the line. He'd tangled with a coyote trap.

Coyotes were, perhaps, the single most serious threat to the lifestyle of Scottsdale. The treacherous beasts would slink into the peaceful neighborhoods under cover of night. They'd devour the small pets Scottsdalians typically kept. God knew the coyotes had to be stopped. There'd been no help from City Hall, just a mealymouthed notice with the water bill advising citizens to keep small, feeble, and otherwise vulnerable pets indoors at night. Vigilante types laid traps in the desert. The traps caught the very animals everyone wanted to protect. The coyotes, in fact, now made a practice of eating the trapped pets. It was a fine how do you do.

Magda counted herself lucky. The coyotes had ignored the trapped poodle. Perhaps they'd become finicky eaters or, like the coyotes on the ranch, followed a traditional diet whenever possible. She was certain that no coyote would eat a poodle if lambs were around. Perhaps Scottsdalians should start raising a few lambs.

Magda had worried about Sassy for months. The little sneak had always been an escape artist. Once a week or so, he managed to negotiate the elaborate security system Magda set up. Then, whether he bit a child or rolled in something dead, Magda would face a nasty situation. Now, the jaunts had turned dangerous. Sassy was lucky; he'd gotten away with a mashed leg and bruised ego. His prognosis was guardedly positive. Magda thanked God and crossed herself, despite the fact that she had not been a practicing Catholic for more than forty years. The crossing business added an emphasis Magda felt might help. Sabine crossed himself, and he was as godless an old lapsed Catholic as ever jeered at the pope. If her agnostic husband could cross himself, then so could Magda. It certainly didn't hurt.

The injured Sassy looked uneasily at Mademoiselle Champagne d'Avignon (Champy), Beauchamps de Joies (Joey), and Monsieur Chien d'Andalousie (Moe). The other dogs hovered and loomed over their downed and vulnerable companion, just hoping Magda would leave for a while. Scores would be settled; accounts would be balanced. Sassy knew enough to expect the worst. He trembled and shook in every cell of his small body.

"Oh, look at poor, poor Sassy," said Magda, touched to the core of her abundant sympathy. "Mama won't let those naughty doggies bite her Sassy-Wassy. No, she won't."

Sassy continued to stare warily, his tiny forehead bunched in apprehension. The other dogs growled and barked, full of hateful anticipation. Sassy's wounded leg troubled them. The sight of it made them want to kill him. Of course, they had always wanted to kill him. The injury was both further provocation and a unique opportunity. Magda's protective presence exasperated the dogs. They milled nervously, growling and baring their small, sharp teeth.

Magda was getting tired of the skulking and looming. "You

all just get out of here and leave poor Sassy alone, you little boogers," she said, making a shooing gesture. The dogs responded immediately. They trotted out of the bathroom/hospital ward. Magda closed the door, at which they instantly began to bark and scratch. It occurred to Magda that they were going to wake the Colonel. Well, she thought, if he's going to drink like that and then need to stay over, he'll like it or lump it. She did not feel that the Colonel necessarily deserved a good night's sleep.

She returned to icing Sassy's leg. The timer was on the blink, stopped at eighteen minutes. Who knows how long the ice had been on. Best, she decided, to leave it on another fifteen minutes. To comfort poor Sassy she sang him a song.

Ooo ooo ooo la la la la
You did me wrong
When you went out to play
Because I almost lost you
What a price to pay . . . I'm crying
Ooo ooo baby baby
Ooo ooo baby baby

The song, pointed as it was, never failed to relieve the nervous preoccupations Sassy had endured since his unfortunate injury. Magda had used singing for years as a specific for sick, wounded, or emotionally fragile children and animals. She had a clear, lovely voice and near perfect pitch. It worked for Sassy, as it'd worked for perhaps a dozen of Magda's earlier charges. Sassy's favorite parts were the "ooo ooo" sections, and he managed to produce a feeble but life-affirming bark at those points in the song.

It was, in fact, at one of those points that the door burst open. The space suddenly filled with the exiled poodles and the Colonel, a brown, leathery man in McKenzie clan plaid boxer shorts. On top of his otherwise bald head, seven or eight strands of silver hair stood straight up, bringing the man's height to a full five feet eight inches. Like the small dogs, the Colonel seemed agitated. His eyes rolled, his arms flailed. It struck Magda that her neighbor resembled Popeye's paramour, Olive Oyl. There were obvious differences to be sure, but the resemblance was striking. Thin limbs with knobbed joints; frenzied movements; sputtering, hysterical speech; she'd put her finger on it. Furthermore, she reflected, the resemblance was not merely physical. The man had Olive Oyl's extreme emotional excitability. Magda looked at him with some dismay. What on earth could be the problem? Sassy had a rather similar fit whenever Magda wore her straw hat for gardening. It couldn't be that. Did he need to use the bathroom?

The Colonel kicked at the dogs (Magda frowned) and continued to sputter.

"The gun, gun, wha . . . wha . . . where do you keep the god . . . ggggod-damned gun."

It is always annoying to have quiet times with injured pets interrupted by retired, drunken colonels demanding guns. This is particularly true when the retired colonel's very presence in the home is unsolicited and he is kicking at prizewinning poodles. Magda felt that an explanation should be forthcoming. Casting a withering gaze on the man, she waited. Having the Colonel around made Magda realize how fortunate she'd been to marry Sabine. She did not like the Colonel very much. In unguarded moments, this lonely man was vulnerable, childlike. He liked her, and that was flattering. He had a bunch of dogs, some sort of hunting hounds. He worked with them every day and seemed to care for them. Magda liked that. Still, his politics were horrible, and he was a narrow, opinionated man. On top of all that, he was a randy old goat, as horny as he was unappealing. Despite his many flaws, to Magda he was another needy mammal, touchingly stark in his solitude. She'd given him the benefit of the doubt and managed (barely) to tolerate him. It'd take very little poodle kicking to change things. She continued to glare.

The Colonel had seen this expression before, and he did not like it. He was better acquainted, in fact, with the expression than with Magda. Women on three continents had taught him. This look signaled a bitter scene in the offing. Images of such scenes flooded his mind and had an oddly calming effect. He took a deep breath and closed his red-rimmed eyes. Retired Colonel Jordan McKenzie had a bad headache. What a time for the revolutionists to strike! Diabolical! He struggled to get a grip. He had to approach the situation calmly, soberly, with deliberation . . . and a weapon! That was priority number one. Get armed and allow a lifetime of military training, experience, and know-how to pay off. Why didn't this woman tell him where to find the gun? He'd asked in plain terms!

Magda did have a gun. It was a nice big one, an old 45-caliber Mauser pistol. Sabine had given it to her when she began staying in Arizona year-round, insisting that she'd need it for self-defense. She used it to prop the window open in the garage bathroom. She'd taped it there with duct tape. There was a box of bullets somewhere, perhaps in the thread drawer with the sewing machine bobbins. Not that she was about to provide the Colonel with a gun, bullets, or any such thing! What on earth was wrong with him?

At this point, Magda noticed that the doorbell was ringing. Indeed, it'd rung nineteen or twenty times in, perhaps, three seconds.

"VJ!" she shouted, recognizing her baby's impatient approach. She pushed past the Colonel and ran toward the front door. She shouted back at the Colonel to keep the ice on Sassy for five minutes more. The uninjured dogs were at her heels shrieking in delight, fear, and generalized hyperstimulation. Moe peed all over the rug, leaving a trail behind them.

The Colonel made a motion as though to hit the cowering Sassy. He grabbed the ice bag and applied it to his own head. If the revolution had begun, if the blacks and Mexicans were at the door, they'd just have to kill everyone, he guessed. The reds had taken over anyway. Socialism, dead and buried in the former Soviet Union, was on the march in Arizona. There wasn't really much more to lose. He began to feel sentimental about his death, what a great person he'd been, what a staunch soldier and fearsome opponent. At least he knew where he'd be buried and under what circumstances. Another white cross on the field of America's best.

On blistered feet, Ev Crume made gradual progress across the wet, tepid lawn. "Hefty," as his mother always said, he tried with small success to step lightly. The wet grass failed to soothe, but was better than the flagstone walk. The distance to the front door approached infinity. Ev got to the porch just as Magda threw open the door and grabbed VJ.

In Ev's view, Magda was a rather daunting person. She was tall, full-figured, sharp-witted, outspoken, and given to extravagant dress. The women in Ev's family contrasted in every particular. Ev approached the porch warily. Light poured out onto the lawn. Magda was dressed in a white satin robe. She was surrounded by shrieking poodles that bounced viciously.

In her mid-sixties, Magda was almost as attractive as Rosa. Her abundant red hair was as alarming and alluring as it'd always been during the twenty years Ev had known the Eckleberrys. He snuck furtive glances, feasting his eyes on Magda's full, luscious lips, the peachy glow of her surprisingly elastic skin, the kind sparkle of her odd, almost violet eyes. Aroused and anxious, his pulse quickened. Ev, to his discomfort, had always been drawn to both Magda and Rosa. It pained him. They were his best friend's mom and sis! What would VJ say if he knew? What kind of friend would be hot for his buddy's mom, his sis? A bad one, he supposed, but he couldn't help it. It was embarrassing. He was inevitably clumsy and tongue-tied around either of them but did generally save his most humiliating displays for Rosa. This one would be tough to top.

At Magda's orders VJ helped Ev into the house. They sat

him on a sofa in the den. A wizened, sunbaked, angry-faced prune of a man materialized like a wraith out of the bathroom, gazing sourly on the scene. Magda hustled about, issuing further orders and producing Diet Cokes. Ev would have an ice pack for his "poor tender little feetsies," she promised, as soon as Sassy's time was up. She strode off to find bedding and various accessories that VJ and Ev would need if they managed to get to bed before dawn.

VJ followed, talking about ostriches and waving his arms. Ev was left under the supervision of the Colonel.

"You're lucky you didn't try to get into my house at three in the morning," the Colonel snarled. "I'd have blowed your ass away and had the job of dragging your fat carcass inside. Of course, you'd have never got by my dogs; I've got real dogs."

Ev was far from attentive to the Colonel's remonstration. It was cool, cool, and he was in an air-conditioned revery. Luckily, the Colonel was not the kind of man who required or even wanted responses to his pronouncements. He did manage to learn that Ev was a student at UNM.

"University of New Marxism," the Colonel snarled. "That's what I called it when I was stationed at Kirtland."

Ev managed a lame smile. He supposed the Colonel was razzing him. Ev always did his best to be a good sport. He was too exhausted to try very hard.

Magda continued to bustle. Congratulating herself for getting Sassy's swollen leg at least minimally iced, she set about organizing the assembled bedding and seeing to Ev's poor burned feet. Ev just watched. Virg had taken his place in his mother's entourage, behind Champy and in front of Moe. Ev could hear his staccato sales pitch on meat practically free of cholesterol; eggs that were delicious, nutritious, and huge; leather that was durable and stylish. Ev was again impressed. VJ was not much of a reader, but he'd certainly absorbed that article on ostriches.

Magda was by no means pleased to hear VJ's hyperactive

monologue on ostriches. Surrounded by her own animals, she nonetheless wondered what she could have done to leave a son with a need to surround himself with gigantic, obnoxious, and perversely flightless birds. While she did her various tasks, she made a frank assessment of her last born. He was skinny, Lord, skinnier than ever. Wasn't he ever going to fill out? And his clothes: brand-new, stiff jeans and an acutely ugly cowboy shirt of a purple hue not found in nature. He was far too alert for 4:00 A.M. This boy had a look of eccentricity. It made her tense, like she might hyperventilate. When he was younger, she hadn't worried. Instead, she had treated him like a foal.

There's a period in the life of all equines when a colt doesn't know a thing but to run, and run he will, not a brain in his head. A person simply has to endure that time without fighting the little horse too much or yielding to the temptation to abuse it into mannerly behavior. Magda had thought of VJ that way and had maintained her maternal optimism in spite of the fiascoes the boy had breezed through. But he was twenty-two now and she was getting nervous. The trip to Nevada was beginning to take on a great deal of importance. The ranch needed some TLC, that was certain, as lazy as Sabine was getting. It was nine-tenths shut down and would be falling apart if it weren't for Rosa. But . . . Rosa . . . , well, perhaps Sabine had some ideas. And then there was VJ. All it took was one look to see the obvious. She and Sabine *had* to do something about Virgil Jose. Sabine's solution of chasing the boy around with a salad fork had not had a particularly good outcome.

VJ continued on about the ostrich-raising business. Getting a cool response made him nervous, and he tried harder than ever to talk up his idea. The certain knowledge that this approach was futile did not help. He talked on, unable to stop, more convinced than ever that his mother's apparently happy, successful life in Scottsdale was nothing but a brave front. The proof of it was the Colonel. She had to be desperate to depend on an evil old buzzard like that for her emotional needs.

Ev had gone to sleep about five minutes after he hit the couch, and VJ was aware of the Colonel lurking in the background with his ears hanging out while VJ talked ostrich. Already uneasy, the specter of Colonel McKenzie made him positively taut with nervous tension.

"And one of these days, there'll be a futures market for ostrich eggs," VJ was saying. "That's when the smart investors will get out of the business of eggs."

The Colonel, unable to restrain himself any longer, butted in. "Young man, you've been talking some of the most harebrained foolishness I've heard in my life. Get a job, for Christ's sake. Join the god-damned army if they'll take you. Get a life! By the way, Magda, Fatty's already asleep. Just throw a coverlet or parachute over the son of a bitch and let it go at that. What do these boys expect, showing up at three in the morning?"

Magda felt her jaw tighten and her ears get hot. This was the second time the Colonel had butted in when she was occupied. He had disrupted her attempt to care for dear Sassy. Now he had the nerve to insult her boy and, even worse, Ev, down for the count with his poor blistered feet! She also recalled the infuriating image of the Colonel kicking at the little dogs while demanding firearms. All of the emotion that'd been building—her concern for VJ, her sadness for her poor little hurt Sassy, and her sympathy for the footsore young man on her couch—turned instantly into rage. She placed her hands on her hips, turned slowly, and bore down on the Colonel with a look that made him wince.

"Colonel McKenzie," she said slowly. Her voice quivered with the effort to maintain decorum. "I invited you for dinner and a couple of drinks. You got drunk and were not fit to drive. I offered you my hospitality. I've been a tolerant woman." She strode in his direction, her index finger in a position the Colonel called "locked and loaded."

"But everybody has a limit. When you stand in my home, display your coarse manners, and criticize my boy, you've gone too far." She poked him in the chest with her finger. "It's time for you to go now, and I mean *right* now, without another word. I could pinch your head off, you old toot. VJ, you go move your pickup. Colonel McKenzie needs to get his car out."

The Colonel knew enough to decide instantly. He'd leave, by God. The situation had become intolerable. The so-called dogs this woman chose to surround herself with were bad enough. All of a sudden, here at three in the morning, a crowd of young fat-asses and meatheads shows up talking about ostriches. It's irritating to have young chowderheads yammering about ostriches in the middle of the night. It'd be bad anytime, but a man has more stamina for such things in the early evening, for example. Magda was not showing proper appreciation for the organizing, civilizing influence he brought to her household. For the time being, then, he'd withdraw the favor of both his presence and forthright counsel. Anyway, he had to feed his dogs at five.

He accompanied Magda's son out to the driveway where a nice new, blue one-ton Ford pickup with dual rear tires was parked behind the Cherokee. The Colonel was impressed. That Ford was one nice little buggy. Perhaps he'd misjudged the boy.

"Son," he said, "that is a beautiful vehicle you've got there. What kind of engine you got?"

"Well, sir," VJ said, his voice buttery with pride, "you might call it overpowered, but for my money, I like a few mules in the stall. It's a four-twelve. Not a trailer made it won't pull."

The Colonel was practically purring with admiration. The boy was certainly sound in the area of motor vehicles, however suspect this ostrich business might be.

"You know what I like about that truck?" the Colonel asked,

beaming at the pickup shining there in the streetlight. "The lines, young man. I do hate those damned king cabs or super-cabs or whatever name the car pimps give the damned things. They spoil the appearance of the vehicle. Now yours there, you won't find a vehicle in Maricopa County any prettier."

"I'd drive a Datsun before I'd have a king cab," VJ said ear-nestly. Maybe he'd been a bit hasty in his judgment of the Colonel, obviously a man of taste. Rarely had VJ encountered anyone having sentiments that matched his own so com-pletely. Stirred, VJ had his first twinge of uncertainty about the ostrich project. "Harebrained foolishness," that's what the Colonel had said. Could a man be so penetrating, so right about one thing and so wrong as regards something else? The Colonel's judgment made Virg uneasy. For several moments the men stood united in their admiration for Virgil's pickup.

"I'm Colonel Jordan McKenzie," the older man finally said, jamming his hand toward VJ. "I don't recall that we were properly introduced." They shook hands. "Listen, young man, I said some harsh words in there about your livestock scheme. Don't let it get to you. Maybe I was a little sour at having to get up at three in the morning." His voice trailed off.

"Aw," said VJ, shrugging it off. "It's not an idea most people like much, at least not at first. I probably don't do it justice when I talk it up." He walked to his pickup and unlocked the door.

"Just one more thing," the Colonel said after him. "If you had to choose, who would you say was the country's finest race car driver?"

VJ did not hesitate. This was a subject without ambiguity. "Richard Petty," he said, "hands down."

In the dark, VJ probably did not see the huge smile that spread across the Colonel's face. Moments like this were rare, but in such moments, Colonel Jordan McKenzie almost wished he'd fathered sons. As he drove past VJ, who'd pulled out of the driveway and was waiting to pull back in, the Colonel stuck his arm out the window and gave the young man the thumbs-up. Magda, he thought, had thrown a good pup after all.

Back inside, VJ was surprised to see his mother still bustling. She was assembling suitcases and doggie travel kennels.

"That Colonel McKenzie is not such a bad old guy," VJ said to his mother, wondering what on earth she was doing.

"Well," said Magda, "I'm glad you find him agreeable. He'll be driving me and the dogs to Nevada tomorrow. We'll caravan up to your daddy's party. Now you quit gawking like that and get some sleep. We've all got to be on the road by nine or we could miss the party. You know your sisters and how they'll react if *you're* not there on time. It doesn't matter so much with me. They only half expect me. I was noncommittal when Rosa called."

VJ was perplexed. He could have sworn his mother had just thrown the Colonel out on his ear.

"The Colonel?" he said, his jaw hanging in confusion.

"Don't stand there and gape, VJ. I swear, you look like an idiot child. While you were out there admiring your pickup, I called the Colonel's number and left a message on his machine. I certainly wasn't going to talk to the old goat."

CHAPTER FOUR

■ ■ ■

Rosa Margarita Eckleberry took one step back, put her hands on her hips, cast her chin toward the featureless horizon, and sighted down her nose. Her father wallowed in the dirt beneath the trailer hitch of a red-and-white pin-striped livestock trailer. The words "Sherry Baby," lettered in red, graced the side of the trailer and imparted an unexpected lyric dimension to the otherwise prosaic scene. Wheezing and grunting, Sabine attempted to secure the trailer's safety chains to the frame of his pickup. The enterprise was demanding. As is customary, the chains were a sixteenth of an inch too short to work as designed. They had to be jury-rigged each time the trailer was used, and Sabine could never remember how.

The trial-and-error procedure allowed Rosa to make a frank assessment of her father's physical condition. In the first place, the old man was getting to be a real tub. His belly didn't even go down anymore when he lay on his back. His old black

34

belt was at least four feet long. It was buckled, snugly buckled, even straining, at the last hole. That belt told the tale:
thirty or so years of indulgence in wine, potatoes, olive oil,
and fat-marbled meat. A long series of worn buckle holes
marked the ancient belt. Sabine, a thrifty man, had worn the
belt for as long as Rosa could remember, and Rosa remembered that belt with great bitterness from early childhood.
The old man grunted.

"Daisy," he said, "give Daddy that ball-peen hammer. It's
right there in the box." Shortened through the years from
"Rosie Daisy" to "Ro-daisy," and "Ro-daisy-o" (in her cowgirl
years), "Daisy" was Sabine's special name for his third and
youngest daughter.

Rosa got the hammer out of the box and handed it to him.
"You're not going to lengthen that chain by beating it," she
said, "so get out from under there. Just throw those darned
chains around the ball."

Sabine replied with a grunt and struck the frame smartly.
Slabs of dried mud fell to the ground. Two such slabs, the size
and consistency of bricks, fell onto Sabine's chest. Given his
girth, they didn't gain much momentum. The extra space allowed the chains to slip into place, not the exact place they
ought to have gone, but "close enough for who it's for," as
Sabine liked to say. Finished, the old sheep rancher was faced
with the task of extricating himself from his supine position
beneath the hitch. This was no picnic. Quite a lot of kicking,
clawing, scooting, and grunting was required, along with a
curse or two to expedite the project. Rosa watched, ever more
concerned with her father's well-being.

The situation annoyed her in so many ways that she was
left, for a moment, speechless. Sabine struggled to his feet as
that moment passed. "Dad . . . ," she opened her mouth only
to be interrupted by her father, who stood dusting himself off.

"*Mandonas*," he said, "that's what I've raised, *puras mandonas*. In Spanish, that's a bossy woman, a harpy, a shrew. You're

getting to be just like your sisters that way. It's an ugly habit for a pretty girl." He took out a large bandanna and wiped at his sweating brow. Rosa looked at him, drew a deep breath, and decided not to waste it. The "girl" business; there was just no use telling him she didn't like it, not to call her Daisy, to lose weight, to quit smoking cigars, to get Virgil Jose to help run the ranch. She and her sisters tried their best to boss the old guy. This was because he needed bossing, the recalcitrant old devil. Rosa was resigned. The bossing was far from effective. At best and with constant effort, the three sisters were occasionally able to curb their father's most extravagant excesses and hinder his more impetuous plans. It had been useless to tell him what a harebrained idea it was to get those donkeys.

Sabine Eckleberry, like his son, had fallen under the thrall of an article in *Stockman's Universe*. Sandwiched between features on milo silage and contrivances that prevented water tanks from freezing over was a story entitled, "Cutting Coyote Depredations the Natural Way: Guard Burros for Sheep and Goats." Rosa had seen her father poring over the article on dozens of occasions, whiling away idle hours drinking wine and dreaming of cozy sheep, sleeping peacefully while benevolent burros kept watch. Months of meditation behind him, Sabine was ready. The soiled and wine-stained *Stockman's Universe* took its place in the stratigraphic sediment that had accumulated through the decades in the old man's "office," a corner of the front room. That office! Rosa was convinced that the household would be improved if the office were dynamited.

Though out of sight, the article on burros was certainly not out of mind. Old Sabine, according to his daughters, was the one out of his mind. He told them that he'd thought it through, done his homework, and was, by God, ready to have some donkeys.

Rosa was not the kind of woman to be silenced by the mere futility of her position. The old man hefted himself into the pickup cab, and Rosa took up her post as shotgun.

"Daddy, the ranchers in this state have been whining for years about the wild mustangs and burros. How many times have I heard it? Some old geezer looking out at the poor grass and blaming the damned feral horses and donkeys. What happens? The government rounds them up to get rid of them, and the fool ranchers fall all over themselves adopting them. How are they going to help with coyotes? Two years ago they were the same as coyotes: pests. What, have they mended their ways in two years?"

Sabine was putting the pedal to the metal. He always loved to speed when he was pulling a trailer. It made such a grand cloud of dust.

"Daisy, you know something? In Spain, they move the sheep all the time. They use big mastiffs to run off the wolves. You never saw such grass. These little collies we use here are pretty good, you know, but they're so small. They can't do too much with the coyotes. I thought about getting mastiffs, but with dogs, I don't know, it's always something. My father once tried mastiffs, and those dogs just needed too much care. It covered him up. There's plenty of donkeys in Spain, too. Little tiny guys. They've got the cutest little hooves you ever saw. It reminds me of my father to have some donkeys. I don't know why I never thought of it before. These wild burros here, they're bigger, you know, and they can't stand a dog or coyote. But I don't care if it works, not really. Maybe I just want to look out of my office and see a burro taking a crap."

It was always Spain. All the old man's irrational behavior had to do with Spain. He was seventy-one years old and was born in Nevada. His father, though, was an immigrant Basque from Spain. Just before World War Two, Sabine's father, Joanes Eckleberry, sent Sabine away so he wouldn't get drafted. The Americans wouldn't fight for Spain, so his boy wouldn't fight for America. Sabine argued bitterly with old Joanes but did as he was told. He was supposed to stay in Argentina with an uncle and a bunch of cousins until the war was over. Instead, he left Argentina almost immediately with four of those crazy cousins. They headed for Europe and the war. They ended up in Spain and embraced the traditions of their Basque heritage. They became smugglers, robbing and stealing from the fascist government on the one hand and sabotaging German and Italian boats on the other.

According to family stories, Sabine and his Argentine cousins were soon terrorizing the coasts with a commandeered submarine. They were not much better than pirates. When the war in Europe was won, Sabine returned to Nevada. Joanes had died while he was gone. They'd clashed bitterly at the time of Sabine's departure, and no opportunity remained for reconciliation. Sabine lived with regrets. He always tried to do things he thought his father would have done. It was his legacy, and he had money, war plunder, plenty of it. In 1946, he bought a thirty-thousand-acre ranch. He likewise paid tribute to his father by always voting socialist—and making a big deal out of it. This infuriated and disgraced his daughters, especially Felice, who was an active Republican of the American rather than the Spanish variety.

Rosa associated the donkey project with socialism. Sabine's crazy cousins had big ranches in Argentina with llamas, alpacas, mules, pheasants, peacocks, fighting cocks, parrots, guinea pigs, and donkeys, as well as sheep and cattle, and those cousins, all of them, were certainly socialists, or worse.

Rosa remembered the year her second cousins showed up from Argentina for the christening of Celia's baby, Courtney. The cousins came to celebrate Sabine's first grandchild. They were the most godless, irreligious reprobates she'd ever seen, yet they left their own families to come to a christening in a church they claimed to despise. Six months they stayed, drinking wine, singing war songs, and gambling down in Reno. They were all filthy rich from war plunder and lacked the decent restraints that slender means exact. In Rosa's view, it just wasn't right for such a bunch of rowdy old pinkos to have so much money. It wasn't dignified.

Since that infamous visit, Sabine was always threatening to "go see some real grass" down on the Pampas. Rosa was glad Argentina was so far away. He got into enough mischief close to home.

Rosa wished that this tedious donkey business was a little closer to home. They'd be on the road for at least ten hours. God knew how long it'd take to get wild donkeys to load into the trailer. Sabine would have gone on his own if Rosa hadn't put her foot down. A trip like that, at his age! He couldn't make the ninety minutes down to Reno without getting the nods. In ten hours, he'd fall asleep and kill himself for sure. Now, he would merely exhaust himself and spoil the birthday party.

Ev Crume had faithfully promised Rosa that he'd have Virg there for the party. Ev was one of the few people Rosa could rely on. VJ *would* be there, and Rosa wanted her father alert and in a peacemaking mood.

They drove about forty-five minutes before they hit the paved road. Finally able to be heard without shouting, Rosa began to list objections to the burros. She'd gone through it all before, and she was certain it'd do no good, but she felt compelled to give it one last shot.

"Think of the hoof care," she said.

"They go barefoot," he said. "They're easy keepers. They'll be on rocks quite a bit. All we'll have to do is rasp them once in a while."

"I guess they'll just let you pick up their feet right away."

"I'll teach them."

"They're stubborn!"

"Nope, cautious."

"They'll tear stuff up."

"Can't be any worse than sheep."

"They're wild. They might hurt you."

"The convicts have them halter broke."

"They'll bray, make a racket."

"No donkey alive is as rackety as a bossy daughter."

"You won't ever be able to get rid of them if they don't work out. Who'll buy them?"

"If they don't work out, I'll teach them to pull the shepherds' wagons."

"Don't get me started on those damned shepherds' wagons. I can't see why you keep them. Their day's come and gone, Daddy; none of the shepherds will stay in them. Look at the money you spend renting trailers. You could sell those darned old sheep wagons to a museum or something and use the money to buy a proper trailer for the shepherds. You drive on the ranch, and it looks like Hollywood's here shooting a movie. Those wagons are strewn everywhere, junking up the place. How many wagons have we got—ten, twelve?"

"We've got nine, and money down on number ten."

"What? You're buying another one?! Da-dee! How do you expect me to keep the books in order when you have money down here and there? It's as bad as the way you hire shepherds without telling me. We put the word out that I do the hiring, and still you . . ."

Sabine, picturing the wagon in question, was not listening very closely to Rosa's points about the business. The girl was doing a good job with the business, but that didn't mean he needed to attend to her every concern.

"You know, it's a real nice one," he said, "real cabinets inside, not a nail, not a screw, real cabinets. Daisy, you just can't pass up something like that for three hundred dollars. I'm planning to get rid of some of the others. But wouldn't one of those wagons look great all fixed up with a team of six or eight donkeys?"

"Six, eight? Daddy, where did you come up with six or eight? We're picking up four, right? Four that we don't need?"

"We will need more, Daisy-o. We'll need a donkey for every four hundred sheep."

"Good, that means we need none. I count about twenty head in the kitchen pen. Otherwise we've got none."

"We're a sheep ranch, my dear. We'll have sheep and plenty of them when I decide that the market's about to improve. We need the donkeys ready to go in anticipation."

"Like hell. It won't work!"

"You know, Daisy, it's no wonder to me that you still haven't got a husband. No matter how much a man may curse and swear oaths, it's not something he'll admire in a woman. Now, no one may say a word, but they start to think of you different, like you were one of their hunting and drinking buddies, rather than a girl to respect and court and marry."

"I'll marry when I damned please, and I'll speak the way I hear language spoken around me. We're not talking about my lack of husbands, a topic I consider my own concern; we're talking about a seventy-year-old man working with wild animals that are known to be stubborn, irascible, and unpredictable."

"I've spent my entire seventy-one years dealing with wild, stubborn, irascible, unpredictable animals, and I have to admit the worst of them were daughters."

"Any of those qualities us girls got, we got in a watered-down form from you. I guess you're right, you're the perfect man to work with donkeys; you'll know their every instinct."

"Anyway, you see, we're going to need more of them. They'll work out. They'll cut losses. And I mean it about a team to pull one of the shepherds' wagons. A man's got to have six or eight of them, minimum."

"Surely, you don't plan to do the foot care yourself?

"Surely I do. A few rasps every six months or so is all they'll need. No need for the expense of a farrier. Those burros are easy keepers."

"You are as tight as you are contrary. You'll throw your back out."

"Daisy, it sounds like you're leading up to a point about these donkeys. I could swear you're fixing to lodge some kind of protest. Spit it out, girl; your father didn't teach his girls to be shy about their opinions."

The old man set the cruise control to seventy, lit a cigar, took a long pull, and let it out with a sigh, drawing the smoke deftly into his nose as he exhaled. He gave his daughter a big wink. It was one of the most elegant, concentrated expressions of defiance imaginable. This man would have donkeys, and as many as he found suitable.

CHAPTER FIVE

■ ■ ■

There is no denying the beauty of the Nevada landscape. "Spare" is a word that tends to crop up in the descriptions. The pure mineral beauty of cliff, stone, and soil is not spoiled by a clutter of vegetation. A person can see a long, long way. The view from the window of a truck changes but slowly, and despite the aesthetic quality of the vistas, it can be boring country to cross. Luckily, Rosa and Sabine were able to while away several potentially boring hours arguing about donkeys.

The conversation demonstrated that old Sabine surely had not raised his daughter to be shy about expressing her opinions. For fairness, though, one must add that although Sabine's daughters stated their views without hesitation, Sabine seldom listened.

They arrived at the prison around midday. Sabine drove up to the guard post and told the young man that he was there to pick up four burros. The young man walked out onto the

43

pavement and pointed to a painted line just behind the pick-up's rear wheels.

"Have to stop in back of the line," he said.

A large utility vehicle marked A Acme Laundry pulled behind Sabine's rig. The guard walked toward the sentry booth.

Sabine was confused.

"Me or the truck?" he said, walking around the pickup to stand behind the line.

"Truck."

The A Acme truck was too close. Sabine asked the driver to back up a few feet. The driver was listening to Rush Limbaugh on the radio. He moved. Sabine managed to get the "Sherry Baby" rig into the proper spot behind the painted line. The guard walked up with two clipboards.

"Here's a few forms you'll need to fill out. You've got some time. No visitors can come in while the prisoners go to the cafeteria for lunch, which is in five minutes. You don't have time to complete the forms before lunch break, so it'll be an hour and a half before you can go in."

"We've finished the forms already." Sabine had worked through identical forms that the Bureau of Land Management sent with the Wild Horse and Burro Adoption Packet. He'd spent hours laboriously completing the six or seven necessary forms. There were forms to get into the prison, forms to get the truck and trailer into the prison, forms for Rosa, forms for provisional adoption of four burros, forms for federal relinquishment of four burros, forms allowing state inspection of the burros' new living quarters, and forms certifying the burros' age, sex, and general health. Sabine showed the guard the forms and followed him to the sentry shack. Sabine did not want to sit at the gate of the prison for much longer.

The guard looked at the forms. He scrutinized them in every conceivable way. Finally, he picked up the sentry shack phone. The driver of the laundry truck turned his rig off, got out and lay down, leaning against the front tire while he ate his lunch. He had the radio cranked to top volume, still tuned to Rush Limbaugh. Sabine was in a terrible state, looking at his wristwatch, chewing at his cigar. He did not think he could endure an hour and a half. He had things to do, fish to fry, and it could take time loading those donkeys.

After some minutes waiting silently on the phone, some minutes discussing the forms with unseen superiors, and some minutes reviewing Sabine's forms, the guard hung up the phone and turned to Sabine.

"Can't take 'em," he said.

Sabine felt a tightness in his throat; his pulse began to race dangerously.

"What?" he choked out, unable to believe what he'd heard. "The BLM sent those forms with a letter that said I had to fill them out and present them here."

"Nope. Can't take 'em. You have to fill out these forms here." He handed Sabine a sheaf of forms and a clipboard that had a pencil hanging from it.

Sabine looked at the forms. White dots danced ludicrously before him. He could see Rosa in the pickup craning her neck to see what was keeping him. The forms were identical to the forms he'd labored over for hours the night before.

"But," he said, "these are the same forms. I already filled out these forms."

"Can't take 'em."

Sabine felt the blood vessels in his skull engorge. His strong heart pounded those vessels as though assessing their soundness, their susceptibility to aneurism. For the moment, at least, the walls held.

A loud whistle sounded, obviously announcing lunchtime at the penitentiary. The guard smiled.

"There you go, Mr. Eckleberry, gate's closed until one-thirty. You'll have plenty of time to complete these forms."

"But why? I've already got *these* filled out, and they're exactly the same, exactly."

"Can't take 'em. Those are the old forms. As of the first of

August those forms were obsolete. The BLM sent you the old forms. Those on the clipboard are the new forms. We're required to take the new forms."

Inside, Sabine began to give up; his blood pressure dropped into safe margins. Honor obliged him to persevere. The guard must not see that he had won. Sabine continued to reason with him.

"But the old forms are exactly the same. See, the information, all the questions, exactly the same. How can you say these are the old forms?"

The guard sighed, deeply annoyed at the persistence of the old man. Marshaling his patience, he took the first page of the first form from Sabine's stack of filled forms and compared it to the apparently identical blank form.

"See," he said, pointing at a cluster of tiny letters in the lower left corner of the form, "this one is GSX-RE1 p.1; that's the one you filled out. Now the one we need is this one." He pointed to the lower left corner of the blank form. "GSX-RE2 p.1," he read, "that's the one we need, the revised GSX forms."

Sabine looked. It was true, but aside from the RE1-RE2 contrast, the forms were identical.

"But these forms are exactly the same," Sabine observed. He was now relaxed, reconciled to a long wait.

"Can't take 'em," the guard concluded. "Anyway, the girl has to fill out her own visitor forms and leave some ID with us. You all have almost an hour and a half to finish up, plenty of time."

Sabine walked back to the pickup. His legs felt wobbly; the energy was just about drained out of him.

Rosa watched her father approach the pickup. God, the man looked old, weak. Maybe this would show him that he needed help with the ranch. He got into the truck and told her about the forms and how they had to wait an hour and a half to go get the donkeys.

Rosa tried to cheer him.

"Well, let's split the pile of forms. You've already done all the work. All we have to do is copy."

Sabine agreed sourly and they began. To Rosa's immense irritation, the old guy began muttering about anarchism and the Spanish Civil War. He was not even slightly interested in politics, that was the aggravating thing. If he really had deep convictions, it'd be different. Instead, he had just enough familiarity with eccentric politics to truly embarrass his daughters.

The day had turned hot. Sabine was starving. He'd had a small breakfast at six, three eggs, a couple of sweet rolls, and a quart of milk, barely enough to sustain him through the morning. The driver of the laundry truck finished his lunch but continued to listen to his radio. Sabine was losing stamina. The noise was almost too much to bear. It is never easy to complete redundant forms while Rush Limbaugh boasts at top volume. The conditions were far from conducive to the cheerful demeanor Sabine had maintained through the long drive from the ranch. Finally though, they finished the forms. Sabine was about finished as well. He felt every one of his seventy-one years and then some. He was tired, hot, and hungry. His shirt was wet. The squealing of Rush Limbaugh made the situation grim beyond words.

Rosa had been waiting for such a moment. The lessons of Desert Storm were far from lost on Rosa Eckleberry. She'd been in high school during Desert Storm and had seen it all on the evening news and CNN. She was familiar with the "surgical strikes," the "smart bombs," the Tomahawk Cruise missiles stalking the streets of Baghdad, sensing vulnerability, "softening up" the stout defenses of the enemy. It's a foolish young woman who does not bring such lessons to conflicts and engagements with her father. Rosa Eckleberry was nobody's fool.

She gathered up the finished forms, organized them into proper order, and turned to old Sabine. "I guess it's going to be donkeys for you. It'll be a good thing, I suppose. You'll have a big time doing the training. I can just see you. Up at six to feed, working with them so they'll lift their feet and not kick you in the head, getting them used to the sheep, seeing that they work as they should with the sheep, doing the doctoring, floating their teeth, walking the fences to see that there's no place they could injure themselves, and so on. Daddy, you've talked me into it. It's a big challenge, a project you need. It'll keep you young."

Sabine had enjoyed arguing with his daughter about the donkeys. Her enthusiasm was another thing. God. They hadn't even seen the donkeys and already he was utterly exhausted. He'd forgotten about floating teeth. It wasn't necessarily easy to file the teeth of an animal that was used to it. With horses it was always hard, and it was unlikely to be much fun with burros, especially wild burros that'd never even seen a curry brush, much less a tooth file.

"I hope those donkeys load nice," Rosa said merrily. "We still have quite a drive, and then we've got to unload the little devils, don't we, and get some hay and water to them as well. Long day ahead, huh, Daddy?"

Sabine grunted.

"You know, I was thinking, Daddy, now that you're going to have this donkey project, you'll have to make up with Virgil Jose and get him back to run the ranch."

There, she'd launched it, the smart bomb, the surgical strike. Now she could relax and give the old man the help he needed with the donkeys.

At some moments in life, the small distractions of the present suddenly cease to vex. Sabine had been hot, hungry, harried. At the mention of his son, all this evaporated. Unable to do otherwise, Sabine imagined Virgil Jose running the ranch. This vision was so appalling that the present miseries seemed almost pleasant by comparison. It would be easier by far to endure Rush Limbaugh's self-righteous carping than to have to listen to VJ go on without commas about his latest big scheme. Sabine had been feeling the burden of his full seventy-one years even before Rosa broached the topic of Virgil Jose and the ranch. Now he felt at least a hundred. Oh! That boy!

"Daisy," he said, his voice faltering, "we've discussed it and the answer's no. The boy is a meathead."

Now on the face of it, Sabine's view was undeniably accurate. Rosa, however, had seized the advantage. Now was the time to summon her capacities to urge her view on her reluctant father. She was not about to back down. "Almost every ranch in Nevada is run by meatheads," she said, "and you have to admit that VJ is good with sheep."

"He's the best shepherd I've ever seen. That doesn't mean that I can tolerate his shenanigans. . . . That terrible Jojobalueca ordeal? Those morons are still calling collect from Australia."

Rosa thought about the Jojobalueca enterprise. It had not been pleasant, but she did not think it particularly relevant. "If he has some responsibility, he won't have time for that kind of thing."

"He'll make time." As Sabine argued, the color began to return to his visage.

"The fact remains . . ."

"What? The fact remains that your little brother is a nincompoop, a crackpot. Let's just dig a hole and bury me right here. They probably have a form for it. I'll fill out the form, you dig. I'd rather just spare myself the agony of a slow death by aggravation."

"Boy, you do have some opinion of your offspring. Me and my sisters are *mandonas* and Virgil Jose's a meathead. You manage to put up with Felice, Celia, and me. You can put up with VJ and you have to. He needs to learn the business."

Sabine drew a deep breath and considered his daughter. What a pistol she was. "Daisy, you and your sisters are stubborn, rackety, and bossy. Those are terrible flaws, but at least the three of you are level-headed."

"VJ's level-headed." Rosa shifted the ground of engagement. "He wouldn't have let that business with the guard and paperwork get him down."

Poor Sabine, he was still shaky from that ordeal. Unhappily, he imagined VJ dealing with the prison guard and the forms. Rosa was right. VJ'd manage it with a laugh and probably charm his way in. He'd be on his way north already. He'd have a trailer full of donkeys and not a care in the world. There was no denying the boy had energy and enthusiasm. People liked him.

"He is the most exasperating human being I have ever known." Sabine silently excepted his father. Rosa had no way to know how exasperating Joanes had been. "It doesn't matter how great he is with sheep. He thinks he's above all that, he's too good to work with the woolies."

"When's the last time you worked with sheep?" Rosa could not resist this jab. Sabine ignored it.

"All I can say is that my life has been peaceful since the day I ran that boy off the ranch. I guess that's over. You, Felice, and Celia are going to make it hell on earth, I suppose, until I bring him back to ruin my digestion. That's what my birthday party is all about, isn't it?"

It was, of course, but Rosa felt no need to continue the discussion further. She'd completed her mission, dropped the bomb, and it had found its mark. Now to the business at hand. There were forms to finish and superfluous donkeys to load for the long drive back to the ranch. Rosa sat with her father and filled out the forms to the cheery sounds of Rush Limbaugh distorting facts in the background.

Finally in the parking area of the Mustang and Burro Adoption Complex, Sabine took in the scene. To the north, the Big House loomed over the landscape. The prison was a stark monolith festooned with razor wire and tricked out with the customary appointments of prison architecture. Just south of the prison was the complex of corrals and stables the Bureau of Land Management used for the Wild Horse and Burro Adoption Program.

"You know, Daisy, prison's just the place for these animals." Sabine got out of the pickup and ambled up the walk toward a double-wide trailer that housed the BLM offices. Rosa alighted and came close to losing her balance. The air was thick with horsey smells and a cacophony of shouts, neighs, and, yes, a booming and raucous spasm of distant braying. Rosa felt momentarily overwhelmed. As she regained her composure and rushed to catch up with Sabine, Rosa was uncertain as to whether Sabine was referring to the hundreds of mustangs that infested the corrals (there were only a few burros) or the dozens of convicts that were working with the horses. Sabine didn't explain. He strode to the trailer and presented his paperwork to the program administrator, a round, balding, tobacco-chewing gnome in jeans and a western-cut corduroy sport coat. Just the sight of that jacket made Rosa feel how uncomfortably hot the day had become. The gnome had a name tag that identified him as "Howard Brumbelow, Director." He had a sign on his desk that indicated "The Buck Stops Here." The trailer was teeming with people, but Brumbelow seemed to be the only civilian among the uniformed guards and jumpsuited convicts. Reading the forms, Brumbelow led Sabine and Rosa to a pair of folding chairs. Inside and out, the adoption area was an entirely male scene, and Rosa was attracting a lot of attention. She stayed close to Sabine and tried to avoid making eye contact with anyone.

Brumbelow considered the forms with a frown. Sabine felt a palsy developing in his chest. "Something wrong?"

Brumbelow grunted and spoke. "No, naw, no, it's just fine. I was just puzzled as to why you filled out two sets of forms." Sabine told him.

"Ridiculous," said Brumbelow. "Sure we got new forms, but we're sending the old ones out as long as they last. It's one of Vice President Gore's ways to save the government money. The forms are exactly the same, old or new."

Rosa noticed that the little man had to work hard to suppress a smile when Sabine regaled him with the story of the guard who could not "take 'em." It was clear that bureaucratic absurdities amused Mr. Brumbelow.

The paperwork was in order, "doubly so," as Brumbelow pointed out. He went on to say that he'd gotten Sabine's letter some weeks earlier and had set a number of prisoners to the task of halter-breaking burros. He thought that eight or nine burros were available for adoption. Sabine could take his pick. The burros were already separated out from the mass of animals and were waiting in the adoption area along with their handlers. Flaco, a trustee who'd worked with a couple of the burros, would show Sabine and Rosa the way. Once they decided which animals they wanted, they could come back and get the "pink slips" on those particular animals. Then they could load the donkeys and take them.

Probably because Sabine and Rosa walked by several hundred horses on the way to the burro pen, the donkeys looked really small. Rosa had to admit that the little herd was precious. Rosa had not realized that donkeys were so varied in their coloring. The little group had a couple of duns, a roan, a black, and a spotted, pintolike fellow. The donkeys were much fuzzier than the sleek horses. And then there were the ears! They were so long and gave the little beasts an exaggerated appearance of attentiveness. They all stood together in the far corner of the pen. They seemed to know something was afoot. They faced the humans with their long ears pricked, alert but not uneasy.

The choice was not difficult. There were two jacks. *Stockman's Universe* was firm on the point that jacks are not reliable enough to leave with sheep. You cannot depend on a jack for anything if there is a jennet or mare within whiffing distance. There was also a small gray jennet with an adorable foal at foot, a small character with a fluffy head and spindly little legs. Sabine did not want a jennet with a small foal. *Stockman's Universe* opined that the maternal instincts of donkeys are so powerful that a jennet with a small foal would simply not have the free attention to care for a bunch of sheep. That left four burros—two geldings and a jennet with a large foal, probably at least a yearling. Rosa was glad to note that Sabine's little herd sported quite a mix of the colors available. The jennet with the foal was a classic gray dun with a black cross on her back, black ear tips, and subtly black-striped legs. The foal was identical in coloring, a slightly miniaturized copy of his mom. The younger gelding was a roan, with lots of white hairs and red hairs along with the ubiquitous gray. The older gelding was the huskiest of the four. He was a beauty, black with red highlights.

The inmates put the jacks and the mother with the little foal into a common corral with a bunch of mustangs. The inmates who'd trained Sabine's burros stayed. They haltered the burros and led them to a gate at the end of the pen. This was a small pen, and it featured a squeeze chute for loading animals into trailers. Once in the small pen, the inmates took the halters off and made their good-byes to the animals. It was, for Rosa, an affecting and completely unexpected scene. These men without women had neither leered nor made comments. Now they were quietly petting the animals they had trained. One very tough-looking guy, a big-boned fellow, arms covered with tattoos and face covered with five-o'clock shadow, cradled the yearling's head in his arms and gave it a kiss on the nose. Rosa actually got a lump in her throat watching the curiously tender scene. Sabine hustled off to finish the paperwork. This left Rosa alone with Flaco.

Watching his fellow prisoners with the donkeys, Flaco spoke. "I guess I'm lucky, at least for the day. I been working the jenny and the baby. I call her Cleopatra. She's smarter than most people. The baby is Tony. He thinks I'm a toothing toy. It makes me miss my kids. I train horses too, but the horses are crazy. They'll do anything. The burros are all . . . coming up and putting their head on you."

Flaco lapsed into silence watching the inmates and the burros. One by one, the inmates finished their good-byes and walked away.

"The guys get to like the animals," Flaco said. "You come the first time because it's a change, a way to see some new scenery. The animals grow on you. Pretty soon, it's almost like they're yours, like family or something."

Suddenly Sabine was back, brimming over with enthusiasm. "Those ears," he said, "just look at those ears!"

"I don't know if Howard told you," Flaco directed this to Sabine, "these guys are Panamint burros from Death Valley. Miners brought in their grandmas and grandpas and let them go when the mines played out or they went crazy or got killed or something. The BLM was just fixing to shoot these little guys. Somebody pitched a bitch, so I got to see what a burro is like. I don't know why they can't just leave them alone."

"I don't know why they can't leave anyone or anything alone." Sabine pressed his lips together. Sabine was impressed with Flaco, and he'd been impressed with Howard Brumbelow. It was clear that Flaco, like VJ, had an intuitive expertise with animals. It was clear that Brumbelow liked the burros, mustangs, and inmates. In Howard Brumbelow, Sabine sensed a kindred spirit.

Sabine was always able to forget that he was a rich man, a huge landowner and capitalist. He always pulled for the underdog, the proletariat. Donkeys were certainly proletarian animals. Rosa was correct in her association of the burros with socialism.

With the squeeze chute and ramp, the animals loaded easily. Sabine and Rosa both wondered what kind of rodeo would take place when they tried to load the beasts without the benefit of these aids. Sabine often had the sheep trucked from one part of the ranch to another. The donkeys would have to go too. They would have to load easily and certainly.

Very much against her will, Rosa found herself more and more interested in the donkeys and the uses Sabine had in mind for them. She'd gone through a horsey period when she was in high school. She'd stayed away from them since. She liked horses, but they were too big and hyperemotional, animals that made no sense. They were irrationally obedient. They'd run themselves almost to death if you said run. They were too hysterical. Let the wind ruffle the edge of a garbage sack and a horse could panic and practically explode. There were just too many ways for such an animal to harm itself and those close by. At seventeen Rosa lost her obsession with horses. Then, she went through a period of having sex with stupid guys. It didn't last long, but it did end the horsey phase. She knew a lot about horses, and she missed Pumpkin. She'd never rekindled her fervent affection for the big beasts, but she did have a soft spot for equines.

The possibility that burros actually would guard sheep was intriguing. It was just a matter of time before Sabine began to spend his winters with Mom in Scottsdale. Someone would have to know about donkeys if he managed to get them guarding the sheep. Well, those concerns would keep. Rosa Eckleberry had a pressing and very difficult task to perform. She had to help Sabine recover. She had hit him with the suggestion that VJ should run the ranch at a moment of great fatigue and aggravation. She had exploited the moment. That was all well and good. It would not do to have him feeling feeble and morose for his party. He would need all his powers intact to deal with VJ.

Rosa could not allow him to exhaust himself, and this was a dilemma. The donkeys were loaded. The business at the penitentiary was complete, but the long drive home, the un-

loading, and ancillary work still loomed. How could he recover his energy and composure with so much work still in
front of him? Honestly, he was impossible. Getting those burros the day before the big party, what an idea! She supposed
she could unload the animals and get them hayed and wa-
tered. She also supposed she could drive. Old Sabine handed
over the keys to the truck so easily that Rosa knew things had
gone badly downhill.

CHAPTER SIX

■ ■ ■

Retired Colonel Jordan McKenzie awoke in his Scottsdale digs feeling the full weight of his four and sixty years. Dismissing the possibility that the eight highballs had anything to do with it, he did his early-morning workout fighting the pain. His temples pounded. Small, hot explosions spread like napalm through his central nervous system as he put his dogs through their paces. He fought his way along the dirt roads of the Sonoran Desert, suffering, while the dawn sent hot pink walls of morning light through the Scottsdale skies. The Colonel was a disciplined man. He drank the occasional highball (sometimes more than one), but practiced moderation. Drunken displays were for the weak, the unworthy, the lax and slovenly, not for colonels. He certainly did *not* have a hangover.

Still, Colonel McKenzie's pain was real, and it worried him. He could barely shout his customary oaths at his dogs. He did shout, he had to shout, that slacker Sanborn saw to that. The goldbricking turd was trying, as always, to cut corners and loaf his way along, letting the other dogs break the morning headwind. The Colonel managed to shout but lacked the gusto to achieve the volume he liked. All he could produce were dry, perfunctory barks.

"Move it, Sanborn, you lazy sack of shit," and "Sanborn, I'm going to, by Christ, shoot you." He yelled halfheartedly, following the blueticks as best he could, bunched in pain and aggravation.

This was not a hangover. This was woman trouble. This was what happened when you did a woman the courtesy of staying over to provide the protection that only a man can provide. You end up having your rest ruined by half-wits, lard-asses, and yapping damned poodles. How they grace those snarling, glorified rats with the noble name of dog was a mystery that surpassed belief. Even the worst of the species, like that slacker Sanborn, deserved to be called dog. And Sanborn, miserable Sanborn, was worth fifty poodles, the mannerless yappers!

He should have known. Maybe he was getting soft. Any woman who kept poodles was going to be bad news. Was he that lonesome? Was he so hard up that he was going to stand for being thrown out of the house by a poodle lover? No, not by a long shot. The scales were falling from his eyes. Magda, for all her good looks, fine cooking, and independent nature (he did like that spunk in a woman!), was yesterday's bad news. She'd crawl back to him, and he'd put it to her, "It's either those god-damned dogs or me." That'd show her.

He got back home at seven, kenneled the dogs, fed them, microwaved some water for instant coffee, got his corn flakes, and switched on the TV. He was so excited about dumping Magda that his headache vanished. Diane Sawyer was on *Good Morning America* talking to a retired army general in Texas. This looked interesting. He turned it up.

The guy was talking about his retirement, how wonderful it was, how rich he was getting, how satisfied he was with his new enterprise. He gave Diane a pair of fancy cowboy boots. The boots retailed for around six hundred dollars a pair, and every sale sent around three hundred dollars' profit straight to this retired army guy. "Ratites," he said, "are the best business opportunity available for someone who has a little money to invest and likes a rural lifestyle." The camera panned over (by God!) a bunch of ostriches and some smaller birds that the Colonel didn't recognize.

That's what Magda's whelp, the one with the nice pickup and the sound view of Richard Petty, had been yammering about at three in the morning! He recalled the situation. He'd obviously misjudged the boy, but what do you expect, three in the morning, poodles everywhere, left-wing college students cluttering the living room. Even the most discerning mind would have an understandable lapse in such circumstances. His patience had been tried, severely tried. Perhaps he'd have an opportunity to talk with the boy when Magda crawled back. Maybe he'd just put off the ultimatum about the poodles long enough to find out how much the boy knew about this ratite thing. He finished the corn flakes as Diane Sawyer wrapped up the feature. She surely was a fine-looking babe, even if she was a communist. Hell, the Colonel was open-minded. He'd even bought one of Jane Fonda's exercise videos. That Ted Turner sure knew where to wick his candle. If you were rich enough, that's what you could do, reach out and take what you wanted and politics be damned.

The red light on the Colonel's answering machine was on. Magda, he guessed, was already crawling back. The message was long, probably full of weeping apologies and pleas for for-giveness. A contented grin broke across his brown, wrinkled features as he rewound the tape. The grin, however self-satis-fied, was short-lived. Magda's voice was strong, loud, almost booming, lacking the feeble, supplicating tones of contrition.

"Colonel McKenzie," she said, "Magda Eckleberry here. We need to get straight. I sent you home for many good reasons. First, I invited you over for dinner and, perhaps, quiet conversation. I did not invite you over so that you could drink yourself into a besotted stupor. I ask that you contain yourself in the future. Second, there is no excuse for your behavior toward my dogs. Drunk or sober, I expect you to treat my dogs with kindness, respect, and common courtesy. Third, my son and his friend are guests in my house. Young Ev is a fine young man I have known for many years. I will not have him insulted under my roof, and I certainly will not have my only son, whom I dearly love, insulted. I feel that you owe both of them an apology. Any further contact between you and me is, in fact, going to depend on you making those apologies.

"I am very angry with you, but I am not, after all, a vindictive woman. Everyone makes mistakes, and I realize that I have to make some allowances. It is, after all, nearly four A.M., and I know that elderly people are seldom at their best at this hour.

"So, angry as I am, I am willing to offer provisional forgiveness. Apologize to VJ as a start. Why don't you come by here at eight forty-five tomorrow morning. I've decided to drive to Nevada along with the boys. You can come along. It will do you good to get out of your rut. All you seem to do is swill down booze and run those poor hounds of yours. I'd like for you to drive. It'd be a favor that would partially make up for your behavior this evening. I'll be taking the dogs and need to be free to nurse poor Sassy. You'll like my husband, he was in World War Two. We'll come back Friday or Saturday. I can leave instructions for Marti, the girl who works for me. She'll see that your dogs are fed and exercised. 'Bye for now. Please do not call before eight tomorrow. I'm turning my phone off. Hope you're not too hungover."

Colonel McKenzie's face changed color a number of times during the course of the message. Magda's words annoyed him so thoroughly that he felt, for a moment, overwhelmed, defeated. Next, he was aware of the drumming of his pulse in his temples. Taking a deep breath, the Colonel stepped back and peeled off a few quick karate kicks, neutralizing the enemy one imagines in solo workouts. He took another deep breath, proud that he was learning to master his rages. He weathered the episode bravely, damaging neither his furniture nor his fists. Now he could think. The Colonel was a realist and proud of it. He could not perform the mental gymnastics necessary to characterize Magda's message as "crawling back." Nope, but she was up to something, and the Colonel figured that he'd best just cool his jets for the time being. He supposed that he ought to go on along with her to Nevada. The prospect of meeting Magda's husband was not particularly delightful, but if he went, he could keep his options open with the woman and find out about this ostrich business. It'd be painless enough. He'd already put up with those damned poodles for some months; a few more days wouldn't matter. Besides, he'd already apologized to the boy. Of course, he was not doing another damned thing, and he was lonesome. He'd never have the satisfaction of seeing Magda crawl back if he didn't hang around. He'd have to resist the temptation to put the needle into old Blubber-butt. Luckily, that one had slept through his ration of insults. No need to apologize to *him*. Magda really got her claws out when it came to her cubs, even the honorary ones. She sure was a saucy number.

Ev did sleep well. Not only did he sleep through the Colonel's insults but also through most of Magda's ministrations to his blistered feet. She'd popped the blisters, iced the inflammation, and then wrapped the feet in cotton, lightly secured by gauze. Ev slept until eight, when he was awakened by the unmistakable sound of poodles driven to manic hysteria by the psychic knowledge that they'd soon be in Nevada chasing sheep. Ev did not mind. He'd had a splendid, nourishing repose. He was cool and in his depths felt that he required nothing more of this existence. Let others strive for fame, wealth, power, and social position. Just let him, Ev Crume, live a life of simplicity, a life lived out in blessed breezes of refrigerated air. VJ could solo to Nevada. Ev would stay on. He'd make a way for himself so long as he didn't have to go outside.

Young Crume's conviction that he had awakened in paradise was fortified by the smell of breakfast wafting on chilled breezes from the kitchen. He swung himself into a sitting position and considered his bandaged feet. They felt fine. Ev wondered, though. What would happen when he put his weight on those feet? He had no concrete aspirations in that direction, but the blended scents of eggs, toast, coffee, and other delights exerted nascent pressure on the young man. He placed a cocooned foot onto the unforgiving but trendy flagstone floor. Hmm. Not bad. By degrees he put weight on his feet, first one, then the other, then both together. Within a quarter hour Ev was standing on his own. He was smiling. It was like a miracle. He'd really healed up in just that few hours. Sure, he'd have to take it easy, but it really wasn't so bad. He was grateful, happy. His heart surged in his chest with warmth for Magda and the climate-control system that, he now felt, had healing powers. The irrationality of this conviction made Ev feel uncomfortable as he made his slow, careful way to the kitchen. As an educated person, he insisted on faith grounded in reason. On the other hand, he was stirred. He recalled the sweet, drowsy, drifting-into-sleep image of Magda on her knees tending to his poor, burned feet. She was so tender, so careful, so concerned that he be comfortable and insulated from anything that would pain his feet. Magda had turned the air conditioner on, opened the vent, and set the thermostat. Ev's feet had healed in the breezes she summoned. There was no getting around it, but then that was Magda's way. She'd always been kind and made great efforts to make Ev feel better. She was an extraordinary woman, VJ's mom. It was a shame, Ev felt, that he was always such a tongue-tied nitwit around her.

The kitchen Ev entered was full of activity. It had the feel of a command post, the nerve center of some great campaign. In the midst of the activity Magda loomed, pacing three steps, turn, three steps, turn, talking to someone on the phone. My God, thought Ev, just exactly like VJ pacing in that little apartment so few hours ago. Ev blushed. VJ's pacing had been a demonstration of robotic distraction. Magda's movement up and down her kitchen was a vision of sensuality. Her pacing involved undulation. She was wearing a blue silk or satin house dress that adhered to her body. With one hand she held the phone to her ear and with the other hand she stroked and combed at her auburn hair with her long fingers. Ev had to hunch over to hide the evidence of his carnal reaction.

VJ was there, teasing the frantic poodles and having his breakfast. Ev could not believe how much VJ could eat sometimes and how little he would eat in other circumstances. At any rate, he was obviously taking advantage of the maternal care and restoring his depleted tissues. Ev followed suit.

Magda was quick to note that Ev was getting around pretty well. The trauma to his feet had certainly not affected his appetite. Sassy was not so lucky. He was off his feed and hobbling around miserably. The one good thing was that the other dogs sensed the impending trip to Nevada. They were running wild and nutso all over the house. They had taken Ev's and VJ's boots out in the yard to pee on them but were, mercifully, ignoring poor Sassy.

Magda had slept until almost seven-thirty. Three and a half hours' sleep in a stretch was not bad. At some points in her life such a sustained rest would have seemed an unattainable luxury. She was pleased at how simple and satisfying her life in Scottsdale had become. Why, she was able to just take off, just like that. Nothing to it. All she had to do was call Marti and have her come in to clip dogs and keep the boutique open; call and reschedule four clients who insisted on her particular attentions for their pets; call the vice chairperson of the ad hoc committee for a Safe Scottsdale for Our Pets (SSOP) and fill her in on the agenda for the meeting Magda would miss; call Herb Mole, SSOP's volunteer lawyer, and leave a message to hold off on the letter to the City Council; call Marti again and remind her about the Colonel's dogs, in particular not to let Sanborn loaf during the exercise runs; call Celia in Nevada, having gotten no answer from Rosa or Sabine at the ranch, to let the Nevada contingent know she, VJ, Ev, the Colonel, and her four poodles were on their way to Nevada and would arrive sometime around ten in the evening (give or take a couple of hours); ice Sassy's leg; make a good wholesome breakfast for the boys; pack a lunch; do a couple of loads of laundry; pack her clothes; run out to buy a present for Sabine (who was, as Celia put it, "going ape-shit and getting a bunch of donkeys at his age"); wrap Sabine's gift (four fancy cotton lead ropes for the donkeys); call a feed store in Reno to see that they had the special dog food Sassy had to have for his convalescence; and call young Morton Gelb next door to have him come in to feed the fish and birds, as well as run the TV for the birds, while she was gone. Because of Ev's feet, she felt that she also had to inventory the first-aid kit she kept in the car, making sure there was a roll of cotton. This reminded her to stop at a Walgreen's and buy a decent first-aid kit to give VJ for his pickup. She knew better than to expect that he'd have thought to buy one. As always, she'd had to fight some on the phone with Celia, and that had put her a little behind. When Ev came in for breakfast, Magda was almost ready. She did have to retrieve the boys' boots and hose the dog pee off them. Otherwise, she was ready to load up as soon as the Colonel arrived. She remembered her life at the Nevada ranch, what had been involved to organize something as small as an overnight trip to Reno. It was weeks just getting ready and weeks more for the routines to recover from the disruption.

It was nice to have things so simple, so easy to take care of. It gave her time to watch VJ and Ev have their breakfast. This was one of the great pleasures of Magda's morning. She loved to eat, and she loved to watch while others tucked in. People were really not very different from animals, and all were at their most vulnerable in the act of eating.

Unfortunately, VJ was entertaining himself through a leisurely breakfast by teasing Magda's dogs. Moe was always terribly insecure about changes in the day's routine. VJ found that he could make a certain face at Moe that drove the poor dog into neurotic fits, digging at the floor, cringing, and spinning circles in a pathetic attempt to ingratiate himself with this new, threatening person. Initially, the face VJ made was quite a production. He would tighten his lips, puff his cheeks, and roll his eyes. During the course of the meal, he refined the grimace. Finally all he had to do was tighten his lips as though he were going to make the face. Moe was taking no chances. The poor thing was wearing himself out. Now, finished with the preparations and ready to join the boys for coffee, Magda could do something about it.

"VJ," she said, "now you quit teasing poor Moe. You're going to give him a nervous breakdown. He'll be sick on the trip if you keep it up."

VJ quit. He'd just been passing time. In regards to his mother's pets, he had neither malice nor compassion. He figured the dogs would all be sick on the trip anyway.

"So," he said, "when are you and Daddy getting back together?"

Ev started with alarm at VJ's tactlessness. Magda answered without a blink.

"As soon as his resistance wears down. A couple of years maybe. Anyway, I don't want to live with him year-round, you know that. I am not going to live on that ranch again, not ever, but I think eventually he will have the good sense to winter with me here in Scottsdale and spend his summers in Nevada with you and the girls."

Magda smiled, noting that Moe had settled down and entirely relaxed. He sat at VJ's feet as though VJ was his best friend and the soul of kindness. VJ had a peculiar charisma. Animals always liked him. VJ soothed the world's beasts. He spoke to correct his mother's assumption that he'd soon be living in Nevada.

"Maybe I won't be in Nevada. I kind of like New Mexico. It's a better place for my ostrich business. State legislature there provides some tax incentives, and the climate is . . . well, you know what Nevada is."

Magda smiled at Ev but directed her remarks to VJ.

"Tax breaks," she said. "You sound just like Colonel McKenzie. Taxes this, taxes that. I swear he thinks that the way to heaven is paved with tax breaks. Do you have a girlfriend, VJ? I mean anyone special?"

"Nope, I'm leaving that to my business manager. He has one, ol' four-eyes Susie. She's a student just like him, Mama. She's not much to look at," he winked, "but she makes up for it by being mean."

"Doggone it, VJ, don't you start in on Susan. Missus Eckleberry, er, I mean Miz Zumwalt. Uhhh. Susan is . . . a girl. Virgil Jose calls her my girlfriend. She's . . . " Instead of finishing his sentence Everett simply blushed.

"I'm sure Susan is a fine young woman if she's *your* little friend," said Magda, responding to Ev's obvious distress. "I just wish VJ would show some interest in long-term relationships. You know, VJ, that girls are drawn to you. Why do you get so distracted?"

VJ said nothing but began whistling Elvis's version of "My Way." Virgil Jose was very talented at whistling, punctuating the tune with arpeggios and other smart-ass flourishes. Magda shook her head. What an exasperating child! "Virgil Jose," she said, "what you are doing is not smart, and it is not funny. It was your father that made you like this. He put you out with that horrible old Golfrido and all those shepherds. And look at you." She shook her head. VJ was wearing brand-new jeans with the tags still attached, an extravagant blue-and-yellow-striped cowboy shirt, probably expensive, undoubtedly his idea of high fashion, and sweat socks of that god-awful pink color that comes when you wash whites and colors together. He was such a good-looking boy, too. Why couldn't he . . . And poor Ev. Now there was a boy in need of supervision. If VJ looked eccentric, then Ev was simply shabby, right out of the K-mart bins. Magda felt that Ev's poor choice of apparel was his girlfriend's fault. VJ had said she was "mean." Evidently, she was not nearly mean enough. Magda could not understand what was wrong with young girls. Rosa was the exception. When *she* had a gander at Laurel and Hardy here, they'd find out about mean, all right.

This revery was interrupted by honking. Magda recognized the signature of the Colonel: long, persistent, increasingly irritated (and irritating!) honks from the expensive Klaxon horn he'd had specially installed on the Cherokee. The dogs, hearing that familiar and hated sound, went into paroxysms.

"That'd be the Colonel," Magda explained to the boys, who looked at one another blankly, wondering why a semi truck would be making a delivery in a residential neighborhood.

"Gather your things. I'll go out back and get your boots. The dogs took them out to piddle on them. Ev, you won't be wearing your boots anyway. Put your socks on over the bandaging. You seem to be getting around. Your feet will be okay if you are careful."

There really was not much to gather. VJ just had to throw his paper bag into the pickup. Ev had slept in his clothes and hadn't even unloaded his suitcase. VJ noted that his mom had assembled her things by the front door. There probably was not quite enough to last a year, but it was still an impressive pile.

The Colonel was evidently going to honk his horn indefinitely. Magda and VJ went out so the Colonel would see them and stop honking. Ev paid a visit to the bathroom.

Seeing Magda and VJ, the Colonel smiled broadly. She was

wearing that swishy satin thing that gave him such a bone. He was ready to roll. He'd serviced the Cherokee, gassed it, pulled one of the seats out, and put a couple of cages for the dogs in the back. Best to take the Cherokee. Magda had a Ford Crown Victoria station wagon that did not even merit consideration. That vehicle was to genuine cars what the damned poodles were to genuine dogs. It had a mushy ride and even with the 390 seemed underpowered. As Magda and VJ approached, the Colonel cranked down his window.

"Listen, Son, like I said last night, I regret the harsh words. I was in an irritable mood, I guess."

"Oh," VJ said, beginning to twirl his hair, "everyone reacts like that, at least at first."

"Well, let's get loaded. Magda, if I am going to drive, I want to take the Cherokee. That damned Ford drives mushy, and it's a glorified bucket of bolts . . ."

Magda, frowning, interrupted. "Certainly we can take your precious Cherokee, but there is no reason to start the cracks about the Ford. It's a perfect car for me, and I'll thank you to keep your comments to yourself. Remember, you're still on thin ice."

The loading was quite an efficient process. Even the dogs seemed to sense that it was time to get serious. By nine, the black Cherokee and the blue pickup were headed down Camelback Road toward the freeway. Magda insisted that Ev ride in the air-conditioned comfort of the Cherokee along with her, the Colonel, and the poodles. For the time being, VJ was on his own in the pickup.

CHAPTER SEVEN

■ ■ ■

Thank goodness for long summer days and air-conditioned pickups. Rosa was driving north, driving fast, and feeling better by the mile. The old man was in that quiet corner of heaven made possible by cholesterol and alcohol. He was smoking a massive cigar. Sherry Baby was brimming over with feral donkeys. The midsummer sun was organizing itself to begin the slow job of setting in the northwestern sky. The ranch was maybe three hours distant; not bad, all in all.

Rosa, like her father and brother, loved to drive and loved to drive fast. The farther she drove, the better she felt. Like her father on the trip down, she settled on a modest eighty-five as the proper speed for towing donkeys. God, it was a nice pickup. She couldn't fault the old man on his choice of trucks, that was for sure. Having achieved a triumph in her relations with her father, Rosa was inclined toward generosity, a certain relaxation of judgment. What a great old guy! What a grand day it'd been! Sure, there were more donkeys involved in things than she'd have preferred, but that was a given. The old boy was going to have donkeys whether or not anyone exploited the situation. In Rosa's mind, one of the great challenges of life had to do with using the momentum of the inevitable to push along your projects, and Rosa had some projects to push along.

She wanted her folks back together, for example. This meant that Sabine had to begin turning over the work of the ranch to her and VJ, which meant that VJ needed to be at the ranch. Rosa was doing as much as she could do already. Sabine set up the business in a complex, idiosyncratic, and quixotic fashion. Running his affairs was a labor-intensive endeavor. VJ was an exasperating boy but really no more exasperating than his father. He had energy to spare and learned quickly when it suited him. Rosa would see that it suited him. So project number one was getting VJ back on the ranch, and Rosa had moved it along nicely. She'd hit the old man at a weak moment. He didn't even argue. The white flag simply went up in his old eyes, and he seemed to wither, looking haggard and drawn.

This withering and drawing was alarming at first, and Rosa wondered if the onslaught, successful as it was, had been too much. Then she remembered how long it'd been since breakfast. She was the daughter of Magda Zumwalt-Eckleberry, and she'd always paid close attention to her mother's supervision of the old man. If Sabine slipped into pessimism, melancholy, Magda would feed him. Rosa, relying on maternal wisdom, had done just that.

Just outside the prison she'd stopped at a phone booth. She phoned ahead to a steakhouse in Caldwell and ordered four steak sandwiches, a loaf of garlic bread, an order of sauteed onions, and two bottles of Sangre de Toro red table wine. She likewise asked that they assemble the package to go, along with the largest cigar available, a disposable table cloth, plastic utensils, napkins, and paper cups for the wine. It was the kind of meal Sabine would have eaten twice a day if left to his own devices, a terrible meal. As first aid to a foundered ego, it had been perfect. The toxins had paradoxically restored the color in Sabine's cheeks, the defiance to his carriage, and the smart-aleck cracks to his conversation. "*Una vez al año*," he'd happily chirped, "*no hace daño.*"

He was right, once a year wouldn't hurt. Sabine tended to use this proverb once or twice a week in what Rosa felt was a horribly self-deceptive way. Not deceiving herself, she played the percentages and crossed her fingers. The meal would *probably* not cause a hypertensive episode. She told herself that it was worth the risk. The old guy had a birthday party coming up.

The meal certainly worked its magic. Afterward, Sabine lit his terrible cigar. He was a new man.

"This is a poor excuse for a cigar," he said, smiling broadly and puffing at the poisonous, ropelike stogie. "Look here, Daisy, at the package. It says 'nontobacco ingredients added.' The world is going downhill, *mi hijita.*"

"It smells, Daddy, like those nontobacco ingredients must be dog shit."

"I told you about that language, Daisy. It's no good. No one likes to hear a nice-looking girl talking about dog shit."

"I was talking about the cigar, that *eau de pooch*. Anyway, if you don't like it, throw it out and do us both a favor."

"No, Daisy, you don't understand. The cigar is not bad for what it is, but the truth of the matter is that you cannot buy a real cigar in most places anymore. This is the best we can do, and it is not altogether bad. But it's not a cigar, not really. It lacks integrity. You still have to go to Cuba for a real cigar, or at least Santo Domingo."

Rosa rolled her eyes. If he wasn't despondent, he was argumentative.

"Did you notice the broken ear on the jenny?" he asked,

pulling deeply on the unsound panatela. "Damned sorry rodeo cowboys did that with roping practice. They just roped, abused, and then abandoned her in the desert where she found her pals. You know, it's possible to read an animal just like an archaeologist reads the traces of history in rocks. You can read an animal's past right in its body. At some time in her life, that old girl has been on a ranch full of meatheads, probably your high school boyfriends."

Rosa felt a warm glow in her belly. The old boy was feeling himself again. And he was right. It was certainly possible to see Sabine Eckleberry's past in his body. He sat there on the edge of his seat, his fat old body about to explode with exuberance. Aggression, obstinance, and intensity showed in every cell, as did the obvious history of indulgence in red meat, red wine, and garrulous conversation. Rosa smiled as so many times before she had frowned.

"Daddy," she said, "it's been a while since high school. I've grown out of the cowboy phase."

"Looks to me like you're out of the *boy* phase, Daisy. Why don't you do some things to make yourself . . . I mean, put yourself in the company of some nice young men once in a while?"

"I've got my own pace, Daddy, and my own notion of what's nice. Let's not get started on that. I did notice the broken ear. It gives her a sad look. You don't have to be an archaeologist to see sad."

Sabine was well into the second bottle of Sangre de Toro. The restorative effect of the wine made the old Basque more inclined to philosophy than badgering his daughter. Badgering Daisy was a thankless task, and Sabine figured it could wait. Daisy showed no signs of changing one iota. The work would be there when he got back to it. He could take it up again at his leisure, small doubt of that.

"You know what I like about those donkeys?"

"No, Daddy, is it that they are stubborn and irascible?"

"Daisy, be serious. Do you know what it is?"

Rosa did not know. She now felt that the donkeys were somehow perfect for the old man at this point in his life. Rosa thought they were pretty little animals, but she doubted that Sabine liked them because they were pretty.

"No, what is it?"

"What I like is that they are trash animals. They've always been the animals of the poor, and now they are not even wanted by the poor. But they don't know that. They have dignity. Did you notice the gelding, the black one, sure of his strength, his power, just like a young soldier, a guerrilla fighter, a revolutionary? I'm going to name that boy Che, after Che Guevara. You *know* that Che Guevara was a great man."

"Daddy, stop it. Why do you always have to talk like a communist? You've told me about Che Guevara a hundred times. I knew these donkeys had something to do with crazy politics. So you are thinking of these donkeys as terrorists, Basque separatists maybe, a little cell for you to train to blow up boutiques in Madrid? Don't embarrass everybody. Name him something like Bojangles."

"Bojangles? Oh, Daisy, no, no. That little guy is *fuerte*, dignified. It's got to be something like Che, or maybe Bolívar."

"Bolívar's not bad; you could still call him Bo."

"*Ay mi hija,* you don't understand. Here, think of the trainer, the guy they called Flaco."

"Yeah, what about him?"

"He is a trash human, just like the donkeys are trash animals. *Mira,* here's this guy, Daisy. He's got tattoos. He's got that little cross by his thumb. Isn't anyone going to hire him, *ever,* and you know he sees to that. He's got that way of walking says '*y la tuya, cabrón.*' He's probably a killer or something. Anyway, did you notice how good he was with the animals, how much they liked him, how well they responded? It's lucky guys like that don't have the atom bomb. If guys like him ever stop destroying themselves, there will be a revolution, not just crazy men blowing up boutiques.

"Watch people, Daisy. Their true nature comes out when

they deal with what's beneath them. Anybody can be nice to those above them. Think of the holy rollers sucking up to God. Think of the way people kowtow to the rich and powerful. It means nothing. Then think of Flaco in that hell there, how kind he is to those donkeys and horses. You know he has nothing to gain from those creatures, they'll never hire him, they'll never get him out of there."

Rosa watched the rearview mirror. The sun was getting ready to set and taking its own good time at it. There was no hurry. In July, the Nevada sun can afford to be fussy with aesthetic details. A local thunderstorm fifty miles east had been drawn into the project for dramatic emphasis. Some wispy strings of cloud were there at the horizon for the color phase, but Rosa expected them to be withdrawn, perhaps at the last minute. Shadows of telephone poles fell across the highway at an angle. This gave a nice rhythm to driving, especially since Sabine was droning on. The rhythm of speech created a counterpoint to the rhythm of light. It was a very nice effect, even as a backdrop for Sabine's crackpot theories.

She did not much like the direction of the conversation. It was interesting, but annoyingly eccentric. The only other person she knew who talked like this was VJ, and *that* was disturbing. The pace was different, but the feel of the *charla* was the same. As much as the two of them would deny it, they were just alike. The words were different, but the music was the same. Father and son, they were oddballs, both of them. All her life, Rosa had dreamed of an ordinary existence, an ordinary family, with an ordinary father, thinking ordinary American thoughts, in ordinary English, not Spanish, and certainly not Euzkadi. VJ was just as bad in English as the old man in any tongue. Recollection of this sobering fact now dampened Rosa's sense of triumph. It was galling to her to be working so hard to get VJ back on the ranch. She ran the ranch just fine for the most part. Sure, she needed someone with a bit more brawn from time to time, but it needn't be her brother. She'd maybe forgiven, but would never forget, the incident with the snakeskin. A girl can never really feel the same about a brother who involves his trusting sister in a fraud involving the skin of someone's deceased pet python.

It was a miracle she hadn't landed in prison because of that snake attack stunt VJ had pulled. That would have probably made her father happy. He evidently admired convicted criminals. Rosa was annoyed at the way he talked about Flaco, and she was annoyed at herself for being so friendly with the convict. The guy was a thug, probably a gangbanger, a stereotypical pachuco. He did have a way with the animals, he had a nice smile, and he was respectful to her. He did not leer and make sideways comments like some of the other convicts. But in the final analysis, the guy was just another loser, skinny, withdrawn, but holding himself in that defiant, contemptuous way Sabine so admired. Flaco had made her nervous. She was glad to put both him and the prison behind her, and she drove on enjoying the rhythm of the road and enduring her father, who continued his dissertation.

"The thing I liked about Flaco is the way he has molded himself into the kind of person whose very existence is an offense to those in power. He makes people nervous and he makes animals relax. I've noticed that about the best shepherds, and I have to admit it, Virgil Jose is like that. Not a criminal, I don't mean he is the same as a murderer, but face it, he makes people nervous and he makes animals relax. It's a beautiful thing. He's the best damned shepherd I ever saw.

"Anyway, I love the way nobody knows what to do about the wild burros and mustangs. They are trash like Flaco. They make people nervous, and they offend the powerful. Just think of old Donnell and his Arabians. Those horses are worth twenty, thirty thousand and on up, but they are as dumb as a handful of marbles. Imagine. Here I pay three hundred dollars to adopt four burros, and even the foal has more sense than those brainless, overbred Arabians. That will offend Mr. Donnell, *mi hija*, and it's one thing I like about them."

"Great, Daddy, all that fine talk about them running off

coyotes was just an excuse, I guess. What you really like is offending your neighbors. That is so infantile. Why don't you just go moon Mr. Donnell or something. That would offend him and would be a lot less trouble." Rosa smiled. The image of Sabine mooning the Donnell ranch house was one to savor.

"I don't want to offend anyone. It's the burro nature, I'm talking about, that draws me to them. It's my misfortune, maybe, but I like that spirit. It's the same with you. You have your spirit, Daisy, and I like it."

"Well, don't count on me to run off coyotes."

"Did you notice how each of those donkeys had a particular way of doing things? The jenny made her way so delicate, while Che just blundered and barged here and there, knocking the others around. The foal had this superior, smart-aleck way he held his head, and the gray gelding was nervous, watching, waiting, worrying, seeing that everything was okay and finally following the others. He was looking around all the time."

"No, Daddy, I was mainly noticing the colors, I guess. I have to admit they're pretty little animals, and they do seem bright-eyed and intelligent."

"Well, we've got Flaco and the others to thank for that, at least partly. The training has left them with their self-respect. The jenny is wary and has a negative outlook, but no one can blame her for that. Look at what the damned ropers did to her ear."

"You don't know how she got that ear broken. Maybe another donkey grabbed it and bit it like that."

"Nope, that's an injury of abuse. I tell you, you can see it in her body. The body doesn't lie. Did you see how she hunches her shoulders and peers around? It's like she's always expecting someone to show up with a two-by-four. I'm going to show her to VJ, he's so down on sheeping. Maybe he'll see what that rodeoing he admires so much is really all about. Hell, those idiots even rope goats. Treat an animal like that!

They should just take those who'd do such a thing and force them to rope and hog-tie one another at rodeos. I'd pay big to see that."

He paused, shaking his head and picturing the unfortunate burro. "When VJ sees that jenny, maybe he'll quit disgracing us. *Dios mio,* my son a cowboy!"

Well, Sabine was right about that. Rosa guessed that the cowboy phase was inevitable. To her shame, she'd certainly had hers. "Ride 'em hard and leave them sweatin'" was one cowboy beau's characterization of the act of love. She was glad to have all that behind her.

They talked a while about naming the burros. Sabine, of course, would have his way. The black one would be Che, against all objections. The worrisome gray would be Capitán, because he reminded Sabine of a military commander he'd known in Spain. The jenny would be Vera. Sabine said he was certain that a black man would name her Vera. Rosa pointed out that Sabine was not black. Sabine ignored his daughter and went on. Blacks, he said, are America's most downtrodden people. They would have the best names for donkeys. The foal would be Elvis because of his smart-aleckiness. Rosa had to laugh. At least "Elvis" was a Nevada name. She surprised herself. She'd argued about the names as though she cared a damn.

The energy the old man expended in the consideration of names had left him pretty depleted, and he had sucked down the second bottle of Sangre de Toro. Rosa was not surprised when she noticed him nodding off, just as the sun sank with resolution beneath the southwestern horizon.

It was about ten when they pulled up to the ranch. Rosa sent Sabine straight in to bed and was again concerned. He did not argue. He did not insist on getting the donkeys unloaded. He just did as he was told and went silently in to bed. His energy really was flagging. He was showing his age. Rosa saw this as confirmation. It really was time to get VJ back on the ranch. Old Sabine often wilted at the mere mention of work. Even driving and arguing wore him out.

The prospect of unloading the donkeys was admittedly daunting. Loading them had been a chore despite the squeeze chute at the prison and plenty of help from the prisoners, BLM people, and guards. Unloading them was likely to pose a problem or two, especially since Rosa would have to do it on her own.

There was a fifty-acre pen just in front of the house. Sabine called it the kitchen pen. He kept the sheep he meant to slaughter for the table in that pen. It was a likely place to put donkeys. Sabine often kept huge numbers of sheep there during shearing time, so it was quite secure. Rosa hadn't looked at it closely for a while, but it was the best-fenced pen anywhere near the house. Sabine had the little corral west of the house full of the damned old covered wagons he was collecting. Any animal worth its salt would get into mischief within two or three minutes in that corral, and Rosa had the feeling that the donkeys might have a talent for mischief. She'd just drive Sherry Baby into the kitchen pen, unload the donkeys, and then put the trailer into its spot in the barn. She was going to need the pickup bright and early and preferred to have the trailer safely stowed.

The moon was just this side of a quarter moon and waxing, but it was still dark as hell. Rosa eased on into the pen, cut the engine, stepped out, and opened the trailer. The donkeys, loose in the trailer, were all crowded at the other end, away from the door. They were motionless. They made no noise, but their ears were straight up. That was one alert bunch of donkeys, Rosa reflected. They were obviously not going to simply jump out of the trailer.

Rosa decided she'd try driving them out. She went around to the front where the burros were huddled and pounded on the metal sides of the trailer.

Rosa had listened to Sabine rhapsodize about donkeys for

months, and she knew the fundamentals of the breed. Donkeys are animals that have a conservative nature. They are slow to be convinced of the wisdom of change. The enterprise of getting into that small, cramped, unfamiliar space to leave the happy surroundings of the prison was not something they warmed to easily. It took quite a number of people employing quite a number of persuasive tactics to convince the burros to get into the trailer. Rosa did not understand what had finally worked. People had tried reason, sweet talk, bribes of alfalfa pellets and apples, baby talk, threats, force in the form of pulling on halters, limitation of options via the squeeze chute, encouragement from the rear via pushing, pleas, stern swats to the butt, and even ventriloquism. One of the convicts, a paper-hanging check artist who'd worked his ventriloquism act at Circus Circus in better days, had cast a pitiful imitation of a braying donkey into the trailer thinking that would attract the animals. The four donkeys, all herded down the squeeze chute together, had stood on the ramp and stared at the three-eighths-inch aperture between the ramp and the trailer. They were content, it seemed, to make a life's work of this activity and resisted all attempts to get them across that tiny crack and into the trailer. Finally, the collective patience of the onlookers and helpers was just about exhausted. Talk turned to topics such as two-by-fours and summary execution. Twenty-odd people were standing around contemplating violence when the jenny raised her head, snorted, and walked nonchalantly into the trailer, followed closely by her peers. The foal hesitated a few minutes more, but finally followed, unwilling, in the final analysis, to be left behind. It looked to Rosa like the burros studied the situation until they felt comfortable, then acted. These animals were different from horses.

So Rosa did not expect her beating on the sides of the trailer to have much effect. She tried it anyway. Sure enough, the donkeys did not budge. As reluctant as they'd been to get into the trailer, they'd evidently developed quite an affection for it. Yes, it was small. Yes, it did force a donkey into close contact with other donkeys, some of whom were inevitably repugnant, but it had the kind of known, safe quality to it that burros universally appreciate. Contrast the familiar ambiance of the trailer with the unknown, the inky, stinky, sheep-smelling abyss that suddenly yawned open with a terrible creaking. And then there was the added indignity. A small, annoying human stood in the open door issuing orders and making a racket. No burro is going to be so foolish as to simply leave a place that has proved secure for the dark and untested unknown, however loud and annoying humans become.

The burros believed in the wait-and-see approach to things and were determined to huddle together, hold their ears at full attention, and stare into the depths of the Nevada night. The others, in fact, looked to the jenny for guidance. The jenny did not move. She did not believe in squandering her energies in unnecessary agitation. A person familiar with don-keys and attentive to their ways might have noticed a subtle tightening of muscles around old Vera's muzzle that brought her lips together with the firmness that denotes resolution. Indeed, Vera tightened her bodily apertures, both fore and aft, instinctively electing to make her stand, if need be, in that cramped yet familiar space. Taking their cue, the other don-keys shrank toward the far end of the trailer and lapsed into a state of profound inertia. They had a peaceful look as though swayed by the wisdom of Vera's policy into a kind of hiber-nation.

Sabine had been right. "Vera" was the right name after all. The old doll had a stalwart quality no doubt shared by many Veras throughout history. It was something Rosa admired, de-spite the problems it posed. There was no use in trying to convince any of the other donkeys to leave the trailer. Vera would have to be first. She'd follow the foal were he to leave, but the little guy was behind her, clamped to the floor and leaning heavily against the maternal flank. Nope, it had to be her.

Rosa did not *have* to do anything. A lesser person might simply walk away secure in the knowledge that the donkeys would eventually leave the trailer on their own. Indeed, the animals were able to smell the welcome scent of fresh grass beneath the offensive sheep musk that hung about the field. No donkey in recorded history is known to have starved in an open trailer in the middle of a pasture. Eventually, following their own promptings, trailered burros will leave that paradise of familiarity in the interests of a much needed meal. Rosa, however, was not the kind of woman to leave donkeys lollygagging in a trailer all night. She meant to put that trailer where it belonged and then go to her repose, confident that she would be able to use the truck at her convenience without having to deal with donkeys and trailers before breakfast.

A battle of wills was obviously shaping up when a familiar, far-off sound cut into the silence of the rural Nevada night. It was low and far away but persistent. Honk! Honk, honk, honk, honkhonk, honk, honkhonk, honk, honk! Honk! Honk, honk, honkhonk, honk, honkhonk, honk, honk! Honk! Honk, honk, honk, honkhonk, honk, honkhonk, honk, honk! Rosa listened closely, and a huge smile spread across her face. VJ, she thought . . . and Ev! It was VJ for sure. No other human on earth would honk like that coming down that dirt road. Ev had done it! Rosa forgot about extracting burros from trailers. She performed a short but energetic bit of choreography to the mixed interest of the four donkeys and threw the halter she'd selected for Vera back into the tack box. The donkeys would have to get out of the trailer on their own. She'd make VJ give her his truck in the morning and put the trailer away. It'd be a fine project for him. The relationship with Vera could be put on hold. The inevitable confrontation would wait.

She walked out of the kitchen pen and shut the gate. As

fast as VJ always drove, he'd be there any second, and Ev would surely be with him. Rosa smiled again, a broad, fond smile that went with a rush of warmth to her face. That Ev, she thought, what a cutie with his pudgy body and earnest ways!

The burros stood quietly in the trailer. For a while there was a lot of action, action that the burros were content to avoid. A noisy vehicle drove up delivering blaring, rhythmic blasts of superfluous sound. Doors were slammed. People laughed and talked, backed by the yapping of small, obnoxious dogs. Before long another vehicle arrived. The sounds continued. Screen doors slammed, odd lights went on, and fearsome shadows danced across the pen. By degrees, however, the flurry of energy died down. The humans went into their lair and stayed. The donkeys waited a half hour or so in the dark, quiet night before Vera stepped into the pasture. The other animals followed. They were in a good place. There was a lot of good grass and a minimal contingent of the small, revolting animals the burros had smelled. Rosa hadn't paid any particular attention to the usual cluster of sheep in the kitchen pen. Vera and her long-eared companions were not given to such oversights. They saw the little woolies a couple of hundred yards away, huddled against the fence in the southwest corner of the pen. While the other donkeys grazed eagerly, Vera walked casually down to the stupid, panicky little coterie of sheep. She grabbed a small one, a lamb, by the scruff of the neck. She tossed it over the fence. Startled by its new situation in the world, the lamb jumped up and began running up and down the fence bleating loudly. The sheep became agitated, and with the lamb's mother in the lead, they managed, against all odds, to push their way under the stout fence. This unexpected stroke of fortune made the pen tidy and comfy for burros. Satisfied, Vera drifted back to join the other burros, contentedly grazing through the serene quiet of the Nevada night.

CHAPTER EIGHT

■ ■ ■

Few aficionados of sheep would characterize their favorite creatures as intelligent. Honest advocates must pass over the term. Luckily, sheep enthusiasts are able to find plenty of positive and accurate adjectives for these praiseworthy beasts. "Docile," "content," "peaceful," "humble," "gentle," "meek," and "compliant" are words found, for example, in *Stockman's Universe* articles devoted to the needs and nature of sheep. "Quick-witted," "practical," and "astute" rarely appear. Though experts agree that sheep are not intellectually gifted, some suggest that intelligence may well be less desirable than other talents. Sheep do have a quality of persistence that invariably excites admiration. Biologists attest to the importance of this modest trait, so crucial to the essential soundness of the breed.

When Vera inconsiderately ejected the small lamb from Sabine's kitchen pen, the nine remaining sheep showed this quality of persistence. Unable to bear separation from the frightened lamb, they were able to muster the determination to defeat the stout fence. They dived at it again and again, slowly wearing away the soil. Around 2:00 A.M. they began to squirt under the implacable fence. One by one, they joined their tiny, bleating companion. Joyfully reunited, the little flock stuck together through the night. Gradually, they drifted toward the complex of houses and outbuildings that formed the vital center of Sabine Eckleberry's ranch.

They had fond feelings for those buildings and admired the two-legged creatures that inhabited the place. The two-legged creatures were scary sometimes but were mostly nice. They brought food. The grateful sheep harbored warm sentiments toward the humans. While those humans slept, the sheep approached one of the buildings Sabine had once used to store grain. Ev and the Colonel had left various of their things in the shed: suitcases, a tape player, and a number of the Colonel's magazines (*Hustler* and *Penthouse*). They wanted their valuables safe and out of the weather. The door was shut, posing the kind of problem that sheep resolve through cooperation and resolution.

They crowded together against the door. The sense of confinement was frightening, and the sheep closest to the door momentarily panicked, jumping against the portal. The others fell back for a moment, and they all breathed hard, reassembling their composure. Then, for the second time, they approached the latched door. Again, the animals nearest the door became nervous and panicked. This went on for a while. The sheep had achieved a consensus. They were committed to the activity of pushing against the shut door and were quite willing to stay at it for hours. This was not necessary. In a moment of panic, one or more of the sheep bumped into the door handle, releasing the latch. The sheep crowded into the room and took up the happy task of slowly inspecting and dismantling the packages that Ev and the Colonel had stored there. They tested the contents for edibility and proceeded to eat what they could. Sheep are not fond of novelty, but these had spent several hours away from the lush grass of the kitchen pen. They were famished and willing to experiment. The recorder tapes and cords were not particularly tasty but had a texture several of the sheep did finally appreciate. Other sheep chewed on various wardrobe items, while one brave ewe chewed at the pages of Colonel McKenzie's magazines.

True to her resolve, Rosa Eckleberry was abroad early. She had the keys to VJ's pickup and a promise that VJ would move Sherry Baby to the usual spot. Rosa enjoyed the early hours. She liked the chill that invariably sharpened her senses. It was a time when she felt intensely alive, caressed by the warm rays of the rising, strengthening sun. She liked the oblique quality of morning light, soft yet crisp, awaking the earth. She strolled about the houses and outbuildings, taking time to enjoy the sight of happy donkeys grazing in the far end of the kitchen pen. At dawn there'd been the usual clamor of birds, excited out of their limited wits by the prospect of another day.

Rosa walked and quietly ate her typical breakfast, a peanut butter and honey sandwich. The world was full of small soft noises, the rustle of an almost imperceptible breeze, the distant whistle of a train miles from the ranch, the gentle sound of sheep, bleating and bumping in one of the outbuildings. Hearing the sheep, Rosa's dark eyes narrowed. Sure enough, she was hearing the unmistakable sounds of sheep, sheep that were somewhere near the ranch house. Moving in that direction, her gait became purposeful.

As hundreds of young men scattered through the county had noted for years, Rosa Margarita Eckleberry was an unusually attractive young woman. She was not at all tall but somehow seemed so. She was a woman who stood tall and covered ground when so inclined. Shapely in a robust way, her figure showed curves that defied the emaciated fashions of her time. She was Magda's girl, all right, less heavy than her mother but full-figured in her tight jeans and checkered shirt. A home-ec teacher had once characterized her as "too busty," as though large, full breasts were somehow unrefined. Few men are aware of the precise and rigid standards women bring to bear as they scrutinize one another. The men of rural Nevada universally appreciated Rosa as arguably the most attractive woman in Basque County. Feminine judgment, however, was little swayed by male opinion. The edict of the teacher resounded through Rosa's life. She was too busty.

She was also preoccupied with the unexpected sounds of sheep. She strode toward those sounds wondering why in the *hell* Sabine was allowing animals so close to the house. She was annoyed. She had been thinking about Ev. He'd turned into such a fine, responsible young man. He was so earnest and good-hearted that he was just about irresistible. She'd given him a big kiss the night before, when he'd arrived with that terrible man. She meant to welcome him to the ranch, to thank him for everything. It *had* been a longer, more lingering kiss than she'd intended. Rosa was embarrassed and a little disturbed at her loss of decorum. Still, she thought she'd probably kiss him some more when the opportunity arose. The only faults Rosa could find with Ev had to do with immaturity. He was clumsy and shy, but that would pass as he succeeded with his various endeavors. He was smart and quiet and decent. He had none of the vices Rosa'd found to her dismay in most of the men that'd come courting. His taste in clothing was horrible, but that was not all bad. Other women were less likely to notice his fine qualities. He really just needed to have a woman along when he shopped, that was all, and of course he carried more bulk than he ought, but give him half an hour of exercise a day and *grrr*, he'd be a hunk. He was halfway to being a hunk anyway, and he had a vulnerability to him that just about made Rosa nuts thinking about it. While she thought about it, she noticed with a blush that her panties were a little damp.

It was with some reluctance, then, that she focused her attention on the sounds of sheep coming, astoundingly, from one of the outbuildings. Sheep were not supposed to be in that building! She went to the tack shed and picked up one of the many *makila* staffs that the shepherds all used. Thus equipped, she walked back to the storage shed and looked inside. Sure enough, there they were. There were about twenty of them. Someone (maybe Ev!) had left luggage and equipment. The sheep had been busy. They'd chewed electrical cords and scattered clothing that she recognized as belonging to Everett. Rosa bent to gather the clothing and assess the damage. Although Rosa was not exactly a snoop, she was opportunistic. She was not about to neglect this unprecedented opportunity to look through Ev's things. VJ had mentioned that Ev had a girlfriend, and Rosa wondered if she would find a photograph. Happily, the depredations of the sheep were such that she just *had* to gather the scattered possessions. Nothing had been damaged too much. Sure, a couple of cords were beyond salvage but . . . What on earth? The sheep had just about demolished a couple of magazines. She picked one up and set it back down immediately. She took a step away, blushing to the tips of her ears. She gasped and almost lost her footing. The rank images pushed roughly into her consciousness and had a seismic effect, disrupting her sense of balance and well-being. God! It was pornography.

Thinking of these magazines, their uses, and the degraded situation of the women in the photos, Rosa was disgusted and a little queasy. Steeling herself to the task, she reexamined the chewed porn and allowed anger to replace the shock and confusion. She was not the kind to tolerate such things. Most of the photos were half eaten, but there was still sufficient evidence to affront and anger milder women than Rosa. The clothes nearby looked like Ev's. She had to be sure. Surely VJ wouldn't buy this filth. She looked at the tag on a tote bag. EVERETT CRUME. It gave his Albuquerque address. Rosa felt angry prickles go up her neck. Ev!

Attempting to regain her composure, she concentrated on the practical task of moving the sheep and tried to forget the images from the magazine. Unfortunately, the former task was too easy and the latter utterly impossible. The sheep ambled right out of the shed and with just a bit of urging were happy to relocate to the kitchen pen.

Rosa was stunned and close to tears. The thought of Ev poring over those photographs was almost too much to bear. As she closed the gate to the pen, she set her jaw and felt grimly relieved. It was actually lucky, a blessing to find out before . . .

She found VJ's pickup and started it. How annoyingly typical; VJ was almost out of gas. There was enough to get to the highway, but she'd have to stop at the first station.

How could she have been so stupid and naive? It was embarrassing. She knew men. How could she have supposed that Ev Crume was any different from any of the rest of them? She was better than twenty-four years old and was still dumb. Not as dumb now, she thought sadly, as she'd been just a half hour earlier. She pulled away from the ranch house, fishtailing the pickup and wishing she could just keep going.

Gray, lop-eared, and cynical, Vera had watched Rosa return the sheep to the kitchen pen. She was far from pleased. The sheep stayed right there by the gate, pressed up against the fence like a bunch of idiots. Their smell, a noxious wall of puerile anxiety and senseless need, offended Vera's delicate nostrils. It was more than a donkey could stand. As Rosa pulled away, Vera sauntered over to the sorry, bleating sheep, seized the luckless little lamb by the scruff of the neck, and ejected him once more from the pen. The others formed a confused, frightened knot emitting their ridiculous squeaks. They didn't even run. They just stood there under Vera's withering gaze like a parcel of dopes. Several minutes passed. The flock gradually realized the lamb had once again been torn from their midst and deposited on the other side of the fence. Acting on this worrying information, they started diving and hurtling themselves against the fence that separated them from their companion. Despite their supposed lack of gray matter, the night's lesson was not lost on these sheep. They now knew about the fence and quickly displaced enough soil to get under. Vera watched. However pleasing it was to have the sheep gone, their exit was a revolting spectacle. She walked away in disgust.

Reunited and free, the sheep drifted off, once again, toward the houses. Vera relaxed and began to graze. All was right, once again, in the world. Unencumbered by a bunch of stinky, brainless sheep, a donkey could enjoy the morning and the ample fresh grass that grew in the pen.

CHAPTER NINE

■ ■ ■

A birthday was bad enough. The celebration was something Sabine could truly dread. A holiday celebrating the pure fact of one's birth and continued existence would have made a lot of sense. Despite the state of the world, Sabine was very glad to have been born. Unfortunately, the counting mania eclipsed other, more positive possibilities. As far as Sabine could see, specters of deterioration, debility, senility, sickness, and death haunted American birthdays. Sure, they were nice for children who could not wait for passing years to yield them adult powers and advantages. Being ten was definitely better than being nine, something to be happy about. It was ludicrous, on the other hand, to go into ecstasies over being seventy-two rather than merely seventy-one. It was bad enough to head for your inevitable grave without your entire community happily pointing out the mileposts while gorging on cake.

Birthdays were dicey at best, and this one was going to be

a real doozy. The first wave of the entourage had arrived during the night. Sabine knew from the honking that VJ was among the madding crowd. He was still quite annoyed with the boy and would not tolerate much in the way of shenanigans. Sabine had gotten up early, ready to linger like a gentleman over his morning coffee. More than anything he was looking forward to feasting his eyes on grazing donkeys. Unfortunately, the house was already crawling. There was a wizened American-style fascist; a harebrained son who was going on without commas about ostriches; and a sassy, independent wife stalking about and taking charge, trailing a swarming gaggle of poodles that ebbed and flowed like a hysterical tidal flood in her wake. Young Ev Crume was present as well, the only calming influence. He'd always been a nice, level-headed boy, a good influence on Virgil Jose. Sabine had always liked him. Unfortunately, the poor young fellow was limping. He'd evidently developed gout. How can a man savor the addition of four noble donkeys to his estate in such a madhouse?

The presence of VJ was ominous. Sabine had, at the last family celebration, ejected the exasperating young ninny from the property. He'd not asked him back, either, but there he was, twirling his hair into a matted mess and prattling about ostriches. Sabine's ears prickled with anger; his stomach began to knot. The girls had obviously done this for him on his birthday. Bossy, conniving, controlling, *mandonas*, all of them. Here he was, old and vulnerable, brought to bay, immobilized like a god-damn maypole while his daughters danced around him running his life. It wasn't VJ's fault; he was a noodle, a dreamer. He didn't have a conniving bone in his body, but Lord, those daughters. Their big campaign at present was getting VJ on the ranch. Ultimately, of course, they wanted Sabine and Magda back together.

The idea wasn't half bad on the face of it, but it involved going and living with her in that hell of poodles, citrus fruits, and old people they had down there in Arizona. How human life could be sustained in such a place was beyond Sabine's ability to imagine. The one advantage would be the notable lack of daughters infesting the place. Magda, now there was a woman that knew something. And there was only one of her, in contrast to the girls, who were always fresh for the onslaught, resting in twos, while the third worked him over. Magda knew what he liked and he knew what she liked. They'd learned through the years to be easy on each other. Those girls though, they only knew what he *should* like, and they made a full-time occupation out of seeing that he got it, like a damned family birthday party when all in the world he wanted was to enjoy his new burros. Having to endure a birthday party was a bit much for a man who was feeling delicate in the aftermath of red meat, cigars, and Sangre de Toro.

The most perplexing thing was the military presence that'd come to dominate the household in the early hours. This Colonel McKenzie was barging about like he owned the place, blathering about sheep. Sabine supposed that the presence of sheep on a sheep ranch was too much for the military mind to grasp. Sabine would speak to him about it eventually. First, though, he had to absorb these changes and work out inner conflicts. He'd been up since Rosa had roared off, slinging gravel in all directions, at six. It was now eight, he'd not yet spoken, and conversation was not in his immediate plans.

VJ, on the other hand, had plenty to say. He was putting together his plan for a visit to the ostrich ranch up at Stansville. The Colonel had decided to go along. Ev limped through the front room. Sabine was sitting there staring at cold coffee and fighting the urge to actually listen to what VJ was talking about. VJ was standing in his shorts a few feet from his father. He had a towel in his hand and had obviously put off his morning shower to talk ostrich.

"I may come back with some eggs, Daddy, it all depends. If the price is right, I may do it. I may have to buy an incubator, too, if they won't let me borrow one of theirs but they probably will, depending on how far along the eggs are and if they have any hens actually sitting."

Ev, like the mute Sabine, had little enthusiasm for the topic. He was thinking of Rosa. He was unhappy that she'd gone, but at least he'd have time to clean himself up a bit and put on a fresh shirt before she got back. His feet were a little better, but they did slow him up. He walked down toward the shed to get his tote bag. He had a nice shirt in there. Magda and the poodles roared by.

"Morning, Ev, I'm taking the dogs out for a walk. God, I love this place! What a morning! Look at Sassy! His leg is a whole lot better. How are your feet?"

"A little better. Thanks for helping me with the bandages and all; it made a big difference. I don't suppose, though, I'll be doing much dancing for a while."

Magda smiled. She had such a nice smile. Rosa had inherited that same big, face-breaking grin. It'd pop out on her once in a while, too. Ev had never thought quite so much about Rosa as he had since they arrived. She'd been so glad to see him. At first he thought that she was probably just glad to see VJ and the glad was rubbing off a bit on him. Still, she'd seemed so particularly grateful to him. Then she'd surprised him with a kiss, a *really* big lingering, hungry sort of kiss. She had kissed VJ first, a sisterly kiss. Ev had expected a similar perfunctory peck. He just about passed out when he first realized she was probing his lips with her tongue. Wow! So now what? The situation was divine but perplexing. He was not a pound lighter or an iota more handsome than he'd been the last time he'd seen her. She hadn't kissed him like that then. In all the years of his silent yearning, she'd never seemed interested. Like a man confronting a windfall fortune, Ev Crume finally had a problem he could enjoy.

Footsore and pleasantly confused, Ev decided to get his things. They'd stowed everything in one of the outbuildings, a storage shed. Hobbling into this shed, he found to his dismay that sheep had gotten inside and torn into his tote bag. They'd ruined the cord to his razor charger, along with his Walkman cords. His clothes were slobbered but intact. To his amusement, the sheep had torn up, destroyed, and half-eaten old Colonel McKenzie's dirty mags. Smiling, he walked out of the shed carrying the tote.

On the long drive from Scottsdale to the Nevada ranch, the Colonel had bored, disgusted, and embarrassed Ev with the *Hustler* and *Penthouse* photos. Ev had a period of devotion to *Playboy* when he was in high school. He still bought the swim-suit edition of *Sports Illustrated* every year, but he'd never seen *Penthouse* before. The Colonel subscribed to *Penthouse* and the even sleazier *Hustler*. Ev had done most of the driving from Arizona, and Colonel McKenzie kept risking their lives, sticking select pages into Ev's line of vision. "Take a gander at that action, Fat Boy," he'd say. Or, "Think you'll ever get into anything like that?" or, "This one can warm my ears with her thighs any day of the year!" and etc. Ev had been mortified beyond endurance at the Colonel's suggestions and insinuations. He was glad no one else had been present.

A tragic principle of human existence is that injury cries out for reinjury. Leaving the storage shed, Ev stepped on wounded feet into an unexpected maelstrom of shrill noises, hurtling forms, and sharp hooves. Champy, Joey, and Moe had discovered sheep and turned that discovery into a chase. Yapping and snarling, the dogs contracted themselves into tight little balls and took off, attaining top speed almost instantly. Only Sassy, slowed by his own sad injury, lagged behind, near Magda, who made her best speed in pursuit. "Stop this foolishness and come here right now!" she shouted.

Trapped in the narrows between the shed and parked vehicles, Ev was buffeted by the speedier sheep, one of which stepped on his right foot. This was quite painful. Trying to get away, he hopped on his left foot, which was still tender. He lost his balance as the second wave, the slower, more desperate sheep, plowed into him. He kept his equilibrium for a moment in a churning sea of dirty wool and then went down heavily, along with several straggling sheep. Speeding poodles, unprepared for the opportunity to actually catch the fleeing sheep, tried without success to avoid the pileup. Magda and Sassy arrived in time to witness the aftermath of the collision, a confused, panicky knot of poodles and sheep swarming busily over one another and the supine form of the fallen Ev.

The sheep regained their feet, if not their composure, rather quickly and made a graceless exit, following their more fortunate peers, who waited nervously on the front porch of the house. Champy, Joey, and Moe, shaky and whimpering, sought the safety of their protectress. Ev was left alone, dazed, and down on his back, wondering what had hit him. He took a deep breath. Whatever that had been, it hadn't killed him. His right foot, though, hurt like the very devil. He pulled himself to a sitting position.

Magda was winded and angry. The ranch was going to pot. What was Sabine doing, letting sheep run near the house like that? She was mad at the dogs and scolded them mercilessly as they cowered in shame and regret. She knew it was not the dogs' fault, but she just couldn't help it, the darned little snips, chasing those sheep like that, not stopping or even looking back when she called. Having to scold her dogs made her even madder at Sabine. Sassy was gloating. There was not much he enjoyed more than bearing witness to the punishment of others. He was not, however, spared for long. "You're not one bit better than the rest of them, either, Sassy, so you don't need to smirk like that. I saw you; you were running just as fast as you could!"

Magda was so angry with her poodles and her husband that for a moment she actually forgot about poor Ev. He was several feet away from the chastened poodles, straining and struggling, lurching painfully to his feet. Magda's lifelong habit of caregiving belatedly kicked in when she stopped scolding long enough to notice his distress. The poor boy had been at the bottom of that roiling mass of mammalian frenzy. Tenderly offering him a shoulder to lean on, she helped him back to the house.

A few minutes later, Ev was seated in Sabine's favorite chair, a battered Lazyboy recliner, with his feet up and re-bandaged. He wasn't really injured, but his right foot was pretty sore. Magda was cross-examining Sabine about the sheep.

"I had them in the kitchen pen," he said. "Why the hell would I have them running loose? Daisy must have left the gate open last night when we put the donkeys out there." Colonel McKenzie, quick to side with the prosecution, stuck his head in the front door.

"Gate's closed. No fresh tracks leading away anywhere near the gate. I'd say the sheep have been out a while. I tried to tell you earlier. I don't know why the hell some people won't listen!"

Sabine did recall the annoying militarist squawking some-thing about sheep while Sabine was attempting to have his coffee.

"Butt out, pip-squeak."

"Okay, Sabine, that's enough of that. The Colonel was kind enough to help drive me up here so I could come to your birthday party. I'll not have you insulting him. And Colonel, why don't you stay out of this? At your age you should know enough to stay out of discussions between husband and wife."

"All I said . . . " Magda's eyes stopped the sentence and sent the Colonel scooting onto the porch. He shouted that he'd keep an eye on the sheep. A couple of minutes later, Sabine and Magda emerged and with the Colonel's help shooed the nervous sheep toward the kitchen pen.

The spotted donkey foal, the one Sabine had decided to call Elvis, did not share his mother's frosty contempt for sheep.

He'd maintained the characteristically cautious burro reserve since arriving at the ranch. Grazing all night had calmed his nerves and filled his young body with the giddy calories of high-protein pasture grass. Like his namesake, Elvis was ready to rock. He'd been harassing his mother since sunup, nipping at her, attempting to nurse or mount, and making a general nuisance of himself. Old Vera was not much of a play-mate, and she'd come up short on patience, disciplining Elvis severely several times. He was feeling a bit sulky and picked-on when he spied the humans inserting the funny-looking little stinkies into the pen. He took one look and decided it was party time.

Elvis and Vera had been grazing a couple of hundred yards from the pen's main gate. When Elvis noticed the novel com-bination of humans and sheep swarming nearby, he acted im-mediately. Breaking into a high-headed gallop, he ran straight toward Sabine and the others, closing the gap very quickly.

Vera had been annoyed with her foal, but that was hardly remarkable. He was an annoying foal and she was a grouchy mother. When he bolted toward the humans, however, all of Vera's profuse maternal instincts suddenly activated. She was instantly at a dead run, determined to place her body between her foal and the dangers that the humans at the end of the pasture might represent.

The sheep, still uneasy from the harrowing poodle inci-dent, scattered at the sight of the onrushing donkeys. Sabine moved gingerly to close the gate. Suddenly, the air pulsed with a sound that the Colonel at first thought was a foghorn. It was not. It was the full, clear roar of the burro Sabine called Che. Che had taken note of the activity and, like Vera and Elvis, was running toward the humans at top speed, braying impres-sively. Che, like Vera, was a donkey who took his adult respon-sibilities seriously. If the humans threatened to do something to the idiotic foal, Che would put a stop to it.

The situation resolved itself quickly. Vera caught and passed

Elvis. Wielding her butt expertly, she check-blocked Elvis and kept him away from the humans. Che took advantage of the angle of pursuit. He passed mother and foal and moved to shield them from whatever danger the humans could pose. He used his own butt to check-block Vera, diverting both mother and foal away from the humans. Vera kicked and hissed at him. Elvis circled back to make a snorting, bucking pass at a couple of sheep that were running toward the far end of the pen. Vera stopped about twenty yards shy of the gate and began to graze. Having satisfied himself that all was well and his duty discharged, Che walked up to the gate and put his head over the fence, obviously hoping that Sabine, Magda, or the Colonel would feed or pet him. He was in luck.

"Oh, look how sweet he is. What a good boy! You take good care of your herd, don't you, you little sweetie?" Magda was only too happy to pet the burro and scratch his ears. The Colonel was badly shaken by the sudden onslaught of donkeys and the high-volume blast that had issued from the little beast. He stepped back, well away from the creature.

Sabine was unconcerned. He'd enjoyed the situation. It was a pleasure to see the foal run and kick up his heels. He examined the ground in front of the gate. The Colonel was not much of a tracker, but he had been right. Besides the tracks the sheep had just made, there were nearly fresh, dew-filled tracks leading into, not out of the pen. Sabine figured that there had to be a hole in the fence somewhere, though on cursory inspection, he couldn't see it. He'd have to take a good look later, or better yet, let VJ do it. It was a perplexing damned thing. Someone, maybe Daisy, had driven the sheep into the pen before the dews had sopped the ground. It didn't make sense. Could they have gotten out twice?

Magda scratched Che and reflected on the chaotic situation of the ranch. The place was going downhill. She was convinced that Sabine's failing powers were the problem. This was a real lapse, sheep wandering near the house. It was definitely time to get VJ back to the ranch, which would not be easy. She did not know how to shift the boy's focus, but she had to think of something. He *had* to give up this unfortunate obsession with ostriches, and the sooner the better. Sabine obviously needed his son's help.

The Colonel was disgusted. This was some ranch. Chaos reigned. Outside the military there was evidently no justice whatsoever. How could a slovenly, swarthy, foreign-looking slacker like Sabine end up with a woman like Magda and the riches to own a ranch like this? The question ate at him.

Lost in their private thoughts, the three of them watched the donkeys graze near the trailer. Before long they were joined by VJ, who wore no shirt and was still toweling off his head. "Well," he said to the Colonel, "ready to go on up to Stansville?" The Colonel was ready. "First I've got to put up this horse trailer. Well, I'll be damned, Daddy, donkeys. I bet you got them as guards for the sheep. You didn't get any jacks did you? If you did, you'd better get Norton out here to geld them. The jacks aren't trustworthy enough, and say, you'd bettered separate them from the sheep for a few days. Put them in pens next to each other so the donkeys can see the sheep and vice versa. That way they can get used to each other. It helps if they buddy up somehow. God, those sheep look nervous. What you been doing to them? They'll have scours if they don't calm down. Those donkeys are nice animals. I wonder how they'd do with ostriches?" He walked around toweling his head, expecting no response.

Sabine said nothing while Magda recounted her story of the dogs, the sheep, and the accident with Ev. Sabine did not listen with much interest. He was thinking about VJ's comments on the sheep. The boy was impressive in his one massive talent. No shepherd alive was more sensitive to sheep than Virgil Jose. He was able to determine at three hundred yards that the sheep were nervous. How did he do it? As far as Sabine could see, the sheep looked exactly as they always looked, sort of contented in a dull way. There is not much in the demeanor of sheep to suggest changes in their inner lives. VJ was right about the donkeys, too. Sabine had simply forgotten the *Stockman's Universe* suggestion that the donkeys be separated from the sheep but visible in an adjacent field. VJ had obviously read the same article, an article *he* remembered. Sabine found this annoying, but kept his mouth shut.

Virgil Jose loved the ranch. On the ranch, he always had tons of energy. Instead of getting out of bed at ten or after, like he did in Albuquerque, VJ was often up at dawn or even earlier. He liked to sleep late but couldn't contain himself. Besides, he had fish to fry before the party. It was an hour's drive to Stansville, and Rosa wanted him back by four. He was also concerned about the sheep. Excitement is not the kind of thing that one associates with thriving sheep, and those sheep sure looked agitated.

"I'll give those woolies a once-over before we take off. Give me a half hour, Colonel McKenzie. Is that okay?"

The Colonel nodded, a minimalist response.

"Virgil, don't forget that you told Daisy you'd put the trailer away, and I'd appreciate it if you'd walk the fence in the kitchen pen to see how those damned sheep have been getting out." Sabine didn't want any further discussion with Virgil Jose. He turned and walked toward the house. He took about five steps, stopped, and turned.

"Magda, it's nice that you came. You look a wonder. I don't know how you do it. You are the prettiest thing I've seen in months." He smiled a big smile, turned, and walked on into the house.

The Colonel wondered how Sabine had ever fathered as bright a boy as VJ. The man was a sentimental old fool. He was right about Magda, of course, but he didn't have any tact. Colonel McKenzie felt that compliments were a bit indecent. The present situation was a good example. What could a man say to a woman in such circumstances? "Oh, yeah, I think so too," would not quite cut it. It was an awkward moment.

"Guess I'll service the vehicle, VJ. We'll take the Cherokee, if you don't mind. I don't much like the idea of three of us in the pickup." He turned on his heel, ducked his head, and took off at double-time, furious at Sabine. Magda watched him go, oblivious to his agitation but amused at his speed and efficiency.

"VJ, I think it's time for you to make peace with your father and get your fanny back to this ranch. He can't handle it anymore."

"Hell he can't, and what about Rosa? Give Rosa her head and she'll own the whole state and make more money than Reno. 'Sides, I got fish to fry. I want to get Ev set up in the ostrich business, Mama. The poor fella barely gets by, and his folks are starting to fail. They live in this little old trailer and just drive around to wherever it happens to be warm. Poor old Ev has watched our family be rich his whole life. Doesn't he deserve a break?"

Magda saw that there was no use trying to talk to VJ for the time being. It was even worse than she'd feared. Ev's parents were probably the happiest, most contented people on earth. They'd sold their house at Earl's retirement and did exactly as they damned pleased, which was travel. They had a bumper sticker on their Winnebago that said, "Spending Our Children's Inheritance."

Magda knew VJ. If anything could fix his intent, it was altruism. Certainly, in this case it was misplaced, but you'd never convince him. He was truly generous, willing to work like a dog and suffer real privation in the interest of others. It was a fine trait in a boy, but when would he develop the judgment to go with it?

"Your poor father deserves a break. Ev's a bright, responsible young man who's going to do just fine as long as he stays away from ostriches, TV quiz shows, and things of that ilk." Magda knew that she shouldn't say this kind of thing to VJ. It would just make him more determined. He'd want to prove her wrong.

"Mama, let's not discuss it now. I'm still pretty much in the research phase. Let's just have Daddy's birthday today. With the sisses on the way, he has to put up with me for the time being, but he's not exactly jumping for joy. Anyway, I've got these chores to do before we run up to Stansville." He vaulted the fence and walked toward the nervous sheep.

CHAPTER TEN

■ ■ ■

When Rosa ran into Fanny Ulibarri, she acted on instinct. Fanny was working at Dan's Tack Shack, where Rosa stopped to buy Sabine's birthday present, halters for the donkeys. Fanny was a tall, robust girl with dark eyes and hair. Rosa had known Fanny since grade school and had always liked this sweet, good-natured person. True, Rosa would never describe her friend as quick-witted, clever, or astute, but Fanny did have the qualities of firm persistence and unforeseen yet focused intelligence that often wins the day. Rosa enjoyed Fanny's spirited conversation "in small doses" but understood how others found her tedious. Like most small-town American women in their early twenties, Fanny was on the rebound from her failed first marriage.

"Don't tell me you're getting into Arabians?" Fanny asked. The halters Rosa had selected were Arabian sized. Arabians have little pinheads all going to mane on thousand-pound bodies. Burros have a more practical arrangement, Arabian-sized heads on modest five- or six-hundred-pound bodies.

"No, these are for some BLM donkeys my daddy adopted. I wanted to get him some nice halters for his birthday. Knowing him, he'd just jury-rig up some rope halters. They'll look cute in these."

"Gift wrap?"

"Gift wrap? Since when do you do gift wrap? Doesn't seem like Dan. Fanny, I've got to say, you work for the stingiest man in Nevada."

"Tell me about it. Between paychecks I forget. No, it's true, someone must have died and willed him a bunch of wrapping paper. It's hard to imagine him buying it. Anyway, he told me to wrap gift purchases if people wanted. It's not enough that I sit back here making him money all day, he's got to figure out how to get more work out of me, and this is one of his big ideas. Not that I mind. It gets boring standing here like I was part of the damned register. It's the awfullest wrapping paper you ever saw, though. I couldn't blame you for not wanting it. Lookee here, uuuuuugleeee!"

Indeed the paper was appalling. Horrible Day-Glo stripes on a mustard-colored background. Rosa smiled.

"No, go ahead. Put them all in one box and wrap it. I want to see if Daddy tries to save that paper."

"Now, that's a depressing thought. . . . Who all's down for the party?" Fanny said this in what she thought was a casual, offhand way. Rosa was not fooled. She noted the sudden avoidance of eye contact, the intemperate flurry of wrapping. Rosa knew the limited possibilities a single girl faced in Basque County. All of the men were either married or sorry, and mostly both. Oh, this was turning out very well, very well indeed.

"Well, pretty much the whole tribe. Mama's up from Arizona. Celia and Felice are coming with all their kids. Virgil Jose showed up with Ev Crume, the pervert."

"Good God, those uncles of yours won't be there, will they?"

Fanny's nose wrinkled and her face darkened as she thought of those disreputable old bums and what a bad name they gave the Basque community the last time they came around.

"Lord no. It's christenings they seem to like. Anyway, they're *great*-uncles." Rosa wished there were other qualifiers she could add. The word "great" did not sufficiently distance the old scoundrels.

"So Virgil Jose has made up with your dad?" Again the avoidance, the forced casualness. Rosa was delighted.

"Well, not exactly. But we figure maybe since it's Daddy's birthday and all. . . . Why don't you come to the party? VJ always liked you, Fanny." This was true in only the most technical sense. VJ loved life and loved the world. As an undifferentiated component of the world, VJ loved Fanny, not that he ever precisely noted or acknowledged her existence.

Fanny blushed; she'd always found Rosa's younger brother exciting. His being two years younger than her had made a difference in high school . . . but high school years had passed away.

"Well, I have to work."

"Just come on out when you close up. I told Celia and Felice four o'clock, but with all the kids they've got they'll never be on time. If you close up at five, you could be at the ranch well before six."

"You think I'd have time to change, do myself up a bit?"

Rosa evaluated the evidence and decided that it would be a very good idea for Fanny to do herself up a bit.

"Sure, six-thirty should still be plenty early."

"Great, I'll be there. Maybe if it gets slow, I'll shut this place at four." Fanny handed Rosa the package. It was the worst wrapping job Rosa had ever seen, but then, as ugly as the paper was, nothing could make matters much worse.

Rosa knew that Fanny was a long shot, but the project was still worth a try. What Fanny lacked in brains, she more than recovered in single-mindedness and quiet, almost ruthless determination. If Fanny had any luck with VJ, it'd slow his momentum and tend to keep him in Nevada. If he fell in love with her, well, a sister could hope. A woman like Fanny would anchor him, slow him down, and then . . . Fanny always had looked up to Rosa. Rosa felt that Fanny would be the perfect sister-in-law, a natural ally who would always be sympathetic to Rosa's views. VJ had never been unfriendly to Fanny. This seemed hopeful, but then VJ was never unfriendly to anyone. As far as Rosa knew, VJ had never paid Fanny any particular attention. But that didn't mean much, either. He never paid particular attention to any potential sweetheart. VJ was not much of a ladies' man, a shortcoming that was entirely his doing. Women had always loved him, from elderly aunts, to babysitters, to girls his own age, on down to his nieces, who adored him and competed for his attention. VJ was mostly oblivious. He lacked persistence of attention and had neither instinct nor training in the fine art of making his admirers feel special. He seldom dated.

This desultory interest in women had left the field advantageously open, and Fanny did have points that VJ would surely admire. Fanny still affected the cowgirl look that Rosa had abandoned. The fashion featured skin-tight jeans that tended to draw attention to a woman's behind. In Rosa's view, the Ulibarri derriere was a bit vast for her cowgirl affectations. VJ, however, was certain to see Fanny's fashion statement in a positive light. This was exasperating on the one hand and fortunate on the other.

Rosa assessed Fanny's charms with the harshness women reserve for other women. The truth of the matter, however, is that Rosa had always felt quite indulgent of Fanny's lapses in taste. The high point of their many double dates with Earl and Merle, the Eddington twins, had been the ladies' room hysterics that the sincere, slow-witted "simpleton twins" inevitably caused. Rosa had really enjoyed going to the ladies' room with Fanny. Fanny was sweet, kind, and, in her own way, smart. When nervous, Fanny talked compulsively, engaging both Rosa's sympathy and her annoyance. Fanny was a pretty, pretty girl. Rosa loved her hair and the curve of her hip. Rosa was short and liked the lines of "Long, Tall Fanny." One did wonder, though, why she was so bent on accentuating her humongous butt by cramming it into red, turquoise, or purple jeans that were always a size or two too small.

A hopeful point was that Fanny had a parrot named Abe, after Abraham in the Bible. VJ might well be interested in a woman with a parrot. It was the kind of thing that'd speak to his imagination. It'd give Fanny a way to get him into a conversation. Rosa was afraid that if Fanny did not get VJ into a conversation, she'd end up going into one of her hyperactive monologues. If she did that, big butt and all, she'd drive him away. That's where the parrot came in. If VJ showed interest in the parrot, Fanny would relax. When Fanny relaxed, there was not a sweeter, more winning, and attractive girl any-where.

Rosa left the tack shop with a feeling of satisfaction. She had her present for Sabine and had set a snare for VJ. It was just ten past nine in the morning. Who could say what she might accomplish by party time? VJ and Sabine were lucky to have a woman like her in the family. The pleasant glow was nice, but sat on top of the pit in her stomach when she thought, inadvertently, of Everett Crume. What a disgusting hypocrite! She'd given him that kiss and meant it too. How humiliating! That young man was going to get his comeup-pance, and Rosa Margarita Eckleberry was not going to cut him slack, not an inch. She felt the back of her neck get hot. To think of how she'd been picturing things, the future. Well, live and learn.

For Ev, the only thing that made the trip to the ostrich ranch at Stansville bearable was the recalled image of Rosa's kiss. If

Rosa had stayed at the ranch instead of running off to do her "party shopping," Ev would have passed on the trek. VJ talked him into going, though, and it was, he supposed, a bit better than sitting around the ranch dwelling on the pain in his right foot. The presence of the Colonel, though, made it a close call.

Driving his own vehicle, the Colonel assumed an attitude of command. He was damned interested in this ostrich business. He had his money invested wisely. When they mustered him out of the air force, they'd flown him to LA with several other officers for a workshop on financial planning and investment. The Colonel chose astutely and had a solid portfolio. It seemed cowardly and unimaginative, but the yield was there. He'd wondered, though, what a man with a little scrotum and a bold strategy could do with that money.

The day was beautiful, stark and hot. The sky was immense, endless lovely blue. They sped over highways that shimmered and vibrated as the day heated up. Inside the Cherokee, it was cool. The Colonel played tapes of Frank Sinatra, "I've Got You Under My Skin." There was no traffic to speak of, and the music was nice. Ev had Rosa Eckleberry under his skin. Unfortunately, the Colonel was determined to drown out his own music. He started in on Ev.

"So they've got a business school at the university, do they? That's rich, a Marxist business school. What do they have, classes in Wealth Redistribution One-oh-one? Figure to be a businessman?"

Ev felt his jaw muscles begin to tense. He reminded himself that he needed to respect older people, an increasingly difficult proposition with the Colonel. At the very least, though, he needed to show patience and forbearance.

"I don't know, I guess so. I'm taking management, and the business school is a good one. It's not Marxist. It's all about the market, competition."

"Tell me about it, Fatty. Every god-damned day of the world

they had protesters there at Kirtland's gates. Every one of those clowns was from the university. University of New Marxism, that's what I call it."

"I know."

"Oh, you know, do you? I didn't see your ass out there."

"No, and you won't. Ninety-nine percent of the students are completely apolitical."

"Yeah, and that's the trouble. Sorry little wimps! At least the god-damn reds had the scrotum to take a stand. So what do they teach you about business?"

VJ piped up. "That business school there is something, Colonel McKenzie. Competitive, oooweee baby! Robert O. Anderson put the place on the map! Ol' Ev there won't say much, but he's a hell of a student. He's got about a four-point grade point and knows all there is on financial management and stuff like that. He's going to handle the business end of the ostrich enterprise. All I need to do is raise the beasts while Ev mints money out of it. He'll get me a critical path with flow charts and everything. All those big companies are just clawing each other to death to hire him, intern him, let him make them money. He knows that downward sloping demand stuff forwards and back, that's the kind of school it is. When they call that thing a business school, they mean business and that's a take. I admit that his girlfriend Susie is a communist. Bad-looking too, but serious. Had ol' Ev on a short tether for a while there."

"Susan is not and never was my girlfriend, Virgil. I told you that a dozen times. And anyway, she's a feminist, not a communist."

"I stand corrected, Evertly Ev. I never knew women got so rude and mean with guys they just know casually."

"VJ, it's not rude. It's being assertive. She's not used to it and goes overboard. I don't want to talk about Susan; she just lives in the same building, that's all."

"She talks nasty too."

"That's just the way college students talk."

"Well, you're a college boy. You don't talk like that, and anyway she's a girl."

Ev just shook his head. "Girls aren't *girls* anymore, VJ. You think Rosa is a *girl*?"

"Rosa, Ev, is something different. She's a force of nature or something. All my sisses are like that, as you well know."

Ev thought of VJ's sisters and drew a deep breath. Each of them was a piece of work in her own right, yet their real power emerged when they pooled their substantial resources. VJ thought he could do anything he set his mind to, but he was wrong in that. His sisters felt that they could accomplish anything they agreed on, but *they* were one hundred percent on the money.

"I'm still interested in what College Boy there can tell an old retired military bird like me about business, if he knows so damned much. 'Buy low, sell high,' that it, Lard? Now here's downward sloping demand for you." He clawed obscenely at his crotch. "Speaking of which, everything you boys heard about Oriental women is true."

Ev was in pain. The impulse to throttle Colonel McKenzie was so powerful that he had to summon all his strength to resist that urge. The inner struggle took a toll. Loading up on Juicy Fruit, he bit his tongue and gave an involuntary groan. The Colonel reacted.

"Listen, Fatty, I'll have no disrespect out of the likes of you. So can it and tell me what Anderson Business School thinks of this ostrich business."

Ev was glad that the conversation was turning away from the topics that sparked the Colonel's most objectionable views and behavior. He was eager to respond. This would give him another chance to trot out the objections to the ostrich fiasco. The more he was able to do this, the more likely it was that VJ might eventually listen. Why the hell the Colonel wanted to know anything about ostriches was a question Ev did not care to go into. The old toot looked kind of like an ostrich with that thin neck, big beak, and ornery expression. Ev actually smiled at the comparison.

"Can't tell you a thing about the business, because there is none. The operant word is 'scam.' A business provides goods or services to the marketplace. This creates jobs and wealth. This ostrich thing has no product, no goods, no services. It creates neither wealth nor employment. It does take wealth from the hands of people like VJ and transfers it to people up the food chain. It's carnivorous. It's nothing but people selling each other ostriches to use to breed ostriches to sell to other people to breed ostriches. There are a few dandy pairs of over-priced boots around, but there is no real product."

"VJ, you got yourself a hell of a manager here. Listen to him. 'Operant word,' my ass. Every successful enterprise was like that at the start. That's when there's opportunity, boy."

"That's the good thing about ol' Ev, though; he's conservative that way. It's his role. I'm the one that'll take the risks, get it going. Ev'll manage the going concern once the shekels start drifting in. He makes me think, gives me some questions to ask these ostrich people. He's got a good point about needing a product. I hired him to dig in his heels."

Hired?! This was worse than Ev had thought.

The Colonel snorted. As a man who loved military life, he'd hated, loathed, and despised the military pencil pushers and bean counters. These myopic bottom-liners did their best to curtail the development of imaginative weapons. They'd killed his favorite, a little radar-controlled missile that burrowed through the earth and came up underneath facilities and just vaporized them. What a weapon! And the soulless, unimaginative, number-crunching dwarves bloody well killed it, just because of a petty cost overrun. Like the geniuses behind that missile, VJ was a boy with imagination, and here was this young communist lard-ass trampling all over it!

Fewer than thirty-six hours previous, the Colonel had referred to VJ's idea of raising ostriches as "the most hare-brained foolishness" he'd ever heard in his life. This may not have been literally true. The Colonel had lived a long time and had encountered a good deal of harebrained foolishness. The ostrich notion *was* a good fit in that category. The idea had not improved during those thirty-six hours, but the Colonel's view obviously had. VJ's admiration of Richard Petty made a difference, and so did the feature on *Good Morning America*. Ev's arguments against the notion convinced the Colonel utterly. If the bean counters and pencil pushers were against it, it had to be good!

"Is that what they teach you at business school? To be negative, to sit on your hands when opportunity knocks? All that verbiage is pure theory, straight out of the book. When you have a little practical experience, you'll know that sometimes you have to, by God, operate out of intuition. You've got to be decisive. It's maybe smart to look as close as Fat Boy suggests, but it's also cowardly."

The Colonel thought of his own safe, conservative portfolio and blushed. Minimize risk! Hell, if a man lives like that, he might as well die and get it over with!

"I look at it as balance," VJ said. "I need Ev even if he doesn't agree with me. He makes me think."

Ev doubted this. It was kind of funny, though. If the Colonel kept it up, VJ might actually start thinking.

The farm was not, of course, right in the town of Stansville; not much was. Stansville was merely the nearest metropolis. Ten miles north of Stansville they turned onto a dirt road, opened and closed a gate, and knew immediately that they'd correctly followed the directions. An ostrich stood in the middle of the road.

The first sight of an actual ostrich is inevitably a powerful experience for those who have been considering the creatures in the abstract. "Shock" and "awe" are words that suggest themselves as descriptive of that experience.

In Everett Crume this shock and awe had other emotional colorings that made the experience resonate in his subconscious. "Horror" is not too strong a term to use in characterizing Ev's reaction. The sight of that bird shook Everett's long-held belief that nature was a benevolent, maternal force. Something about having an ostrich in the middle of a dirt road in northern Nevada sent an icy rush up Ev's spine. Here was evidence, compelling evidence, of the malevolent caprices nature had seen fit to loose upon the earth and nurture through the millennia. The creature was huge, so huge that Ev gasped and looked about for something to offer a comparison point, to give scale. It towered above the Cherokee. Long scaly legs emerged from a body that resembled an oversized black tutu. Those legs ended with grotesque clawed feet that had to be as big as baseball mitts. A small, angry head capped a long neck and snaked about in restless menace. Eyes—avian, reptilian eyes—scanned the Cherokee as though assessing the Colonel's pride as a possible meal.

The sight was threatening. A 3.92 grade-point average, however impressive to corporations in the Fortune 500, had done nothing to prepare Ev for this. Instinctively, the troubled, footsore young man sought refuge in religion. He called aloud on his god in this hour of affliction.

"Jesus Christ!"

Although the bird could not possibly have heard this cry for spiritual succor, it buckled its knees as though to pray. Its enormous body shook with exertion, and slowly, over a minute or two, something began to emerge. It was a bird dropping. It hit the ground with a heavy splat. The bird followed this production with an impressive encore, a high-pressure stream of a milky yellow liquid. The creature had relieved itself in spectacular fashion. The dropping was a rather poorly integrated mass of brownish green material. It reminded Ev of a meatloaf, a small meatloaf to be sure, but impressive. There must have been at least a half gallon of the gravylike liquid.

Its labor complete, the bird then pulled itself up to its full height (maybe nine or ten feet), extended its neck, and opened its sharp, brutal beak. The sound that issued from that beak seemed to shake the Cherokee to its steel-belted radials. It was a sudden, deep, guttural howl that was ear-numbingly loud. The cry tapered off gradually, a reverse crescendo of sorrowful and furious indignation.

When Zebulon Pike first gazed upon the peak that was to bear his name, he regarded that mighty mountain in silence. He felt awe, admiration, and finally a kind of horror at the magnitude and the inhumanity of this mountain. He later wrote that mortal man would never climb this monstrous peak. No one can say that the feelings that stirred Everett Crume were any less profound than those that animated the mighty frame of Pike. Ev's hushed and silent awe was, perhaps, the precise emotion that invariably grips those who behold a natural wonder.

The bird, having delivered itself of the impressive poop and the savage cry that announced it to the world, turned and walked slowly away. It strolled the perimeter of a chain-link fence, ambling along with its head high, aloof, showing no sign of the relief and pleasure mammals ordinarily experience at such times. VJ, Ev, and the Colonel gaped when the bird stopped and pecked at the boulder-strewn ground. A moment later, something caught the light, something the bird had retrieved from an apparent hiding place among the boulders beside the fence.

"Look!" Ev gasped. "He's got someone's watch. What's he doing with a watch?"

The Colonel strained his eyes. For the love of God, College Boy was right. The bird had a watch. What more could a person say? Colonel McKenzie had been tense watching the bird. He found Ev's inquiry annoying.

"Well, what the hell do you think? Maybe he was just on his way to the pawnshop. Maybe he comes down here to the gate to sell things to passers-by. Maybe he has an appointment he doesn't want to miss. Maybe he's going to eat up hours and shit out minutes. Maybe he's been to business school and knows all about downward sloping demand. Maybe his broker said 'sell,' and here he is at the gate ready to follow that advice. Maybe he just likes to know the time of day." The Colonel forced a nervous falsetto laugh that broke into a fit of coughing. "Damned thing looks like a feathered pig on stilts." He sputtered.

Ev had enough free attention to be surprised at the Colonel's outburst. For the first time since they'd met, the Colonel showed wit, humor. It was evidently a shock reaction of some sort.

VJ did not seem to hear. He gaped after the bird, lapsing into a revery, lost in thoughts of his prospective venture.

Soon the ostrich was out of sight, down the fence, following whatever inner urges prompted action. VJ, Ev, and the Colonel simply watched as the bird disappeared.

Finally mustering his resolution, the Colonel drove on.

Ev tried to be light.

"You have to be glad the things don't fly."

"Yeah," VJ finally replied, "that's a take. Hey. Everything's gotta go, though. Whaddaya expect." Sudden, unbidden visions of nice innocuous little sheep turds paraded along VJ's stream of consciousness.

The Colonel, ever concerned with logistics, had practical concerns. "I wonder how many times a day the creatures lay those bricks?"

VJ knew. "Oh, about fifteen to twenty. They are birds and all. I sure hadn't imagined there'd be so much of it, though. Maybe the volume is different at different times of day or something. I can't believe they'd produce twenty of those a day. They've got a feed conversion rate of two to one; they're mighty efficient. Cattle convert feed at twelve to one. They poop out ninety-two percent of what they eat. Ostriches only poop out fifty percent of what they eat."

"They must eat pretty well, then," was Ev's dry reply. As

they drove on, he noticed an inordinate number of meatloaf-sized mounds all equal to, if not bigger than, the one the bird had made for them.

"Well, College Boy," the Colonel piped up, "tell us about *your* conversion ratio. How many hours of Marxism do you have to sit through to produce each sentence of the bullshit you drop about your downward sloping demand, your guns 'n butter, and your creation and transfer of wealth?" The Colonel fumed. This boy needed a dose of military toughness.

About a quarter mile or so beyond the gate, the Cherokee arrived at the apparent center of the operation. The Womynscraft Ostrich Ranch included a large, smartly designed manufactured home that was set rather cunningly against a small hill. There were, by VJ's estimate, fifty acres, fenced with eight-foot chain link. The new metal barn was larger than the manufactured ranch house. There were wooden outbuildings scattered here and there that obviously predated both house and barn, and a little teardrop trailer up the hill from the house. An enclosed water tank was on top of the hill, obviously supplying gravity-fed water to the complex. Two husky women in overalls were using a scaffold and working together to reroof one of the outbuildings. An extraordinarily thin, elderly man in a baseball cap sat in a folding chair at the foot of the scaffold and watched. There were no ostriches in evidence, but the ground was littered with the unmistakable signs of their tenancy.

The women climbed down the scaffold as VJ, Ev, and the Colonel got out of the car. An unfamiliar aroma surprised Ev's nostrils. He'd once lived in an old apartment that'd partially flooded when a phone call interrupted his bath preparations and the tub had run over. The ranch smelled a lot like that wet carpet.

Tina and Jessie introduced themselves and Bert, Jessie's father. Bert lived in the little trailer. Tina was the talker, and talk she did. VJ listened and played with his hair. The Colonel asked questions nervously. Tina had a ring in her left nostril, and Colonel McKenzie couldn't take his eyes off of it. Ev watched Jessie. She was not husky at all really. It was the overalls that'd produced that impression. She was tall, maybe five foot eleven, and light complected. She had a blond crew cut with a purple streak. She kept looking at her watch and trying to catch Tina's eye. She was casting her partner a nasty look. Finally she stalked back toward the scaffold.

"Next time, call." She got on the scaffold, turned her back to the company, and went back to roofing the shed.

Tina just laughed. "Don't mind her; nothing pleases her, nothing. No, no, honey, you just lay shingles and feel sorry for yourself. I've got birds to sell. At least I assume you boys are here to talk turkey, har har."

To Ev's infinite distress, VJ was there to "talk turkey," and so, it turned out, was the Colonel.

Tina had a proved breeding pair, Samson and Delilah, that she was willing to part with at the sacrifice price of sixty thousand dollars. Leaving Jessie laying shingles to beat the band, Tina showed everyone around. Sixty thousand? Did she really mean dollars? The figure stunned Everett, who limped along, his face bunched and troubled. Bert tagged along, bending Ev's ear about the injustices he suffered at the hands of his daughter, who took him out of the rest home and put him in the trailer. He'd been one of the few men at the rest home and really the only one who wasn't senile or mean. The old dolls just loved him, he said. So up shows Jessie, all guilty about him crammed in that home. Does she listen to him? No, and she was just like her mother in that and how he'd ever managed to outlive her was beyond him and now here he was in that trailer while Jessie and Tina had their lifestyle and . . .

Ev, reminded of his great-uncle, tried his best to at least give the impression that he was listening, even though his right foot was as sore as a boil and he was worried about VJ.

When they entered the metal barn, the smell was so thick, so dense, and so foul that it was like running into a wall. Tina stopped and breathed deeply, her eyes closed and her head thrown back. "Ahhh, just take it in, boys; that smell is the smell of money."

Bert was evidently not the kind of person given to metaphor. "Actually," he said in an aside to Ev, "it's the smell of bird poop." This was difficult to deny.

The building was occupied by ostriches at all stages of development. There were incubators with eggs, little chicken-sized fuzz balls, ugly half-fledged three footers, three-quarter-sized adolescents, and near-adults that towered and dominated the barn space. The barn was divided into sections that segregated the different sizes from one another. It was a very big operation. There were at least thirty incubators going and some pretty sophisticated automation, food and water dishes that filled automatically. Someone, Ev concluded, had put *beaucoup* bucks into the operation.

The Colonel was impressed. This ranch put the place on *Good Morning America* to shame. Still, it was doubtful that any ranch, however well capitalized, could be supplying Cartier wristwatches to their breeding stock. "We saw one of your animals at the gate. I think you ought to know it was carrying a wristwatch around."

"Him, not it; that was Samson. He's had that watch for a couple of months now. We had some people out. Turned out to be a bunch of time-wasting looky-looks. Samson was free, as usual, and was wandering around over by the house. Guy was over there trying to feed Samson a kiwi fruit. Samson didn't think much of the kiwi fruit but the watch intrigued him. He grabbed ahold of it and busted it right off the guy's wrist. The guy started bellering, and Samson hauled butt. He gave the guy a little kick as he was leaving, too, right in the chest. The fellow must have startled Samson, because that ostrich was smokin'. They can hit sixty miles an hour, you know.

"Anyway, knocked the breath out of the guy. There he was on the ground turning purple and doing this, just like a fish." Tina did a cruel pantomime of a person in extremis, fighting for breath. She giggled.

"Guy had it coming, I figured, and Samson just tapped him. What a wuss. So anyway, he catches his breath and starts in screaming about a lawsuit. So I took him down here and showed him this."

She indicated a sign that read as follows: THE NEVADA STATE LEGAL CODE RECOGNIZES OSTRICHES AND OTHER RATITES AS IN-HERENTLY DANGEROUS EXOTIC ANIMALS. CITIZENS WHO ENTER INTO A POSTED AREA WHERE OSTRICHES AND/OR OTHER RATITES ARE KEPT DO SO AT THEIR OWN RISK AND IMPLICITLY AGREE TO HOLD HARMLESS THE OWNERS AND HANDLERS OF THE BIRDS MAINTAINED WITHIN THAT POSTED AREA AS REGARDS ANY INJURY OR PROPERTY LOSS SUSTAINED THROUGH CONTACT OF ANY SORT WITH THE AFOREMENTIONED OSTRICHES OR OTHER RATITES.

"The guy was a real wimp. If Samson'd really kicked, the guy would be dead, like the rottweiler that dug under the fence and got in here. Samson kicked that dog big time. Dog looked like a Morten Andersen field goal: long, straight, and right through the uprights. Dead before he even hit. Anyway, the little tap and the missing watch gave the wuss a good excuse to leave without buying anything. Samson has had that watch for a couple of months now. He hides it and then goes and gets it. God knows where he keeps it."

Ev had trouble following the story. The smell was nauseating in the July heat. It didn't seem to bother Tina, VJ, or the Colonel, but Ev could not take it. He looked around for as long as he could, maybe five minutes, and then limped heavily outside, followed by Bert.

"Gimpy?"

"No, I just got my feet burned on pavement down in Phoenix and then some sheep stepped on the right one here in Nevada."

"Well, don't go to Utah then, some of them big, fat old Mormon women will stomp on your feet if you do. I lived for better than a year at a home in Utah, Brigham City, and the fact is that those Mormon women do not miss many meals. I was always thinking that one of those old babes was gonna go wobbly on me and I'd end up crushed. One of 'em give me a big hug once, popped my back, straightened it out too, I swear I stand two inches taller, but you know a man doesn't like to go around figuring he's like to get crushed, not that it's . . ."

Unconsciously Ev tuned the old man out. He figured that Bert was probably right. The foot was just spoiling for further injury. He was getting gloomy about his feet. He should have stayed at the sheep ranch under Magda's care. He made his way back to the Cherokee and found it locked. He thought about easing himself up on the hood, but found that it was not only too high but also red-hot. He came close to burning his hands on it. Bert, sensing Ev's needs and vulnerability, went and got the folding chair. Ev put the chair in the shade of the Cherokee and dropped into it like he was made of lead. Bert hunkered down, determined to keep him company. The two of them watched Jessie roof the shed. From the barn, then the house, then the fields, they could hear the low murmur of Tina pitching ostriches. Ev screwed up his mouth. He sniffed, aware that his nose was, happily, becoming de-sensitized to the acrid musk of the ostriches. He grunted. He cast withering glances in the direction of Tina's voice. As Tina led VJ and the Colonel back into the barn, Bert nodded in her direction.

"A lesson to you, boy: never own anything you have to paint or feed. Fact of the matter is that these gals—they're gals but they call themselves womyn with a *y*, if that don't beat anything you ever knew of—these gals work more than a person ought. It makes a man of leisure like myself tired just watching them. Figure it out. They got enough money to buy all this, then they got enough to not buy it and take it easy. They got their lifestyle, why not enjoy it? Nope, can't be done, gotta roof a damned shed for these . . ."

Ev was stunned. "Never own anything you have to feed or paint," the old guy had said. Ev could not recall ever having heard better advice. (More than once in the course of his sometimes troubled existence Ev remembered old Bert's astonishing admonition. He never adopted this wise code, but he always thought about it when he took on new responsibilities. Everything, it seemed, needed to be fed or painted. Ostriches do not need to be painted. That is one of the very few unalloyed advantages of the species.)

When they left Womynscraft Ostrich Ranch, the three companions took with them the strong but now unnoticed smell that had adhered to their clothes. They also took an ostrich egg in an incubator. This, VJ informed Ev, was a birthday present for Sabine. It'd cost seven hundred dollars, after lengthy negotiations with Tina. The incubator was a loan. VJ would bring it back when the egg hatched—or buy more eggs. The Colonel had lent VJ the money. They needed to get the egg to Sabine's within a couple of hours and then crank up the incubator. Tina claimed the incubators were insulated well enough to hold the temperature within the needed parameters for at least three hours. The drive up had taken an hour and twenty-two minutes. They had a margin.

As they pulled away, Tina and Jessie (who had become quite friendly when she learned that they'd bought an egg) waved good-bye along with Bert. Tina made a pantomime motion of dialing a telephone. She'd given VJ reams of computer printout on ostrich husbandry and had also insisted that he call her every two or three days until the egg hatched. At that point, he was to call her every day for a while. She guaranteed the egg. She'd replace it if it didn't hatch. Samson and Delilah, it seemed, were legendary in ostrich circles as true breeders. Their eggs were better than ninety percent gravid. Tina made out that it'd been a real privilege, almost an omen, that they'd seen Samson taking a crap near the gate. They didn't see him on the way out, which struck Ev as an even better omen.

Ev was just waiting for the Colonel to make some crack about Tina and Jessie, but the old soldier just drove, oddly quiet and reflective. VJ, too, was quiet. He'd gotten himself in a jam. He had to have a present for Sabine, and it'd worried him all day. He was a bit short of funds. He'd spent every dime he owned on gas for the trip. The Colonel had offered to loan him the money for the egg, and now that's all he had to give his dad for his birthday. It was kind of a funny birthday present, and there was a very good chance it'd make Sabine mad. If that happened, an unfortunate incident, like the escapade with the fork, might well ensue. The old boy was probably still a bit touchy about the Jojobalueca business.

Probably, VJ reasoned, it'd be better to tell Sabine that he was going to raise the ostrich and find it a mate before actually leaving it at the ranch. But then, where was he going to raise it, and how was he going to get it back to New Mexico? It would have been smarter to buy an egg in New Mexico, probably, but what's done was done. It was due to hatch any day, so maybe he could stay there with it at the ranch until it hatched and then take it to New Mexico. He'd just have to see. Sabine did have those donkeys, after all. Maybe the idea of an ostrich would appeal to the old man. He'd surely have read the articles in *Stockman's Universe*. At least Sabine would know something, at least it was animal husbandry. Anyway, if the old Basque didn't like the gift, it'd sort of serve him right for being so damned slow to let go of a nickel. It was his fault, after all, that Magda had to work her fingers to the bone clipping those damned Scottsdale poodles. It'd be a treat to see the old guy's startled expression when he took his first gander at the egg. That had to be worth the price, right there.

CHAPTER ELEVEN

■ ■ ■

Virgil Jose Eckleberry shared with his father a sense of dread and foreboding as regards family celebrations. Though neither would or could have articulated the conviction, both sensed that family celebrations were conspiratorial affairs arranged by the distaff side to bring the Eckleberry men into line. For this reason, VJ was quiet and reflective on the drive back to the ranch. He kept picturing Celia and Felice in their separate cars closing in on the ranch. They'd bring rafts of children and whatever pets were at hand. Downtrodden, potentially rebellious husbands might or might not be along. It was a sobering, intimidating image. Rosa was already at the ranch and doing quite an adequate job of sistering for VJ's money. The habit of command was a strong feature in her approach to things, and this was in no way diminished by the presence of Magda. In fact, both women were worse, if that can be imagined, in one another's presence. They imparted a rather martial air to their surroundings and seldom fell into the kind of competition that VJ or Sabine could exploit in the interest of liberty. Put Celia and Felice on top of that and the situation would reach critical mass. No man on earth could withstand the combined strength.

Although VJ rode along with a growing sense of foreboding, he did not fully grasp the character of his situation. Young men bearing unwanted ostrich eggs typically experience crises of confidence when they face such odds. VJ, as a representative of that small class, was certainly no exception. An ostrich egg is the size of a football and weighs some three pounds. It is a difficult thing to conceal from judgmental sisters, particularly when that egg must be cared for and coddled. The clock was running and there was no way to avoid discovery, no way to get the incubator set up in a surreptitious fashion. Nope, he'd just have to brass it out in the face of them all, Magda, Sabine, Rosa, Felice, Celia, and the nieces and nephews that were sure to penetrate every nook and cranny at the ranch. The egg had to be incubated. The incubator had to be plugged in; extension cords had to be strung. Timing was of the essence. The egg simply had to be under incubation within the three hours Tina had specified. Whatever abuse this entailed would have to be borne with all the grace he could muster.

The drive from Womynscraft Ostrich Ranch back toward Sabine's place was quiet. Ev huddled in the shotgun seat, his mind divided. Happy thoughts of that extravagant kiss from Rosa battled somber déjà vu. How many times would he bear witness to Virgil Jose's bent enthusiasms? Would he grow old thus, posing fruitless objections to doomed schemes? Was it his fate to lobby for reason in the face of madcap folly? He supposed so.

VJ, normally the very soul and spirit of madcap folly, sat alone in the back, his eyes searching the horizon as though for guidance. The realization of a dream is a sobering experience.

The Colonel drove in silence, lost in sour thoughts of

scrubbed weapons and cowardly investments. Speculation, he noted, was a young man's game, and getting old was hell. In addition, the project of forcing Magda to crawl back to him was not going particularly well. "Magda, well, Jesus!" Twice the Colonel pounded unexpectedly on the steering wheel, uttering this oath and giving his passengers a bad start.

On Nevada State Highway 34 there is a Fina service station near the turnoff to Sabine's ranch. Colonel McKenzie guided the Cherokee into the station and pulled to the full-service pumps.

"I gotta piss like a racehorse," he explained.

Ev did not, but he was glad to stop. A Diet Coke and a Butterfinger might just hit the spot. It was an awful thing to be driving through Nevada with an egg. It awakened memories of Susan back at the UNM in Albuquerque going on about existential absurdity and dread. Happily, existential dread is simply no match for the restorative powers of Coke, even Diet Coke, and Butterfingers.

VJ did not want to stop, not even for a Butterfinger. His face was knotted with concern. The clock was running. He watched the Colonel stride toward the bathroom as Custer must have watched the deployment of the first large contingent of Sioux at the Little Bighorn.

The attendant who filled the tank coincidentally had an Indian headband-style bandage around his sore head. Earlier in the day he'd thrown a crescent wrench at a tire that was not coming off its rim as quickly as he'd felt that it ought. The wrench hit the tire and bounced right back, swatting him a good one, right on the ear. The ear had hurt badly all day. When the skinny old guy in the Cherokee jumped out and headed for the shitter, the bandaged man forgot his pain. An appalling stink issued from the Jeep. Strong and dense, the stink drove all petty preoccupations from his mind. He wondered that the driver made such haste toward the restroom. It was obviously too late to matter.

While the attendant pumped gas, glorying as seldom before

in the smell of gasoline, the passengers got out. The fat guy made a beeline for the candy machines. The skinny one paced up and down, straining over toward the men's room as though his impatience would hurry the old guy. It was astounding. The men, all three of them, gave off the same, truly insupportable stink. He could scarcely credit that human beings could smell so bad. He hoped that his wife never ingested the particular beans or cabbage or split pea soup that had produced such devastating results. Five minutes of the smell was about the limit as far as he was concerned, and he was glad to finish the business with the old guy so they could leave. His eyes were beginning to water. The Cherokee pulled back onto the highway, leaving the attendant with his sore ear and a new perspective on the olfactory possibilities of the human condition.

Ev was puzzled as he washed down the last crumbs of his Butterfinger. "What was wrong with that guy? He was breathing funny."

"Probably he was a business major at a communist university, Fat Boy, all out of breath from talking on and on like he knows everything there is to know. Someone evidently gave him a cuff on the ear to shut his smart mouth." The Colonel's mood improved when he emptied his bladder.

VJ said nothing. Even though he knew that they had better than two hours to negotiate twenty miles of dirt road, he was worried.

Sabine spent a happy day after all. The sight of Magda's poodles inadvertently catching up to the panicky fallen sheep had turned the day around for him. It was too bad, of course, that the sheep had trampled over young Crume's sore feet, but at least they hadn't trampled over Sabine's feet, and the scene was highly entertaining. It was worth an injury, especially an injury to someone else, a young person who would heal readily. Of course, none of the sheep got hurt. Sheep were hearty. It took something spectacular, like hurtling off a cliff or walking in front of a train, to injure sheep. They did do these things fairly regularly, but small collisions with chunky humans were no threat.

It had also been a treat to see Magda run jiggling up to save and then scold her babies. Sabine liked a bit of jiggle on a woman, and Magda had jiggled a bit for him in her day. A man could hope she'd give him a bit of a jiggle before his birthday passed. She was his wife and all. She had good sense about VJ and the girls and almost everything else save poodles and Arizona, but allowances could be made. He did love her and could hope for some kissing and pickle-tickle later on. Who knew what might develop? He felt hopeful, optimistic.

When Magda regained her composure, she steeled herself for strife and located Sabine on the porch. "What on earth," she said, "did you think you were doing when you threw VJ off of this ranch? I don't know which is more infantile, your stunt with the fork or his ostrich reaction." Did Sabine bellow in rage as he was wont when confronted with such inquiries? Did he lapse into stony, entrenched silence and fortify his resolve with a defiant midmorning snifter of Sangre de Toro? No, the old sheep rancher simply recalled the exquisite image of his voluptuous wife rushing to separate sheep from poodles and smiled with the sure knowledge that he lived in a beautiful world.

They managed, therefore, to agree on VJ. They talked about him for almost an hour, taking advantage of his absence, off on his ostrich quest with Ev and the Colonel. He was an exasperating boy and required a lot of conversation. At the end there was an accord that had eluded them for several years.

"He needs responsibility. When I was his age I was navigating a submarine. Where do those nutty ideas come from? What does he need with such animals?"

Magda thought of the donkeys and grinned. VJ was not the only Eckleberry with nutty ideas and absurd animals. "It'd take you, Sabine, to equate responsibility with defiance of your father and piracy on the high seas. Navigating a submarine, indeed. I suppose that's what you'd have your boy doing, pitching in with a bunch of crazed vagabonds like your cousins to waylay hapless merchant ships and steal everything in sight. It's no mystery to me where Virgil's nutty ideas come from, and I wish you wouldn't use that word. I won't have it. He's an inventive, creative boy and his ideas are imaginative, not nutty. He is so good-hearted. He thinks he can use this ostrich idea to help people."

Sabine noted the cracks about piracy and his Argentinian cousins and chose, for the time being, to let them pass. The boy needed sheep, many, many sheep. That would straighten him up. What was this business about helping others all about?

"Help people? Help who? How?"

"Well, me for one, Sabine. Our boy thinks you're awfully tight. He figures I'm suffering poverty so profound that I've had to turn to poodle clipping for my daily bread."

"Well, he may have a piece of the truth after all. I don't know why you have to have that kind of business. It gives everybody the wrong idea."

"I don't care what sort of idea it gives anybody but me. It gives me the idea that I'm happy and can run a business that turns a nice profit, but let's not start in on that. The point is that he has a touching, if misguided, concern for my well-being."

Sabine was losing concentration, beginning to picture a better world. Lately these reveries always included donkeys. It was difficult to imagine a better world that lacked donkeys. While Magda talked, for example, he pictured VJ on the high prairie tending sheep. It was on the leased land many miles from the house. For several years, Sabine had opted against wintering his sheep. In a world where you could sell fattened sheep in the fall, invest the money in 120-day CDs, and then buy lean sheep in the spring, wintering the animals had seemed unnecessary, a bother. On the other hand, keeping the sheep all winter, the traditional ewe and lamb operation, had its attractions. It'd mean profits from the increase in the number of animals from year to year. That was the way the ranching should be done, and VJ could do it. Sabine thought of his herds increasing under VJ's care. It was a beautiful thought and of course included donkeys.

The boy would have one of the shepherds' wagons, completely tricked out and stocked to the ceiling. He'd have a couple of donkeys with him to pull the wagon, guard the herd, and run off predators. He'd be off alone there with the sheep for months, miles away! It'd be perfect, better than military school. Sheep had to be the perfect animal for developing responsibility. The gaps in their intelligence constantly astounded Sabine, who'd lived with sheep as his close companions for the larger part of his life. If they got any stupider, they'd need the help of shepherds to fill their lungs with air and then exhale rather than asphyxiate. A shepherd has to have an intuitive, almost psychic grasp of herd dynamics, or he has to keep his wits and watch the woolies constantly. It's just short of a miracle that sheep have not gone extinct. They are inadvertently suicidal animals, who will walk off a cliff in great crowds following one of their companions who'd accidentally fallen. It takes work to keep them out of jams. It takes concentration or it takes intuition. Virgil Jose was visionary, easily distracted. His talent as a shepherd came from intuition and empathy rather than vigilance. VJ was wonderful with sheep. Sabine meant to see that VJ spent some quality time with a huge herd of sheep. His talents were wasted on his idiot groom job in Albuquerque, and they'd be even more wasted on ostrich husbandry. It had to be sheep, lots of them.

Magda had her ideas, an agenda she was looking for an opportunity to push. She wanted Sabine to allow the boy to run the ranch with Rosa. She wanted to get old Sabine the hell out of there. The perfect thing would be to have Sabine come winter in Arizona, leaving the kids in charge. To her surprise, Sabine broached the subject.

"I've made a decision about Virgil Jose, Magda, and I need to have you behind me on this. I'm going to ask him to stop all the foolishness. There is work, winter work, here on this ranch, and he is eventually going to have to learn how it goes. I say the sooner, the better. I also figure that it's got to be on his own with real responsibility. That means distance from his old man. I don't expect I'll have a whole lot of contact with him. From November to at least mid-March, I won't even see him. While he's freezing out on those winter grounds, he'll not need me looking over his shoulder. I plan to winter warm for once."

Magda couldn't have imagined that this conversation would be so easy, that Sabine would be so reasonable. She knew Sabine missed her but never would have guessed he would agree so readily to absent himself from the ranch for the winter. Even before she moved to Arizona, she'd tried to get him to winter there. Finally, she guessed, it'd registered. He'd probably been wanting to come to Arizona for years and been just too stubborn to admit it.

"You'll get no arguments from me. I've been thinking the same thing. He needs your trust, and he doesn't need you around watching his every move. Besides, you do have to think of your own comfort. You can't take the cold the way you used to."

Boy, Magda was right there. The last thing Sabine wanted to do was spend any time snooping around a herd of sheep in the dead of the Nevada winter. Especially up on the high prairie where he was planning to send the boy. Nope, he'd not stray too far from the fireplace and the Sangre de Toro. Small danger of that. Daisy could continue to handle the business, including the trips into town on frigid days. He might even be able to induce Magda to come for an extended midwinter visit. Anyone would get sick of the damned orange trees and swimming pools.

"No need," he said, "for me to freeze my butt anymore when I've got a couple of hot-blooded kids like Virgil Jose and Daisy. Let the young fight the cold."

Sabine and Magda shared a fond gaze, thinking of how nicely the other was mellowing with age. Humming to herself, Magda went off to ice Sassy's leg. Sabine was ecstatic.

There were the details, of course, to work out, details that would include reconciliation with the boy. That'd be delicate, since Sabine had no intention of making the slightest apology for assaulting his son with a fork. The young fool had actually wanted money for that Jojobalueca nightmare! *Money!* On top of driving Sabine to the brink of a nervous breakdown, he'd wanted *money* for his efforts and had the nerve to bring it up at dinner! If Sabine had grabbed a knife, that'd be different; knife assaults constitute a real breakdown of paternal protocol. But, given the provocation, Sabine had shown almost saintly forbearance. Choosing the humble salad fork to emphasize his firm resolve to drive the boy from the house, he'd passed on butter knives, steak knives, and a wicked, bone-handled carving knife that littered the tabletop. While not exactly proud of having menaced his only son with a salad fork, he did consider it a very measured and appropriate reaction. Any right-thinking father faced with the situation would've done the same.

In the heat of the moment, Sabine had possibly gone too far. He had sworn a fateful promise to disinherit VJ. Rosa, Felice, and Celia had let their father know many times, in many ways, that this had been much more than the situation warranted. Maybe it'd been excessive, but maybe not. After all, he'd not really changed his will. It'd been gratifying to see VJ's flight, and Sabine had enjoyed a couple of months of relative peace. Still, there was no denying the brutal truth. The incident with the fork had cast a pall, strained relations. Sabine would need to confront the issue and work to create more amicable father-son communications. Only then could he begin demanding that the boy care for a thousand head of sheep.

He'd deal with all that later. Now he'd just survive his birthday and coast on how well he was getting along with Magda. Finally, she'd wised up and quit harping at him about going to Arizona. Despite her apparent success in the poodle-clipping business, perhaps she was thinking about moving back to Nevada. Maybe she'd at least come for a few weeks in January when not much was shaking. With VJ safely occupied with a huge herd of sheep, he and Magda could have themselves quite a lovey time during those long nights.

With the VJ situation settled, Magda and Sabine went their own ways until late afternoon when people started showing up for the party. Magda iced Sassy's leg, took a walk with the other poodles, and called Arizona to check on business concerns. Sabine walked the fences of the kitchen pen wondering how the sheep were managing to escape. He also spent time with the donkeys, watching them graze, haltering them with some practical rope halters he'd quickly fashioned, attempting (without success) to do a little hoof work, and attaining a state of great serenity. The burros, especially Che, were wonderful creatures, friendly and curious without the servility of dogs. They were solid, centered beasts and allowed Sabine to handle them. With regard to picking up their feet, however, they were consistent and firm in their refusal. Sabine admired both their persistence and their courtesy. He would pick up a hoof, and Che would simply put it back down. The movement was deliberate, emphatic, yet without rancor. There was no nonsense, none of the rearing and backward somersault foolishness Sabine had sometimes seen with horses. He had the feeling that Che would eventually allow him to pick up his feet and do the hoof work. This would follow Che's timetable and sense of donkey protocol.

The animals were surprisingly affectionate. Che, still

barely halter-trained, had lived wild for years, remote from human contact. Amazingly, he had walked up to Sabine, rested his big head on Sabine's shoulder, and let the man mess with him for a good half hour. Sabine liked the way that, excepting the sudden, explosive fits of braying, the donkeys never seemed to lose their dignity. They were decorous animals with a strong sense of tradition. They observed proprieties. There was obviously a proper sequence in the unfolding of relations between them and the human species. Che would allow Sabine to pick up his feet after a decent interval of introduction and earned trust. Until then, the burro would firmly refuse. Sabine began to understand the reputation for stubbornness. Yet the animals were not stubborn. They simply held their own views on pace. They were sweet and had soft, velvety noses. Sabine learned these essential truths of the breed on his first day as a novice owner.

Around three in the afternoon, while VJ, Ev, and the Colonel were unknowingly absorbing the adhesive stink of the Womynscraft ostriches, a lull fell over the Eckleberry compound. Powerful inner forces and mysterious atmospheric conditions drove Sabine into the hammock that'd hung, abandoned for weeks, on the porch. The trip to the prison had taken a toll, and the old man felt a good deal of anticipatory fatigue whenever he thought of his birthday celebration. The talk with Magda had eased his mind, contact with the donkeys had further relaxed the aging Basque, and an afternoon tumbler of Sangre de Toro made its own soporific contribution. Thus primed, Sabine climbed into his hammock at 2:45 with a fresh edition of *Stockman's Universe* (it had a feature article on cost analysis and protein content of seventeen commercial feeds for horses, cattle, sheep, and hogs). At 2:47 he slipped into the land of nod.

Magda, who'd made an afternoon nap a feature of her daily routine, was already asleep, nude and comely in the darkened bedroom she'd formerly used for reading and during rare periods of conflict with her husband. There was nothing inadvertent about Magda's nap. As true believers of the Islamic faith turn six times daily toward Mecca for prayer, Magda Zumwalt-Eckleberry turned at 1:30 each day to repose. This was quite a project, involving, as it did, a shower followed by the liberal application of oils and elixirs of various kinds. Blindfolded, ears plugged with stopples of specially manufactured wax, and greased from waist to forehead with Oil of Olay, Magda always napped for at least an hour, the bed surrounded by poodles who knew enough to stay on the floor, each in his or her own proper place. Magda enjoyed her preparations and found them relaxing. She was still tired from the long drive.

The crowd of humans had dispersed. Some were still around, but their lair grew quiet. The donkeys, having grazed for the better part of thirteen hours, were contented and full. Like Magda and Sabine, the burros in the kitchen pen sought cool, quiet spots some distance from one another and slept through the warm afternoon, disturbed by nothing save the occasional bleat or baa from the nearby sheep.

Those sheep had been busy. The donkey Vera had given the lone half-grown lamb new and startling experiences. Twice she'd thrown the little mite out of the kitchen pen. So impressed were the lamb's sheep companions that they'd twice pushed through the fence in sympathy. Twice then, humans had spotted the perplexed sheep and herded them into the pen with the donkey that'd started it all. This kind of thing is inevitably draining. The sheep were physically fatigued and emotionally fragile.

During the course of the long, hot summer day the sheep slowly regained their composure. Understanding their distress, VJ had cooed and petted them soothingly before leaving with Ev and the Colonel. He'd also given each of the sheep a couple of alfalfa pellets, so calming to frayed nerves. By midday the sheep were back to normal. They'd forgotten that any burro had ever thrown a lamb over any fence, and they'd forgotten the terrible little dogs and the frightening wreck that'd started the day. For sheep, forgetting is the work of a moment, but they'd spent much of the day slowly calming down, as anxiety gradually and inexplicably dissipated. Finally, they were relaxed enough to begin grazing and did so, quietly at first but with increasing enthusiasm. By three, their bleating had awakened Vera one time too many. A burro will tolerate only so much. Stirred into unsolicited wakefulness, she strolled to the small cabal of sheep that bleated conspiracy against the far fence of the kitchen pen. She went to work and actually threw two of them over the fence, the lamb and one of the smaller ewes. Now habituated, the other sheep pushed their way under the fence, which distended and then snapped back into place. Vera watched with satisfaction. She drifted back toward the house, finding the shade of a good-sized white oak that grew just outside the fence. There, a comfortable distance from the other donkeys and unmolested by the sounds of sheep, Vera lay down on the cool grass and slept on her side.

The sheep, outside of their pasture for the third time, were anxious and confused for the third time. This time they avoided civilization. Guided by inclinations impossible to fathom, they headed toward the cutbanks of the small stream that drained the canyon. Too nervous to graze, they covered ground and covered it fast. They reached the stream, crossed it, and turned upstream. They walked without hesitation, as though determined to reach the headwaters by nightfall.

Around four in the afternoon, things in both the human world and the natural world began shifting. Thunderheads forming for hours over the mountains to the north began rolling down the valleys. It was probably atmospheric pressure, but it felt like all nature was responding to the birthday celebration that

loomed in the immediate future. Shorebirds, peeps, and kil-
deer, after standing for hours, suddenly took flight. A stiff
breeze out of the north whipped up and sent a brood of dust
devils skittering across the wide space of the valley. Sabine
Eckleberry awoke from a dream of arguing with his father,
while his daughter Felice, forty-two miles away, eased the
pink Cadillac up to ninety and slapped at her children in the
back seat. Meanwhile, her sister Rosa gave Fanny Ulibarri a
cell phone call to suggest that she bring her parrot Abraham
to the party.

Rosa carried the accouterments of the party in the back of
VJ's pickup. It'd taken her the day to assemble everything, but
the deeds were finally done. Nothing remained except to return to the ranch and prepare for the onslaught. Her sisters
were hurtling toward the ranch, narrowing the distance at
least a mile each minute. The image of hurtling sisters made
Rosa feel a bit giddy. Off and on during the course of the day,
Rosa had allowed her thoughts to return angrily to Everett
Crume and his disgusting porn. At present, she needed mental discipline. She had to dismiss both images and emotions.
Armies were on the move, and the world girded itself in expec-
tation.

The party had a character and momentum. It'd begun early
with an anticipatory form that'd drawn VJ and Ev from the
torpid routines of the New Mexico summer and pushed them,
albeit circuitously, toward Nevada. The energy field of the
party created convergence. At 5:17, for example, Fanny Ulibarri, driving a tan Ford pickup, turned off Nevada State Road
31 onto a dirt road that followed the valley of a small stream
to the Eckleberry Ranch, some nineteen miles distant. A dark
Jeep Cherokee shared that same dirt road with Felice Han-
son's pink Brougham Cadillac and her sister Celia's silver Mercedes four-door. The Mercedes, like the Cadillac that preceded
it by a mile or so, was clotted with children and sped down
the dirt road angrily, seemingly offended by the paucity of
pavement. Felice, slapping at the dog and children while

slowing the Caddy to a modest fifty-five, reached into her vast pink-and-white-striped canvas purse and extracted a handful of radishes soaked in brine. How like Daddy, she thought, to live out his days nineteen miles down a dirt road. She resigned herself to the snail's pace and ate radishes.

All parties involve surprises of one kind or another. As Felice rounded a familiar bend and crossed the one rickety bridge over the small creek, a bunch of sheep bolted across the road in front of her. Swallowing a whole radish, she swerved left to avoid killing her father's sheep, hit a soft spot on the shoulder, and proceeded to lose control of the vehicle. The Caddy spun lazily back to the center of the road, spun again, veering to the right. Felice was one of those people who seek the mean by crowding the extremes. As a driver, she tended to overcorrect. The Cadillac did a desultory doughnut or two and then left the road with no apparent intention of ever returning. The big boat bumped heavily over the prairie. All of the kids were wearing their seat belts but still got jostled. They started bawling. Kronen, an Irish setter with the intelligence of an orange pip, lost control of his bladder. Felice was glad to have stopped the spinning and fishtailing. The prairie wasn't much worse than the road, and she managed to get the Caddy stopped within a few hundred yards, just as her sister Celia, driving the Mercedes, crossed the bridge.

Celia stopped the Mercedes at the point that the Cadillac had left the road. She got out, shielded her eyes against the sun, and regarded the inert Cadillac, which sat issuing forth bawling children some distance away. Celia was a stout woman in her midthirties. She wore an arresting lavender paisley muumuu. She stood peering toward the Cadillac, frowning at the children and finally the dog that leaked from that unseemly vessel. VJ, Ev, and the Colonel joined her. They'd just arrived in the Cherokee. She regarded them without surprise. Her nose curled.

"My God, VJ, what is that stink? I swear it's going to gag me. Stand downwind, all of you!"

The men moved sheepishly to her aft side.

"Felice just about turned her car over. Look at it. Look at those damned kids." She regarded the Colonel.

"My sister has the worst-behaved kids that were ever born. Sweet Jesus, I love her dearly, but those kids of hers, look at them!"

Celia's own kids were, by decree, confined to the Mercedes. There were four of them, two boys and two girls. They were amusing themselves by punching one another's arms, claiming that right through a game known as "flinching."

The Colonel was speechless. He'd not known that he stunk and was uncertain as to how to cope with that apparent reality. The smell of the ostriches must have clung to them somehow.

VJ immediately started arguing.

"What stink? We don't stink. You must be smelling the creosote."

"VJ, don't you argue with me. That is the worst smell I've smelled in my life. Now, I don't know nor care what you've been doing, and I'll thank you to allow me to draw my conclusions. I suppose I can trust my nose to let me know if something or someone stinks, and little brother, you stink. Look at Felice there. How is she ever going to get that obscene boat out of that field? The only reason she got that car is that damned Mary Kay business. She'll drive us all crazy. What is that stink anyway? It's like concentrated chicken shit, pardon my French."

"It must be the ostriches."

The explanation evidently satisfied Celia. She didn't mention the smell again but did take care to see that VJ and his friends remained downwind.

The sheep that Felice had swerved to avoid were long gone, single-mindedly following the little stream. They were, however, vividly present in Felice's thoughts and conversation. She marched her children along, away from the stranded

Cadillac. Enthused with his sudden freedom, Kronen ranged around here and there, galumphing at top speed. It was more than a little humiliating for Felice to cross the distance toward her siblings and the knot of hangers-on about them. She blamed her father. Living down that damned dirt road still, at his age, not to mention allowing unsupervised sheep to force motorists into the boonies! Now she would have to pile her children into Celia's car, which was already, no doubt, crammed with those brats Celia had spawned. Felice loved her sister dearly but had to admit that she'd raised the worst bunch of kids that ever sassed and whined.

Felice was two years older than her sister. She was thin and had the highest metabolic level among the Eckleberrys. She used as much energy in an ordinary conversation as most people would use to tear down a brick wall. One of the top-producing Mary Kay Cosmetics representatives in Nevada, Felice was dressed to the nines in heels and a blue business suit with wide lapels and a starched white shirt. She wore a modest blue satin scarf, ascot-style, around her neck. She'd have known poor Celia at a mile's distance in that horrible muumuu. God, it had enough fabric for a tent. Just like her mother, that was Celia: no taste, no instinct for grooming. If she could just get her to a Mary Kay seminar, they might be able to do something. Fat as she was, she did have a sweet face. At least she seemed to have left her pomeranians at home. God, what awful animals, pooping like they did into that long fur; they were scarcely better than Sabine's car-wrecking sheep.

VJ watched his eldest sister approach. It was impressive how well she could negotiate the prairie in her high heels. He was a little anxious about the ostrich egg. There was still plenty of time, really, to get to the ranch and get the incubator set up, but he did like a margin of error. He'd just checked the egg and imagined that he'd felt a tremor. Back at Womynscraft he'd listened to the heartbeat of the egg-bound infant through a stethoscope. The idea of it hatching filled him with excitement and apprehension. As Felice approached, he drummed his fingers on the hood of the Mercedes.

Felice's children had quit crying and were, instead, complaining of the distance they'd had to walk across the field. Felice ignored them. Kronen, sniffing wildly, covered ground, slowed to three-quarter speed, and leapt onto Ev, striking him in the chest, licking at his face and snuffling all over him while Felice yelled at him to get away. The Colonel, as was his habit in such circumstances, kicked at the big dog. He missed, but the incident did not escape Felice's scrutiny. Who was this old turd who was kicking at her puppy!?! She was too frazzled to act, but the incident provided a first impression of the Colonel that would prove indelible.

"What on earth is that smell? My God, VJ. First I've got Daddy's sheep running me off the road and now it's you. That is the foulest stench I have ever smelled. What is this, some kind of a macho club? You don't bathe or wipe your butts for six months? And for God's sake, quit beating on the car. What is this, Celia? What is going on at this ranch? I wouldn't have thought that Rosa would let it get this far. I mean, Daddy's eccentricities are bad enough."

"It's ostriches, Felice." VJ quit drumming his fingers on the hood of the Mercedes. He was always stunned and humbled when confronted with his older sisters. "We were at an ostrich ranch and I guess we picked up a bit of the scent of the animals."

"Well, if that is a bit, I'd hate to smell a bunch. You busters are going to have to bury those clothes, I'll tell you that for sure. If Rosa lets any of you in the house, I'll quit claiming her as my sister. See that car? Your daddy's sheep wrecked that car. They're running wild, I guess. I suppose his politics have rubbed off on his sheeping. What did I do in my last life to get born into this family, an anarchist father and a brother who's taken up stinking as a life's work? And who [to the Colonel] the hell are you and how dare you kick my dog? You look old enough to know better, but I guess there's no fool like an old fool. And by the way, who is going to drive me and my children to the ranch? I'm not riding with you." She pointed her chin at VJ, Ev, and the Colonel. "Celia, send your kids with them and give me and my kids a ride."

Celia frowned and extended her several chins toward her sister. In the end, though, she hesitated. She decided to cut Felice some slack. The near crash had obviously stressed her out. Besides, Felice was a Republican, and Celia worried that the requisite hypocrisy was exacting a fearful toll on her elder sis. She fought down the urge to battle. Still, Celia would draw the line at forcing her children to ride to the ranch in that rolling gas chamber with VJ, chunky little old Everett Crume, and that stinking reprobate they'd apparently picked up in some adopt-a-smelly-old-geezer program. Celia was convinced, despite VJ's theory on ostriches, that the Colonel was the source of the offending odor.

The Colonel, though unaware of Celia's judgments, was livid. How could this pair of harridans be Magda's daughters? What would shut them up?

"I am retired Colonel Jordan McKenzie" was at last all he could think to say. Limited though this contribution was, the principals utterly ignored it.

Celia offered to run her kids up to the ranch and come back for Felice, her kids, and Kronen. She was glad she'd been wise enough to leave her dogs at home. Their coats were so long and fine that they'd have probably absorbed that terrible smell.

Felice agreed. Her kids started griping about having to wait, but they'd been griping anyway about the wreck and the long walk they'd made back to the road.

The Colonel rallied. His tough-mindedness returned, along with a grim martial determination to do a job right, regardless of rewards or lack thereof.

"This Jeep can haul that car out of there," he asserted. "Now, you women go ahead to the party. Make the two trips if you have to. I'll drive on in to drop off young VJ here as well. He has a valuable egg and needs to set up an incubator. The college boy and I will come back and get that Cadillac. We'll tow her in whether she seems roadworthy or not. Somebody probably ought to give the car the once-over. Something might have shaken loose."

Everyone agreed. The Colonel was still unredeemed, as far as Felice was concerned. Bringing in the Cadillac might have made up for the stink, but in no way made up for kicking so viciously at Kronen, the poor puppy.

Sabine awoke with a terrible start. Where the hell was Rosa? His daughter Celia's silver Mercedes roared up the driveway, honking "La Cucaracha." Like VJ, Celia announced her arrivals with a characteristic flourish. The Mercedes careened to a stop, and Sabine watched the vehicle disgorge four children. It then backed up, lurched around, and roared away, narrowly avoiding a collision with the Jeep Cherokee that the Arizona general drove. The Jeep stopped. Ev and VJ got out. A terrible smell wafted up the driveway and onto the porch where Sabine struggled to maintain a sitting position in his hammock. Young Ev Crume unloaded some unrecognizable equipment into one of the outbuildings and got back into the Jeep. VJ walked from building to building with an egg the size of a large cantaloupe. Like the Mercedes, the Jeep backed up and roared away. VJ continued to wander around with the egg. Suddenly Sabine lurched, nearly falling out of the hammock. Courtney and Laurel, two of Celia's girls, were on the porch, clawing at him and chanting, "Grandpa, Grandpa, Grandpa, Grandpa."

Sabine struggled to a half-sitting posture in the swinging hammock in time to see a young woman he only half recognized emerge from a tan pickup. She wore a white cowboy hat, a revealing buff satin blouse, and skin-tight turquoise jeans. She was carrying a parrot. The birthday party, Sabine realized, had begun. God, what was that smell?

CHAPTER TWELVE

■ ■ ■

Sabine's unstated view was that a man's seventy-second birthday party ought to be a sedate affair, offering a man of maturity opportunities for quiet reflection. The family agreed. Each of them, Magda, Rosa, Celia, Felice, or VJ, would've said so right out. Unfortunately, they were an excitable lot, and nothing excited them more than a family get-together. Despite their best intentions, the family acted in every conceivable way to unleash the forces of chaos.

Bearing witness to the arrival and departure of an astonishing flurry of vehicles, Sabine was still half asleep. Despite the lingering effect of his nap, he spared no effort to extricate himself from his hammock. Grandchildren scattered, leaving off the "Grandpa, Grandpa, Grandpa" chant to take up the characteristic calls of their breed (shrieks, giggles, and feigned farts). Hard telling how many there'd been, probably around seventy, though he'd been able to positively ID only two of them, part of Celia's offering to the party ambiance.

143

Cars were still coming and going outside. Rosa was in the kitchen doing something that apparently involved a jackhammer and a set of cymbals. VJ was visible in the distance, wandering around among the outbuildings. Magda marched into the room with the tall girl he'd seen arrive. Magda sure looked good. The excitement of the impending party was apparent in her face. She had a small, turned-up nose and bright, flashing eyes that were hazel in color and penetrating without being obtrusive. Her buxom figure filled her silky caftan and practically smoked with sensuality. As to the girl looming over his wife, well, he'd not, evidently, dreamed her after all. Those colors were real, the parrot likewise. Magda introduced her. My God, she was Golfrido Ulibarri's girl, Fanny. Rosa had invited her.

Magda hustled fetchingly off to help Rosie Daisy with the jackhammer and percussion work in the kitchen, leaving Sabine to shake off the cobwebs from his nap by making conversation with Fanny, a girl he'd known since her baptism. He'd never have recognized her. He'd seen her a number of times during her growing years, giggling with Rosa and avoiding all conversation with adults. He could not recall ever having spoken to the girl and wondered what he was getting into. Luckily, the task of conversing with Fanny Ulibarri did not demand much effort. Rich smells of basil and baking pastries wafted in from the kitchen. Sabine breathed deeply. Thus fortified, he surrendered himself to the task.

"Well, happy birthday, Mr. Eckleberry. Here I am. Rosa stopped at the shop today, and we got to talking. She ended up asking me out, and I told her I'd love to come since I remember you from when I was a little girl. Now, why she wanted me to bring Abraham to your party, I can't say, but she called special to ask me to bring him along.

"He just loves to go out. They really are such social animals, and I'm just not enough company for him. It makes me feel terrible. If I'd work with him a bit, he'd learn anything, even though he is a very old bird. Nobody knows how old he is. The vet told me that no one knows for sure how long the different parrot species can live. Abraham talks, but he hasn't said how old he is. He has lots of words in English, some in Spanish, and even a few in Euzkadi that Daddy taught him before he died. Daddy, I mean, but I guess you know that, since you can see that Abraham is not dead yet.

"Speaking of Daddy, the last time I think I saw you was at his funeral. Can you believe he's been dead four years? I just can't. Sometimes I wake up and still expect to see him in his truck with his old dog. It was wrong of Mama to have that dog put to sleep when Daddy died. It wasn't the dog's fault. But you know Mama. 'My dog now,' she said and hauled the poor old thing off to Doctor Decker's. Sure the dog was blind, but who's to say his life wasn't worth living? Mama always disliked that dog, even when he could see."

While Fanny talked of her late father and his late dog, VJ, wearing a short, threadbare bathrobe and a pair of thongs, came into the room. He made the briefest hello to his father and said nothing to Fanny, a girl he had difficulty placing. She seemed familiar, but VJ had trouble thinking of anything except the ostrich egg and how he needed to get it into the incubator.

Earlier, when VJ'd arrived back from Womynscraft, Rosa had smelled him at a distance. She shouted a terse order that he immediately shower in the wool sluicing pits. He did as he was told. Even with the shower, he had a bit of a time margin. He decided not to fight Rosa on the shower issue. He would not allow anything to get him crosswise with his closest sis, not with Celia and Felice lurking and looming over the ranch. He was worried about the egg, though. He needed extension cords and had maybe twenty minutes.

Sabine wondered if VJ recognized Golfrido's girl. Maybe he ought to say something that would jog the boy's memory. He decided against it. The sight of VJ in that bathrobe was so annoying that it made Sabine light-headed. The boy was wandering around the room with a vacant expression, staring at the walls. He was making Golfrido's girl nervous, that was plain. The poor girl was pulling at her left earlobe. She was talking faster, and her voice was high and tense.

"Anyway," she said with sideways glances at VJ, who was removing the extension cord to Sabine's lamp, "since you've been to Argentina, maybe you can tell me about Abraham. His species is native to South America. Come to think of it, though, I think the vet said Bolivia or Mexico or something like that. Is that near Argentina? I suppose not. Anyway, I've done some arithmetic and figure that Abraham has to be at least two or three hundred years old. Can you imagine, three hundred years old and he's still going strong, breeding and everything? I know he's *that* old because he talks about Simón Bolívar. What he says is, 'Bolívar, *hijo de la gran puta.*' He'll be just shrieking and then all of a sudden he'll start in on Bolívar. I figure he had to have learned that from one of his owners, probably a Spanish governor or someone like that who hated Bolívar. I knew that name, Bolívar, from school but I couldn't remember much. I didn't pay much attention to my history class in high school except that I thought the teacher was cute. Anyway, I looked up Bolívar in the encyclopedia and found out that he died in 1830. That means that Abraham is at least that old and maybe a heck of a lot older. He says some stuff that Daddy always thought was gibberish, but I think it's Indian words maybe from the times before the conquistadores. There's a legend that these parrots let themselves get captured on purpose. They stay with the Indians and learn human speech. Once they know it, they escape and teach the language to the other parrots. You can walk through the jungle and hear conversations all over the place. I guess, though, all they ever talk about is food, fighting, and mating. They're obsessed with sex, at it all the time. They don't, like, talk about sports or anything, unless you think of their sex lives and fights as like sports for them." She stopped talking.

VJ, preoccupied with the quest for extension cords, had walked between his father and Fanny. There was an awkward moment of silence as VJ realized that he ought to speak. Luckily, the woman had been talking about birds. He spoke, "With ostriches it's different. They have sports, races, you know, with jockeys and everything." He had come up with a couple of extension cords. He wanted to go outside, to get the incubator set up. This girl, though, was in his path, gabbing at the old man. God, the old guy looked crabby; you could stack cordwood on his old lip. Speaking of lip, who was that girl? Fanny, he finally recalled, was one of Rosa's pals. Had been forever. She seemed startled that he'd spoken of ostriches. Despite long connection with the family, she had not, apparently, heard of his ostrich preoccupation. Later on, he'd have to fill her in. Pretty girl, he thought, quite a dresser, too. The parrot, too, was intriguing. Sabine, he supposed, was boring her; she sure looked nervous. He'd have to come back and rescue her as soon as he got the incubator hooked up.

Fanny was panicky, starting to hyperventilate, seeing spots in front of her eyes. She was keeping her eyes averted, away from VJ, who was almost undressed! In such situations, Fanny invariably sought refuge in words. She simply talked until she regained her shattered composure. She stared into Sabine's eyes, fearing eye contact with VJ, and pressed on.

"People think fighting, like wrestling and boxing, are great sports. I don't know why. It makes me sick. My ex-husband took me down to Caesar's Palace to see some black people fight. It was disgusting, I thought. They were just boys, probably couldn't even buy a drink or play the slots or anything and there were all these guys like my husband making bets and drinking till their eyes swole up. They swilled down the booze and walked around before the fight acting like big shots. They hollered all during the fight and smoked cigars. My ex-husband had never smoked a cigar in his life, but he did then and I think it ended up making him barf, along with all the booze. I'd like to see all those guys digging ditches or working at a car wash. It was a disgrace, all the money those idiots wasted. I guess the black kids got some of it but I can't imagine it was worth it. There's not enough money on earth to make me whale on somebody so people like *that* could watch. I think the cops ought to round them all up and put big signs on them that say 'Big shot, caught drunk' and force them to go around with a garbage bag and a little sharp stick cleaning the streets so you could drive by and honk at them. The police could hire young black boys like the ones that fought to guard them and see that they got all the trash up off the streets.

"Parrots' fights are just a bunch of bluff, shrieking and biting at each other. Daddy always said that Abraham tried to kill Isaac, one of the hand-feds we got when we bred him seven or eight years ago when I was still in high school. It wasn't really true. Daddy just made it up because he thought it was so funny. I didn't think it was a bit funny to make fun of animals just because their names are in the Bible. Daddy, though, never thought much of the Church. Abraham is sweet and very affectionate. I like him better than I ever liked my ex, I'll tell you that for a take. He's nicer, cleaner, and probably smarter. I saw this thing at the A&P that really made me think. It was in a *National Enquirer,* which I never read, but I caught sight of this article about this lady in Colombia and how she was suing her vet for six or ten million dollars. The vet made some kind of mistake and the woman's parrot died. You know, come to think of it she had a Basque name too; it was something like Vizcaina or Viscarra."

Sabine shifted his considerable bulk from his right leg to his left. Fanny's story failed to grip, and his thoughts returned unbidden to his fork assault on VJ. The boy had so deserved it! He was so exasperating. Here he was, barely civil to Golfrido's girl, who was obviously very nervous and talking hysterically. If VJ had any manners, he'd converse with this girl and relieve an old man of the burden. Instead, the boy continued his bizarre behavior. He was collecting extension cords.

With no better option, Fanny continued the story from the tabloid. "Anyway, this lady, maybe Mrs. Izcarria it was, claimed that her dead husband had reincarnated into the form of that bird and that she'd lived with that bird as her true spouse for seventeen years. The vet's incompetence had killed her husband and left twenty-nine grandchildren crying for their *abuelito*. The courts only awarded her eight hundred thirty thousand dollars though. A story like that, it makes you think, doesn't it?

"I was wishing that Daddy could get reincarnated into Abraham, but I don't think it's possible even if I believed in reincarnation. I think the soul would have to pass to something just being born or hatching out. If Daddy got reincarnated into a baby parrot, then I could get him and hand-feed him; that's what they do with the babies.

"I just hate to think of Daddy in purgatory. It'd be a lot nicer for him if he could end up being a parrot, even if it was just a baby parrot. It just makes me sick, thinking of God ordering people off to purgatory."

VJ nibbled at his lower lip until it hurt. This woman was evidently going to block the door and talk indefinitely. He had cords for the incubator, but what good would that do if he were stuck for an eternity listening to this admittedly fetching motormouth talk theology? He couldn't risk delaying any longer. He had to get to that egg. He pushed past Fanny onto the porch. "Sorry," he said, "but I'm going to be sick." It was almost true. If he'd delayed much longer, both he and Fanny would have gotten sick from pure nervousness.

Sabine's head was beginning to hurt. It felt like *he* was in purgatory. The one bright spot was that VJ had gone. He didn't even want to know why the ninny had taken the extension cords to his lamps. He watched the bird while Golfrido's girl talked on. The bird looked like old Golfrido, only better; its eyes were brighter, more intelligent. But then, Golfrido was always drunk on bootlegger liquor or that rotgut wine his wife made and sold by the gallon to all the lushes and shepherds. The bird was impressive. It was a green that seemed to vibrate. Sabine could see how it could seem special. All the stuff about the bird being two hundred years old and talking Indian languages, though, was a lot of bull. How could she know that the bird talked in any language? The bird would never get a word in edgewise as far as he could see. VJ's sudden, incredibly rude departure had, for a moment, silenced the girl. Sabine now had an opportunity to wedge a word in himself. He felt an obligation to set the girl straight about the bird. The silence felt awkward. The girl had large, and to Sabine's eye, comely breasts that strained at the buff satin blouse. Sabine was having a tough time battling the impulse to abandon all civility and simply stare. The silence made it worse. His eyes kept returning to Fanny's bosom. He needed to speak up, take refuge in conversation. At any rate, the girl should not be allowed to continue to believe such absurdities about the damned parrot. It was bad enough for the poor thing to have had Golfrido for her father. Her undeniable charms did not nearly make up for that misfortune.

"Listen, *mi hijita*," he said in a soft, kind voice, "can the bird say his own name?"

Fanny shook her head absently as though something failed to register. "He can say 'Abraham' but he doesn't do it very often."

"Well," said Sabine, "just because he can say 'Abraham,' does that mean he was alive when Lincoln was president?"

Fanny stared at Sabine and pursed her lips. What was the point? What did Lincoln have to do with anything? She was too overcome by VJ's behavior and visions of her father in purgatory to pay much attention to the old guy's puzzling tangent.

Sabine could see that his line of reasoning was making no impression. He gave a sigh and dropped it. "Anyway," he said, "don't take religion too seriously." He thought of Golfrido in purgatory and smiled. That chiseling old bandit would be in hell rather than purgatory should Church dogma prove true.

Unfortunately, it wouldn't. All it did was manufacture fear to control the masses. Sabine took the view that if all the bishops in Spain had been shot on the spot during the war, the place would've gained a good deal in virtue. He supposed that this opinion put his soul in peril. The thought amused him.

Fanny was comforted. It was always reassuring to talk to an old man like Sabine, even if he did go off on tangents about Abe Lincoln. He had that olive oil and wine smell about him, just like her father. She had blathered on. It was something she just couldn't seem to control when she was nervous. She was really, really nervous about VJ. It was obvious that Rosa was setting them up. It'd been nice to converse with their father, calming. He was an attentive old man, and he wasn't always eyeing her breasts like some old men.

Sabine, free of the need to talk about the parrot, warmed to one of *his* favorite topics. If the Church was a whited sepulcher, a corrupt and pernicious institution, it was not his fault. If his views on the Church embarrassed and aggravated his daughters, that did not make them less accurate. As a man of some experience in the world, he felt he owed the next generation the benefit of his opinion.

"No," he said, "don't take religion too seriously. Poor people like you and me are gasoline for the Church. It's a machine of power. People are nothing. We're just another renewable resource, *mi hijita,* better than an oil field. Just think of the ten million little *quincenera* girls all over the world, doing their beads tonight and worrying about going to hell if they get on the pill or pop in a diaphragm. You think the Church gives a damn about poor people like us? In fifty years we'll have people standing on top of one another, everybody starving, and still the bishops will drive around with sound trucks encouraging everyone to keep reproducing for them. It's a religion of ass kissing, *mi hijita,* and old Golfrido was never a *lambe.* So don't worry about it. If he's in purgatory, he's probably found the bootleggers by now; he had that gift, you know."

While Sabine talked, Fanny's mouth dropped and hung. She was stunned and forgot how nervous she was. The old toot had a lot of nerve talking about being poor. Everyone knew he was as rich as Croesus and as tight as Scrooge. He reminded her of her father. There were things about that old devil! It was sad how true Sabine's smart-alecky crack about bootleggers had been. Oh! She could have slapped his superior old face when he said that! But she couldn't. She couldn't defend her father. As much as she missed him, she did not miss his quirks, prejudices, and vices. That was the trouble with old people. They seem nice for a while and then launch into some tirade or reveal some nasty habit and spoil everything. She was not about to humor Rosa's dad by listening any longer.

"I think I'll see if I can help Rosa in the kitchen. No reason for Mrs. Eckleberry to have to do anything as long as I'm here. Here, would you keep Abraham for a while? You've got no earrings, so he'll behave himself."

She left the room with the speed of an aviator bailing out of a plane she could no longer control. Sabine stood suddenly alone in the middle of the room with a parrot on his shoulder. He was still only a few feet from the hammock and had been awake for only ten minutes. He already needed a rest. Fat chance. He went over to his desk and filled a coffee cup with Sangre de Toro. As his children arrived and the house began to fill, more than one party-goer noted that the old man, often accused of piracy for his wartime exploits, truly looked like an old buccaneer, fresh from his hammock, complete with his parrot and grog.

VJ was finally at peace. He put the incubator into the only room he felt was secure from his many nieces and nephews. He plugged it in and looked about the room. It was plenty big, two queen-sized beds and plenty of floor space. Sure, it was the room Ev shared with the Colonel, but why would they mind? The incubator made no noise. The room smelled a bit of ostrich from the egg. Because he'd continued to handle the egg, a slight poultry odor lingered, as well, like an aura around Virgil Jose. He didn't care. He was blissed out just watching the incubator, twisting his hair, and singing

Volare, oh oh.
Cantare, doodle-ee-oh.
Dee-dah-dee-duh-duh dee duh
Dah-deedle-dee-doh-dah
Dah-dah-duh-duh-duh peace of mind.
Doodle-duh-duh confusion
Doodle-duh-duh illusion dee-die.
Just like birds of a feather
A rainbow forever we'll find.
Nel bibbity-boppity-boo
Nel bibbity-boppity-boo

VJ was a happy man. He'd found a case of Sangre de Toro in one of the outbuildings while looking for a spot for the incubator. The packing list showed that it'd been shipped nearly ten years ago. VJ went all warm inside. It'd be a present for his father's birthday. No way the old man would remember that case. Sabine was not the kind to let good wine sit for ten years. It'd just gotten misplaced and forgotten. Now VJ wouldn't have to even mention the egg. The wine would constitute a huge peace offering.

He'd soon be back in his father's good graces. He'd hauled the wine up to the room where the Colonel, Ev, and now the ostrich egg were quartered. He was pleased that the egg was situated and was in no hurry to rejoin the massing throng at the house. The party was off to a hectic start in his opinion. The place had been as noisy as a stamping plant, and it'd been embarrassing to be in that bathrobe listening to Fanny Ulibarri. The bathrobe was so thin and so short that he'd felt very uneasy. It was no fun having that good-looking woman so obviously having to avoid looking down his front while she talked about the longevity and sex lives of parrots.

He lingered, therefore, in solitude, away from the madding crowd, allowing the neck knots of anxiety to melt away in serene confidence that his egg was properly situated. He spent the most pleasant moments he could recall watching the egg through the clear cover of the incubator. People continued to arrive for the party. The house was alive with a loud and increasingly merry din provided by his mother, sisters, nieces, nephews, and Rosa's good-looking friend. "Fanny," right name for her, that was for certain. He did like the fit of her jeans! God, though, that gal could talk. She was maybe a bit deficient on the listening end and had not shown adequate interest in ostriches. The fault, he supposed, had been the bathrobe. The bathrobe had made her nervous and she was stiff from the effort of not looking down his front, just like old Sabine was stiff with the effort of not staring at her breasts. No wonder she'd lacked enthusiasm for ostriches. It'd been a tense situation, even for VJ, and he was not having to avoid staring at anything. Such situations are always a strain, especially when a person is trying to get his ostrich egg properly situated.

VJ decided that it was time for him to get dressed properly. He was intrigued with Fanny Ulibarri and was still trying to place her (could old Golfrido be her father?). He tried to remember. The name was no help. Throw a rock in Basque County and you'd probably hit someone named Ulibarri. Her mention of an estranged husband made it even more uncertain. Maybe she'd married one of the numerous Ulibarris and had, unaccountably, kept his name. VJ had worked several summers under the supervision of Golfrido Ulibarri and could not recall the old shepherd ever mentioning a daughter, but that didn't mean he didn't have one, or ten, or a scattering of them from Utah to Montana. Golfrido talked about sheep, gambling, and hunting, not daughters. The girl had mentioned her father . . . something about laughing at the parrot. VJ had never known Golfrido to laugh at a parrot, but it wouldn't have been entirely out of character. VJ was eager to know more about the parrot, and he also meant to draw Fanny out on the subject of ostriches. She seemed to know an awful lot about parrots, and her parrot obviously adored her and thrived under her care.

She did have an adhesive quality that VJ found alarming. She had apparently glommed onto poor old Sabine when he was still groggy from his nap. VJ was the kind of person who always liked the option of a quick exit from a suddenly dicey conversation. Still, he wanted to talk to her, and didn't exactly know why. Well, he knew part of it, the stirrings of his old John Thomas that was threatening to turn his threadbare bathrobe into a sort of pup tent. He certainly wanted to be wearing something more than that old bathrobe for the next encounter with the girl, that was clear. Still, he stalled, lolling on the bed. He was in no hurry to get back to the party and Fanny U. The only partially explicable desire to connect with the woman (pretty as she was) made him nervous.

Sitting with the incubator helped to soothe his frayed nerves. One nice thing about ostrich eggs, they are ever quiet and considerate companions. Eggs do not attach themselves to a person and talk ad nauseam about parrots and reincarnation. That parrot sure looked funny as hell on old Sabine. Smiling to himself, humming "Volare," and thinking pleasant thoughts of happily hatching ostriches, Virgil Jose assembled his powers for the party.

Earlier, while VJ had been setting up the incubator, he heard Ev and the Colonel drive up. The Colonel had ferried Felice, her children, and Kronen to the house, leaving Ev with the Cadillac. Taking it slowly, Ev had been able to start the Cadillac and drive it by degrees across the prairie to the road. The vehicle was apparently undamaged. Ev met the Colonel, who was driving back with the idea of towing the Caddy. The Colonel brought the Cherokee to a skidding, gravel-throwing stop and regarded Ev with the popped eyes and opened mouth of feigned surprise.

"Well," he said, "I am amazed. You managed to get that boat off of the shoals. I guess your socialist education has not rendered all of the initiative out of you. Drive it on in, Son. I'll follow in case the damned thing breaks down after all."

Ev drove, humiliated at the pleasure he'd felt when the Colonel addressed him "Son." It was the first time since they'd met in Arizona that the Colonel had chosen a term that was not an insult. The Cadillac smelled strongly of dog pee. Ev accepted this with bitter resignation. It'd add complexity to the ostrich fragrance that evidently enveloped him.

When they arrived, Rosa was there to meet them. She'd already dealt with VJ; her sisters reported that Ev and the Colonel smelled just as bad. It irked her to have to talk to Ev, however bad he smelled, but she was just going to have to get up on her hind legs and do it. From her vantage point in the kitchen she was able to see the road. The dust of the approaching vehicle gave her plenty of warning, plenty of time to prepare. She walked down to the driveway and waited.

Unfortunately, Rosa was not able to prepare herself for the flood of emotions that suffused her small, handsome body when Ev Crume actually hobbled toward her from the Cadillac beaming a huge, affectionate smile. Her heart raced. Beneath her blouse she endured a four-alarm blush on her chest and neck. She staggered a step as though someone had walloped her one upside the head. Images from the magazines came unbidden to mind, and the mixed feelings coalesced into anger. Rosa Eckleberry was not ordinarily vulnerable to sudden rages and did not, therefore, have much experience stifling or containing the unsolicited dynamo.

Towering rage transformed Rosa's countenance. Recovering quickly from her initial stagger step, she bore down on

Ev, covering ground in long, deliberate strides. Though first
out of the car, the Colonel wisely stood aside. Unlike Ev, the
Colonel had seen a number of enraged women; he knew the
signs. As Rosa bore down on the shyly smiling Ev, even he
could see that something was amiss. Rosa's jaw was so tight
that the muscles of her neck stood like balanced pencils on
her collarbone. A muscle in her cheek twitched intermit-
tently, and her lips pulled away from her teeth. She held her
shoulders stiffly and clutched her hands into fists. Ev's smile
froze on his face. Rosa allowed the momentum of her double-
time march to propel her. She stopped just six inches from
Ev's chin. Pausing, she closed her eyes, took a deep breath,
and raised both hands to her temples. She combed backward
through her long hair and opened her eyes to pin the hapless
Ev to the spot, like a bug to a blotter. He seemed to shrink.

"Everett Crume," she growled through clenched teeth,
"you are to remove your clothes and burn them. You can also
put your gross, disgusting habits aside for your stay at this
ranch, you dirty-minded sleaze-bucket. Don't you dare act surprised either; you know exactly what I'm talking about. I've
known you since you and VJ were in third grade together, and
I never thought I would see you sink into the slime. That's
what gets me. And you act like such a saint, like you're better
than VJ. VJ goes off half-cocked but he's not a gross pig. You
are such a hypocrite." She put her hands, still balled into fists,
on her hips and held her ground, angling farther into Ev's
space. Every muscle in her upper body was taut with the effort of self-restraint. It was obvious that she was mobilized for
physical engagement.

Ev stood by the pink Cadillac with the broad, open, affectionate grin frozen in the muscles of his face. As Rosa moved
that fraction of an inch toward him, he was shaken with the
understanding that this woman might strike him. She certainly wanted to. It was obviously taking every fiber of restraint in her small frame to master the urge. This was only a

degree or two less startling than the kiss she'd given him. He moved back and tried without success to speak.

"Haupt, haupt, haupt."

"You don't need to bark your pathetic excuses at me, you obscene jerk," she said. "And you needn't flinch like that either. I'm not going to hit you. The Basques are getting civilized. I just want to serve notice. Just forget any ideas of making advances toward me. I kissed you yesterday. I meant it and I regret it. I can't take it back, but I've washed my mouth out a dozen times. I was responding to the man I thought you were rather than the scumbag you've turned out to be. I guarantee you that I will not make the mistake again." She bit her lip and stopped. She was breathing hard, almost panting, through dilated nostrils.

Somewhere in her being, Rosa knew what was happening. She'd locked down a crowd of powerful and very mixed emotions. Now that they had finally broken loose, they'd rushed for the exit marked "anger." Disappointment had opened the door, and she sensed that fear still lurked.

She turned her gaze to the Colonel, who stood, as invisibly as he could, a few feet beyond Ev. She spoke in bland tones. "You heard what I said about the clothes, Colonel McKenzie. Please burn them. You can take a shower in that building over there. It's a barn that we use for sheep sluicing when we shear. It's got hot water, and I'll see that you have towels and washcloths. That goes for you too, Mr. Crume," she snapped, the fury returning to her voice. "This is my father's birthday and I don't want it spoiled. I'll say no more about this, but I expect you to muster the decency to respect my wishes. If you try anything, you'll get a good slap, I promise you that."

She turned on her heel and was gone, slamming the front door with a bone-jarring crash. The screen door slammed as well, kind of a sound shadow to the explosion that preceded it.

The Colonel said nothing. The scene was deeply disturbing to the old soldier. His being was compromised, conflicted, torn by a mixture of glee and horror at the scene he'd witnessed. Naked fear likewise gripped his wizened form. The women in this family ought to, by God, have warning labels, he thought. He began unbuttoning his shirt. Best to get the clothes burned quick. He'd been tempted to protest, but as an old soldier he knew better. The ground here was not favorable, and the opposing force had the advantage of both momentum and superior firepower. Yes, he and the boy should burn their clothes right sharply, shower as instructed, and attend the damned party. For his part, he should take immediate steps to put off the looming conflict with Magda. He needed to rethink things. The very notion of Magda crawling back to him now seemed ridiculous. Magda was nice, a tolerant woman all in all. Her tongue was rough from time to time, but nothing like he'd seen from her daughters. How had such a sweet woman spawned such a litter of harridans?

A few minutes after her outburst, Rosa sat stiff, pinched, and rigid at the kitchen table. She was shocked at her behavior. She couldn't recall ever having talked to anyone like that. Objectively, she knew that Ev's apparent obsession with porn wasn't really that bad. It certainly was not unusual. Something had taken over when she saw him standing there, just radiating love in her direction. That big sweet face, those honest eyes, that kindly disposition, all false, so false. All day she'd pictured him hustling off to a bathroom with one of those magazines tucked under his arm. Well, she'd sort it out later.

The order to burn their clothing, though, where on earth had that come from? The smell was not *that* bad. But that's where the indignation had taken her. All she'd done with VJ was tell him to stay downwind, get his clothes into the washer, and get a shower. But then, VJ had not polluted himself with porn. As the adrenaline ebbed, she was not exactly sorry that the men were burning their clothes. She was aware that she'd gone rather over the top and had no idea what she should do next.

The kitchen was a good place to reassemble her composure. She could stay to herself for a few minutes, take some deep breaths, and keep an eye on the progress of the party. She could hear Fanny talking to Magda about parrots. Sabine was playing with his grandchildren. All he did was gripe about them, but whenever the kids showed up they all made a beeline for the old man, and he entertained them for hours. He egged them on and encouraged wild behavior. Celia and Felice were often irritated with Sabine at such times, especially Felice, who was so damned conventional. Rosa breathed deeply. Somehow watching her dad play with the kids helped her to reestablish her equilibrium. Practical concerns now crowded her mind. The party was on, and there was work to be done. She grabbed a turkey baster, filled it with the olive oil–basil sauce, opened the oven, and thoroughly basted the popping, sputtering leg of lamb. The blast of heat and the gorgeous mingled smells of meat, oil, and garnish worked magic on Rosa Eckleberry. In a world where such pleasant sensations lurked everywhere, how could things be long out of harmony?

VJ still lay on the bed that Magda had assigned to Ev. He was thinking. He'd been there with the egg, the incubator, and his own peace of mind since he heard the vehicles drive up. He would soon have to explain to Ev and the Colonel about the incubator, why he had to have it in their room. At present, it was nice just to lie there and watch the egg. Unsolicited images of Fanny Ulibarri continued to prey on his mind. Listening to her had just about drained him. Still, some of the stuff she'd said about her parrot was interesting now that he had time to think. If an ostrich could live to seventy, then a smart bird like a parrot could conceivably live even longer. It made sense. Still, the idea that Abraham was more than two hundred years old was hard to believe, and he wondered if Fanny had any further evidence. He'd have to restrain himself from asking her about it. That woman talked plenty. She did not need encouragement.

Ev came into the room naked to the waist, clutching a towel about him. He was too agitated to have much regard for Virgil Jose's inner life. The sight of VJ, in fact, irritated him. Ev was further irritated to see the incubator set up in the room he shared with the Colonel. VJ's decision to set the device in the space where Ev had initially placed his suitcase further aggravated the offense. Ev also noted that someone, probably VJ, had put a case of wine right in the middle of his bed. Things were stacking up. Ev was so devastated by the scene with Rosa that he lacked the stamina to raise even the smallest protest. He couldn't even think about it. Instead, he grieved the loss of his clothes.

Under orders of the most imperious kind, he'd burned his second-best pair of jeans, a cheap but almost new shirt, and a pair of jockey shorts that were not exactly new but still had a lot of use left in them, his best pair in fact. Now, VJ had tossed his suitcase roughly aside, providing, no doubt, some further insult to Ev's tattered wardrobe. Not that it mattered. The clothes Ev had folded so nicely before the trip were rumpled and sheep-slobbered even before VJ had flung the bag into the corner. He'd end up wearing the sheep-slobbered clothes. What could it matter if they were wrinkled? No one cared what he looked like anyway. Too demoralized to protest, Ev lay down on the floor next to his suitcase and stared at the ceiling, wondering that he could even care about wrinkled clothes.

The Colonel, having regained his composure and disposition in the shower, strode in cackling. He spoke to VJ.

"I don't know what Tubby there did to your sister, but she sure reamed him out good. You'd better find out what it was he did. You could end up having to whip him. He probably tried something. He's the kind that'll try to grab a big feel when no one's looking. I saw her give him that big smooch yesterday, looked like he took a yard of tongue; probably gave him big ideas. He sure was pleased with himself." The Colonel was wearing a towel that matched Ev's. He dropped it and put on a fresh pair of McKenzie tartan boxer shorts. He was practically glowing with pleasure.

Ev moaned. VJ quit twisting his hair. His mouth dropped open, and he strained, trying to remember Rosa kissing Ev. He couldn't. He looked at Ev and tried to imagine him "trying something" with Rosa, maybe "grabbing a big feel." The image was difficult to summon. Thus experiencing brainlock, VJ found his mind wandering unbidden to the happy situation of the ostrich egg. It was such a relief to have it settled in and incubating. His mouth still hanging open, VJ shifted his gaze to the incubator. It had a small red light that glowed to show that all was well. A warm little smell emanated soothingly from the little paradise for fetal ostriches VJ had so lovingly created.

Ev breathed deeply, attempting to rally his energies. The burns on the soles of his feet were throbbing a bit, emblematic of his profound sense of vulnerability. He finally managed to speak.

"Well, he's right about one thing. She did lay into me pretty good. I wish I knew why. I haven't really even seen Rosa since we first got here. That kiss did make me feel pretty good, but it was not . . . like *he* makes it out, dirty. And that's what I don't understand about what she said. She said I had filthy habits and that kissing me that way was a big mistake. There was some other stuff too. 'Scumbag,' 'sleaze-bucket,' 'obscene jerk,' and 'hypocrite' were words that came up. She told me she'd slap me if I tried to kiss her or anything."

VJ was still having a hard time getting up to speed. "That is a little radical, even for Rosa. Doggone, are you sweet on Rosa? If you are, I can't say that it's a very hopeful sign, her talking about filthy habits. I mean . . . she says things, she's sassy. But filthy habits? Scumbag? Obscene jerk? I don't know. It's hard to see much room to move if she's saying . . . Yup, hard to put a good spin on it. Damn, though, you look like hell. I never knew you had a crush on Rosa. She's *older* than you!"

"I never had time to get a crush on her, and she's only eighteen months older than me. Until now, your mother and Rosa have always been nice to me, and I never thought, I never thought anything until yesterday. I was just working toward getting a crush on her. I don't know what could have set her against me like that." Ev's upper lip quivered, and for one brief, horrible moment, VJ thought he was going to start bawling. Lord, he looked awful, wallering on the floor, miserable with his hair licked down, plastered to his head, lying there next to his pitiful suitcase. This was bad. It put the whole ostrich project up for grabs. What good would it do to make Ev rich if he was going to mope and waller like that and be unhappy? VJ reached down and patted his friend on the shoulder. Poor old Ev. VJ bit his lip. He was about to bawl himself.

The spectacle of Ev's misery even affected the Colonel. "Son," he said, "don't let it get to you. Life's too god-damned short for sniveling. Cut your losses and move on. Magda spoke highly of you. She told me to leave you alone. Well, that's not my way. I'm an old army bird, so don't let my razzing get to you either. I'll by God razz your ass if it suits me. It'll help make a man out of you. College kids could all use a dose of toughness. What you and I ought to do while we're in Nevada is sneak off for a few hours and spend some time with the whores. That'll give you some perspective."

Ev moaned. VJ and the Colonel between them had some of the worst ideas imaginable.

VJ once again rested his eyes on the incubating egg. He couldn't help but feel good. The more he thought about his sister's outburst, oddly enough, the better he felt. Old Ev had evidently shaken loose some pretty powerful feelings. Somehow, everything was going to work out fine. VJ knew it, and he knew that he could probably do much to keep things moving in the right direction. That smell, that warm little smell. Life, pure potential, was stirring in that egg. VJ had an intuition about it. That egg would surely play a crucial role in poor old Ev's eventual, inevitable happiness.

Nourished by visions of his friend's happy future, VJ came out of his revery. "We'd better all get dressed and shake a leg. The old man's party is going full bore. We'd best get over there. The women will have the old boy run up the flagpole. Rosa is fixing a big meal, and then it's happy birthday time. I'm not giving him the egg, after all, at least not just yet. I've got a case of wine for him. We can say it's from all three of us."

VJ hustled back to the main house still in his bathrobe. He had some clean clothes in his old room that he'd forgotten during the months since his sudden departure. He felt like a genius. Having the wine be a collective present from "the guys" would defray some of the criticism his sisters were certain to level at him for catering to Sabine's vices. It was perfect.

The Colonel smiled, thinking about the whores while he finished dressing. Having seen Magda's daughters, the Colonel was ready to spend some time with women who knew how to behave themselves. They had some fine whores in Nevada, he knew that. He was shaving in preparation for the party, dragging the razor across his old face with gusto. He'd get him one that looked like Jane Fonda or, better yet, Diane Sawyer. Why, it gave him a bone just thinking about it. He'd show that damned Magda. A nice pay-and-play girl would also get him over the bad taste in his mouth that remained from the visit to Womynscraft, as well as the rude treatment he'd endured at the hands of the Eckleberry women. That one gal at Womynscraft had been a real corker; terrible shame she was a lesbo. One thing about a gal that peddles her ass, she keeps things simple and she usually gives value. A man can feel pretty secure with a woman like that. It'd also be worth the trip just to see the young lard with the whores. The Colonel was beginning to warm to Ev. They'd endured terrible abuse together at the rough tongues of VJ's sisters; the Colonel tended instinctively to draw closer to embattled companions. The whores would be very nice to Ev. They'd be entertained with a bright, young, bashful boy. He probably still had his cherry, and it was evidently safe from VJ's sis. Young Crume had already dragged his sorry butt up to the party. He'd go and he'd slip the boy a note while he had it in mind. The Colonel retrieved a notepad and pen from his suitcase and wrote, brimming over with goodwill: "As discussed, we'll visit the local poontang palace after the party breaks up. I know that a cocksman like you can't go too long without it. Meet me at the Jeep at 20:30."

He stuck the note in his pocket and marched over to the ranch house and the party. He smiled broadly, pleased with himself. He was going to be nicer to that boy than Magda could have dreamed. The smile disappeared when he stepped into the room where the party was in progress. He cast a jaundiced eye on old Sabine, who looked the fool with his big belly, that parrot, and all those damned kids. How Magda could ever have fallen for a bozo like that was beyond Colonel McKenzie's ability to comprehend. But then, he'd always known it; woman's love, like the vagrant dew, was apt to settle on a pile of dog shit.

CHAPTER THIRTEEN

■ ■ ■

Sabine, to his great surprise, was actually enjoying the party. VJ provided a good deal of amusement alternately chasing and then dodging Golfrido's girl. He danced and feinted and reminded his father of Muhammad Ali. He was avoiding the corners and twirling his hair while Fanny bore down on him talking nonstop about the parrot, her dead sainted father, and her divorce. Lord, the boy looked just terrible in that damned clown shirt. Cowboy fashions got more ridiculous every year. This shirt was in the style the marketing pimps called "brush-popper." It was so damned gaudy that the brush evidently popped in horror when any of the idiots who wore the things were around. VJ looked like a scarecrow covered with a collapsed hot-air balloon. He was a handsome boy, but so thin. Sabine considered his son. It was no wonder he was scrawny. His brain had to be burning calories constantly to come up with all those plans and schemes. Ostriches! VJ was trying,

against all odds, to turn the topic of conversation with Golfrido's girl in the direction of ostriches. The shirt, though;
there was no excuse. Sabine would have to take him to the
men's store in town and buy him some new shirts.

Felice and Celia had their cars situated and their kids unloaded. Sabine had not seen either of them, but he knew they
were there. The party was barely started and already they were
fighting. Felice's little Heather had rubbed her cousin Courtney's face in the sand. Celia gave Heather a swat on the fanny,
and the sisters were off. At least they weren't fighting about
Mary Kay cosmetics and tortured bunny rabbits, like they had
at Christmas. They were in the kitchen. Sabine could hear
the whole thing. Felice was shouting at Celia, who comforted
a hysterical Courtney.

"Don't you ever again lay a hand on my daughter, Celia, not
unless you want to get your lights punched out. I don't care if
you are my sister."

Ever since Rosa was born, Celia and Felice had fought. It
made Sabine feel guilty, since Rosa had always been his favorite, his *consentida*. They used to fight over clothes, who was
wearing whose, and so on. Now they fought in defense of
their kids. Sabine was not entirely displeased that someone
had rubbed Courtney's face in the sand. She'd been one of the
little monsters who'd shaken him awake chanting "Grandpa"
at him. It was small-minded of him, he knew, to gloat over a
child's pain, but he figured he'd manage, somehow, to live
with himself. It was *his* birthday. Later, he'd teach Courtney
a special magic trick to make up for gloating over her misery.
He'd show her how to make sheep turds appear in her mother's pockets and behind her little brother's ears. Magic involving sheep turds always made a big hit with kids and without
fail annoyed their parents. Sabine liked both sides of the
equation and figured that the parental annoyance was a key
factor in the popularity of the modest pellets.

It was quite a party. Sabine, reflecting on the event some

hours hence, was impressed, awed. He had to respect and admire humanity and humbly applaud the capacities of the species. His family, the people he loved, had drawn more drama from the celebration of his birthday than he'd have believed possible.

At some point, the party achieved momentum. Very early on, of course, he'd begun fortifying himself with sustaining bumpers of Sangre de Toro. Despite this precaution, the ebb and flow of family took a toll. The party flowed into the kitchen, out onto the porch, down to the kitchen pen, back to the front room, and back again, inevitably, to the kitchen. The women were constantly snapping photographs and shouting orders. The flashing, along with the constant movement, was overwhelming for an old man of quiet habits. People kept taking Sabine aside. He was "aside" so much that he probably missed a good deal of the party. This was a fortunate thing as far as he was concerned. He saw enough. The asides were predictable. Rosa, Celia, and Felice worked on him to bury the hatchet and get VJ back on the ranch. Since he'd already decided to do so, the encounters lacked the customary tension.

Rosa waylaid him at the kitchen pen and played up the whole topic of the burros they were petting. If Sabine actually wanted to train the burros, he would need VJ around to pick up the slack in other areas. Hell, he needed VJ around to pick up slack in other areas anyway. There were probably fifty miles of fence wire hanging to the ground, and they were going to be covered up with hay even though it was grass hay and they only had to do two cuttings. If VJ were on the ranch, *he* could either fix the equipment and cut it himself or hire it cut. Either way they'd need to sell most of it and VJ could do that as well. Rosa knew how much Sabine hated the hay headache. It meant having to hire help and supervise the whole tedious operation. Sabine was doing a very half-assed job of it. VJ would do better. Besides all that, VJ could probably even help with the burros. She forced Sabine to admit that VJ was good with animals. She also pointed out that whereas Sabine was old, VJ was young. It was amusing to see her in action. One crucial and accurate point she hammered home was that Sabine had been too exhausted even to unload the donkeys on their arrival the previous night. She built her case. She was also concerned about Sabine's attention to detail in regards to the tiny herd that kept escaping from the kitchen pen. She was managing the business, and Sabine was supposed to manage the livestock. "If you can't keep track of twenty sheep, Daddy, what are you going to do when I go out and buy two or three thousand? Who's going to drench, inoculate, see to birthings, manage the shearing? You're so damned cheap, you'll bellyache till doomsday if you have to hire all of it done. The ranch can't make money if we don't run sheep, and if we don't make a better effort to keep it a working ranch it'll start to lose value."

"If that happens, I'll hear from Felice. That girl is awfully sensitive to anything that might threaten the inheritance she figures she's got coming." Sabine couldn't resist a comment or two further. "Look, the ranch won't make any money if we do run sheep. Since we can make as little money with twenty as we would with three thousand, why should we have more than twenty? Just to multiply the opportunities to actually lose fifty or sixty thousand dollars? It don't compute, Daisy. Anyway, we're plenty busy with just the ranch. I'll go flush thirty thousand dollars down the toilet, save us the trouble of having sheep, and still come out ahead of where we'd have been if we'd bought a bunch."

It was getting dark, and Sabine was getting tired of Rosa's comments. She was distracting him from the task of petting his donkeys! He decided that he might as well go back to the house. He wasn't getting to have any quiet time with the longears. He turned and walked slowly up the drive to the house. Rosa followed.

Rosa said that she supposed it didn't truly matter since Sabine was able to lose twenty easily enough. Conceding her father's point about the market, Rosa went on to point out that the market would eventually return and they'd want sheep. She'd hire the shepherds, but as a woman, she'd lack the authority to boss the *machitos*. She claimed that she did not trust Sabine's ability to fix his attention. "At your age, Daddy, you should be able to do what you want, ignore the sheep. VJ is the best shepherd in Nevada. Everyone knows his ability, and even the old guys respect him. They'd take all the bossing he could dish out. So take advantage of the fact that he drove eight or nine hundred miles to come to your party. Eat a little crow and send him after those sheep you allowed to escape."

Sabine was actually able to listen to this manipulation with tolerant equanimity. This was an enjoyable, if novel, sensation. Rosa had scarcely finished her last scathing sentence when Celia took over. She intercepted Sabine at the door as Rosa rushed to check on something, probably cake. Cake smells made Sabine salivate, and he was looking forward to a big slab.

Celia prefaced her remarks by stating that, as Sabine knew, she loved her sister dearly and respected her accomplishments. Felice, she said, was quite a businesswoman. She was the top Mary Kay Cosmetics distributor in Nevada and made just boatloads of money. The preface complete, Celia came to the point. She wondered whether Sabine had noticed how badly Felice's kids behaved. Sabine was able to answer truthfully that yes, he'd noticed. (Felice's kids were monsters. Magda had caught Felice's Jeffy attempting to put a small firecracker known as a ladyfinger into her poodle Moe's little anus. Sabine had annoyed his wife, wondering aloud if the measure might cure the dog of dragging his butt along the floor.) At any rate, Celia began to berate Sabine for having what she called a hands-off attitude toward his grandchildren. He should do something more than simply entertain and play with the children.

"I'm really worried about Felice's kids," she said, "especially Jeffy. You could help. You could take her aside and urge her to set boundaries, discipline. That'd be help, Daddy, support. If you'd just get VJ back on this ranch you could visit Felice, follow up, make a real difference in the lives of those kids."

Sabine said nothing. He wondered when the zinger was coming. He had to admire Celia. She was the most level-headed of all of them. Sure she was fat, but was that an afflic-tion? At least she wasn't a nitwit, a Republican, or a foul-mouthed *machita*. In fact, in Sabine's view, Celia's fat had a softening effect on her as her girth expanded through the years. She was a kind girl with her double chins and tentlike dresses. She was every bit as bossy and manipulative as her sisters, of course, but with Celia, it was somehow easier to take. He smiled.

Celia considered her father. Was the old buster going senile on her? He had the sappiest grin on his face. She spoke. "I don't know, Daddy. I think you're slipping. Those sheep! How'd they get out? Is your kitchen-pen fence as bad as the rest of your fencing? Shouldn't someone get them in? Don't you have any shepherds working for you? Why are you raising that Sudan grass? They'll be hopped up all the time on that stuff. Those sheep are a menace; they're out there right now, probably forcing another car off the road. If VJ was here, there'd be no sheep wandering the roads, and you'd have two cuttings of alfalfa under your belt. That Sudan grass, unbe-lievable."

Well, Sabine smiled to himself, there was the zinger he'd known was coming.

Sabine felt peaceful, secure in the knowledge that he'd soon have VJ, assisted by a crack team of guard burros, run-ning a couple thousand sheep. Despite what he'd said to Rosa, he did need the sheep. His plans for VJ depended on sheep, and every sheep he managed to keep was one he did not have to buy. He almost told Celia these plans. This big block of a daughter took some resisting. Long experience, however, had made Sabine wary. As long as he held his own counsel, he maintained a tiny advantage in his relations with his daughters. He should not give it up just because Celia was nicer than Felice and had her mother's pretty face. It was also very annoying to have to hear how VJ would take better care of the sheep. He bit his lip thinking of the idiot sheep. Their escape had sure put him one down. It was true, of course, that sheep in VJ's care do not end up heading for Reno, but it was also profoundly annoying. He wondered if he was ever going to get in the house. Rosa had pushed on by, leaving Sabine on the porch and Celia blocking the door. For a moment it looked like a standoff. Sabine just stood there waiting for Celia to move while Celia stood there waiting for her father to capitulate.

The standoff ended when another altercation between Courtney and Heather broke out. Celia rushed inside to protect her daughter, and Sabine slipped in behind her. The tearful, hair-pulling scene led to yet another confrontation between Celia and Felice. Sabine, ever opportunistic, was able to slip into the kitchen and snag a piece of cake (it was a sponge cake with a tangy lime-orange cream cheese frosting). He was heading to the table for another, in fact, when Felice buttonholed him and led him into his office. She was flushed from the recent flare-up and still bitter about Celia swatting Courtney. In Felice's view, Celia was obviously neglecting the basics. Her kids were spoiled, snotty little brats, and as much as Celia threw money at them (money she didn't *really* have to throw), they were unhappy and all headed for emotional problems and probably crime, drugs. Sabine admitted candidly that Celia's kids were as ill-behaved as any he'd ever encountered. Felice went on that Sabine had the opportunity to model parental skills for Celia. He'd set limits with VJ. That was good. Now, however, was the time to show forgiveness. VJ had respected the boundaries his father set and had obviously learned from his mistakes. Sabine should act quickly to reward VJ's compliance and willingness. If Sabine invited him back, allowed him to take responsibility, he'd succeed. It'd help Celia to see the effectiveness of setting limits with kids.

Up to this point in the conversation, Sabine had been amused. It was funny to see the way Felice and Celia brought their fight into the strategies for working on the old man. Unfortunately, Felice did not stop there. She was always the one to give her dad that extra push. Sabine's politics irked Felice. She had an important position in a Republican women's group and worried that word of Sabine's eccentricities would reach that group and embarrass her. "You've always made a big deal about your socialism and the way you fought the fascists in the war. I have my own ideas. You know that I'm a Republican and a good Catholic, but I did listen to you and I expect you to live up to the ideals you preach. If you don't take VJ back on the ranch, give him responsibilities, and let him know you could learn to trust his judgment, then you'll be little better than a tyrant in your own family. How can you square that with your politics, Daddy? You have to deal with your family from authority, but it has to be enlightened authority or no one will respect you. When you tell Celia, for example, that she needs to reduce, how is she going to take you seriously? No, Daddy, you've got to make your politics real for once. And by the way, speaking of losing weight, you'd best steer clear of rich foods like that cake or you won't be able to cram into those pants much longer. No wonder you don't have the energy to keep your sheep contained. Loose sheep are more than a cash drain, Daddy; they're a menace. Someone could have been killed. The fences on this property are a disgrace. You're so tight you won't hire somebody to mend fences and so ornery you ran Virgil Jose off the ranch with a fork. It's a wonder you quit stuffing your face long enough to do it. Now your free fence mender's gone and you're too stubborn to apologize and bring him back. Some socialist you are!"

Felice had nearly done it. Sabine had thought that in this

situation, he was immune to the girls' manipulations. He was going to do what they asked, after all. He'd already made up his mind. Despite all this, he almost came unglued. The "real for once" was too much of an affront, whatever the circumstances. He'd been patient for years with Felice. Her habit of carrying radishes in her pockets and purse was profoundly annoying. That was the way, she always said, that she stayed slim. He'd also had to put up with her misguided politics. There were worse things than having a Republican in the family, although at the moment he'd have a difficult time saying what. And how on earth did she expect him to tell Celia to slim down? Not that anyone was ever shy about telling him to lose weight.

One thing Sabine utterly confirmed on his seventy-second birthday was that he had the nerviest, bossiest three daughters ever spawned. They could make him mad even when he was determined to follow their wishes. The nerve of them, the cheek, the effrontery! He actually saw red and tasted bile when Felice did the "real for once" business. As a younger man, he would have reversed his decision to have VJ move back to the ranch. But he didn't. He was old and he wanted his wife back. It was that simple. It was sobering, though, to see the stratagems his girls used to work him. He would extract vengeance of some sort. He wasn't that old. He'd go out and mend the damned fences himself. He'd work with the hay crew he was going to have to hire. At the first opportunity, he'd tuck into a huge wedge of his birthday cake right under Felice's nose. Then he'd eat the icing that lined the cake pan. He'd lick his fingers and make lots of noise. That'd show her. She could stuff a few of her damned radishes into her ears . . . or elsewhere.

Yes, he almost lost his composure. Angry shouts began to form in his throat. It'd been a close thing, but a scene erupted in the other room that usurped his burgeoning rage. He'd seen the buildup. The Arizona general had handed young

Crume a note of some sort and drifted off listening to Fanny Ulibarri sing the praises of that reprobate Golfrido. Ev read the note and turned about ten shades of scarlet. Shaking his head, Ev gave the note to VJ, who smiled at first and then laughed out loud. He read the note several times, put it in his pocket, pulled it out, read it once more, and then set it on the table. Sabine had wondered, idly, why the Colonel had given Ev a note when he could have spoken. Almost immediately, however, Sabine forgot about the note, and VJ must have forgotten it as well. The boy evidently left the note on the table, since that's where Rosa found it. She was clearing off the dishes after cake when she chanced upon the note. Sabine was about to shout at Felice and refute the unjustified accusations when Rosa went ballistic.

The process involved some fairly alarming attacks on Ev Crume. This concerned Sabine. The Crume boy was, after all, a longtime family friend, as well as a guest under their roof. Sabine liked the young man and appreciated his calming effect on VJ. He was also surprised that Rosa would cause such a scene at the party. Like everyone else, Sabine followed the angry shouts into the dining room. Rosa had the Crume boy cornered and was shouting at him to leave the house at once and to leave her little brother alone. "You disgust me," she said, "and I never knew until just now what a bad influence you've been on my brother." With that she threw the note into Ev's horrified face, turned on her heel, and left the room.

Sabine had to smile, watching this distressing scene. How many times in his marriage had Magda turned on her heel, in just that fashion, to stalk from that very room, using the same measured tread? Lord, that girl was her mother's daughter from the toenails on up. But what on earth was going on?

Ev took the note, closed his eyes, and uttered a deep animal groan, the kind of sound that would issue from a Cape buffalo that's sustained a mortal wound. He made his exit, so defeated and dispirited that he seemed to drain out of the room at ankle height, heading, no doubt, for the room he shared with the Arizona general.

Before any clarification or sorting out of the troubling scene, Ev was back with news that an egg of some sort was hatching. Sabine's vague fears were taking shape! VJ had gone off half-cocked and bought an ostrich egg, now hatching. The party collectively moved to Ev's room. Sabine, the kids, dogs, Fanny, Abraham, Magda, Ev, VJ, the warring elder sisters, and finally Rosa crammed into the room. Kids were shouting, shoving one another, and bursting into tears. Felice and Celia argued about the kids' pushings and proddings. Poodles were yapping, first at the incubator, then at any promising target. Fanny launched into a story about how Abraham's son Isaac was the lone hatchling of a nine-egg brood and that she suspected her father of encouraging Abraham to attack poor little Isaac. Abraham himself shrieked in terror and tried to get on top of Fanny's head, noting that poodles were lunging and snapping at him. Sabine wondered about the newborn ostrich; what opinion of the world would a creature form with *this* as its birth experience?

Colonel McKenzie had moved the incubator onto Ev's bed and opened it. There, in the midst of the hullabaloo, a retired colonel and a wet, newly hatched baby ostrich were considering one another.

Sabine was struck for the second time in as many hours by the unexpected similarity between the faces of birds and humans. Colonel McKenzie, the Arizona general, looked very like that newly hatched ostrich. Colonel McKenzie was watching the ostrich closely, chewing his upper lip. The soggy ostrich, scraggly, splayed out, and exhausted from its work to break out of the egg, was watching Colonel McKenzie with even closer, more intense attention. The bird's eye had luster and focused on the Colonel, excluding all others. It looked to Sabine like the bird was conveying affection, love for the old militarist. VJ, steeped in the *Stockman's Universe* article on ostriches, noted the process and recognized what was afoot.

"Jesus, the bird is bonding to you, Colonel McKenzie."

Acting with the resolution of authority, VJ took charge. He alone knew about ostriches. Borrowing a conceit of command from his sisters, he ordered everyone from the room. No one moved. He persisted, explaining the situation. The newborn needed relief from the harsh lights and loud voices. It needed rest and would continue to require the warmth of the incubator for many hours, until it was fluffy and well dried.

The crowd began to thin down. VJ looked at man and bird and worried. He hadn't dreamed that the egg would hatch before he'd read the folder of photocopied information Jessie'd handed him as they left Womynscraft. He motioned to the Colonel, who was clearly reluctant to leave. Finally, though, the Colonel did tear himself away from the chick. He strode back into the party smiling and proud that the ostrich had showed such instinctive good sense in its bonding preferences.

Magda had watched the Colonel closely and felt her maternal heartstrings stirred. She pursed her lips. Why did she befriend the Colonel? He was, after all, a political troglodyte, an utter sexist, and a randy old goat whose passes were coarse attempts to cop feels, pop her panty elastic, and hike her dress up. She dealt with him easily enough; a word, a glare, or a sharp little kick would always serve to cool his jets. Still, his persistence was annoying, and his constant, obvious state of arousal was actually nerve-wracking.

She knew of his taste for the soft and not-so-soft porn that was primly stacked on the nightstand next to his bed. This would have little appeal to VJ as long as his mind was on ostriches. That sort of influence, however, could be corrosive to a vulnerable boy like young Everett. It was distasteful. It made her lip curl. Yet it was rather standard. She'd learned to be patient with male vices. Still, why should she in this case?

The Colonel was not family. There were no ties of loyalty obliging her to tolerate the old goat. And the way he treated his hounds! He was worse than Hitler. And yet, she helped him get porcupine quills out of Sanborn, his laziest, most dull-witted hound; she let him come by twice a week to hose off her patio; and though she wouldn't enter his house, she invited him for a meal and drinks every week or two. Why on earth? He even had a musky smell about him that she didn't like, and that was before he, Ev, and VJ showed up reeking of ostrich!

Watching him with the newly hatched chick provided Magda with startling insights into her own puzzling behavior. Why, she put up with the old buster out of pity. He was a childless man with a strong need to father; that's what put him into the military. And now he was as proud of himself and that little ostrich as any young father coming out of the infant viewing area of a hospital. It was touching, and Magda actually felt a little catch in her throat as she watched him strut out of the room. Bonding was evidently something that worked both ways.

Sabine kept his eye on Magda all evening. He had his hopes. Maybe with all this drawing aside that was so much the fashion, he'd be able to draw Magda aside. They could, perhaps, read a bit with the lights out, play a few rounds of hide the sausage. Good God, she looked fearsome good. If ever there was anyone who was sexy sixties, it was his wife! She was always able to summon the energies he'd feared would ultimately ebb. She'd been a bit cool with him since the separation. Against all reason, she resented his refusal to move with her to Arizona. Anyone could see that Sabine was too fat to live a decent life in Arizona. How could he run around in a swimsuit and a tan all the time like they did down there?

Despite all this, she was miffed, and it'd been nearly impossible to get in her pants. The separation sharpened Sabine's desire to the point of discomfort. Whenever she was around, the old man felt that adolescent misery of the lower abdomen known as blue balls. From time to time he sought relief in familiar quarters, the famous Ms. Palms and her five sisters. It felt undignified, to revive such schoolboy expedients at his age. What if Rosa came into the bathroom and caught him at it?

The hatching of the ostrich egg was the high point of the evening. Sabine was happy to have his birthday upstaged. As the crowd pressed back into the living room, he was able finally to grab that second piece of cake he'd promised himself. He showed Felice, too, just how much he thought of her impertinence. Right under her nose he slathered a pint or so of that good Borden's full-bore vanilla ice cream onto the generous mound of cake he'd cut. The party wound down. Magda and Rosa went into a spasm of industry delivering bedding to the many bedrooms. The grandkids put on a fine, seemingly coordinated chorus of whining and complaining that had the effect of uniting Celia and Felice at the end of the evening in shared disgust with their own offspring.

Magda was here, Magda was there, trailing her small flock of poodles in her wake and looking as fetching as could be. She was wearing a paisley head scarf and one of her white flowing outfits, all silky and revealing. Looking at her, Sabine wondered if she was braless. It was not likely, but she certainly bounced with a bit of lilt and jiggle as she bustled by with loads of sheets and bedclothes.

Rosa's bustling was subdued. Like her mother, she'd noted those magazines contaminating the room that Ev shared with the Colonel and the ostrich. They were under a shaving kit on a nightstand on the Colonel's side of the room, the same horrible magazines she'd saved from the sheep. Someone had taken the time to assemble the magazines and deal with the sheep damage. Could the magazines belong to the Colonel? She'd find out, even if she had to ask VJ. She continued to help her mother with the bedding.

Magda considered her youngest daughter. She could not

pass up the opportunity to address the young woman's appalling breach in good manners. "That was a fine thing the way that you yelled at poor Ev, Rosa! I don't know what he did, but I can't imagine that it warranted that. It looks to me like you should be showing that boy some gratitude. He got VJ here, didn't he? And he is always sensible, always helping your brother to see reason."

Rosa's eyes flashed. The rage she'd experienced earlier began to rise again. Her jaw tightened, and her lips once again pulled away from her teeth. "Mama," she almost shouted, "he's dirty-minded. So you think he's such a good influence on VJ, do you? Just tonight I found a note. Everett Crume was trying to entice your baby into going with him to a *whorehouse!* I guess he couldn't even wait until after Daddy's party."

"What on earth? A note? A whorehouse?"

Rosa Margarita Eckleberry caught her mother's eye as they bustled down the hall, both of them burdened with bedclothes. A tear made its way down her cheek. She balled her fists and dropped her load of blankets. Magda picked them up and hustled her into the bedroom Celia would soon take.

Celia was down the hall, lecturing her children. "If the three of you can't behave for one night away from home, if you can't keep from fighting and whining for three hours on your grandfather's birthday, then I don't see how we can take five days away from home to go to Disneyland." Magda did some mental calculations. Celia was barely into the threat phase of the lecture. She'd work her way toward guilt, her strong suit. Magda could count on at least twenty minutes for a heart-to-heart with Rosa. Something was definitely stirring, if little old tough-nut Rosa was bawling. The shouting at Ev had been a bit excessive, especially for Rosa, but had sent up no maternal warning flags. The entire family was prone to outbursts of shouting. With this girl, however, tears, even just a few, were another matter. It was just like with Champy. That dog was always throwing up, and it meant nothing. But if he ever turned his nose up at food, you knew something was wrong.

Magda set her daughter on the bed and sat beside her, caressing her back and holding her around the shoulders. Rosa leaned against her, wetting her satiny outfit with warm tears. Magda smiled. Rosa still had the sweet cut-grass breath she'd had as a little girl. The tears had their season. When Rosa quit crying, her mother spoke.

"Okay, what's it all about?"

"It's that damned Ev. I was so glad he was here. I kissed him. I just meant it to be a friendly kiss out of gratitude for getting VJ to the ranch. I don't know what happened, but I just kept kissing him."

Magda held Rosa hard against her. She did not want her daughter to see the huge smile that crinkled her face. This was wonderful news; Rosa's behavior made perfect sense. She was at least halfway in love with that fine young man!

Mistaking her mother's strong hug for maternal empathy, Rosa continued. "It was unsettling but exciting. It was like I just lost control. It was as big a surprise to me as it was to him. And Mama, I thought *he* was going to pass out." She laughed haltingly and then cried a bit more as she realized that it was not *exactly* a surprise to her. She'd been appreciating, then enjoying, then eyeing Ev for some time, at least a year. She'd been reserved. The gratitude they all felt changed by slow degrees into affection that'd gradually grown quite warm. The kiss forced her to confront unacknowledged feelings that'd grown inside.

"Then this morning I was walking around thinking that I was a little in love with him. I thought about how long it's been since I let a man near me. I felt that Ev was someone I knew, someone I could trust. I was thinking I didn't mind if he was tubby. That bunch of Daddy's sheep had got out of the kitchen pen and got into the shed where Ev had his luggage. He had those porn magazines, Mama; you saw them, terrible pictures that he probably uses when he plays with himself. I was upset all day. So I let him have it. I let him know that as far as I was concerned I was taking my kiss back. You should have seen the look on his face, pure fear. There he was wearing those gruesome off-brand jeans. God, he stank from those ostriches. He smelled even worse than Virg. It would have been funny if it hadn't been so awful." Rosa had another period of interspersed laughing and crying. Magda laughed as well and released her daughter. Rosa rolled around on the bed convulsed with laughter, then tears, then laughter again. Magda ducked into the nearest bathroom and came back with a glass of water.

"Thanks, Mommy."

Magda looked at her youngest daughter with incredulity. Mommy? Oh boy, head for the hills. The last time Rosa had called her Mommy was during that beautiful interlude in an infant's life that occurs just before the terrible twos.

"I don't know why I'm getting so upset. Here, look at this note." Rosa had found the note on the floor where Ev had dropped it in the wake of the confrontation. Magda took the crumpled paper and read: "As discussed, we'll visit the local poontang palace after the party breaks up. I know that a cocksman like you can't go too long without it. Meet me at the Jeep at 20:30."

Magda recognized the small, defiant writing. The Colonel had left dozens of notes for her in the past several months. All of Colonel McKenzie's notes were annoying for one reason or another. It did confirm her suspicion that the Colonel was having a corrupting influence on Ev. But happily, Rosa was mistaken. The magazines certainly belonged to the Colonel, and there was nothing but the Colonel's insulting, belittling innuendo to suggest that Ev had agreed to go to the whorehouse.

"I saw Ev give that to VJ," Rosa said. "Right under Daddy's roof, Ev was trying to get VJ to go with him to visit prostitutes." Magda was relieved to note an edge of anger creeping back into her daughter's voice. Having opened up like that, she'd surely have to lash out, and Magda prepared herself for the explosion. She spoke.

"No, honey. I don't know why Ev was giving this note to VJ, but I do know he didn't write it. That is Colonel McKenzie's handwriting, and notice how he refers to military time. And the magazines you found belong to the Colonel, not Everett. The Colonel is, excuse the expression, a horny old goat. I have to keep my wits about me all the time. He's always trying something."

The information took a minute to sink in. Rosa experienced a moment of intense, sickening embarrassment. Her eyes widened. Her pulse quickened. Her blood pressure soared as the capillaries in her extremities constricted in unison. A powerful blast of adrenaline suffused her system. Her jaw muscles tightened, tightened, tightened. She considered her mother.

"How dare you bring a man like that into this house!" It was Magda's fault! If Magda had not brought that horrible man into the family home, Rosa would never have made those disastrous, humiliating mistakes. She glared at her mother and found her wanting. Mama was not even a Basque, after all. She was soft and had poor judgment. Rosa raised her voice. "It's bad enough that you left me and Daddy alone here. Then you come dragging a sex fiend into the family home! I'll bet he was never in the armed forces either. They wouldn't let a filthy-minded man like that become an officer. You just call him a colonel to try to make him seem respectable. I can't believe you'd be having an affair with someone like that, someone who is corrupting your own son."

Magda drew air slowly into her lungs. Mother and daughter were now back into utterly familiar emotional territory. Magda was startled that anyone would think she was having an affair with the Colonel. It was good to know. Rosa was probably not the only person harboring the notion. Still, the righteous indignation was annoying. Rosa could be a little pill.

"Rosa," she said, "go ahead and be mad at me. God knows I probably deserve it more than young Crume. You have a point about the Colonel, even though I am *not* having an affair with him. He's really just a lonely old guy. He seems more obnoxious than everyone else because he never learned how to disguise his nasty side. At least he doesn't get any worse as you get to know him. In fact, it's his nicer side that you get to know slowly. But my God, Daughter, what kind of a mind have you got, all full of lurid affairs? Your fantasy life is probably worse than the Colonel's porn. You're getting to be quite the prissy little prude, Rosa, and prudes are the ones obsessed with filth. So just don't do it, honey; it's not your nature."

"So you know my nature?" Rosa was still on the boil. She listened to her mom—she always did—but maintained her indignation.

"Honey, I installed your nature. I know your nature better than I know my own. What I don't know is how you got hurt or scared enough to develop this prudishness. It really is unbecoming, my dear. It's not a wonder that you don't manage to hold a steady beau. Men get nervous when women look at them, judge them, get down on them about their natural urges."

Rosa was still mad, but she did have to laugh. Sabine thought she was drifting into spinsterhood because she had such a foul mouth. Now here's Magda blaming it on prudishness. It was funny but . . . that "don't manage to hold a steady beau" business? What a cheap crack! Feeling her blood rise, she strained to moderate her response.

"It's not prudishness," she said. "I'm confused and nervous and I'm wanting you and Daddy back together and I want VJ back on the ranch. I run it *alone*, Mama. Daddy's just into hobby ranching now, and that's fine, but the place deserves better. It needs care, it needs attention. I brought Fanny Ulibarri out here hoping she'd waylay VJ, get his mind on her instead of the ostriches. I was actually hoping she'd seduce him. So I've got all this in my head along with the work of the party, and all of a sudden I'm getting ga-ga over Ev. When I kissed him, Mama, I really lost it. I almost couldn't stop. Some prude! It was shameless, right in front of VJ and that terrible man. I don't think I would have been so harsh with him today if I'd been able to control myself last night. Something about those magazines, though, did set me off."

She started to tear up again.

"I guess I've really blown it."

Magda had to admit that this was true. Rosa had provided an impressive display of righteous wrath. Poor Ev was naturally sensitive and had been even more vulnerable than usual because of his blistered feet. If Rosa's ferocious and unfathomable attacks did not scar the boy for life, they'd certainly stun him into a terrified withdrawal that could last for months.

"Well . . . those things are difficult to unsay, Rosa, but at least you didn't say anything about his weight. I think he's very sensitive about his weight."

"I guess that is a bright spot, all right. I also didn't say anything about his horrible clothes or the way he stunk of ostrich even after his shower. Why, he's probably just brimming over with gratitude because of the horrible things I didn't say to him. I mean, Mama, I did show some restraint. Those jeans he wears are so hideous."

"Yeah, you were restrained, all right. You made him burn those jeans."

Both women lay on the bed and laughed until it hurt, listing terrible insults Rosa hadn't included in her attacks on Ev. Rosa cried again and then laughed more. Finally, though, Magda decided that they should get back to work. Celia would soon be coming to bed. Having worked hard to reduce her children to tears of remorse, guilt, and shame, she'd then spend a weary quarter hour or so building them back up. She'd be none too pleased to find Rosa and Magda on her bed in a hysterical laughing jag. Magda was keenly aware of the errors she'd made with poor Celia, who was, at that very moment, making identical errors with her children.

So Magda sent Rosa along to bed, saying that she'd deliver the rest of the bedding, batten down the hatches, and spend some time with the birthday boy so he wouldn't feel neglected. Rosa was tired, wrung out, practically a zombie. She did as her mother suggested, passing Celia, who'd left her children happy, but emotionally exhausted, in their beds.

Magda found Sabine on the porch drinking wine and looking at the stars that spread across the moonless night, unmolested by city lights.

"So take me on a walk around your ranch, handsome," she said.

Sabine was happy to take his wife's arm for a nighttime stroll. They walked by the kitchen pen and thought of the sheep that were missing. Those damned sheep! They'd certainly become a thorn in his side all of a sudden. He hadn't had any trouble at all with that bunch until everybody showed up ready to pass judgment on his failing powers. No wonder he'd never liked sheep. Well, someone would have to find them, bring them back, and then study the kitchen pen to find out how they were getting out. He'd already walked the fence once and hadn't found any breaks. He'd have to get VJ on it. Sabine was momentarily annoyed, but this passed. Animals are always annoying. Breakouts, disease, destruction, and frustration are part of any livestock business, and losses are unavoidable. At least none of these were dead yet, as far as he knew.

The sight of his new donkeys was soothing for Sabine, and he was able to restrain himself from making any nasty cracks about Magda's poodles. Magda told him about Rosa and Ev, but Sabine did not find the topic particularly interesting; the lack of sheep in the kitchen pen was too distracting. Ev was a good boy, always had been. Rosa was a live wire; that's the way she was. Ev would either handle it or drag up and move on down the line. Maybe Sabine would help out a little with a carefully placed word or two for Rosa. His Rosie Daisy was a pretty girl and sure to find a husband, in spite of her temper and her vulgar mouth. She could certainly do worse than the Crume boy and probably would if left entirely to her own devices. In temperament and to some extent looks, she was a lot like her mom. Magda, of course, had much better judgment as regards men.

Magda was a wonderful woman, Sabine's proof of his own superior judgment. She was very snuggly and affectionate. She knew him, understood why he wanted to have the donkeys, that he wanted to look at them, get to know what they were like. As they watched those donkeys graze in the dark, under a dazzling sky, Magda told Sabine that she'd given her bedroom to Felice's boy Eric for the night. Sabine smiled broadly. It'd been quite a seventy-second after all. Now he would return to the house and make love to his wife for the first time in, perhaps, a year. Sabine felt that his luck had changed when he got those donkeys.

CHAPTER FOURTEEN

■ ■ ■

It is always annoying to have to face the fact that you've been a horse's ass. It's generally easier to go on being a horse's ass. History is full of examples.

Virgil Jose Eckleberry, however, was not a shirker. He was not metabolically suited for craft or evasion. He felt that a man has to face facts. This is best done in the hours just before or just after dawn. VJ was not one to defy tradition.

On the day after Sabine's birthday, Virgil Jose awoke at 5:30 A.M., long before the gentleman's hour of 9 or 10 that he preferred. This was, at first, annoying. For several days running, he'd gotten up at an ungodly early hour for one reason or another. It was happening again. He'd decided to sleep on the floor of Ev and the Colonel's room, next to the incubator. He'd expected some peace, a good night's sleep on a hard floor. He hoped that he could cause the young ostrich to transfer affections and bond to him.

Evidently, though, a person couldn't count on anything anymore. Old Sabine was letting the ranch go to hell. He was raising Sudan grass so he wouldn't have but two cuttings. Fences were down and outbuildings were left open. Sheep were leaking out of their pens, untrained guard donkeys were infesting the place showing no sign of guarding anything, and now Sabine had gotten something that made a racket so that a person couldn't sleep. My God, it sounded like a dozen barn cats in a plastic trash can! Whatever it was, it was penned way too close to the house. What on earth could Sabine be thinking? If VJ hadn't known better, he'd have sworn that the animals were in the room with him.

As it turned out, this would've been an accurate observation. VJ came slowly awake, realizing by degrees that the animal sounds were, indeed, close at hand. He sprang to his feet and snapped on the light. Had a raccoon, coyote, wolverine, or other vicious predator crept into the room to get the defenseless little ostrich? Well, no. The little incubator was vibrating and dancing about on the floor as though alive. VJ felt a tightness in his belly, an unpleasant, familiar feeling that brought to mind his unfortunate experience in Los Angeles on the *Jeopardy* program. "Tiny fuzzball ostrich" was the surprising answer to what question? Sadly, VJ knew (which was more than he could say for his *Jeopardy* experience). The question was "What in God's name is raising all that hell?"

Ev and the Colonel were both half awake. Both of them let VJ know that they were far from happy that he'd turned on the light. They both blamed him, as well, for the racket. They hadn't agreed on much since they met but were firmly allied on that point. They had consensus. They were half awake and aggravated at VJ.

"Just shut up and go back to sleep," he told them. "I'll turn off the light."

They groaned and tossed, turning toward the walls. One of them, VJ did not know which, farted rather expressively. Trying to ignore both the tension and the new and unpleasant mammalian odor that now filled the room, VJ crawled over to the gyrating incubator and opened it.

If VJ had been able to see the little critter, he would've seen a grapefruit-sized ball of white fuzz. From that ball issued a pair of shiny black and yellow eyes encased in a head the size of an olive that was mounted on a neck that could be compared to a cooked spaghetti noodle. The chick's legs could be similarly compared to straightened paper clips. The legs descended perhaps four inches from the ball of fuzz to the floor of the room. VJ saw none of this. What he saw was motion, a blur. The blur had personality somehow. A head and beak emerged from the blur to grab VJ's high school class ring. He'd left the ring (a pinkie ring) near the floor pallet his mother had made for him. Now the ring was gone and the ostrich with it, running senselessly about the room.

Young Eckleberry did not, of course, know that liberty's great philosopher, John Locke, felt that the mind at birth was a tabula rasa, a blank slate of pure possibility that slowly filled with information and skills during the growth process. Ignoring philosophy, VJ did draw conclusions about ostriches during the first five seconds that his ostrich was out of the incubator. Far from being a tabula rasa, that ostrich was born with inclinations, predispositions. The bird was born to run and born to grab stuff during the process. In terms of the bird's intellect, however, the tabula rasa argument admittedly had merit.

VJ knew something about animals. He was an animal, after all, and knew it. That was one factor. In terms of experience, he had grown up on the ranch, caring for animals night and day. He'd learned a lot. Beyond that, he had an uncanny ability to understand animal anxieties, desires, and preoccupations. This ability might have extended to humans except that people made VJ nervous. With people he was unable to slow down enough to focus his attention effectively. An example of this was Fanny Ulibarri. Cornered, brought to bay during a lull in Sabine's party, VJ had stood longer than he characteristically stood in one spot, attempting to listen to Fanny while he wondered if she would ever stop talking. She was talking about the way her ex-husband had pawned her furs for gambling money. Surely hell would be an eternity of heart-to-heart discussions with this woman. With animals he was more relaxed, even when they did things like grab his class ring and run.

The little ostrich ran. It cared not that bedrooms, even spacious, well-appointed bedrooms, are not designed for running, whether as an athletic endeavor or escape. The bird ran in the face of architectural considerations. VJ knew the impulse. He sensed that unsuccessful attempts to capture the chick could exacerbate the situation. It was running here and there on the floor. It was not frightened but apparently ran for existential reasons. It was running simply because that was its nature, a nature VJ understood. If VJ started chasing it, it would surely attempt to escape, and it might become hysterical, jumping onto beds and crashing into walls. Ev and the Colonel, well, they probably wouldn't think too much of that. Still, he needed to capture the creature. It'd need food and water eventually, and besides, there was something aggravating about the constant motion of the thing, an affront to the dignity of the predawn hour. Surely all beasts that creep and birds that fly tend toward repose in the deep and solemn chamber of night's end. . . . Not this one.

The chick established a course. It ran under and around the beds in a rough figure eight, crossing VJ's pallet every fifteen or twenty seconds. It'd already shit three times, and that was going to be a problem unless he limited the acreage the thing covered. The droppings themselves were aromatic, at least as bad as the stink produced by the humans. It was curious that the little thing had shit in its intestines, not having eaten anything. Its failure to eat the class ring was a hopeful sign, not that it'd given any indication of relinquishing the only ring it'd thus far found.

So VJ faced a dilemma. He needed to capture the bird without scaring it into a ruinous panic. The attempt would have to succeed on the first try. A failure would inevitably cause the little creature to become evasive. It'd be just a champ at evasion, anyone could see that. VJ decided to get a light plastic milk crate. He'd lead the little devil a foot or so and throw the thing over the bird as it attempted to run past. He'd then stack some stuff on top so the little ostrich would be unable to overturn the crate and resume its avocation.

VJ knew there was a plastic milk crate in his father's office. Sabine kept important papers in the crate, like the originals of U.S. Government Form Number GSX-RE1, which he'd filled out so laboriously two days before. VJ made his way into his dad's office. It was the work of a moment to empty the contents of the crate onto the summit of the mountain of junk that covered the old man's desk.

He strode back to the bedroom. The chick was still on task, covering the route with the dedication that drivers, like Richard Petty, bring to the stock car races VJ and the Colonel so appreciated. This unvarying approach gave Virgil Jose a measure of confidence. He watched for a while in the burgeoning light of the day that was beginning, now, to dawn. After several minutes of close study, VJ felt certain he could judge the speed well enough to drop the crate true. With a flick of the wrists that imparted the needed trajectory, the crate arrived at the targeted spot at the exact moment the ostrich attempted to cross that spot. The bird was captured. VJ quickly grabbed a shaving kit and the girly magazines that the Colonel had on his nightstand. He stacked these on top of the crate. He breathed a sigh of relief.

Ev and the Colonel were showing determination; neither of them more than flinched at the sound of the dropping crate. It was a poignant moment for VJ, as he realized the sacrifices he'd have to embrace in the interest of others. He was in the ostrich business. He breathed deeply, his nostrils assailed by the smell of ostrich. He was doing this for his mother, for Ev, for the sheep- and cow-beaten lands of the parched West.

He had a powerful premonition that the husbandry of this bird and his breed would entail a great deal of wakeful attention. The future he faced involved a lot of missed sleep. The bird had a nature to run, and VJ's talent for empathy told him that, likewise, the creature had a nature at odds with human slumber. The article in *Stockman's Universe* had not touched on that characteristic.

Once confined, the bird did drop the ring. VJ reached for it. Suddenly, the subtle movement of the dawning day was broken by an intense flash of pain and a partially throttled shout. Curses issued from inert forms, ebbing gradually into the characteristic silence of the predawn hours. For a moment, VJ did not understand what had happened. The little ostrich had bitten him, delivering a severe pinch to the index finger that'd sought the apparently abandoned ring. VJ did get the ring, but not without cost. It was difficult to believe that a creature that'd been an egg less than eight hours before could bite so hard. VJ tried with little success to imagine the kind of bite a seven-foot-tall, four-hundred-pound adult could deliver.

This was not an auspicious way to begin the day. These events affected young VJ deeply. He began to consider the possibility that he was blowing it badly, using his free will capriciously, acting like a horse's . . . On the face of it, he had to admit, it seemed likely. On deeper reflection, it seemed even more likely.

As the cold light of the distant sun peeked over the dry, jagged mountains to the east, VJ considered ostriches. He supposed that their meat was heavenly, both tasty and healthy. Likewise, he marveled at their economy. They used their feed so much more efficiently than cattle or sheep, gaining weight on much less food. Their hides were valuable; full quill ostrich boots were certainly out of his price range, at least as long as he walked horses for a living. But all this was pretty theoretical.

Other traits were now more compelling. The birds stank. They were costly. They were big enough to be dangerous and did things like kick field goals with large dogs. They grabbed jewelry and fingers. They ran. They bonded to the first motile being they happened to see after hatching and were not inclined to reconsider the decision. Furthermore, one of his aims in the venture was to provide his mother with an independent income. The notion now seemed superfluous. His mom was suddenly all lovey with Sabine, apparently in bed with him at that very moment. VJ supposed that he should be glad, but the idea of his parents in bed together made him nervous. His chest tightened. Magda sure wouldn't need any financial support if she got back with his dad. Beyond that, VJ had wanted to give poor Ev a taste of prosperity. Poor Ev. VJ remembered how optimistic Ev had been lying on the bed before the party. In the cold light of honest reflection, it now looked like the ill-considered ostrich trip had ruined any chances that poor old Evertly Ev might have had for future happiness. Wealth would be but ashes for old Ev now.

And what in God's name had happened to Rosa? Had life alone with old Sabine become such a strain that she'd finally just lost it? He was a cantankerous old elf, but everyone knew that Rosa was his favorite. VJ couldn't imagine that the task of bossing her dad around would take such a toll. Bossing had always come so easily for Rosa. It wasn't as if she wasn't used to it. But something had happened, something had shifted within the small, intense frame of his closest sister. Maybe it'd been a mistake for him to stay away so long. He'd wanted to teach his dad a lesson. No one ever appeared to have done so before, but the long odds had seemed worth it. Rosa's behavior raised questions, doubts. Maybe he should have dodged the fork a bit, apologized, and stuck around.

Rosa would be the perfect woman for Ev. That was for positive. Ev was a guy that seemed to just thrive on bossing. He even let neighbors, like old four-eyes Susie, boss him around. Just imagine how comfortable he'd be taking orders from Rosa, a woman he obviously . . . loved. For his part, Ev would be the perfect fellow for Rosa. VJ was astounded that he'd not noticed this before.

At about seven, Ev woke up. He was alarmed to see VJ staring into the eternal distances out the west window and twisting at his hair. His friend was evidently still utterly obsessed with ostriches. This was going to be even worse than the *Jeopardy* debacle or the business with the python skin. When Ev recalled his own troubles and the events of the previous evening, he gave an involuntary groan that aroused VJ from his state of revery.

"So, it's Rosa, Ev, Rosa!" VJ said without a preamble. "I don't know whether I can stand it if a guy with underwear as holey as those gets to be my brother-in-law. What a guy. Here you convince me that you're all hot and heavy with old four-eyes Susie, whom I in no way approve of as a seemly woman for my buddy, and then you up and go after my sis. Now if I was a proper Basque, I might just have to kill you. I'd at least have to threaten. That's pretty much the custom. When someone wants to marry your sis, if you're Euzkadi proper, you gotta act like you might just have to kill the fellow or at least say something like 'Sir, you have cast your greedy eyes on the stainless virtue of my sister. Should you dishonor my family and besmirch her unsullied honor, I will hunt you down in whatever hole you choose to hide yourself and kill you like a rat.' It's the Basque tradition; just swill down a gallon or so of wine and grab the beret and shotgun. Just wanna let you know, Evertly Ev, what you're getting into when you marry into the Euzkadi."

Ev opened his mouth as though to speak. He was sitting on the edge of his bed, his large frame tense with the effort needed to contain the powerful emotions that threatened his equilibrium. Certainly, his mouth hung open. No one can blame him for that. In such situations, a person has plenty to think about besides muscle tension in the jaw. Ev regarded VJ with that sullen hatred that newly awakened people feel toward those with the poor taste to be wakeful and energetic.

"I have other underwear," he said truthfully. "Rosa made me burn my best pair."

"Well, Ev, I'm certainly glad to hear that you still have underwear options. I guess I'll have to put up with you marrying my sister. I ought to just kill you, no matter how many pairs of shorts you have, but I guess I won't, not yet anyway. Maybe I won't have to pay you so much to manage my affairs if you're going to be family and all."

Ev was wishing he'd had some breakfast before he got up. Breakfast always helped him to cope.

"I want to have breakfast, VJ. Shut up until I've eaten. I'm sick of you and your family."

VJ began whistling "Fly Me to the Moon." After a bar or two he began singing:

Fly me to the moon
And let me sing dee-doodle-doo.
Doodle-dee doo-doodle-dee
Tra-la-la tra-la-la.
In other words, hold my hand.
In other words, la-dee-dah-doo.

While he sang he thought about his sister. That girl needed to get some sense into her head. Maybe it was the damned sheep. Anybody would get ringy, hanging around endlessly while sheep bred. He'd send them off, Rosa and Ev, on a trip to Tahiti or somewhere, maybe Paris, get Rosa away from the ranch and the sheep.

"Ev," he said, ignoring the order to shut up, "do you think that maybe Jamaica would be the place to take Rosa? The sis is under stress at this damned ranch. She's gotten pretty ringy. Maybe you could take her there, get her to smoke a bunch of that Rasta weed and drink a few gallons of rum, get her straightened out."

Ev was beginning to feel a certain amount of stress himself. The mention of the rum made him feel queasy, and he had a bit of a bellyache from the party food. He went to the bathroom.

VJ was unconcerned. It didn't surprise him that Ev woke up crabby. He'd tease him later when it'd be more satisfying. Anyway, there was the ostrich. He needed to find some chicken scratch and a water bowl. The chick had run seventy miles or so. It was bound to be hungry. The scratch feed was in one of the barns. VJ left to find it.

While he was gone, Colonel McKenzie awoke from a dream of baking biscuits. This struck him as odd. He'd never baked a biscuit. From the way the dream had gone, he was glad he'd never done it. He opened his eyes, relieved that he was in bed rather than tending an oven. The first thing he saw was a pair of eyes looking back at him. They were small yellow eyes, eyes that glowed with affection. The Colonel felt warmth in his midriff and thought for a moment that he'd wet the bed. It was touching to the Colonel that the little ostrich liked him. He decided to blow off his morning run. He was on vacation, damn it, and actually wished that he still had the ability to wet the bed. With his prostate, the process of urination had gotten to be a complex, effortful, tedious affair that he blamed on women, especially Magda. He regretted not having made it to the whorehouse. The medium of money was the only way that connecting with women made any sense at all.

Ev walked into the room.

"Morning, Fatty," he said, "and wipe that pitiful expression off your face. God-damned little ninny, don't know when you've got it good. I'll bet you just took a good leak, didn't you?"

Ev, astounded, confessed. "Er, kinda. I always have to go when I get up, and I had quite a bit of punch at the party. I woke up about to pop." His brow furrowed. He did not much like having someone grill him about his morning urinations. It seemed rude.

"Well, there you go, damn you. I just wish to hell I could have the pleasure of taking a good leak, just raring back and letting go. When you spend a good half hour to strain out a few little piddles, like I have to, then you'll kick yourself for being such a sourpuss. Lookee here at this little ostrich here. It just loves me."

Ev looked at the ostrich. The thing was cute in kind of a mindless, feral way, and the Colonel was right. The bird was watching his every move with the concentration of pure love.

Magda was up bright and early, sweeping about the place, trailing yards of fabric and poodles. Sassy's leg was finally on the mend, and he was out for vengeance. The other poodles had made his convalescence hell. Without Magda's constant protection, the others would have fallen on him and killed him in his weakened state. Today, Sassy meant to show the other poodles, miserable dregs that they were, that the alpha dog was back on top and nobody's sweetheart. During the long night, Sassy had not missed Magda's attention to his leg. He could tolerate (barely) the ponderous human lovemaking that filled the room with rich aromas. He slept deeply, dreaming of killing rats, which assumed the shapes of Champy, Joey, and Moe at crucial moments. Awake and chasing after Magda, the others sensed Sassy's mood, deferred to his every snarl, and stayed close to Magda for protection. The hunters had become the hunted.

There is something about multiple orgasms that brings a spring to the step of any lively sixty-six-year-old woman, and Magda was no exception. That Sabine was quite an old stallion. She'd left him cultivating his sated slumbers. She was going to, by golly, enjoy those fine cool hours Nevada provided even in July. She'd thrown on a flowing lilac caftan and had taken a nice walk down to the little stream, around to the sheepless kitchen pen, and finally back toward the compound of ranch buildings and barns.

It was a glorious morning. The sun had risen purple and cast its image into tens of thousands of drops of dew that'd drenched everything, including the four donkeys. Fine beasts those donkeys were too, in Magda's opinion, such wise and intelligent expressions, such long, silky ears. As she approached the compound, Magda was surprised to see her last-born going into one of the feed sheds. Virgil Jose had surprised her with his early rising more than once lately, but the sight of him with a coffee can full of scratch feed at six in the morning was still worthy of comment.

"Good morning, sweetheart. What's got you up at such an early hour?"

"Little ostrich, Mama. He got out of the incubator and I had to catch him. Needs food now, I guess."

The ostrich was not the only one that needed food. Lord, the boy looked skinny, and again that pink shirt! He was barefooted and twisting at his hair like he did, an instant four-alarm worry to any mother. All he needed was the backless gown with his skinny little butt showing and looks-wise he'd fit right in at the psych ward where Magda took the dogs every month for the patients to pet. (Petting the dogs supposedly had therapeutic effects for the psych patients and was good for the dogs as well. They weren't so snippy after all the handling.)

It scared Magda to picture VJ at the psych unit. His eccentricity, his distractability, were so annoying, so upsetting. It was such a shame about the Ulibarri girl, she'd tried so hard but was such a bundle of frayed nerves herself. No one on earth could listen to the poor thing without glazing over.

Magda had to concede that despite VJ's obvious need for

the steadying effect of a female companion, Fanny Ulibarri was a long shot for the position. Her large, solid, man-anchoring butt would never get the kind of notice it deserved as long as she talked like that. She was smitten with VJ, Magda could see that, but she was nervous. She lacked confidence. VJ was a skittish boy. Magda had watched Fanny at the party, gabbing desperately as she attempted to connect. This had provoked VJ into a frenzy of haphazard kinetics: tucking his shirt, stepping back, popping his knuckles, scratching his chin, coughing, and doing lots of the ever popular hair-twisting. VJ's behavior made Fanny even more uneasy. She got more and more obsessive in her oratory and ended up driving the panicky VJ before her from kitchen to living room, to porch, to dining room, and finally even out to the kitchen pen.

It was sad. Fanny was a nice girl, a pretty girl, and an interesting, intelligent girl when she was able to slow down. Magda had known her, of course, practically since her birth and blamed her dead father, old Golfrido, for her temperament. Magda had never known a more elusive man than Golfrido, and that was saying a mouthful. Golfrido was out of the house, camped with sheep or elk hunting or deer hunting or dove hunting or fishing or gambling the damned hand game with the Indians or jake-leg with the Italians all the time, summer, winter, spring, and fall. Magda also supposed, regretfully, that she had no one but herself to blame for VJ's temperament. She was worried about her boy. The psychward image was scary. She prayed, as only mothers can, that handsome as he was, VJ would attract a girl with the resources to hold him. A good woman would inevitably get rid of those hideous cowboy shirts and banish the reek of poultry. VJ had imagination but needed the anchoring and guidance a good woman could provide. Fanny was such a woman. She could do it if she could only relax, slow down, let her many charms operate. Unfortunately, that did not seem likely, thanks to the shabby fathering of that old devil, Golfrido.

Magda stood in VJ's path. She looked at him and gave herself over to worry, actually wringing her hands as the pleasant glow from the night before drained out of her. VJ was alarmed and then annoyed. It is never pleasant to have your mother stand in your way and wring her hands at you. VJ sensed that at any moment his mother was going to say something he didn't want to hear. The only sure way to avoid having her say something would be for him to say something. He cast about for a topic.

"Mama, what is wrong with Rosa?"

"Rosa? Nothing's wrong with Rosa. I can't say when I've ever seen her better. I guess she is going to marry young Ev, and I can't imagine a finer match. I haven't been worrying about Rosa. In fact I was just this minute . . ."

VJ interrupted.

"What do you mean, Mama? She's been just terrible with Ev. Didn't you hear her? She accused him of being a pervert. He's miserable. He'd bolt if he wasn't stuck here. How did she ever get to be such a puritan? I remember how she was when I was a junior, Mama. Rosa had a reputation. Now you'd think she was the Virgin M . . ."

Now it was Magda's turn to interrupt.

"I'd hold it right there, young man. What your sister did or did not do several years ago was no concern of yours then and is no concern of yours now. Whether she knows it or not, she's doing what has to be done. She is letting Everett know that he needs to take steps to make himself fit for a woman. Maybe he's taking those steps, thinking things over. I certainly think he'd be a fine match for Rosa, but *I'm* not contemplating sharing my life with him."

"Well, she has a damned funny way of showing anything."

"Oh, VJ, you don't know a thing. Listen. At their very best, men are drawn in the wrong directions. Just imagine what Ev would be like if he hung out with the Colonel. He'd be out every morning shouting at dogs, living off of beer and Slim

Jims, renting a little unkempt apartment, stoking himself up on porn, and wondering why women wouldn't have anything to do with him. He'd hang out at gun shows and car races. Most role models for little boys are no better than the Colonel, and girls know enough to be wary. Your father is another good example. All *your* life he's been a fine man, a good husband, a wonderful father, an important man who's widely admired and respected." Magda paused and, for dramatic emphasis, drew a deep breath.

"Well, when I met him, he was a pirate. Oh, I know it's a family joke to you, but you weren't confronted with the prospect of marrying him. He seemed truly incorrigible. Well, he wasn't, but he'd sure moved a long way from the mores of decent civilization. Don't ever think I didn't set him a course to run. A woman has to determine whether or not a man can be forged into a husband. Your father, I determined, did have the seeds of decency in him, unruly, arrogant, and egocentric as he was.

"You know, VJ, unmarried men should never have guns or money. I hate to think of the people your father killed fighting in Spain. Oh, sure, he'll say it was war, fighting fascism. But I'll swear, Sabine and those cousins of his! They were like a motorcycle gang. I can imagine the women they managed to find and shack. Thank God I didn't have to endure him while he was actually involved in all that. The point being that he knew when he married me, he had to put an end to his shenanigans."

"What does that have to do with . . . ? Those magazines didn't even belong to Ev."

"It doesn't matter, VJ. Ev has to respond. It's a primitive thing. He's got to get her confidence, show her that he won't run wild, go off half-cocked, like some people I could mention."

VJ was feeling queasy, dizzy, a bit like Ev had felt earlier when VJ was teasing him. It was galling to hear such things before breakfast, especially from his mom. As regards Ev, it didn't make much sense. Ev didn't drink or play the horses or set up Jojobalueca schemes or go to LA to be on *Jeopardy,* or even buy ostriches, damn him.

"What's wrong with *men,* Mama? I never knew you were so down on men. And if you want to criticize me, then just say so."

Magda rolled her eyes, feeling hot anger flush her neck.

"For the love of God, VJ, I'm talking about Ev. Don't invite me to talk about you unless you're ready to sit down for a few hours. I've resisted the temptation to talk about you and your behavior. I can't believe how rude you were to poor Fanny last night. Why you could not hold still for five minutes, let her calm down, and have a nice conversation is beyond me. I cannot say that I envy the young woman you end up with, and all this has nothing to do with being down on men. I'm not down on men. I dearly love men, even old bounders like the Colonel. And I know what men are. They need women to develop emotionally, or they end up like the Colonel, a menace to society. Now I don't think much of Rosa's style, but the impulse was right. She's taking care of herself and her future babies."

Magda moved on. The talk with VJ was getting tiresome, and she had other fish to fry. She swept past her son, trailing lilac satin and poodles. Over her shoulder, she added a postscript, a patented smart bomb so favored by the Eckleberry women.

"Forget about Rosa and Everett, Virgil. You'll soon have enough to think about with this ranch on your hands. Your father will be with me in Arizona for a time, and he's expecting you to manage the ranch. I figure he'll buy a few thousand sheep for you to fatten."

VJ was left literally reeling. It is odd how, in moments of crisis, the mind finds clarity. It has to do, one supposes, with self-preservation.

VJ's eyes were itching. Allergies. He was allergic to the molasses in the chicken feed. Beyond that, the young Basque was keenly aware of the rich poultry smell of ostrich that hung about him. It clung like a dead man's curse to his hair, his clothes, his skin. My God, how he hated that smell.

All this, he realized, was because of the damned ostrich. What madness! Was he destined for this, to be stuck on this, this sheep farm with Fanny Ulibarri poised to swoop down on him any minute? It was too much to bear, even though she was Golfrido's daughter. Worse than the prospect of Fanny Ulibarri showing up to gab were the sheep. Thousands, his mother said; yes, thousands of brainless, pathetic sheep. What animals they were! Appalling! Thousands of bloody sheep and only him between them and oblivion. How is it possible to grasp the despair that young VJ experienced? VJ knew sheep.

No one would ever characterize sheep as creative creatures, but in one endeavor they are incredibly resourceful. They are always finding fresh, exciting new ways to expose themselves to mortal danger. A good example of this was the bunch of sheep that the donkey Vera had so recently ejected from the kitchen pen. They continued to hustle along up the stream, now on one side, now on the other. With determination, sheep can cover ground. They followed the little stream for two more miles. At that spot, four miles from the ranch and fifteen from the highway, there is a railroad bridge across the stream. As is customary, tracks lead in both directions away from the bridge. The tracks are set on cross ties that disrupt the delicate ecology of the topsoil in a way that's auspicious to the growth of Russian thistle (tumbleweeds). Although the passage of trains limited the size of the weeds, their abundance made their size irrelevant. Growing between the tracks, they stretched out both east and west as far as the eye could see.

The sheep were famished. Darting in front of pink Cadillacs does work up an appetite. They began cropping the tumbleweeds, following the train tracks eastward as though resolved to eat their way along that line of nutritious weeds to the New Jersey shore. Two of the sheep were slow to recover from the trauma of being twice ejected from the kitchen pen. Unlike their contented comrades, this pair wandered aimlessly about the tracks, first on one side, then the other. They stayed close to the others, ready to join them on or between the tracks in case of danger.

The little knot of sheep ate tumbleweeds all evening in unconscious celebration of Sabine's birthday. They bedded down where they'd been feeding and awoke invigorated and ready to spend the day slowly eating their way east. Unless someone intervened, a train would be along at about 2:30 P.M. and all the sheep would be killed.

The habits of sheep were at the root of VJ's despair. Drained and dispirited after the conversation with his mother, he'd let the Colonel feed his ostrich. Why not? he thought. Nature had forged a bond. Who was he to pull asunder what nature had knit together? It took energy to defy the course of nature, energy and a cheerful disposition. He had neither. The Colonel wanted to feed the chick. "Fine," VJ said, "go right ahead." He lay down. He had a heavy feeling in his chest. Just breathing was an effort that did not seem entirely justified. It was not yet eight in the morning and every iota of energy had, for the moment, washed out of him. He was unable to summon the ambition even to have his breakfast.

He was thinking about sheep, and although his thoughts were general, he lingered over a notion he'd heard articulated by his father. Sheep should be called an endangered species. Left to their own devices, they'd be extinct in a generation. VJ agreed. In that sense, sheep were like a mirror opposite of Foreman, the alley cat who'd adopted him in Albuquerque. Foreman was practically immortal. He needed nothing and met all his own needs. On a whim he'd decided to befriend VJ, who'd ended up feeling honored. VJ sort of liked sheep.

They were guileless creatures that were often touching in their vulnerability. He was always able to sense their needs and ease their suffering, but how could a person respect them? Felice had nearly killed a bunch of them with her Cadillac. Where on earth had they come from? He could scarcely credit that it'd been the kitchen pen bunch. They'd gotten out twice and had been nervous, restless, when VJ'd inspected them before the trip to Womynscraft. Could they have gotten out again? He'd have to check it out as soon as he rallied himself sufficiently to finish breakfast. At any rate, someone needed to locate the bunch that'd nearly wrecked poor Felice. Things at the ranch were even worse than he'd thought. Sabine might as well go to Arizona; he'd sure let things deteriorate in Nevada.

CHAPTER FIFTEEN

■ ■ ■

A new issue of *Stockman's Universe* arrived on Sabine's birthday. He'd set it aside, wanting to savor it during the especially gratifying solitude he would have once his family cleared out. Sex had changed all that. Sabine awoke rested, sated, with smug loins and cheery testicles. There was nothing he could imagine better than reading *Stockman's Universe* to extend this blissful state. Family be damned. It was his house and he'd, by God, sit and read a magazine at the breakfast table and drink coffee until ten if he damned well wanted. He could then, if it further pleased him, stroll out and spend the remainder of the morning watching donkeys and working up the energy for some siesta-time nookie with the missus.

The idea of watching donkeys was so appealing that Sabine went out on his porch to have an early gander. He stopped by the can and took a quick, profuse, and satisfying leak. Unlike the unfortunate Colonel, Sabine did not strain for dribbles but simply let fly with a glorious stream. He then went out onto the porch wearing only his shorts. He watched Magda. She was leaning up against the kitchen-pen fence watching the donkeys. A warm rush in his belly moved to his face. How had he managed to survive without her? Plenty of women, he supposed, carried into their sixties and beyond a modest nubility, a discreet hypersexuality that'd keep things lively. Lots of women similarly mellowed into good companions. He had to admit that men were the ones most likely to turn irascible and difficult as the years wore on; look at how old Golfrido'd got before he died. The question that remained was: how many women could an old man find who'd share a partiality for fine donkeys? The odds were not promising, and for that reason, Sabine figured he was an extraordinarily lucky man.

The way she watched those burros! There was a kind of purity to it, a perfection of regard, a surrender. She leaned against the fence as though she could remain there content until nightfall. Her entire being communicated that, in her view, nothing on earth was more worth doing than watching those donkeys. She soon walked away, of course; such moments always pass quickly. Magda Zumwalt was one in a million, that was for sure. The miracle was that he was already married to her. He'd let her almost slip away from him, too. He'd damned sure not let that happen again. This conviction was disturbing. Regaining his wife would inevitably compromise his liberty. Life under any roof with any woman meant sacrifice, impoverished options. It was no wonder that most Basques of Sabine's father's generation spent so much time out of doors, under the raw sky, away from their wives. Sabine was ready. He'd go into the thing with open eyes. He'd give up a parcel of freedom, but look what he'd have! What a woman!

While Magda encountered VJ outside the feed shed, Sabine continued to watch the donkeys. It was sure nice having some donkeys in the kitchen pen. A man got sick of just seeing that murky little knot of damned sheep. Sabine had never considered himself a shepherd. He was no good with them. He was a sheep rancher who hired shepherds, men who owned nothing, who had no aptitude for ownership. They simply worked. He took the risks and the profits.

As he reminded himself daily, Sabine was cut out best for a life at sea. That was the Basques. The dull, stalwart ones became shepherds, while the lively ones cut loose and went to sea. He'd made a good start in that direction during the war, but the war ended far too soon. His inability to think of anything better to buy than a sheep ranch probably meant he deserved it. It was about the most unimaginative thing a Basque could do. It was on account of his old man, really. Joanes had been a shepherd all his life. Sabine had bought the ranch because of him. The old man had died owning sixty-five acres and the god-awfullest bunch of patchwork leases you ever saw. What an old dictator. Was it something about the Iberian Peninsula that spawned them? The nerve of the old man, sending him off to Argentina to avoid the draft. Well, Sabine was glad he hadn't been drafted, but he'd hated to have missed the war. In addition to packing the resentful Sabine off on his draft-dodging journey to Argentina, Joanes was inconsiderate enough to die while he was gone. Sabine bore a heavy burden of guilt. He had struck Joanes, raised his hand to him! Joanes, of course, had knocked Sabine around a bit with his *makila*. The parting had been bitter and wordless. Buying the ranch had been Sabine's attempt to atone.

Sabine frowned in the direction of the kitchen pen, aggravated beyond reason at his long-dead father. If the old man had lived six months more, Sabine would have bought a ship or two. After the war there were plenty of surplus vessels around to buy for a song and fix up for commerce! He'd have sailed on into San Francisco harbor and made his father come on board. But no. When he learned that his father was dead, Sabine knew that he had to buy a sheep ranch, the sheep ranch his dad would have liked to leave him. He found this reasoning impossible to explain to anyone who was not a Basque, while there was no need to explain the choice to any Basque of his generation. It was the obvious thing to do. His cousins had all bought sheep ranches as well, and none of them had the excuse of a father to bury. You'd think that one of them would have bought a ship or a small fleet maybe. He supposed that he was the only one who'd really loved the sea. For most Basques in the Americas, money meant five things: sheep, sheep, sheep, sheep, and land for sheep. Well, he had all five and yearned for the free life of the sailor. He thought about it almost every day. Having the donkeys was some consolation. He'd probably never have gotten those donkeys if he'd been a ship skipper, nor Magda, for that matter.

At this point in his reflections, Sabine began to think of the sheep that'd gone missing from the kitchen pen. How on earth they'd managed to escape was beyond his capacity to understand. The kitchen pen was the showpiece of the ranch, meticulously and expensively fenced. Sheep! They can be trapped in a two-sided enclosure. If they blunder into a rock wall that corners around, they cannot figure out what to do. They will stand there and look at that wall until they start dying. They will not simply turn around and walk away. Fence a pen, however, at the cost of several thousand dollars and the damned creatures become escape artists. Now someone would have to find them. That'd be VJ. Annoying though he was, VJ certainly was a champ at finding sheep.

Rosa stood for a moment watching her dad watch her mother watching burros. He was standing there in his shorts. They were holey ones and none of the cleanest either. He was incorrigible. She scanned her father's body, making medical, moral, and aesthetic judgments. From the thinning mane of lank, uncombed hair, through the burgeoning billows of his midriff, and on to his gnarled and troubled feet, the old bird was a mess. Rosa was pleased and relieved that the task of riding herd on the old guy was soon to revert to a real expert.

She felt warm inside, immensely satisfied. Thanks to her, her parents' separation was over. She went into the kitchen and put on coffee.

A few minutes later, Sabine was still there, glaring and frowning at the new pen.

"That new fence offending you, Daddy?"

"Hmm . . . Oh! No, Daisy, it's the sheep; they're gone."

She looked. Sure enough, no sheep had magically appeared. "Maybe they don't like the donkeys, Daddy. They sure have gotten slippery since those donkeys arrived."

"Who the hell knows?" Sabine walked into the kitchen shaking his head and scratching his hairy, pasty chest.

"VJ's going to have to go get them."

"Well, I hope he takes his friend with him."

"Whoa there, Rosie Daisy. Mama tells me you're going to marry that boy."

Rosa felt her knees go all wobbly. Was she still unable to get a grip on herself? "Well, Daddy, he has to ask me first, doesn't he?"

Sabine allowed as to how that *was* customary, if sexist and old-fashioned.

Rosa did not usually take that kind of guff, but she was not usually quite so agitated and vulnerable.

"To tell you the truth, I am so ashamed of how I acted last night that I don't want to run into him. That's why I hope to hell that VJ takes him along."

"I told you about that vulgarity, Daisy; young men don't like it."

Rosa felt a tingling in the palm of her right hand. She imagined how it'd feel to give the old man a good smack upside the head. Dealing with animals, especially horses, you sometimes had to give them a smart little pop to get their attention. The regimen was not likely to make Sabine more biddable but might be worth a try.

"It's all that men of any age *do* like, apparently." She smiled maliciously, getting more and more angry that he was taking advantage of the unhappy situation to harp on her rough language. She fixed him with her coldest stare.

"Anyway, it has nothing to do with me cursing. I never used foul language around Everett. How can . . ."

Sabine watched his youngest daughter. Her complexion had gone motley and her jaw was clamped. Sabine did not like to have his daughters so angry, especially so early in the day. He was still in his shorts, after all, wanting nothing more than a quiet moment to survey his new livestock. Rosa looked mad enough to yell for reinforcements. If Celia and Felice showed up, there'd be hell to pay. All of them carried inexplicable, unreasoning anger toward him.

"Whoa, *mi hijita*," he said, "I was joking. So you're serious about this boy?"

"I guess, Daddy. I just don't know. It's humiliating. I can't control myself. First, I kissed him, and I hadn't meant to do that. It was embarrassing. Later, when I saw that porn, I went ape-shit. It was scary. I couldn't stop myself. I just ripped into him. Now I find out it wasn't even his."

She took a deep breath, let it out through pursed lips, and continued. The source of her attachment to Ev was mystifying, a puzzle that Rosa found alarming. She wanted to explain it, if only to herself.

"I've always thought he was decent, but for years I never paid him a whole lot of attention. I was grateful that he'd helped VJ get out of some jams, but that was all. Now there's something more. I'm drawn to him. He is a very considerate person, and he's so in charge of himself. He knows his mind, he knows what he can do. It's a strength, Daddy; you know, you have it."

"Sure do," Sabine replied. The anger that had almost passed in the earnestness of the conversation flashed up again in Rosa's eyes. Sabine did not seem to notice. He continued, "So, is he good enough for you?"

That was better. The question was proper, paternal. It was also a question she'd considered at length.

"Well, I think so, I guess. We've all known him all his life. He's always been very thoughtful, sincere, and kind, even when VJ got him in that FFA trouble. Mama thinks he's great. He's grown on me all of a sudden, and I guess I've gotten over thinking that I had to have a glamorous guy, a movie-star type. I always talk with him when VJ's off chasing his dreams. I got to where I look forward to VJ's escapades just to have a chance to see Ev. And then when I kissed him . . ."

"No more, *mi hija*, no more. In my father's generation, men reacted in a rage when their daughters . . . You keep the kisses to yourself. What I want to know is *if he is good enough. Me comprendes?"*

"Yes, Daddy, he is." Rosa was suddenly pleased and even a little teary. Emotionally, she was still all over the map.

"Well then, pour him into the funnel."

In moments like this, Rosa remembered with some asperity that her father was still deeply embedded in a foreign culture. "What?" she said, her mouth falling open.

"Close it, Daisy, close it; a pretty girl should not gape like that. I mean the forces of nature are all the same. A funnel uses gravity to direct and control. The outcome is never at issue. Figure it out! Now if that boy is drawn to you, then that force can be used to direct and control. As he gets nearer to you, you see to it that he has fewer and fewer options. Finally he will have but one choice, he will ask the question."

Sabine was making it up on the spot, spinning it out. The coffee that Rosa'd put on filled his nostrils with a rich, thick smell; it was a bit heady.

"All you have to do," he went on, "is form the funnel, the pathway to the marriage bed. You simply have to know yourself, trust your instincts, and show resolve. He cannot help but follow the pull of his nature. Think of those sheepdogs they train in Wyoming. They move those little woolies by sheer strength of will and unfailing intent. They move back and forth to show the sheep the funnel. The sheep follow their inclination to wander and end up in the pen the dog intends for them."

Rosa bit her lip. Just like Sabine to take off on a tangent. She never should have mentioned kissing Everett to her father. The old guy could simply not handle it. It was endearing in a way, however exasperating Sabine might be with his advice. She nodded pensively as though attentive.

Sabine had let his jaws flap. It was the promise of coffee that'd excited the funnel business. Rosa needed no prompting as regards the application of will. As he spoke, Sabine felt an odd sensation, a buzzing in his ears. A moment later he had to sit down. He walked into his "office" and lowered himself heavily into the hammock. He drew a deep breath in his attempt to cope with a startling realization. Magda was sheep-dogging him! Like Ev and the sheep in his story, Sabine was in the funnel. He was moving inexorably toward a given spot, a pen . . . in this case Scottsdale, Arizona.

Rosa was alarmed. One minute, her father had been garrulous, in his customary fashion, full of hot air. Before her eyes he'd seemed to wilt, staggering into his lair and collapsing into his hammock, his skin suddenly pallid and moist.

"I don't have a tan," he said. "How can I sit around swimming pools and talk about operations and investments?" Rosa narrowed her gaze.

"Here, Daddy, let's have breakfast." She wondered whether he might have had a minor stroke. She felt guilty for allowing him to have that steak and cigar on the way back from the penitentiary. It'd been a calculated risk.

Sabine was far from alert to his daughter's concern. He'd just gotten those donkeys; how did Magda expect him to go to Arizona when he had new animals to train?

"Can you and young Crume run this ranch?" he asked.

Now Rosa was truly alarmed. Did he think he was dying?

Was he all right? He certainly looked like a beached whale distending the poor hammock. What was he doing, wandering around giving advice before he'd had a bite of breakfast?

Up close his shorts were utterly revolting. Her mother, thank goodness, would get him to change his shorts every day if he lived. Rosa was starting to feel a bit hysterical. She'd tried to care for him, but there were limits. Those shorts were an indictment. She'd not hesitate to make Everett change his shorts on a daily basis. Why was it so hard for her to insist on an acceptable level of personal hygiene from her father?

"Just look at those shorts," she said.

Sabine looked at his shorts. "I don't own a swimming suit."

At that moment VJ walked into the room looking even more pale and drawn than his father. "Let's have some breakfast, Daddy," he said. "Swimming suit or no, you've got to eat. You look like hammered horse pucky."

Sabine considered his only son, and despite the boy's solicitous behavior, he felt the anger rise bitterly in his throat. The boy was a ninny, good only for shepherding, a terrible disappointment, irredeemable, skinny . . . it was a miracle he'd drawn the attention of Golfrido's girl. Sabine felt that it was a disgrace to have fathered a son who had more attention for ugly, flightless birds than available, interested, and comely women like Fanny Ulibarri. Despite the featherbrained yakety-yak, the girl could be a keeper if VJ gave her half a chance. Now, on top of all that, the boy was evidently in the grips of a neurotic malaise. He had a fresh patch of eczema flaming out on his forehead. Sabine again felt the conviction that he'd been right to threaten the boy with a fork. No one with a fork at hand in such circumstances would have done otherwise.

"You don't look like much yourself, Son," he muttered. He rolled out of the hammock and pulled on a pair of ample denim trousers. He looked wistfully at the copy of *Stockman's Universe* sticking out of the pile of papers and business on his desk. He'd thought it was on top. It was amazing how quickly things piled up. The day had started so well and deteriorated so quickly. He had to face the concrete fact of his situation. Besides having an idiot for a son, his wife was trying to shanghai him to Arizona.

Rosa rushed off to make coffee, distressed that her father was evidently going to spend another day in those indecent shorts.

Ev dressed that morning feeling a good deal of resentment about *his* shorts. VJ had the nerve to criticize his shorts. Here he was awaking in the ashes of futile hopes and VJ decides to ridicule his attachment to Rosa and razz him about his shorts. If Ev was wearing holey shorts, it was VJ's fault. It was his ostrich project that'd sent them off on the chase to Womynscraft. It was his fault that they'd all become permeated to the bone with bouquet of ostrich. Finally, it'd been his bossy, unpredictable, dangerous, and damnably appealing sister who'd forced Ev to burn his best shorts. It was a sad thing to have but one decent pair of shorts, but it was sadder yet to lose them in such a humiliating way. It was intolerable then, to put up with breezy banter about holey shorts. It was a sore point, especially when a certain person's ostrich had made it impossible to get any sleep.

Anyone with the smallest measure of good sense and self-esteem would wash his hands of the entire family, and that's exactly what Ev intended to do. It hurt to give up his hopes, but that's what he got for allowing himself such latitude. He'd yearned for Rosa from afar for longer than he wanted to admit. She was always VJ's beautiful, inaccessible older sister, and that's what she still was! She'd kissed him once, an obvious mistake, and he'd been foolish enough to spin fantasies. It was time to get back to reality. Rosa Eckleberry, for all her fine qualities, was a poor choice anyway for one scrawny, impulsive, unreliable reason. Even if she were the sweetest, most solicitous girl in Nevada, marriage to her would bind a

man forever to her half-wit brother. Ev was not a metaphysi-
cian, but he'd managed to gain a profound understanding of
the nature of hell. Hell was the schemes, insults, and idiot
optimism of Virgil Jose Eckleberry.

Ev crawled into his tight, uncomfortable jeans and limped
about on his still-blistered feet. He wished, in a way, that he'd
burned all his clothes. It was stupid to wear western-style
clothes. It was a holdover from high school and that idiotic
FFA business with VJ. Let VJ dress like a damned cowboy.
Ev had moved on. He was in college, a business major, after
all, and ought to look preppy. He'd probably soon have the
chance. He was, no doubt, reeking of ostrich, having spent the
night with one. Rosa would soon be insisting that he bury,
burn, or otherwise dispose of his remaining clothes. So he'd
be needing a new wardrobe. He envisioned sweaters, blazers,
striped ties.

He pulled a tee shirt over his head. It was a University of
New Mexico "Go Lobos" tee shirt that he liked a lot. It did
not seem to smell. His mood began to improve. The crowd
of colonels and ostriches had thinned out considerably, and
that was certainly a happy turn of events. The Colonel had
dumped the *Penthouse* and *Hustler* magazines off of the milk
crate VJ was using to cage the little ostrich. He'd then set the
creature free. The little ostrich, to Ev's surprise, did not run
about the room. Instead, it focused its attention on the Colonel. It followed him back and forth to the bathroom and finally left when the Colonel left, hustling after the unpleasant
old fart, plainly single-minded in its choice of companions.

By the time Ev headed up to the ranch house for breakfast,
he was brooding and resigned. Eckleberry pathology and eccentricity would concern him no more. Celia and Felice were
sniping at one another while they prepared their expensive
automobiles for the trip home. Felice had sopped up Kronen's
pee and opened the Cadillac's doors and windows so it could
air out. Her kids were whining to leave; they wanted to go

home. Kronen was doing his best to keep tensions high. He was biting at the tires of Celia's Mercedes. Seven or eight children milled around their mothers, playing, shouting, singing, whining, crying. Some were sick, some were cross, and all were outspoken about their concerns. Ev regarded the scene with detached amusement. At least he'd not be fathering reinforcements to the Eckleberry grandchildren's melee.

Felice gave Ev some Mary Kay brochures along with her 800 number and her fax number to give to his mother. Celia was making cracks about the "cult of Mary Kay" Felice had joined. She also had things to say about the way that Mary Kay tested their cosmetics on animals. Just as the conflict was at the point of serious escalation, the donkeys down in the field set up a deafening commotion, braying at the top of their lungs. In Ev's view, it was an appropriate commentary.

Ev smiled his first smile of the morning. He recalled something he'd seen the day before. He'd been sitting in the Cherokee waiting for VJ and the Colonel before taking off for the ostrich ranch. One of the donkeys had caught a sheep, carried it to the fence, and dropped it on the other side. It'd seemed odd, but the demeanor of both donkey and sheep had been quite casual. He'd supposed they were consenting adults. Who was he to stand in judgment? With the Eckleberrys, it paid to adopt a laissez-faire attitude as regards peculiar behavior. If the Eckleberry animals carried one another around, it was certainly not his business. In the subsequent rush of events, he'd forgotten about the incident as the day wore on. The braying brought it back. He'd have to ask Sabine about it. Sabine, he supposed, was the donkey expert. What a family!

At the ranch house, he found VJ and Sabine eating oatmeal at the dining room table. Ev, ever sensitive to subtle colorings of emotion, sensed a certain tension in the room. VJ was in a world of his own, twisting at his hair and taking advantage of the lovely view out the picture window. Sabine pecked at the oatmeal in a desultory fashion, a trencherman obviously off his feed. The table was covered with dirty dishes, the unmistakable remains of Celia's and Felice's tribes' early breakfast. Sabine raised his head and indicated the kitchen with his eyebrows. Ev could find himself some breakfast if that was his ambition.

It was. He walked into the kitchen and came face-to-face with Rosa. She was carrying coffee, three cups.

"Er . . ." he said. It was not much, but certainly embodied his best effort.

"Uh . . ." Rosa replied, likewise giving her all.

Time passed. Rosa stood with her coffee as though her shoes had suddenly adhered to the floor. Ev let his stomach do the talking. It gurgled loudly. He was very hungry.

"Thought I'd have some oatmeal."

"That sounds good." She replied without moving.

"I expect the oatmeal is in one of the cabinets?"

"Yes, the one above the blender."

"Oh."

"Yes, that's the regular oatmeal; you have to cook it five minutes. The kids ate all we cooked. The instant oatmeal is in the cabinet above the microwave. If you can wait, maybe I'll cook another pot of the regular oatmeal. The instant is pretty bad, mushy." Rosa felt like falling to her knees in abject apology. She resisted the impulse. She should have resisted her impulses earlier on. She did not have much talent or grace when it came to emotional outbursts. Instead, she tried to communicate her contrition through her concern that Ev might have to eat mushy oatmeal.

The gesture was almost lost on Everett Crume. He was dying of hunger and mushy oatmeal sounded good. He did not want to wait for Rosa to deliver her coffee and then cook oatmeal at her leisure. He frowned.

"Why don't you have some toast to tide you over," she went on. "There's bread on the cutting board."

Ev was relieved. Now he didn't have to risk an argument by

insisting on instant. "Okay," he said. He sensed, or thought he sensed, a small rapprochement. He needed to respond in kind. "Sleep okay?"

"Yes, fine. How did you sleep?"

"Well, I slept fine, too. VJ kept me up some with the ostrich, but I slept fine when I was able to sleep."

"Good. So I'll be back in a minute and make the oatmeal."

"Okay."

Rosa finally uprooted herself and took the coffee to Celia and Felice, who were preparing their cars for the trip home.

Ev and Rosa's prebreakfast discussion was brief, but what it lacked in length it more than made up for in awkwardness. It was an effortful business that left both of them drained. Ev needed more sustenance than he felt toast would provide. He found the instant oatmeal, sure enough just where Rosa had said it would be. His hands shaking, he managed to fill a bowl and get it into the microwave. If Rosa made more, he'd eat more. For now the instant would do. Sugaring it, he lost count of how many spoons he'd added. He joined VJ and Sabine at the table with a thoroughly sugared bowl of oatmeal.

"So you think you are going to marry my daughter, you son of a bitch?" Sabine said blandly.

The tone of the statement was so mild that Ev concluded Sabine hadn't really said what it sounded like he said.

"Sir?"

"I said, So you think you are going to marry my daughter, you son of a bitch?"

It had indeed sounded like that. Ev was at a loss. What a thing to say! The topic seemed to cheer VJ. He smiled broadly at his old friend.

"Oh," Ev was finally able to say. He took a bite and let the question loom in the harrowing silence. He swallowed the oatmeal without even noticing the high sugar content. "Mr. Eckleberry," he finally said, "I can't talk until I finish my breakfast."

Sabine did not reply but slurped at his coffee. He was glad that Ev had joined them. It took his mind off of Arizona.

VJ began whistling "Fly Me to the Moon."

Ev ate his oatmeal in a robotic fashion, wondering if Rosa had heard Sabine's question. He could see her sitting just beyond the screen door on the porch. She was drinking her coffee and taking the morning sun. Rosa was trying to regain her composure. She'd forgotten about having volunteered to make oatmeal.

In that light, the sideways light of a summer morning in the high desert, Rosa Eckleberry gave off a glow like precious metal. Small wonder, Ev thought, that Sabine would be protective, hostile to prospective suitors. Who could be worthy of such a woman? It was sad that he was mistaken. Ev did not think he was going to marry Rosa. All of this, naturally, was more of VJ's doing. They'd kissed once and VJ considered them engaged. No doubt he'd shared his conclusion with Sabine. The oatmeal fortified Ev. He went to the kitchen and got himself a cup of coffee. When he returned, he spoke.

"Mr. Eckleberry," he said, "I haven't even dated your daughter. I might have liked to, but, to put it mildly, she isn't interested. When we arrived, Rosa and I greeted one another with a kiss that . . . well, it didn't come to anything. VJ seems to have jumped to some conclusions based on that greeting. If I wanted to marry a girl, I would do her and her family the courtesy of courting her openly."

Sabine did not reply at once, but he was impressed. The boy was very nicely spoken and seemed sincere. Why wasn't VJ able to absorb some small percentage of these qualities? Well, perhaps he would in time. It was clear to Sabine that Rosa was in love with this youngster and would probably marry him. Things could happen, of course, to change that, but she'd moved further in that direction than he'd have believed possible on the day they got the donkeys. As regards Ev, Sabine had, of course, known him practically since infancy as

VJ's best friend, but he hadn't assessed the boy as a prospective son-in-law. He needed to probe a bit more, but felt optimistic. Magda felt that young Crume was a good bet, and that counted for a lot.

"Well, young man," he said enjoying himself again, "maybe you're right and I do have a mistaken impression. I am an old man. I'll check it out. But I figure it's possible that *you* might just be wrong one way or another. Maybe you ought to check it out too."

Sabine felt very much the patriarch as he concluded his conversation with young Crume. It was a new role in relation to this boy. It warmed Sabine, braced him. He straightened his shoulders and wondered if he shouldn't, after all, grow a moustache. If he was going to continue to act like Anthony Quinn, then he might as well look the part. Young Crume had obviously benefited enormously from the discussion. He'd come in hunched, dispirited, and flabby. Now he stood erect, met Sabine's gaze, and had a solid, stout appearance. A marshmallow had changed, before Sabine's eyes, into a pillar. Sabine noted that he'd relied entirely on Magda's assessment of the young man. Sure he'd continue to run tests, like the son-of-a-bitch test, just for form's sake, but he wouldn't really need to. Magda's word was all it took, and she'd told him during a brief interlude in their night of passion that Everett was just the one for Rosa. The conversation with Rosa had pretty much cinched it. Sabine trusted Rosa almost as much as he trusted Magda. Rosa was bossy, but most men, Sabine knew full well, needed a ration, a healthy ration, of bossing. Sadly, bossing was a resource that few men were wise enough to appreciate. Few managed to reap the benefits that a strongly voiced feminine directive could provide. Bossy women clarified things. Sabine himself seldom obeyed them but always appreciated the gesture. Most men either fought or caved. Everett would manage. Rosa would keep him honest, but she'd not take him over. He could hold the line.

It was time to find Magda. Sabine had business of his own to settle, now that he'd exerted some chiropractics into the little block that'd developed between Rosa and young Crume.

Ev stood silently, astounded, impressed, and giddy. He did not have to ask for a translation. Mr. Eckleberry had given him permission and encouragement. If he could engage Rosa's affections, Sabine would support rather than hinder the match.

"You boys drink coffee for a while, if you want," Sabine said at length. "I have some business with my wife and a magazine to read. VJ, I'd like for you to find the little bunch of sheep that I was keeping in the kitchen pen. They got out sometime yesterday. You might walk the fence when you get back. I can't understand how and where they are getting out. That fence ought to be the most secure fence in the county. It is damned well the most expensive. If you can spare some time away from your bird, I'd appreciate it."

VJ mumbled in assent. There was something wrong there. It was unlike VJ to be so quiet. It made Sabine a little uneasy. His customary enthusiasm was half-baked but predictable. It was not like VJ to go through breakfast without an exasperating outburst or two.

Ev spoke up. "The donkeys have been dropping the sheep over the fence. I saw the large gray one doing it yesterday." Now it was Sabine's turn to gape.

VJ came out of his fog. "Didn't you read those articles, Daddy? You're supposed to keep the burros and sheep separate for a while. You put them in separate pens, right next to each other, until they get used to being together. Then, one by one, you separate the donkeys. You put each of them with a few hundred sheep separate from each other. There are reasons for those procedures, Daddy. Can't you see that it irritates donkeys to all of a sudden have a bunch of fool sheep underfoot? I remember reading about that trick with the sheep. Donkeys are not real patient with sheep, not at first. I swear, this place is going to hell, Daddy. If you want those donkeys to work, you have to put in the time to do the introductions properly. All you've been doing is working on getting Mama into the hammock with you. It was obvious that those sheep were ready to spook and run. I noticed that they were ringy the minute I laid eyes on 'em. I'd better get going. I'll need to take the twenty-foot livestock trailer. They probably covered fifty miles just out of sheer nervousness. I'll bet it was them that ran Felice off the road yesterday. I'll get them. I got nothing better to do anyway. The Colonel's got the ostrich and I am going to call the project quits. I'll see if the Colonel wants the bird. If not, I'll take it back to Tina and Jessie. I don't suppose they'll give the money back but I don't care. Any fool can see that it's not going to work." He walked out the door, strode to his pickup, started it, and drove carefully off, giving Celia and Felice, who were still arguing with one another while attempting to load and leave, a wide berth.

Sabine and Everett watched with matching startled expressions. Neither of them could recall VJ behaving in such a fashion. There was something eerie in the way he'd driven out of the driveway. He hadn't even raised any dust.

"What on earth," Sabine said, speaking not so much to Everett as to the universe at large, "could that ostrich chick have done to him?"

"I don't know," Ev replied in the same grave tone. "Something." The men stood for a while, watching VJ's pickup move sedately away. It was an unsettling sight.

Rosa managed to slip away unnoticed while her father was talking to Everett. She was still blushing, and her heart was pounding. She could even feel her pulse in her nipples, and that was very weird. Naturally, she found herself drawn to the donkeys. There is almost nothing more calming to a person in a high state of agitation than a few moments of watching donkeys. Petting donkeys, in fact, is an activity known to have superior soothing powers. Although Rosa would not have been able to articulate these laws of nature, she sensed their truth on an intuitive level.

Bo was already her favorite. She wanted to stroke his ears and avoid Vera. She had an unresolved power struggle, after all, with Vera, a struggle she was not at all sure she could win. Anyway, she just didn't feel like conflict of any kind. Vera's inner sweetness rested inside a shell of nervous irascibility. Elvis and Capitán were okay but just didn't have the solid appeal of little old Bo. She was very offended that her father wanted to name him Che. You don't name a sweetheart after a warrior, and little Bo was a sweetheart, pure affection and contentment. The move had alarmed him but did not change his nature. He'd adapted and was at present as content with life as it is possible for a creature to be. Who could name such an animal after a revolutionary? If ever any being was completely complacent and satisfied with the status quo, it was this little black burro.

Just as Sabine had watched Magda watching the donkeys earlier that morning, Everett watched Rosa petting Bo, stroking his ears, allowing him to nuzzle her hair. Although the temperament of youth intensified the passion of the young man, Ev's experience mirrored Sabine's earlier revelation. How he had managed to survive so long without this woman mystified him. Until Ev watched Rosa petting Bo, he had been merely drawn to her. He longed for her as he'd longed for her when he was eight. Watching her in the kitchen pen, he felt a surge of sudden insight that added astounding new dimensions to his boyish yearnings. His sight dimmed and his heart raced as he realized that she was one in a million and that he was wildly, irredeemably in love. Every cell in his body announced it and began a spontaneous celebration. Poor Ev had trouble keeping his feet. That trouble intensified when he tried to walk. It was a shaky business but had to be done. Using powers he didn't know he had, he managed to make it all the way to the kitchen pen without sustaining a fall. It was a kind of miracle, especially since his feet were still paining him considerably. As he clambered over the expensive fence, however, his luck ran out. He fell heavily, but with a good deal of futile flailing. He landed smack on his back. He hit the ground with a good deal of force. Every molecule of air left his lungs, sending his chest muscles into a surprised and offended spasm.

Rosa was perhaps fifty yards away from Everett when he fell. She'd been so involved in petting Bo that she'd not seen Ev coming. When he fell, he dealt the earth a shivering blow that was followed by the sound made when a steam locomotive's piston moves. She responded immediately and was at Ev's side in seconds. The fall had been a great surprise to the celebrating cells. Needing air, they set up an immediate clamor. Ev opened his mouth to little effect. The wind was knocked out of him. Rosa took his hand in hers and gave it a squeeze. The combination of desperation, fear, pain, and intense happiness was too much for his large body to sustain for very long, although it seemed an eternity. His body sorted it all out rather quickly in clock time, and he drew a breath. He squeezed back on Rosa's hand and drew her toward him.

The kiss was a very tame, chaste affair compared to the lascivious display they'd made of themselves two days before. This short, sweet kiss was the most loving touch either of them had ever known. Their lips parted, and they spent a long time absorbing one another with their eyes. When they finally, by degrees, began to notice their surroundings, they saw that the four donkeys had gathered around them at the distance of no more than ten feet. Donkeys are worrisome creatures in times of crisis. They were alarmed that Ev had fallen. They were concerned that he'd barely moved and perplexed at the behavior of the other human. To donkeys, humans are interesting, often busy creatures, and it pays to keep an eye on them.

Just as Ev fell over the fence, Sabine chanced to take a

gander down at the kitchen pen. He was hoping to see his donkeys. The scene he witnessed would be with him until the day he died as an image of perfected earthly harmony and order. He saw the fall. He saw the single reserved kiss. He saw the young couple hand in hand, staring into one another's eyes, surrounded by an honor guard of benevolent donkeys. Getting those donkeys, he concluded, was one of the best decisions he'd ever made.

CHAPTER SIXTEEN

■ ■ ■

Yes, Sabine was getting goofy with pride in his donkeys. When Everett fell into the kitchen pen Sabine was alarmed, the fall was so heavy, the boy hit the ground so squarely. Marshaling his resources to go help young Crume, Sabine noted with relief that Rosa'd seen Ev fall and would be, no doubt, the first to his aid. Sabine quickly concluded that his help would be unnecessary, perhaps unwanted. He'd simply keep an eye on the boy, who lay like a birthing draft mare just inside the fence. Rosa arrived. As she tended to Ev's various needs, Sabine saw the donkeys converge on the downed man. Their concern was obvious and utterly altruistic. Rosa's solicitude was noble. Still, no woman wants to see her future husband break his neck by falling over a fence. The donkeys, having no such stake, stayed the course regardless. They kept a vigil. At length, Rosa stood up, and with infinite care, caution, and more main strength than Sabine would have expected from his younger daughter, she helped the still shaken, limping Everett Crume to his feet. The couple made their way toward the gate with Ev leaning a bit on Rosa. The donkeys followed. The entourage stopped from time to time for Rosa to stroke Ev's cheek or put her hand on his forehead. Only when the couple left the pen to sit beneath a tree nearby did the four burros return to the crucial business of grazing. Sabine was satisfied. It was nice, in a way, that the boy had fallen. It gave Sabine an opportunity to see his donkeys' stalwart reaction to an emergency.

Donkeys are noble, humane creatures. When, for example, through carelessness, misadventure, or harsh fate, a rider falls from a donkey's back, the donkey will stop. Often, the animal will then help the fallen rider in any number of ways. If the rider, for example, is disoriented or confused, his donkey will know what to do. Count on a donkey to get you home in times of adversity. Horses, by contrast, are apt to blithely depart when their rider sustains a fall. Horses like to cover ground and often have a laissez-faire attitude toward their riders. If humans insist on hurtling themselves to the ground and then want to lie there unconscious or groaning, most horses feel that they should be allowed to do so in complete privacy.

To be fair, even Sabine would admit that burros compare rather unfavorably with their tall cousins in some ways. Donkeys do lack a certain something in the area of speed. Speed can be overrated. Certainly it is not *always* crucial, and in the final analysis, donkeys are such forgiving mounts that a wise minority of knowledgeable equestrians esteem them above both horses and mules.

Seeing the evidence of a compassionate nature in his own animals, Sabine was deeply stirred. He wondered how many intoxicated riders through the millennia owed their long lives to donkeys. A donkey will not just walk off and let his owner, however drunk, die of exposure. Small wonder, Sabine smiled, that churchmen through the ages have invariably chosen donkeys as their preferred mounts.

When Everett fell, Sabine had been looking for Magda. She'd been at the kitchen pen earlier, enjoying the donkeys, petting them, scratching their ears, and so on. Perhaps she'd return. This seemed unlikely as long as Everett and Rosa stayed near the pen. Magda was not the kind of mother who'd butt into intimate situations. Sabine felt an urgent need to speak to his wife. This scheme to get him to Arizona was extremely distressing. He had to put an end to the notion or at least hinder it. He felt impatient, the collar of his shirt was tight, his pants were binding up around the waist, and his fingers smelled of tobacco, an unpleasant sensation that compromised the joy of a morning cigar. Sabine had choices. He could walk the ranch, searching every nook and cranny until he found her. Alternately, he could go inside and read *Stockman's Universe*. Despite his impatience, he decided that the wise course would be to wait. He might very well need all his energies to deal with Magda. Reading would preserve and perhaps even enhance energies that futile searching would certainly squander. A few minutes later, lulled by an informative but somewhat dry article on the economic consequences of the recent vesicular stomatitis quarantine, Sabine fell asleep.

Animals lead lives animated by purposes their owners seldom understand. Magda, for example, did not know that Champy, Joey, Sassy, and Moe were poodles with a mission. She was simply taking a walk, happy that her dogs so enjoyed the path by the stream. The dogs were actually on the trail of the sheep. Magda was pleased that the dogs were getting along with one another so nicely. She'd had a very nice walk, and if the dogs had the stamina to extend it a bit more, then she did too. She was glad that she'd made herself a quick breakfast, a peanut butter and honey sandwich, before taking off. They'd walked over a mile along the creek, and Magda, no longer the athlete she'd been at twenty-five, was getting a little tired, about ready to turn around. She'd seen VJ drive slowly by pulling one of the livestock trailers. This disturbing sight brought her up short. It was not like VJ to poke along like that. Almost at once, she dismissed the thought. Second-guessing VJ was seldom successful.

She was admiring a thick stand of willows when suddenly the four dogs quit sniffing about and took off at a dead run. They circled around the willows and made toward the road that Magda knew was there.

Moving as one, the four poodles charged up to the Colonel, who was one hundred yards to the north. Magda followed the poodles around the willow thicket. She could not see exactly what was going on. There was a flurry of frantic activity. She did see the Colonel grab something off of the ground and hold it to his chest. The four dogs were yammering hysterically, really raising hell. Magda, still dressed in her lilac caftan and flats, covered ground as fast as she could. When she arrived on the scene, the Colonel was under duress. The poodles circled around him like vultures with teeth, barking, lunging, and snapping. They had forgotten about the sheep; that trail was hours old anyway. They'd found something much more exciting. In his arms, the Colonel held the baby ostrich, which was wriggling strenuously and making every effort to bite the delirious poodles. For his part, the purple-faced Colonel was cursing and kicking at the dogs in a hypertensive frenzy. He looked like he might have a stroke.

"Get out of here, you god-damn little shits!" he screamed.

Magda felt a flush of hot anger. The Colonel was developing a nasty habit of kicking at her dogs. She opened her mouth to voice her opinion. She did not speak. In the present situation she did not feel that she could give much scope to her indignation. The dogs were offering undeniable provocation. She had to do something.

It took escalating threats and firm physical intimidation,

but Magda got the dogs under control. In fact, she'd resorted to the ultimate threat: she'd reached dramatically down and come up with a stout stick. Immediately the poodles lost confidence and backed off. Issuing a few halfhearted barks, they ran off in the direction of the house.

"Give me a hand," the Colonel snapped at Magda, the habit of command still obviously strong. "We need to see if those nasty little brutes have gotten to him. I think he's okay, but I'd feel a lot better if we could just give the poor thing a quick once-over."

"What shall I do?"

"Just see if he is wounded. Look close. Here, I'll hold a handful of the fluff. Do you see any blood or bruising?"

She looked closely, nothing. The Colonel grabbed another handful of downy fluff, again nothing. It was a tedious process. The Colonel fretted. "Poor little guy," he said. "Poor, poor little guy."

As far as Magda could see, the ungainly chick was fine, more calm, composed, and a good deal cuter in its homely way than the Colonel. He seemed distraught, going over and over the obviously sound body of the little ostrich.

"I hate to think what could have happened. Those brutes of yours would've lunched him. Poor little guy. I hope this doesn't make him sick. His immunes aren't up yet. It takes days. An attack like this, I don't know. Just imagine. The noise, the terrible fear. A baby bird like this. He's a patsy for those damned bullies."

Magda had heard about all she wanted of the Colonel's hysteria.

"Oh, for the love of God, Colonel McKenzie. They're little dogs! This bird is fine! Put him down and quit worrying at him. You are going to work yourself into a fit of some kind."

The Colonel continued to hold the bird, but he did quit grabbing handfuls of feathers.

"Bullshit, Magda. This could kill the little guy. Caution

pays. An ounce of prevention, you know. The woman at the ranch said that veterinarians don't know squat. These birds are not chickens. All the damned vets know are chickens. Those poodles are a lot bigger than this little guy. Imagine the nasty little shits if they were bigger, lunging and snapping like that. They'd have taken me down. I'll tell you that for a fact. I just thank . . ."

Magda raised her hand. "Enough," she said, putting just a touch of warning emphasis in her voice.

The Colonel stopped. Magda could be unpredictable. The thin old officer fought to regain his military bearing. He was giddy and shaken. He felt wobbly in his legs. The incident had taken a toll. Every impulse that animated life in the Colonel's lank frame sought expression in the worried palaver Magda had stopped. If he were not able to talk about the little ostrich, he might explode from anxiety. His main worry was that the dogs would soon return. He managed to keep his mouth shut, but the effort was costly. A week or so earlier, he'd seen someone on *Oprah* who was convinced that unexpressed emotions caused disease. Unexpressed anger caused ulcers, while unexpressed anxiety led to respiratory problems. Although he could actually almost feel disease taking root in his tissues, he supposed that he'd better defer discussion for a while. He decided instead to share a bit of good news.

"I've named the little guy King Richard," he said.

Magda said nothing. The Colonel had been under something of a strain. He showed every indication of being on the verge of a nervous breakdown. That he'd named VJ's ostrich chick King Richard was not a good sign. She took a step backward. One of the patients Magda and her poodles visited suffered from a naming mania. The poor woman had gone so far as to give names to light sockets and mayonnaise jars. The need to bestow names was just the kind of grandiose gesture she'd expect from the Colonel, if and when he cracked. This King business was a further indication of grandiosity. He was

obviously within whistling distance of losing his grip entirely.
Concerns for her personal safety competed with her impulse
to nurture. After a minute or two of painful silence, she finally spoke.

Now is the winter of our discontent
Made glorious summer by this son of York.

It was the Colonel's turn to look blank and doubt the sanity
of his companion.

"King Richard," she finally said by way of explanation. She
was very pleased with herself. After almost forty years away
from the theater, she'd found the opening lines to *Richard III*
blossoming on her lips. It was disappointing that the Colonel
did not seem to recognize the quote, but he'd probably picked
the name from the recent movie version.

The conversation had somehow veered away from the
point. Puzzled, the Colonel tried again: "I guess I owe you an
apology. I misjudged your boy. You raised a fine young man,
Magda. The boy has integrity, imagination, and generosity. I
am an early riser, and I made no exception this morning. I
wanted to spend time with this little fellow. This chick took
a great shine to me. I guess you knew that. Your boy called it
bonding. I've never seen anything like it. He follows me
around, won't be parted from me. The thought of leaving him
was about to kill this old soldier. The little guy just loves me.
So here we were, walking up the road. I was thinking about
my dogs. I have to be straight. They're a sorry bunch of slack-
ers when you get right down to it. Sanborn is the worst, but
none of them's got half the zotz of this baby ostrich. Thinking
of the damned dogs put me into a piss-poor mood. Dogs are
dogs, no initiative, energy, drive. Yesterday I was talking with
young VJ and Fat Boy . . . I mean his stout friend, the commu
. . . uh, the business student. I recognized something. Since
I retired, I've become the big dog in my pack. That's all. I've
got the gumption for more.

"This trip is a wake-up call. It's time to show some grit. Besides, this little guy might live seventy years. I've got twenty, maybe twenty-five if I don't twink out because of your damned poodles. I got no legacy, no kids, no nothing. My dogs are scared to death of me and probably hate me in their hearts. I've got to make a change, Magda. I don't want this little boy here made into a pair of damned cowboy boots after I've passed on. Shit. I never even thought seriously about passing on. I guess I figured I'd live forever. What could they put on this old soldier's tombstone? 'Alpha male son of a bitch?' I gotta suck it up and get on with it, Magda, make something of my retirement, myself!"

Magda considered the Colonel through half-closed eyelids. The Colonel was not having a nervous breakdown after all. He was having an identity crisis. "So," she said, "you were walking along thinking of all this?" One of the many aggravating things about men in the throes of identity confusion is their maundering *yak yak yak*. The Colonel evidently had a point but required prompting to get it out.

"That's right," he went on. "Then VJ drove past. About a hundred yards down the road, he stopped and backed up. Magda, he gave me little King Richard here. He said that he'd decided against the ostrich business. He was firm in his decision, showed spunk. Then off he went after some sheep that got out of their pen. So I named the little guy. He runs, he just runs and runs, so naturally I named him after Richard Petty . . ."

Magda looked blank, still thinking of Shakespeare.

"Oh, for the love of God, Magda, Richard Petty, Richard god-damned Petty." The Colonel's voice betrayed disbelief and indignation. Didn't this woman understand that this bird, just like the great Richard Petty, was born to run? Never, for the Colonel, had the chasm between the worlds of men and women seemed so profound.

Magda was losing patience. It was wearing along toward

ten. If the Colonel was going to stand in the middle of a dirt road having a belated identity crisis and shouting "Richard Petty," he was going to have to do it alone, particularly on a day growing alarmingly warm. Besides, she was now concerned about her dogs. Perhaps she'd frightened them too badly. They weren't used to having her raise her hand, much less a stick, to them.

"Colonel," she said, "set that ridiculous bird down and walk me back to the ranch. It's getting hot and I'm worn out."

The Colonel did as he was told. He recognized the chain of command. They hiked back toward the house without further discussion. King Richard followed. From time to time, he'd lag a bit to eat a bug. Then he'd sprint to catch up. He possessed amazing speed.

Sabine was awakened first when grandchildren trooped primly in, thanked him for inviting them to his birthday party, and bid him good-bye. This process had dragged out but was certainly pleasant. He did enjoy the kids. They were terribly ill-behaved, but that is not much of a drawback with grandchildren. He didn't have to put up with their antics on a daily basis, and it was fun to see them sassing their domineering mothers. He slept again after his older daughters broke camp. He was not down long, but the repose was profound. When Rosa floated into the house, she was carefree and inattentive to her surroundings. She allowed the screen door to slam with a slap that resonated through the ranch house. Then, she went to work.

The sudden sound woke Sabine from a dream. He'd been in a prizefight, badly overmatched. He'd given the fight everything he had, round after round. He was still standing, but only just; he'd last one round more, two at the most. Between rounds he sat. His trainer talked, giving advice and critique. "You're running," he said, "and you can't punch. Your stuff isn't working. You've got to take some punches. Relax and absorb them. You decide when and where the shots hit. That's how you go the distance. For God's sake, don't fight and don't run."

Sabine seldom remembered dreams. This time, the slamming door woke him so suddenly that the dream stayed with him. He realized immediately that the trainer's advice had applications outside the ring.

He lay there in the hammock feeling a bit feverish. Daytime sleeping always left him flushed and leaden. He breathed deeply and thought about the sounds of the house he'd lived in for almost fifty years. He knew every creak and groan, every rattle and squeak. He listened. Rosa was running water. He knew it was her because she always ran her dishwater exactly the same way. First she turned on the hot water full blast, causing a dull vibration in the deep recesses of the house. Next, she would slap at the water for a few seconds and then turn on the cold, again full blast. Finally, she'd slowly back off on the cold until she had the water to the temperature she wanted.

Picturing Daisy with her hands in warm soapy water brought Sabine a horrible realization. The blow he was evidently going to have to take was her marriage! Theoretically, he'd been hoping that Rosa would soon pair up with a decent young man. In fact, he wanted nothing of the sort. It'd be a cataclysmic disruption at a time when Sabine was craving order, routine. He'd be having to adapt, accept new arrangements. The prospect was ominous. VJ's Jojobalueca venture had just about driven Sabine to a nervous breakdown, and it was nothing compared to the changes in the offing now that Rosa had a beau. . . . A beau! Sabine recalled with a terrible, spasmodic start just what it meant to have a beau, a prospective husband. He realized that if young Crume married Rosa, he would be pressing his carnal urges on her, night and day at least for a while.

No father, no Basque father at any rate, can reflect comfortably on the image of his favorite daughter submitting herself to the erotic blandishments of a young and virile husband, however appropriate and welcome the match. Taking a deep breath to regain his composure, Sabine listened to Rosa wash dishes. He could completely attend to the small movements of his daughter as she filled a sink with water some thirty or forty feet away. It'd be another thing entirely to hear Everett Crume batter the Beautyrest as he groaned and strained at Sabine's *consentidita*, his Rosie Daisy. And what if Rosa moaned, or sobbed, or let out ecstatic little shrieks like her mother? It was not something a man like Sabine could lightly accept or even tolerate.

But what could he do? He supposed that this was his destiny, the strained emotions all men with daughters inevitably face. He'd already been through it with Celia and Felice, an experience that did not help at all. It was going to be even worse with Rosa. At least Celia and Felice had moved away with their useless husbands. Rosa would move hers into the house. With the others, Sabine had gotten some satisfaction from badgering and intimidating the prospective husbands. Only a moron like the Arizona general could enjoy harassing young Crume. Daughters, Sabine reflected darkly, are a curse. You raise them, nurture them, teach them right from wrong, and then young men come to fuck them.

Sabine couldn't stand it. Not under his roof. He rolled violently in the hammock and shut his eyes tight as he grappled with the situation. What a nightmare! He couldn't even stand it when Rosa wanted to talk about kissing. How would he handle it day after day, especially during the feverish rut of the first few months? They were going to take over the running of the ranch. He couldn't very well ask them to stay in the sheeping wagons.

Maybe, after all, he could do something to hinder the match! It was not a done deal yet, and they probably had not yet even had sex. Sabine was sweating. What a humiliation! Could he admit to himself that he'd sabotage his favorite

daughter's future happiness because it made him uncomfortable to know that the prospective couple would be doing it
under his nose? No, selfish as he was, he couldn't do that. He
wished he could. The hell was that he had to admit that he
was seventy-two years old and lacked the maturity to simply
accept that his daughters, like everybody else, were drawn to
that act he so enjoyed and had so eagerly undertaken to give
them life. Sabine had long been aware that humans are absurd creatures. Still, it is no fun having your nose rubbed in
it, and the question remained: what was he to do?

He raised himself to a sitting position. He wasn't getting
any rest; he might as well get up and go look for Magda.
Maybe they could get into a little daytime hanky-panky. As to
his predicament, the solution was actually pretty obvious. He
would simply have to disappear for a while. There was no
other remedy. Maybe he could talk Magda into making a trip
with him. He'd wanted for years to go visit his cousins in Argentina. It was a long shot, but it wouldn't hurt to ask.

If Magda nixed the Argentina idea, maybe it was time for
him to unbend and go spend a few months in Arizona. For
years, he'd played poker with his wife, bluffing, raising, standing pat. Maybe now it was time to switch to chess. He could
lose a castle and capture the queen. Argentina or Arizona,
once he got Magda back, he'd have his own field to plow, his
own erotic urges to satisfy. The young could be damned at
that point.

He swung up out of the hammock and went into the kitchen where Rosa was now making more noise doing dishes
than she'd have made rolling cymbals down a flight of stairs.
Everett was so shaken from his fall and startled at his good
luck that he'd had to go lie down. Rosa reacted differently.
Her trim little body was just brimming over with energy. She
couldn't have napped if her life depended on it. She needed
a project, a target for her energy. Luckily, the kitchen was a
disaster area.

Celia and Felice, for all their arguing, shared the opinion

that their parents had badly spoiled the youngest siblings. In their view, Rosa and VJ were living lives of privilege and idleness. It was the duty of the older sibs to correct and remedy the situation. They devised one method early on and applied it with uniform diligence. They always left boatloads of dirty dishes.

Sometimes this annoyed Rosa, but in general, she didn't mind dishes. It was one of those mindless tasks that are so necessary and satisfying. It was particularly nice at present to have a big mess to clean up. It'd take a while and would help her regain her composure and soothe her love-frayed nerves.

Sabine was still yawning. "My God, Daisy," he shouted, "do you have to drive your old papa deaf just to do the damned dishes?"

"I have to make the noise it takes to do the job. If it bothers you, you can find another spot. You own thirty thousand acres. No one requires you to be underfoot while I'm working."

"I just didn't realize that the activity was so industrial. It's lucky we live in Nevada, I guess. If we lived in a civilized place, we'd get tagged and shut down for zoning violations. We could get in some kind of trouble anyway, I suppose. I don't imagine that the people over in Stansville think much of having the peace of their town disturbed by the racket. Have you seen your mother?"

This kind of palaver often irritated Rosa. Her present mood, though, was so thoroughly ecstatic that she smiled indulgently at her father and ignored his question. Magda could be anywhere.

Sabine's mood had shifted. He enjoyed the banter, but there were limits. "Seriously Rosa, knock it off for a while. I want to talk to you. I'll be going to Arizona sometime soon. You can make all the racket you want then."

Rosa quit stacking dishes immediately. Could she possibly have heard him right? People had been working on Sabine for what seemed like decades, trying to get him to make a trip to

Arizona. He had resisted with some of the tenacity the donkeys had showed at the prison when confronted by the trailer. Rosa had concluded that he would rather die than relent. She'd kept after him mainly for form's sake. The best she'd hoped for was that he'd make concessions enough that Magda would move back to Nevada for six months a year. She'd hoped that her parents would quit threatening one another with divorce, not that she blamed Magda a bit. The old guy was so intractable. She didn't dream that he'd ever capitulate so completely. It was a little scary, if it was true. She sat down at the kitchen table and faced her father. Her stomach was a little queasy and unsettled. She wished she could get to those dishes.

"Daisy," he began, "do you think that you and the faa . . . Everett Crume will be able to run the ranch while I'm with your mother in Arizona?"

Rosa smiled weakly. Her ears were ringing. Sabine looked better, fitter than he had in weeks. He was not a morning person. Characteristically, he started his days slowly, almost painfully. Often he was crabby until eleven or so. She looked at the clock . . . eleven. Still, the transformation was too extravagant to be real. Just minutes before he'd been distressed, disoriented. Even VJ had noticed that something was wrong. How could the old devil's demeanor shift so completely in two hours? Earlier, he'd mentioned something about her and Ev running the ranch; now he was floating the idea a second time. He sat there at the table and looked as vital as a bull. He smiled broadly, put his strong old hands on the table, and looked into her eyes. Rosa blushed a bright red. The raw and obvious affection of father for daughter was powerful, disconcerting in its intensity.

After an extended gap in the conversation that was yet to materialize, Sabine continued. "I've got to go to Arizona," he said, "I don't want to, but I'm a sex slave to your mother, Daisy. I ought to go on *Oprah*. Remember Virgil Jose on *Jeopardy*?

I'm bound to do better than that. It's too bad that they don't have prizes on *Oprah*. I'd clean up! So it looks like you'll have to run the ranch. I'd feel better about it if you had some help, and VJ is a ninny even when he's not off on a wild goose chase. So maybe you should go ahead and marry young Crume. Then we'll probably have two sex slaves in the family. He could go on *Oprah* along with me." Sabine gave an imperceptible wince as he spoke of Rosa's nuptials.

Rosa felt annoyance beginning to supplant her confusion and disorientation. This was a great relief. She'd spent the larger portion of her life annoyed with her father. The feeling was like an old friend. She found she could breathe. Soon she'd be able to talk. She closed her eyes and took in air. "Daddy, I don't want to hear about your love life. What on earth has come over you? Just back up a bit here and start with Arizona."

"Not much to tell. I'm going. I made a decision. I have to do it now, when it's my choice. Alternately, I could fight all of you, Magda, your sisters, and even that ninny VJ, and do it later. I'm too damned old to beat those kinds of odds for long, and the fight would cost me."

"Well, you ought to know, you've been fighting it for at least five years."

"I do, and I've had enough. It'll surprise your mother and give her something to think about. She's been engineering this for years. Well, now she has to deal with it. I am planning to drive back with her tomorrow or whenever she goes. That's all. I haven't worked out any details because I just made up my mind about ten minutes ago. That's why I'm wondering about the ranch. I am not senile enough yet to leave it in VJ's care. I went out on the porch to watch the donkeys for a while earlier this morning. I couldn't help but notice that you and young Crume seemed to be getting along." Sabine had no intention whatsoever of leaving for Arizona the next day. His sudden capitulation would shock everyone so much that he'd have a fleeting but important advantage in various peripheral struggles. All he had to do was keep the dream in mind and remember that his game was chess, not poker.

Rosa was wary. The shift was sudden, too sudden. "Well, don't marry us yet. Besides, all this enthusiasm is a bit unseemly, isn't it? Where's the murderous rage? I'll never forget what you put Celia through when she married, and you were not exactly supportive when Felice made her announcement, either. What would Golfrido say?"

"Golfrido's dead. Young Crume knows what's what. He's practically family already, and he's a very smart boy, not an ox, a *buey* like Celia married or a hillbilly dimwit like Felice's husband. Crume knows where I keep my guns. I've got no need to take him down there and show him what I'd do if he hurt you. He knows. He was around when the other girls married. Besides, if it wasn't for Ev Crume, I'd have probably shot Virgil Jose by this time. He's the only one that VJ listens to even halfway. Unlike Felice's and Celia's husbands, I'd consider young Crume a credit to the family. Virgil Jose is going to need all the help he can get with the business of running this ranch when he finally gets it."

"Honest to God, Daddy, you are such a sexist. What about me? I run the damned ranch already, with no help from VJ. All *you* do anymore is hire unruly shepherds for me to manage, buy shepherds' wagons that no one uses, and crowd the place with half-wild donkeys. I run the ranch. That's a take, Daddy, and I've been running it since before Mama moved to Arizona. I know you can't help it. With the Euzkadi, it's always the son. But I'm not going to sit here and have you tell me that VJ needs Ev to run the ranch. If he needs help, which he certainly does as long as he's doing things like going off to Hollywood to be on *Jeopardy*, then he can let me run the ranch, just as his father has. You are unbelievable. If you're that much a Basque that all you see is your son, then why aren't you Basque enough to go psychotic about your daughter's honor?"

Sabine felt that he had to respond to Rosa's unfair charac-

244

terization of the donkeys. "I saw you down there petting on Che, Daisy-o. You know in your heart that those donkeys are the best addition to this ranch in years. They've only been here a couple of days, and look at how much things have improved. Anyway, what do you expect me to do? You are so ornery, such a *mandona*, that I can't afford to scare young Crume too much. If he bolted, where would you ever find another boy with such a good disposition?"

"Call him Bo, Daddy."

"Everett? Bo? What are you talking about, girl. Bo?"

"The donkey, Daddy, you called him Che."

"Call him Bo if you want to, Daisy; we all have free speech in this country. I plan to call him Che. Anyway, that's exactly what I mean. How many men are open-minded enough to have you bossing them around about how to name their donkeys? Anyway, let me explain to you about VJ. My father always said that you should never divide up land with an inheritance. Life in Euskal Herria went downhill from people dividing the land into tinier and tinier plots. The same thing is happening here. No one will admit it. All the ranchers would rather blame the government, the droughts, the grazing fees, and even the poor damned endangered species when the fact is that better than half of the ranches in this state and probably the whole West are burdened with debt because of the way people divide up their estates when they croak.

"So when I die, the ranch will go to VJ and you. I've got it set up as legally indivisible. Celia and Felice are both rich on their own; the ranch would be nothing but a headache for them. No, the ranch is for you and VJ. I spell it all out in the will. The main thing is that the property is there to run sheep or anything else . . . but you can't parcel it out. I have to face facts; I could live a week or I could live twenty years. Right now VJ is still behaving like a meathead. It wouldn't surprise me to find him sitting on a brood of ostrich eggs. That means I have to think about all this, since he's not showing good sense. I've talked with lawyers and put together a will that substitutes for the good sense the boy should have. For VJ, they put together a trust.

"When I die, you and VJ will have twenty years to sort things out. You can decide to own the ranch together as a partnership. In my view, that'd be best. If not, I am leaving each of you enough money to buy the other one out. Your mom will get plenty, and I'm leaving Felice and Celia a bunch of money too. I'm grateful I don't have to hear Felice gripe about the taxes she'll have to pay and her money going to support welfare bums. If I have to hear much of that, I'll just will it straight to the bums with encouragement to go ahead and buy Cadillacs and booze and have dozens of kids out of wedlock. I *am* going to give a bunch of money to causes Felice is sure to despise.

"You, *mi hija*, have a practical nature and have probably saved me a fortune in legal fees. Your inheritance will come straight, no trust fund, just pure land and money. That's how the will plays out. My mind, though, works differently. In my mind, I think of the ranch going to VJ, and I pour all my worry into the boy. He doesn't even show the good sense to be interested in women. You saw how rude he was to Golfrido's girl. The will shows that I know better, even though I can't keep it in view. You're right, I'm a Basque and I lose perspective when I think of my son.

"It's every child's fate to have to suffer the limitations of their parents, Daisy. You have a father that cannot completely free himself of peasant concerns. I'm not much good at this. I should have been a sailor, but Basque sailors are all what you call sexists. You'll learn a sad lesson when you get old, *mi hija*. No one can be the person they want to be, and it's a mistake beyond a point to even try. My legacy to you has to do with who and what I am and have been, not who I should have been. It's your fate to have a sexist, anarchist Basque pirate for a father. You have to sort it out, not me."

Rosa listened patiently but with increasing annoyance. The muscles in her jaw tightened to the point of spasm.

"Daddy," she said, "that is such a crock."

"I know," he said, "I know. I'm a landlocked sailor, a left-wing capitalist, an anticlerical Catholic agnostic, and an anarchist who spent more than sixty thousand dollars last year for legal advice. In my view, life without hypocrisy would be intolerable. All in the world I want to do now is make love to your mother and train those donkeys to guard the sheep I have never really cared about. Your daddy is a mess, Daisy, but it's your problem that I'm your father, not mine. If you want me to scare your prospective husband, I suppose I could do that much, but my heart won't be in it. You scare him enough yourself."

"Daddy," Rosa said, now exasperated beyond endurance, "shut up. Everything you say is more ridiculous."

By eleven o'clock, the midsummer sun had warmed the fickle desert air of Nevada to a heat of suffocating intensity. Magda and the Colonel were walking down the dirt road toward the house, still perhaps three-quarters of a mile from their goal, when VJ pulled up, trailer full of sheep, and offered them a ride.

Magda was angry with her dogs. Sure, she'd shaken a stick at them, but that was no reason for the little snips to simply disappear. Having led her along the little stream, they'd abandoned her to walk back alone (except for the Colonel and his ostrich). They were, no doubt, resting in cool comfort directly under the air conditioner. The Colonel was angry with himself. It'd gotten too hot to run or even walk comfortably. He never allowed that to happen in Arizona. The heat was debilitating and made him feel like a wimp, an old wimp.

Both of them were more than happy to get a ride from VJ. "These woolies were trying to get run over by a train," he said by way of introduction. "Hop in and I'll give you a ride. The two of you look like you're going to turn into grease spots on this road if you don't get out of this heat pretty soon."

Magda and the Colonel piled in without ceremony. VJ had recovered his cheerful disposition. He was in the mood for conversation. His new passengers were hot, cross, and far from thrilled with his ebullience. Their long, sweaty faces made VJ nervous. He fidgeted, he whistled, he yammered at them about the sheep, a topic they quickly came to resent.

"I knew where they'd be. They were looking to spoil their meat with Russian thistle. I just knew the sheep would head for a big patch. Just think. They're there in the kitchen pen waiting for Daddy to slaughter them one by one for the dinner table. They've got that grass to eat all day so that they stay sweet and tender. It makes them nervous. They don't know why, of course, but it does, especially when Daddy puts a bunch of donkeys in with them. The way they kept getting out was that one of the donkeys would throw a lamb or two over the fence. The rest of them would get panicky and squeeze under. Ev saw it. I just knew they'd end up at the railroad right-of-way. After all that sweet grass, they had an appetite for tumbleweed."

Magda was still annoyed with VJ from their early-morning conversation about Rosa. Now, his crowing, self-congratulatory tone did not sit well at all.

"VJ, shut up."

The Colonel sat there with the baby ostrich on his lap. He was just about to ask VJ whether the bonding of fledgling ostriches lasted into adulthood. He decided, however, to ask later, when Magda wasn't around. He said nothing. The ostrich defecated noisily. The sound was followed by the sulfurous whiff of rotten eggs enveloped in the astringent ammonia of concentrated diaper pail.

When they pulled into the ranch house drive, the only sound was the relentless bleating of sheep. VJ was horrified to see Fanny Ulibarri's mustard-colored Chevrolet pickup dominating the driveway. The sight provided a challenge to the cheerful outlook he had been at such pains to assemble. The pickup did not drive itself through the burgeoning heat. No, Fanny was undoubtedly inside the house. All the cheerfulness in the world could not prevent Fanny from lurking somewhere on the property. Sabine came out of the house. He was smiling and followed by Fanny Ulibarri, who was dolled up in bright-pink pants. She smiled a big, hopeful smile and gave VJ a wiggly fingered wave. Sabine spoke.

"Virgil Jose," he said, "I'm proud of you. Surely you see that you cannot ignore your one talent indefinitely. There's no shepherd alive who could have found these sheep faster than you." He then turned his attention to his wife. "Magda, I've decided to go back to Arizona with you. I need to know when you are going back. I have details to attend to, so I'd appreciate knowing the timetable. I also want to figure out a way to get some of the donkeys down there as soon as I can. I need to train them a bit. You can't just put them in a sheep pen and expect them to behave themselves without supervision. So we may need to buy a different house if you don't have anywhere to put donkeys. Maybe I ought to fly down ahead of you and look at some real estate. By the way, I'm thinking seriously of finally making that trip to Argentina. I'd like you to consider it. The timing would depend on whether or not we'll be having to marry off a daughter."

Magda, who was seldom at a loss for words, was at a loss for words. The Colonel, hot, miserable, and with a lapful of ostrich dung, decided to beat a hasty retreat.

"Need to water the bird," he said, and walked off toward the room he shared with Virg and Ev. The little ostrich stayed right at his heels.

CHAPTER SEVENTEEN

■ ■ ■

Upon reflection, VJ was very pleased. His ostrich enterprise had borne fruit. Sabine and Magda were getting back together. That meant that she could give up the poodle business and stop scratching for every dime. Ev, too, was set, so far as he could see. Rosa was relaxed and peaceful. VJ watched her studying Ev. She parted her lips and just quietly looked at him. Ev made her feel good, and she was not going to give that up.

When she was fifteen and VJ thirteen, Rosa had persuaded Sabine to buy her a horse. Getting the old man to cut loose with a nickel was a task that took perseverance, but at length, she prevailed. For a time, then, she searched. She must have seen half the horses in Nevada. It drove VJ crazy. After the first month or so, he concluded that Rosa had squandered her powers. Sabine was not, after all, going to have to pay for a horse. Rosa would never find a horse that suited her.

Then she found Pumpkin, an entirely unremarkable bay gelding at a horse auction in Stansville. Pumpkin was not one of the auction horses; Rosa found him in a corral nearby. For two weeks she drove to Stansville every day, just to visit Pumpkin. She insisted that this horse was the one she wanted. Everyone in the family tried to talk her out of the notion, pointing out that Pumpkin lacked even the virtue of being for sale. No soap. Rosa would have Pumpkin and finally persuaded the owner to sell him. VJ remembered the way Rosa looked at that horse. She parted her lips slightly, breathed deeply, and allowed all the bunched muscles in her forehead and jaw to relax. She watched Pumpkin with the same relaxed, peaceful expression that she now wore when she watched Ev. VJ realized the expression emerged from firm purpose and confident resolution. It looked to VJ like Ev was going to marry money. He wouldn't need to make it on ostriches.

VJ was impressed with how quickly and completely the ratite enterprise had achieved its ends. Just that morning he'd felt bad that the ostrich business was going to turn out like *Jeopardy* or the Jojobalueca affair. He'd gotten out, his tail between his legs, having hatched but one ostrich. It dawned on him that he'd sensed, almost psychically, that there was nothing further to gain. The business was superfluous. It had been an immense success. Even though the enterprise did not last long enough to generate positive cash flow, it had achieved every objective that VJ had in mind. The annual report for VJ's ostrich business would have to assess profits in the currency of love rather than money, romance rather than finance. Somehow, in ways VJ did not understand, ostriches catalyzed rapprochement between men and women.

VJ realized that he'd placed himself in a terribly risky position. He did not understand romance, but he was making an earnest effort. Through observation, he had concluded that there was a frightening viral quality to affairs of the heart. Fanny Ulibarri was doing a lot of fluttering and jiggling in his direction. He was uncertain that he had stamina. Fanny was a good-looking woman . . . interesting too. She had that parrot. VJ had been too distracted at the party to find out much about the parrot (Lincoln?), but he recalled the intelligent, soulful expression the bird was able to project. VJ also liked Fanny's cowgirl affectations that so accentuated her physical endowments. But the woman drove him crazy. Besides, he had . . . concerns. He was not ready for any serious connection with a woman. He had things to sort out.

He'd known Fanny, like Ev, for practically his entire life. He'd never had to think about her one way or the other; she was a feature of the landscape, Rosa's bud. He'd barely been able to call her by name when she showed up at the party. Now it seemed that the safety net was gone. Fanny was two years older than VJ, just as Rosa was two years older than Ev. Fanny was VJ's sister's friend, just as Ev was Rosa's brother's friend. These frightening parallels gave encouragement to Fanny and intensified the ostrich-induced, infectious condition of the love nest the ranch had suddenly become. Fanny Ulibarri was a menace, a high-octane cowgirl obviously (in retrospect) on the make.

Things had gotten pretty itchy pretty quickly once he arrived home. Magda's ominous words came back to him unbidden. "You'll soon have enough to think about with this ranch on your hands." The words were chilling, especially since Sabine announced his forthcoming move to Arizona. Could it be that Sabine actually wanted him to take the ranch? He'd be at Fanny Ulibarri's mercy. She'd be able to find him anytime she pleased! He'd end up kissing her just to shut her up!

It was lucky he had the sheep to unload. He now wished to hell that it'd taken a bit longer to find and load them. Fanny only had a few minutes. Dan of Dan's Tack Shack had an afternoon of golf on tap and wanted Fanny at the shop by one. She followed VJ down to the kitchen pen.

"I can't believe how stupid I am; I left my earrings right

there by the bathroom sink. Abraham starts going for my earrings when he gets nervous. I bet he's destroyed dozens of my earrings since I got him. I know enough now to get them out when he starts in on them. I read somewhere that a parrot's jaw is so strong that they could actually lift a Cadillac with pure jaw power. Makes you wonder, doesn't it? Why they would want parrots lifting cars, especially Cadillacs, is beyond me. But that's the kind of thing our tax money goes for these days; pure abuse in my opinion. It can't do the birds any good."

VJ was busy. He took a look at the sheep to see that they'd ridden well. He got a long piece of three-quarter-inch plywood that had been fashioned into a ramp for loading sheep. It was reinforced with a thick rubber stall mat. It was heavy, and VJ strained to lift and drag it. Fanny was following him around, talking to him as he bustled. He was glad to be busy. He didn't know how to reply, and the work removed that imperative.

"So anyway, I went and took the earrings out. They were dangly ones, turquoise. I guess I left them right there. I was relieved when I found them. Little dogs like those poodles will get to burying things, sometimes, but I wasn't thinking of dogs when I took the earrings out. I was worried about Abraham. The kids and dogs made him nervous. It seemed like there were a hundred kids at your dad's party and then those dogs your mama has, sneaky little dogs. It even made *me* nervous and I'm not a little bird. Abraham likes to have quiet. He's not used to a lot of chatter. If I'd known about all the kids, not to mention those snippy poodles, I'd have just left Abraham at home. It would have saved me this trip out here."

While Fanny talked, VJ carefully unloaded the sheep from the trailer into the kitchen pen. He decided to stay there with them until Fanny left. He'd need to put the trailer up and then move the donkeys. He'd pen the one, the jenny his dad called Vera, in a corral that adjoined the kitchen pen. He'd let the others roam free. They were devoted to the jenny and wouldn't wander. The burros and the sheep could then stare at one another through the fence. Bonds of familiarity and even affection would grow.

VJ had to smile when Fanny pointed out that Abraham was not used to chatter. When he did so, Fanny averted her eyes and blushed.

"You've got a great way with animals," she said, "a real touch. I was wondering, did you ever get into line dancing down there in New Mexico? Remember back a couple of years when that song 'Achey Breaky Heart' was so big? Well everybody just went ape for line dancing. I guess you were still underage. Anyway, it's still pretty big and they have special nights at some of the clubs where they teach everybody to line dance and then everyone does it and has a lot of fun. The only time of year I do it is in the summer when they open all the windows and doors. The smoke does me in."

VJ felt the first stabs of discomfort behind his eyes. A headache was on the way if something did not change quick. He wondered if Basque women were all like Fanny. VJ had not known many Basque women at all intimately. Magda was not Basque, and his sisters were not anywhere near full-bore Euzkadi. Fanny was full-blooded Basque. She had to be more typically Basque than any of the women in his family. Golfrido had been a more typical specimen than Sabine. Golfrido had no money and was always gone, outdoors, out-of-pocket, following sheep. VJ didn't know Fanny's mother except by reputation. She was said to be a force to reckon with, bossy, controlling, immensely practical, a great money manager and fair vintner. Sabine always said that Marta knew how to get both value and change from every dime she spent. The traditional Basques VJ knew personally were all men, mainly shepherds. They were all eccentric. They wore berets and carried *makila* walking sticks everywhere they went. They were evasive and would never say where they were headed or when they would be back. They were difficult employees, quick to take umbrage, hard to pin down, and mobile. They'd disappear with sheep and be on their own for months on end. It hit VJ with force: maybe the men developed their habits to evade Basque women? Considering Fanny, it made a lot of sense. Even considering his sisters, it made a lot of sense. There was a definite appeal to life with stupid, quiet, biddable little sheep. Applying his attention to the sheep he'd just unloaded, VJ could see that they were distressed. They unloaded okay and went readily into the pen. VJ followed them, and Fanny followed VJ. Once in the pen the sheep did not relax. Instead, they gathered around VJ and Fanny, bleating nervously.

Fanny continued to talk, raising her voice over the loud bleating of the sheep. "Have you ever smelled your clothes when you're taking them off after a night at a club? The cigarette smell is enough to gag a person. I think that they ought to put the manufacturers of cigarettes on trial before Congress and the Supreme Court. The death penalty is too good for them."

VJ was not closely following Fanny's thoughts on the criminal culpability of the tobacco industry. He was picturing the shepherds' wagons that his father was collecting. No apartment, however dark, chaotic, and comfy could compare to the exquisite pleasures that life in a sheep wagon would offer. How efficient they were! Everything a person could need was right at hand. There were dozens of little drawers, niches, cupboards, and closets. The furniture varied from wagon to wagon, but the beds and chairs were invariably comfortable. He regretted that he'd never spent a summer in the high country, living in one of the wagons or even one of the Airstreams. He'd consistently resisted his father's suggestion that he do so. There was always a rodeo or something; he couldn't bear the possibility that he might miss some doings. He bitterly recalled the inane and pointless activities that claimed his youthful summers. He'd listened to a lot of talk, for example, which compared to that he was now hearing from

Fanny. She was pointing out that the capital crimes of the cancer merchants in the tobacco industry were not merely aesthetic.

"I don't mean, of course, that the CEOs should get the death penalty because of getting people's clothes smelly but, you know, people having to go through chemo and everything. If I have to go through chemo, I'm not going to wear any of those turbans. I'm going straight to Congress with my bald head and let them, all of them, see what they caused, not that I ever smoked. Anyway, if you're embarrassed about even going to those dance club cattle calls where they teach you to dance, I'll be glad to teach you a little bit first so you'll have a jump on everyone else."

Hearing Fanny talk, VJ felt that the horizons were collapsing. He'd have to think fast, act fast. Old Chingleput had given him notice on the apartment in Albuquerque. He was outdoors in two or three weeks and needed, therefore, to apply himself to the problem of lodging. With the unanticipated rapid success of the ostrich venture, he was without plans or expectations. Of course, he had wanted to come back to Nevada. He missed the country and wanted to get straight with his father. But his idea was that things would be as before. Rosa and Sabine would run the show, leaving him free to think, experiment, and disappear, Basque style, when it suited him. Things had shifted in an ominous direction.

Everything good, he reflected, casts a dark shadow. He'd set forces in motion with the ostrich business that produced brilliant results. Those same forces now cast the inevitable dark shadow unhappily across his expectations. He could see what he was up against. Magda had told him that Sabine would expect him to manage the ranch when the old man moved to Arizona. Being tied down like that with the responsibility of the ranch was about as bad as being tied down to Fanny Ulibarri, who'd just offered him dance lessons. He realized that she expected a response.

"Well," he finally said, "yeah, yeah . . . I suppose. I've gotta get some things sorted out . . ." His voice trailed away. He kneeled down and began feeding the sheep the alfalfa pellets he'd put in his pocket earlier in case he'd needed food to lure the sheep into the trailer. He petted them and hummed "Volare." This had a calming effect on the sheep, which clustered around him and Fanny, who kneeled beside him and began petting the anxious animals.

"Lordy," she said, "these sheep are beside themselves; looky here, now, lamby-wambies . . .

La lala la lala
A star that I know of
La lala la la lalala
Let us leave this confusion
La lala la lala la la
Lala la lala lala
A rainbow together we'll find.
Volare, lala la la
La lala lala la la."

There is a little-appreciated detail of rural life that is, nonetheless, true: crooning at sheep is a relaxing, calming experience. Doing so with a companion, VJ and Fanny were to find, inevitably builds bonds.

The bleating of the sheep slowly subsided as VJ hummed and Fanny continued to *la lala la la*. Meanwhile, the alfalfa pellets worked their magic. The sheep became tranquil, even dreamy. The donkeys in the far end of the pen were grazing quietly in a reverie of their own. VJ finally stood up, surveyed the scene, and took a deep breath. Soothing the sheep had soothed him. He watched Fanny. She was kneeling, with her eyes closed, petting a lamb, the very lamb, in fact, that Vera kept ejecting from the pen. It was a touching moment, and VJ felt grateful for Fanny's help with the sheep. He couldn't remember seeing a bunch of miserable and nervous animals calm so quickly. Riding in a crowded stock trailer is no picnic and could leave animals anxious and ringy for days. He was impressed and remembered Abraham's obvious devotion.

Fanny stood and faced VJ. Their eyes met.

"I'm sorry I'm such a blabbermouth," she said. "I just get going."

"You're just trying to be nice," VJ found himself saying. "And thank you. You were a big help just now with these spooky woolies. You know it was your dad that used to sing 'Volare' to the sheep. I got it from him."

At the mention of Golfrido, Fanny's eyes filled with tears. She said nothing, but her lip began to quiver. VJ moved toward her without thought or reflection. His eyes likewise filled with tears. He had just been thinking of Golfrido. Golfrido had painstakingly mentored him in shepherding while steering clear of paternal obligations to his own kids. VJ hadn't even bothered to go to his funeral. A tear made its way down VJ's cheek. Knee-deep in sheep, he embraced Fanny and held her while she cried quietly. VJ was deeply stirred, and only part of it had to do with old Golfrido.

"He was a terrible old rip," Fanny said, laying her head unaffectedly on VJ's shoulder.

"Best shepherd I ever knew," VJ said, wiping his nose. "I guess you inherited the touch he had." VJ felt calm. It seemed natural to be holding this lovely big girl. The thought of it would have alarmed him, but he hadn't thought of it.

"Well, I've gotta go. Dan has his golf game. Wouldn't want him to miss his tee time. Thanks, VJ. I don't know when I'll ever get over losing Daddy. He used to sing 'Volare' like that to me when I was a little girl, and I'd think of flying up to the clouds with him. And then he'd be gone with the sheep for six weeks . . ."

"Well, it looks like I gotta be gone with the sheep some myself. I'm working some stuff out. I don't know about those dance lessons, but I would like to see that parrot someday."

"He's a sweet bird. He'd like you eventually, but he's awful jealous. Most of what I've said yesterday and today was pure nerves because I was glad to see you and was hoping you'd stay in Nevada. You come by whenever you want. Mama still makes wine. You could drink wine, and we'd just have to hope that Abraham wouldn't bite you."

This sounded fine to VJ. He'd have to be pretty wary or he was going to get sweet on Fanny just as he'd feared. That prospect seemed far from terrible. What in the hell was old Sabine putting in the water?

Fanny did, finally, have to leave. She was only with VJ at the kitchen pen for ten minutes. Those ten minutes had been both challenging and sobering. They had a lasting quality. VJ would be reprising the interlude for months. When Fanny was gone, VJ put the trailer away, moved the donkeys, and walked the perimeter of the kitchen pen. He found the places where the donkey had thrown the lamb over and the places where the other sheep had leaked out. He tightened the wire, which was distended but intact. The important effect of any fence is psychological. Animals can almost always defeat a fence if they set their minds to it. Paradoxically, the sheep would develop confidence in their fence as they reestablished confidence in themselves. Thanks to the work he and Fanny had done with the sheep, they'd already made strides.

He enjoyed the burros. They were such quiet, undemanding creatures, animals that just exuded contentment and goodwill. He got a curry comb and gave each of the donkeys a brushing. They were just fine as long as he kept the comb up high, away from their legs. It was the kind of thing that continued to soothe his jangled nerves. He was just finishing with the black one that Rosa called Bo when his father joined him. VJ felt that "Bo" was a poor name for the cute little character and "Capitán" for the gray gelding was completely ridiculous. The gray should be Waylon and the sweet black should be Willie.

The two men stood for a time with the donkeys. VJ brushed and Sabine watched. VJ finally broke the silence.

"Daddy," he said, "I'm sorry for teasing you that time. You know, about the Jojobalueca investment."

Sabine was astounded. He was not accustomed to hearing apologies from his offspring. There was not a strong tradition of apology in the Eckleberry family. "Well, yeah, yeah," he said.

VJ hesitated a moment, giving Sabine the opportunity to say something hinting at remorse for the incident with the fork. Sabine noted the opportunity and let it pass.

"So," VJ went on, "you're off for Arizona?"

"Not hardly," Sabine smiled, lighting a cigar. "Your mother's been plotting to get me into that oven for years, but she can't handle anything sudden. Nah, it'll be November, December before I go. If young Crume doesn't break the traces, we'll probably be having another wedding, late fall or early spring. That'd depend on when the boy finishes his degree, I suppose. It's an unknown, and it could play hell with my . . . ugh, plans to drag my fat butt to Arizona. The truth is that now that I've decided to go, I *would* like to be rubbing suntan lotion onto my belly when the first big snow hits this place. We've not yet discussed it, but I know Magda. I'll have plenty of time to get things set here before I traipse off to the capitalist retirement paradise down there. Can you see me by the pool, VJ, checking my stocks on a cell phone?"

The image, VJ admitted, was difficult to summon. He could see that Sabine was going to start in about how he expected VJ to be at the ranch, working with Sabine and Rosa, learning what he needed to know to take over Sabine's role, whatever that was. That's how it would start. Then it'd be him and Rosa working together. It seemed a dreary scenario. He almost wished he was in college like Ev. But God, he damned sure didn't want to major in business. He didn't care about business. He liked things, people, animals. What would be his major? He didn't have a clue. One of the big advantages of not being in college was that he didn't have to choose a major. What he really needed was time. As always, there were plenty of things, like Fanny's parrot (and Fanny herself, for that matter), on his mind, firing his imagination. With time, he'd come up with a project, a direction, a receptacle for his vast energies. How could he buy time without getting bogged in the business end of the ranching operation?

Everyone acquainted with Virgil Jose Eckleberry knew that the young man was resourceful. He was not the sort of person to languish enmeshed in confusion and indecision. He gave his father an appraising gaze. The old bird certainly looked pleased with himself. VJ sighed a sigh, cocked his head, and bit his lip. Sabine was finally getting shed of the sheep business; that's why he was so happy. He'd never been any good at it. He'd never liked it. It'd never suited him. Unlike Fanny's old man, Sabine had no feel for the animals, no grasp of their nature and needs. He was a lousy shepherd and only middling at managing the ranch. All he'd ever been good at, aside from swilling wine and badgering his loved ones, was buying cheap, selling dear, and keeping his money. In fact, the only kind of shepherd Sabine had ever been was a shepherd of stocks and bonds, money market accounts, and arbitrage, whatever that was.

If the old man ever did move to Arizona, he probably *would* end up by a pool smoking cigars and talking to his broker on a cell phone. The image was not nearly as absurd as Sabine let on. VJ was annoyed that despite his father's loudly proclaimed distaste for the free enterprise system, he never let it interfere with his undeniable talent at making boatloads of money. VJ sourly reflected that he himself was the only person in the family with any genuine ability to raise sheep. He was the only one to inherit his grandfather's skill as a shepherd, the only one to have the benefit of Golfrido's supervision. Shepherding was his only unalloyed talent. The brutal truth was that VJ lacked the judgment, patience, and insight that produced effective entrepreneurs.

How ironic: the one thing that was natural and easy was the distasteful husbandry of small woolie animals. Not, of course, that VJ *really* disliked herding sheep. It was fun. It was satisfying to see the goofy little beasts thriving under his care. He always felt peaceful and happy doing the physical work of shepherding. Too bad it was not the visionary enterprise he'd always craved. He could have shown his father a thing or two. It was ridiculous that the old guy had bothered to buy a sheep ranch. That he'd managed to break even for better than forty years seemed like a miracle but was actually due to the efforts of dozens of itinerant Basque shepherds, independent, tough old birds like Golfrido Ulibarri, Fanny's pop.

To say that the veil parted and the white light of truth and reason illuminated the kitchen pen would be overstating to a small degree VJ's experience of the next few minutes. A notion, a direction, an unexpected new possibility suddenly began to gain momentum in young Eckleberry's fevered brain.

Attempting to picture old Sabine sitting at poolside checking his stock portfolio, VJ noted that the old man, rich and propertied as he was, was still a Basque to the eyelids, not *much* different in temperament from Golfrido and some of the shepherds he'd known growing up. He, Virgil Jose Eckleberry, was a Basque too, if not to the eyelids at least to the navel. And what do Basques do to buy time, to avoid unwanted and onerous responsibilities? They go to sea or they escape to the wilderness on the pretext of caring for sheep!

The sea was out. He'd seen it in L.A. when he was there for his truncated *Jeopardy* appearance. The association was unpleasant, plus he didn't even want to think of how the distaff side of the Eckleberry family would react if he announced plans to become a sailor. No, the route was suddenly clear. He'd talk Sabine into giving him a big flock of sheep. Like generations of his forebears, he would disappear into the solitude of shepherding. He'd make a big success of it, and he'd have lots of time to consider his options for the future. This new development with Fanny Ulibarri needed some elbow room. All that girl apparently needed to be really good company was a couple of dozen sheep to calm her down. VJ figured he could always have sheep if the need was there.

VJ knew instantly what was required. It all boiled down to sheep. Sabine had been doing a half-assed, desultory job of ranching for several years. He'd abandoned first the wool business and then the ewe and lamb operation for the simpler buy, fatten, shear, and sell mode. This year he hadn't even gotten *that* together. All he had was the sorry little bunch VJ had just unloaded. VJ would convince Sabine to buy a bunch of ewes with the idea of getting a ewe-lamb operation up and going again. He might need Rosa's support with the old man. Whatever he did, he had to act fast. He had to do something *immediately* or Sabine was going to start in on him about his responsibilities. VJ could deal with a bunch of sheep, but he could not deal with the tedium of managing the affairs of the whole ranch.

"Daddy," he said, "why don't you buy about sixteen hundred young ewes and get the ranch back into a ewe-lamb operation? I'd shepherd them. We've got enough grass in the high country. I figure that this summer's as good a time as any to start up again. They're as cheap as you're ever going to find them. I could stay out there with a dog, the burros, and a sheep wagon. I'd take them on down to the winter range, stay over with them, and run them into the high country when the pastures up there green up nice. I don't want to do it forever, but I'll manage them at least until the first bunch of lambs are old enough to sell. If we don't get some animals on the BLM land, they'll cut our lease allotments."

"They'll cut our lease allotments anyway," Sabine said mechanically. The boy was full of surprises today! Sabine had feared that VJ, despite his lack of experience and good sense, was going to want some say in the management of the ranch. The women in the family had been reckless enough to plant the idea in the young fool's brain. Now this was rich. The boy had articulated almost the precise plan Sabine had hatched.

He never dreamed it would be so easy. Here he'd come out all ready to bully and threaten, and the boy had capitulated without even knowing it.

"I thought you were above running sheep," he accused, quickly adapting. "I would have thought you'd want me to buy a bunch of mangy cows so you could wear those idiot shirts, boots, and hats."

"Nope," VJ replied. "Sheep are what we do here, and anyway, they are less trouble than cows."

"Nope, just littler. Well, I don't know. Sure, they're cheap; do you think that's good? I sure don't. Nobody can make a dime. Why do you think I'm not fattening lambs this summer? It's because you can't make any money on it."

"But with a ewe-lamb approach there'd be increase in numbers, not just weight."

"It doesn't matter. We sell by the pound."

"And the lambs take on weight fastest."

"Ewe-lamb is headachy. The lambs are vulnerable to predators."

"Which, as I hear it, is why you got those donkeys. I think you ought to rename the two geldings. I look at those little boys and I see Willie and Waylon. Besides guarding, I could have the donkeys pull the wagon."

Sabine was overjoyed. This was too good to believe! He was going to get his way and force VJ into concessions at the same time! Those names, though, for Che and Capitán! That kind of harebrained idea was pure VJ, too stupid even to merit commentary. VJ, for his part, was guardedly optimistic. The old man had not rejected the idea.

Sabine was also going to get his digs in. "How about," he said, "your ostrich idea?"

"Oh, that was mainly for Ev. He won't need it now. Remember Pumpkin?"

Sabine did remember Pumpkin. "Yes," he said, "when your sister gets her mind set, she'll bend the world to her inclinations. She accuses me of hobby ranching. But I don't know. I've always felt that it was better to do nothing than to do something stupid. I advise you young people to be realistic going into this thing. Fifty years on this ranch have convinced me that this country's no good for sheep. There's not enough water. With these prices and a market I don't see coming back, we've got the choice of beating it to death, making a quick profit, then selling the degraded, devalued ranch or running a sustainable herd and making no profit. I see no other choice, except getting out of the business. You have to think about that in this market. That's another reason I've got things on hold. I don't mind trying a ewe-lamb operation for a while, but somebody's going to have to rethink the possibilities for this ranch within the next five to seven years. I don't think we can do ewe-lamb for very long unless we really just hobby ranch it and make our money subdividing big parcels into ranchettes for yuppies, and I can't say I've got a lot of stomach for that!" Both men stiffened with disgust.

"Daddy, I was talking with Ev about that on the way up here. That was one of the big selling points of the ostriches. They are much more arid-climate animals than sheep or cattle. But Ev says that there's no product, breeders' market and all, bunch of idiots selling each other birds. Ev is really smart. He thinks all the time. I know that something's got to change, though. I want to spend the winter in the sheep wagon thinking about it. Maybe I'll read, study up on the directions we might take. I figure we might as well do what we know until we come up with the next step."

Sabine was once again astounded. The boy was talking sense. What next? "Those donkeys don't know a thing. You can't even pick up a foot yet, and one of them has been tossing a lamb over the fence. How do you figure they're going to pull a wagon? And I'm not sure four are enough to manage a wagon."

"Daddy, since you're going to be around until November, you'll train them. The only reason you got them is because you want to mess around with them. I don't want to deprive you of that opportunity. We don't need them to pull until I move the flock to winter ground, and we won't much need them to guard until lambing next spring."

"You swear you'll stay with it until lambing's done and we can hire shepherds enough to help with all the lamb problems?"

"I swear, at least that long. I probably ought to stay with it until they're old enough to shear and sell. I thought I made that clear."

"Will you go into Reno with me and let me get you some decent clothes? We'll take young Crume along. Daisy's made him burn his."

"What?!"

"You heard me. If you are going to shepherd, you'll need some decent work clothes. I don't want you scaring sheep to death with those damned rodeo clown outfits you wear."

"I suppose." VJ had not expected this.

"You know, VJ, I wish you'd known your grandfather. He was an old tyrant as pertained to his son, but I think you have a lot in common with him. I spent every late summer of my entire life, up to the time of the war, looking for my father. Every August, my mother would say, 'Sabine, his business has stacked up; go get him.' It'd always take several days to get to the top of the right mountain and find the right flock. He had the gift for understanding animals' needs, and you have that same gift. You won't be a meathead forever, so I guess you have to sharpen the talent you have. We'll get the ewes. Sixteen hundred seems about right. As I recall, each donkey can manage about four hundred."

"Well, Daddy," VJ felt compelled to point out, "we'll need four or five more come lambing."

"You'll have to take that up with Daisy, and you'd best prepare yourself for controversy. By lambing time, I'll be burning myself black in the Arizona sun."

The two men walked back to the ranch house and seated

themselves on the porch. VJ was a little worried about the seven hundred dollars he owed the Colonel for the ostrich egg. He couldn't very well expect the Colonel to forget the loan.

"Daddy," VJ steeled himself, "what kind of wage do your shepherds draw?"

Sabine felt his neck tighten. He knew that sound, that raised inflection on the *eee* sound in "Daddy." It was the sound VJ made when he was preparing to blindside his father. So, he wondered, had VJ set him up? "Depends. Seems like it's fifty dollars a day plus a bonus if the profit's good, which it generally isn't."

"Think you might see your way clear to advancing me a couple of weeks' wages?"

The back of Sabine's head flushed with anger. VJ was going to be VJ after all. "I damned sure will not," he said. "You've got to always push, don't you? It's not, by God's blood, enough that I'm going to drop a couple of hundred thousand dollars into your damned ewe-lamb project. It's not enough that I'll spend a few thousand more outfitting you and buying supplies. It's not enough that I'll have to send you to Wyoming to buy a trained dog. That'll end up costing another thousand by the time you figure in trip expenses. No, nothing's enough. You want an advance on your wages. Well, my view is that you are a member of this family, not a hired hand. I have no plans to pay you a wage."

By God! VJ thought, noting the way Sabine clipped the ends of his words. He'd sounded like that in the minutes leading up to the notorious table-fork assault. VJ had learned something from that incident. He knew that he needed to be careful with his father. The ewe-lamb plan was still tenuous. It would not do to pepper his speech with colorful expressions. Referring to his father as a "tightfisted old skinflint," for example, would be a poor idea, truthful or not. "Stingy sack of shit" was another phrase VJ discarded, despite its definitive quality and alliterative flare. Instead, showing monumental self-mastery, VJ took another tack. "Well, I wasn't really thinking of the wage one way or the other, but I'm in a bind. I borrowed startup money for the ostrich business from the Colonel. I need to pay him back. It just occurred to me. I haven't thought it through."

Sabine puffed air out of his nostrils, noting the tone of apology. "Startup money? For what? You never started. How much?"

"Well, Daddy, it was for the egg. I borrowed the money to buy the egg from the women at Womynscraft. With the incubator and all it came to seven hundred dollars."

Sabine smiled. "Well, I see what young Crume meant. The market is for breeding stock, not omelets," he said mildly. He was relieved. The price of the egg was utterly nonsensical, but that was a given. Seven hundred dollars was a modest figure to surface at the end of one of Virgil Jose's escapades. "I thought you said that the bird belongs to the Arizona general?"

"It does. I gave him the ostrich this morning. The fact that he's got the animal does not release me from my debt. I bought the egg and I borrowed Colonel McKenzie's money to do it. So now I've got to do the right thing." It was VJ's turn to feel relieved.

"Okay. I'll give Colonel McKenzie the money you owe him on one condition."

"Shoot."

"That you get to Albuquerque, tidy up your affairs, and be back here in a week. You are going to work with me for once. We're going to fix up one of these wagons. We're going to teach those donkeys some manners. My belly is too big to do any hoof work. We're going to outfit you for your work, and finally, we're going to buy the ewes, you and me, VJ."

Virgil Jose readily agreed to Sabine's conditions. His preference would have been to delegate to others everything save the shepherding itself. He did see Sabine's point, though; there was more to shepherding than just seeing that the woolies survived.

Sabine was still a little shaken as he handed VJ a check for the Colonel. He'd gotten so mad at VJ that he'd come close to scuttling their agreement. That was why he needed to have the boy around for a time before he took off with the sheep. Sabine needed to work with VJ, see him in action and get to trust whatever judgment the young pup showed. "Get a bottle of that wine you gave me for my birthday and two glasses," he said.

They drank a toast to the project. Mellow tranquility was thus reestablished between father and son. Sabine considered the boy and felt novel sensations. He was suffused with paternal benevolence toward the young man. He felt like he could breathe, like a burden had been lifted from his chest. He poured himself another glass of Sangre de Toro and offered to pour VJ another. VJ declined; he had things on his mind.

Magda, struck dumb when Sabine told her of his intention to come to Arizona, slowly recovered. It is always a shock to win a long-fought battle, and Magda was profoundly disoriented. For all her machinations, she had never really expected to convince Sabine to make the trip to Scottsdale. She'd learned to cope with the disappointment. Now, she would have to cope with Sabine actually coming. It would be a lovely challenge, and she would certainly adjust. She had no intention, however, of putting up with him immediately. If he thought he could change his mind after years of stubbornness and simply waltz into Scottsdale with a trailer full of donkeys and a yo-ho-ho, he certainly had another think coming. Allowing her head to clear, she had waited for him to finish his conversation with VJ. Now was the time to set him straight. She called him into the kitchen.

Standing in the office visualizing a blanket of sheep stretching from horizon to horizon, VJ could hear his mother telling Sabine that he'd have to put off the move to Arizona. At present it was impractical, simply too hot, and besides she needed to do some prepping of the house, and so on. It sounded to VJ like November was a pretty good bet. Hoping to find the Colonel, VJ smiled largely and ambled off to the room where the ostrich had hatched, the room that Ev had shared with the Colonel, VJ, and the ostrich.

Sure enough, the Colonel was there. VJ could hear him singing in an apparent attempt to soothe or encourage the infant ostrich. VJ stopped to listen.

John Henry was a little baby
A-sittin' on his mommy's knee
He picked up a hammer and a little piece of steel
Said this hammer's gonna be the end of me
Good God!
This hammer's gonna be the end of me.
Da da, da, da, da, da, da, da, dada . . .

Clearing his throat to let the Colonel know he was coming, VJ strode into the room. Using the incubator, the plastic milk crate, and a blanket from the bed, the Colonel had fixed a little spot for the ostrich and equipped it with a couple of pie tins with starter scratch and water. VJ opened his mouth to speak. The Colonel quickly shushed him.

"Shhh! shhh! shhh!" he whispered. "Let's talk outside. He had a bad morning, and I've been trying to get him to take a drink."

They walked outside and shut the door. The Colonel's face was a mask of anxiety. He gritted his teeth, and his jaw muscles stood out like golf balls. VJ handed him the check.

"So what in the god-damned hell is that?" the Colonel asked.

VJ took a step back. The Colonel was clearly distressed. VJ did not know why. He reacted to the tone.

"Uhh . . . it's the money you lent me yesterday. I used it for the egg."

The Colonel brandished the check in front of him, waving it back and forth. "Take it! Take the damned thing and make me your price. I'll beat what your old man offers. I guess you figure he's worth more as a chick than he was as an egg? Or is it your old man that wants to milk some money out of the deal? Well, chicken shit as that is, I won't argue with you. Just tell me how much more you want and go to hell. You aren't getting him back." Colonel McKenzie took a menacing step in VJ's direction.

VJ stepped back. "No, that's not it . . . uh . . . it's just that I borrowed the money and intend to pay it back. The bird . . . I'm giving you the bird . . . the ostrich, I mean . . . not the bird like the *bird* . . ."

"King Richard," the Colonel corrected.

"Huh?"

"King bloody Richard! His name! Have you got wax in your god-damn ears?"

"After Richard Petty?"

"Who the hell else? Now what's this? Come at me again on this check. You aren't wanting more money? You don't want the bird back? I realize you got the sales slip and all, but you said . . ."

The Colonel was obviously distressed at the prospect of losing the ostrich. He sure was a suspicious old guy.

"No, he's yours. I just wanted to give you the money I borrowed. My dad gave me the check as an advance against wages. I'm going to shepherd for him."

"Well, why in the god-damned hell didn't you say so? I swear. I barely saved him from those damned vicious little shits your mother keeps and then you walk in with a check from your dad. What was I supposed to think?"

"Look, he's yours. I'll put it in writing. Now take the check. I bought the egg on borrowed money and I'm paying it back. I'm giving you the chick, free and clear. I want you to have him . . . or her."

"Naw, you keep it." He waved the check at VJ. "I'm going to have him, I want him, and I'm already out the money. I don't begrudge a dime of it. I'm planning to ask your mom if I can have half a day to make a run back up to Womynscraft. I want those lesb . . . uh . . . females up there to fill me in on these little critters. I suppose I'll have to buy something so that they don't turn on me."

"No, take the check. Use it to buy another egg."

Colonel McKenzie was sick of the check discussion. He took the direct approach and tore the check into confetti. "There!" he said. "End of discussion."

VJ smiled. He had to kind of admire the gesture. "Like the name," he said.

The Colonel smiled, actually beaming now as he thought of King Richard. "The best," he said. "Oh, I see that your buddy Ev is . . . getting along with your sis. Well, good for him! He's showing better sense than I ever did. Anyway, come on in now. Let's take a look at him, see if he's had a drink."

VJ did not take the Colonel's meaning as regards good sense, but neither did he particularly want to discuss anybody's good sense. Such discussions generally got around to criticism. "So you think you'll try the ostrich business?" he said.

They walked back into the bedroom—ostrich nursery. Perhaps the ostrich had taken the drink the Colonel was so concerned about. He certainly had managed to overturn the water dish, along with the food dish, the incubator, and the milk crate. He had pecked at the blanket and already had a hole worried into it. At the sight of the Colonel, King Richard abandoned the blanket and made a beeline for the Colonel, who smiled indulgently. If VJ hadn't seen it with his own eyes, he'd not have believed that a creature so small could create such a mess in such a short period of time. They couldn't have been out of the room more than a couple of minutes.

"Ostrich business, me? No, no, not really . . . I guess I'll just make King Richard a pet. Look how the little fellow dotes on me. First god-damned thing since my mother that cared a damn for me. I'll see to it that he doesn't end up as boots or cutlets. My main worry is those bloodthirsty poodles. They'll stop at nothing. It wouldn't surprise me a bit if I looked out that door and caught one of them sneaking around right now, hoping for a chance to come in and kill this little guy."

The Colonel reached down and stroked King Richard's head. He scratched the bird's neck in exactly the same way that Fanny U. had scratched Abraham's neck. King Richard obviously enjoyed the attention. VJ bent down and reached his hand out to pet. The bird stiffened, made a hissing noise, and struck like a snake.

"Whoa!" shouted the Colonel. "Step back! He's . . . Those damned dogs have got him nervous." VJ did not have to be told twice. In point of fact he did not have to be told even once. He moved out of pecking range with a modest show of agility. Unconcerned with the mess or the vicious display, Colonel MacKenzie took one of the pie tins to the bathroom and filled it with water.

"What I plan is to just take him back to Arizona with me and fix a place for him. I've got to learn more about the breed. I don't particularly want another one, but I don't want him to be lonely for his kind. I guess I know something about that. Anyway, he'll be cared for. I think I'll move the dogs into the house and redo their kennel for the ostrich. Never had a dog in the house before, but the fact of the matter is that those hounds are not very happy in that damned kennel and they're scared to death of me. A dog can only perform so well when they are operating out of fear."

He put the pie tin on the floor in front of the ostrich. To VJ's surprise the bird drank, pecking at the water and then raising his head so the water would go down his little throat. "Oh, what a good boy!" the Colonel said earnestly.

"Well," VJ said, "sure you won't reconsider taking back the money you loaned me? You never knew I'd give you the chick when you made the loan."

The Colonel took a deep breath. "Sometimes I wonder

what in the hell is wrong with young people. Are you, by God, deaf, VJ? I want to pay for this guy. I want to have laid down my good money for the rights and benefits of full ownership of this ostrich. Is that so damned difficult to grasp? I guess you could pay me back and then I could turn around and buy him from you. Having you keep your lousy money is kind of a shortcut. I would have expected this kind of shit from Fat Boy; he's a socialist. You, though, I thought you had better sense."

VJ was getting a little itchy to leave. He'd only asked about the loan money for form's sake. The Colonel was not through. He looked VJ up and down, shook his head and gave a huge sigh.

"Another thing . . . I'll tell you, boy, the sight of you running away from that girl at the party reminds me of me and what a horse's ass I've been for most of my life. Not now, of course; what girl would chase an old buzzard like me? I mean when I was young."

VJ was getting nervous. His neck was hot. Even though he'd avoided the touchy topic of good sense, the Colonel had managed to turn the conversation toward criticism. He didn't know where the Colonel was going with all this. He was getting as garrulous as old Sabine all of a sudden.

As though to prove the point, the Colonel continued. "I can tell you that it is just the shits to be an old bachelor, especially when your body is breaking down and it takes you a half hour to pee. Take a page out of Fatty's book, boy. Don't walk away from it. Not without looking at it anyway. You were so damned full of your ostrich project that you didn't give that girl a second real look. And look at the outcome. It's me, not you, that King Richard bonded with. Now Fat Boy out there may be soft. He may be a damned red, but it looks like he's smarter than either of us."

VJ had had enough. "Look, leave me alone about that. I like that girl. I guess she likes me. We just this minute finished . . . She . . . Look, it's really my business, isn't it?"

"Well, that's right, but I don't give a rat's ass. It's a free country and I'll say what I damned well please, especially to a kid like you with mush for brains. By the way, you heading back to Albuquerque?"

Now it was VJ's turn to sigh. There was obviously no percentage in arguing. "Just for long enough to get out of my apartment and get back here. Ev'll stay in Albuquerque. He's getting a degree pretty soon. I'm going to run a big bunch of sheep for my dad."

"Well, I expect you'll do a better job than *him*. You'd better get *him* checked for Alzheimer's. By the way, did you find out how that little bunch got loose?"

VJ was spared the necessity of going into it. King Richard relieved himself and went into a very manic mood, darting from bed to bed and literally bouncing off the walls like a pinball. The Colonel hustled to close the cracked door. VJ pushed by and stepped outside. "Gotta go," he said. "Later," the Colonel replied.

Satisfying as the last exchange with the Colonel had been, VJ was feeling a little weary. The prospect of spending several months with sheep rather than people seemed better than ever. He walked up to the house with the idea of just sitting there for a few minutes or using one of the recliners. He was in luck. Ev was there, apparently asleep in a lawn recliner. He'd wandered up to the house to enjoy the gnat-free sanctuary of the screened porch, get a load off of his still-painful feet, and reflect on the astounding shift in his fortunes. He'd been feeling a bit shell-shocked and had closed his eyes in a futile attempt to relax and get on with his altered existence. He heard VJ come up and was playing opossum.

VJ didn't want to disturb Ev if he was actually asleep. He lay down on a recliner that matched Ev's and waited to see if his buddy showed any signs of life.

Lying there, his mind loosened a bit on the Sangre de Toro, and relieved to be out of the company of the Colonel and King Richard, VJ felt something underneath him, evidently a magazine the last tenant of the recliner had been reading. He pulled it out and to his astonishment it was the seminal issue of *Stockman's Universe* with the article on ostrich husbandry. He lay back and thumbed through the worn magazine, eventually scanning through another article, one he barely remembered. It was entitled "The Environmentalist Threat to Our Traditions" and characterized environmentalists as sentimental, unrealistic, and impractical. VJ smiled. This very edition of *Stockman's Universe* featured realistic, practical advice to invest, at great expense, in ostriches. The "Threat to Our Traditions" article also pegged environmentalism as "the last refuge for old-fashioned communists and new-fashioned one-worlders." VJ smiled again and supposed that old Sabine would need to know about environmentalism as his last refuge.

VJ felt warm in the pit of his stomach when he thought about the old man and the . . . traditions *he'd* tried to maintain, picturing his father at his best with his beret, his *makila*, and the tattered Che Guevara tee shirt that he kept to annoy Felice.

VJ wondered whose traditions environmentalists supposedly threatened. Who, exactly, was the "we" of "our traditions." Was it stockmen, westerners, ranchers? Did the "we" include the Basques, the California Mexicans, the various Indians, the bad-ass Hispanics of New Mexico and all of their traditions? VJ had his doubts.

VJ had observed that whenever people blew hot air on the vice of sentimentality, they were getting ready to screw you over. When they harped on about being realistic, it meant that they were going to make a shitload of money in the bargain. He first made this bitter observation at age ten when he sold the little 4-H lamb he'd raised. He'd made a pet of little Cindy and had to see her auctioned off for slaughter. That was being realistic. Since then, VJ had mislaid the talent. No one accused VJ of being realistic. It was not a virtue he chose to cultivate.

"Ev," he asked, noting his friend stir, "do you remember Cindy?"

Ev had relaxed a bit. He was as awake as he'd ever been in his life but was enjoying the opportunity to rest his eyes, as well as his injured feet. When VJ spoke, Ev started. He'd been studiously ignoring VJ's presence. Now VJ was asking about what? Cindy? Who the hell was Cindy? "Well," he answered, "no. Is she . . . ?"

Rosa walked out of the house and joined them. She took Ev's hand casually, proprietorially. "Say what?" she asked.

"Well, Sis, we're going back into a ewe-lamb operation and I'm thinking out loud. Maybe we ought to pay a little more and get stock that'll allow us to keep our options open. Maybe we ought to just ease back toward wool production, maybe even get a weaving and a crafts coop going again in this county. Anyway, I was just talking to the old man and we came up with a plan. I'm going to shepherd for you for a while. Everybody needs a role, an *officio*, like they say in Spanish, and that'll be mine for a while. I guess Ev's is to wait around and see if anyone in the family has the gumption to take a shot at him. Watch the old man, Ev, he's a vicious one with a fork.

"Anyway, last year I was coming in from Texas and I decided to triangulate through Wyoming to fish a little stream I knew. When I got there, the stream was ruined. Some outfit had their animals in there and they'd just beat it to death. It got my nose open. I went to a bar in the closest town and had some beer. I got to talking with the barkeep and aired my views. Some guy overheard. He called me an environmentalist and there was a tussle."

Rosa and Ev smiled. The Wyoming bar brawl and Sabine's trip to Wyoming to retrieve his son from jail were now a staple in the family mythology; tussle, indeed.

Noting the smiles, VJ pressed his lips together and continued. "I do not think much of having trout streams turned into mud holes, and I plan to look at the streamside situation on all our holdings. All that stuff I said about the West being dry country, not suited to cows and sheep . . . it's right! It says it right there in *Stockman's Universe*. It's true even though ostriches are probably not the answer. I still think they may be *part* of the answer, but not for me. But touching on the West being dry, think about this ranch. When we work the ranch, how often does it make money: one year in three or is it one year in five? Figure it out. It looks like we ought to be able to do better. If not, we might as well just stick with Daddy's new practice of not bothering to ranch at all. Covering all those irrigated acres with red-topped cane like Daddy did this year is not going to cut it. It does look pretty though, and I hate like hell to go back to alfalfa. Maybe we need a new approach."

Noting the concern that had crept into the countenances of Ev and Rosa, VJ hurried his points and attempted to reassure. "I don't mean anything radical, like melaleuca trees and ostriches, but we ought to keep an open mind. I've heard of a kind of shell-game thing you can do with sheep, shuffling them around from pasture to pasture all the time. You run 'em on something like timothy or even that damned cane. It costs like hell for fencing unless you use electric fence, and you still have to cut and bale timothy. In the long run, though, it makes up the cost because it's sustainable on all your pasture acres. I plan to do some rumination on the subject next January when I'm stuck on the wintering grounds with sixteen hundred little bleaters. I expect I'll have a lot of time on my hands. Until then, Daddy and I will be buying ewes and a new sheepdog, taming donkeys, and getting everything set up. I reckon I'll have a minute or two to run by and see Fanny's parrot. The old lady, Marta, makes wine—at least that's what Fanny says—and I might want to swill wine and see that parrot in action before heading off to the wintering grounds."

He took a strand of hair between the thumb and index finger of his right hand and began to twist slowly. Ev exchanged glances with Rosa. Both of them were familiar with the signs and felt a combination of relief and dread. The ostrich project was joining the Jojobalueca venture as another of VJ's abandoned enthusiasms. He had a new idea, and he was not known for his moderation. For all his reassuring noises, who knew what excesses were in the offing?

Still, Rosa and Ev were happy. They hugged one another and watched VJ with great affection. It was VJ, after all, who'd brought them together, and they were inclined to feel indulgent. VJ was revitalized. His eyes danced wistfully on the horizon. He began to whistle and then to sing in his whispery, off-key manner.

> He took a hundred pounds of clay,
> And then he said, "Hey, listen,
> I'm gonna fix this world today,
> Because I know what's missin'."
> And then he rolled his big sleeves up
> And a brand-new world began
> De dah de de dah-dah dah-dah dah
> Dah dah dah dah de dah.

"Yup, Evertly Ev, next winter while you're down there in New Mexico, sweating your studies, living your last days as a free man, and contemplating your existence after graduation, I'll be out in the hills with those woolies. A man can do some deep thinking out there."